"Coles's background as a playwright reveals itself in the way she skillfully engages a diverse cast." —*Overcast*

"A profound read, offering up perfectly crafted sentences in the thoughts of the motley cast of characters."
—*Canadian Living*

"*Small Game Hunting* is a singular, beautiful, burning story— not only a piercing page-turner but a sharp and essential portrait of an island and its people in our times that will draw you in and then pull you under. It is an ocean of a book. Not to be missed."
—Elisabeth de Mariaffi, author of *Hysteria*

"No mistake, Megan Gail Coles is a driven, consequential writer who plays for keeps. Her seemingly off-the-cuff voice is controlled and quite intricate, and commands revisiting. *Small Game Hunting at the Local Coward Gun Club* is as important a novel as any that's hit Canadian literature in years."
—Joel Thomas Hynes, author of
We'll All Be Burnt in Our Beds Some Night

"Each character is rendered with such stunning details and unflinching insights that you can't leave this novel's pages without being changed. To read Megan Gail Coles's masterful debut is to become obsessed with it."
—Alicia Elliott, author of
A Mind Spread Out on the Ground

SMALL GAME HUNTING AT THE LOCAL COWARD GUN CLUB

Also by Megan Gail Coles

SMALL GAME HUNTING

AT THE LOCAL
COWARD GUN CLUB

MEGAN GAIL COLES

ANANSI

Warning: Contains scenes of sexual, physical
and psychological violence.

Published in Canada in 2019 by House of Anansi Press Inc.
www.houseofanansi.com

House of Anansi Press is committed to protecting our naturel environment.
This book is made of material from well-managed FSC ® - certified
forests and other controlled sources.

24 23 22 21 20   5 6 7 8 9

Library and Archives Canada Cataloguing in Publication

Coles, Megan, author
Small game hunting at the local coward gun club / Megan
Gail Coles.

Issued in print and electronic formats.
ISBN 978-1-4870-0171-1 (softcover).—ISBN 978-1-4870-0172-8
(EPUB).—ISBN 978-1-4870-0173-5 (Kindle)

I. Title.

PS8605.O4479S63 2019   C813'.6   C2018-901839-9
C2018-901840-2

Book design: Alysia Shewchuk
Cover art: Rebecca Suzanne Haines

We acknowledge for their financial support of our publishing program
the Canada Council for the Arts, the Ontario Arts Council, and the Government
of Canada.

Printed and bound in Canada

I wrote this for myself.

And the beautiful vicious island that makes
and unmakes us.

This might hurt a little. Be brave.

PREP

· · · · ·

OLIVE WAITS BELOW THE sad mural painted in memory of some long ago drowned boy.

She can see up and down Duckworth Street from her perch though there's not much to see this early in the morning. A scattered taxi slogs by carrying fiendish-looking passengers who attempt to discreetly smoke from barely cracked windows. Discretion is a skill they have fallen out with but they don't know that yet. They still fancy themselves stealth, piling four parka-plied humans into a single toilet stall, scarves dangling beneath the door, telling tails on them all.

Volume control is a thing of delusion in the confined spaces they inhabit. It will be years before this is fully realized by those who escape the scene or are thrown into adulthood by overdose or pregnancy. These lucky few will feel overwhelmingly, retroactively embarrassed by their one-time rock star fantasies. Olive can hear them bawling about their supposed betrayals as clouds of tobacco smoke and slurry syllables updraft skyward through the slightly parted window.

But Olive forgives them their make-believe follies.

They are no better or worse than most of the half well-off, half grown-up humans she has met. They are just flawed and vulnerable to the pitch. Olive is no different. She has chased the white dragon into smoky rooms where grad students complained about unkindly thesis feedback while wearing thousand dollar watches. A holiday-tanned winter wrist, a baggie held aloft, another Volvo fob serving key bumps round the ring. Under such circumstances, Olive is for the most part silent. She can pass for one of them until she releases language into the world.

Olive often holds her rural tongue for fear of being found out.

She is not a card-carrying member of the townie majority. Rarely are there other fugitive faces for Olive to hide behind on nights when she wants to get on the go. There was a Mexican painter once. A Russian musician. There was the one Pakistani fellow whose name Olive could never recall. She did not think it was unpronounceable, she just could not pronounce it.

There are lots of words still beyond her reach.

Like Olive can think of no words to describe the pain felt where her pants nearly meet her feet. She winces and tucks her chin farther inside her coat. She tries to push her neck back to save from catching skin in the zipper. She sniffs back hard and swallows a slippery lob. Her grandmother would not approve of hoarding mucus in the body but her grandmother would not approve of much of what she does lately. Olive sighs and swells and swallows spit to slide the lob along.

Ollie my dollie, get a tissue.

Her grandmother's voice is always a program running in the back of her mind. But Olive can't sacrifice a tissue on mere mucus this morning. Her store of napkins is running low and the last time she tried to hock and spit the wind gust blew snot back onto her sleeve. The line of mucus running from her lips to her elbow turned her weak stomach over. A middle-aged woman in a bright blue Canada Goose coat muttered *oh for the love of god* as she hurried past the translucent boundary. This made Olive feel gross.

She swallows that gross feeling down again while she waits.

She can distract herself for a time from the damp soak settling in her heels by watching the craven-faced respectable people meander to their grown-up jobs after a weekend of pretending to be twenty-five. But they are not twenty-five. They are not even thirty-five and feel as such. Most internally promise to stay home with the kids next weekend as they turn their faces to or from the sunshine depending on the quantity of painkillers ingested in the car. This temporary commitment to sobriety is bookended by revolving party systems.

Some relish vitamin D while others resent it.

The division will not last long, though, as the sun already has started to duck back inside the nimbostratus. It will storm again today as surely as the nearly forty will go out again in four days' time. The babysitter will be called. The cat will be let in. They will flee their houses for a little look around.

Get the stink of house off ya.

They will reliably cloak this smell of domestication

in alcohol and nicotine and self-loathing until Monday. Mondays are for quitting everything. Again. Except when it storms on Monday. Then quitting everything is pushed to Tuesday.

Today is such a Tuesday.

The weekend warriors refuse to sell out and so have fully bought in pound for pound.

Olive is just the same. She too had been sold the notion of party drugs as lazy fun and then fast gobbled them hand over fist. Swallow, snort, smoke; ingestion is an irrelevant matter of personal preference and ease. There is no wall to wall them out. Or in. Drug trends are trending along regardless of national media reports daily updating all on their progress east and upward. Olive has watched the same scenes play out on repeat in dark corners of the late night since arriving in Sin Jawns.

They've gone and stashed the kits everywhere to protect against the siren call. A first line of defence kept behind wine bars. Under the bathroom sink. In purses. And Olive knows she must address the long list of reasons why self-medicare is needed to comfort her.

Eventually.

But today, right now, before all else, she must get inside somewhere to prevent worse from happening.

She covets the dashboard heaters inside those coked-up cabs.

Olive hears the latch squeal before the hinges squeak. A black arm heaves garbage bags onto the sidewalk one after the other. There are so many. More waste than is normal. Food that went off during the previous day's storm is now bagged and tossed out for collectors who will not come until it fully clears. Olive worries the birds will have at it.

Omi will be blamed for the weather's interference in the city schedule if he doesn't re-collect it. Olive wills him to remember so he won't get in trouble. Omi is from Nigeria. Olive thinks he is her age but she can't be sure. She has been trying to figure out how to ask without seeming ignorant or making him angry. She has never seen him angry but is still afraid ignorant questions might jeopardize their friendship. She didn't even know they were friends until he said. One day weeks ago while she was waiting for Iris, he approached her on the sidewalk.

Girl, you okay?

Olive didn't know how to answer this honestly so shook her head.

Omi was staring at her skeptically. She worried there was something on her face. In her teeth. She dug through her pockets hoping he would think her busy searching out some important thing. She muttered quietly to the ground before adding *I'm good* as a hurried afterthought.

Excuse me?

I'm good!

Olive had barked much too loudly. Omi put up his palms in mock terror.

You good. Got it.

Olive then pretended to investigate the fraying fringe on a bag that had been new when it had not been hers. She bashful blushed at the ground.

Hey, where you from?

Here.

Sure, but where's your family from?

Around the bay.

Around what bay?

What?

What's your bay called?

There's no bay.

There's no bay?

I mean, there are lots of bays. I mean, it's more of a peninsula.

Olive held up her left pinky and left thumb while watching her other digits labour to curl tightly into her palm's pad. A gesture she learned in adolescence had quickly become reflex. She pinched her left pinky with her right forefinger and thumb before quickly unsnapping the clasp to correct her constant mistake. Olive swung her wrist around to flash knuckles facing out at Omi, who watched her waiting with growing curiosity. Olive recoiled her central digits once more for effect and popped her beloved peninsulas.

This is Newfoundland.

She pinched her left thumb and forefinger.

We're here.

She then reached over the interior to pinch her pinky and wiggle it a bit.

I'm from up here.

They both stood quietly transfixed by Olive's wiggling pinky until she stopped wiggling it. She stood there looking at her held little finger wondering what to say next.

So . . . you all white?

And Olive had not known how to answer this direct question dredging through the whole of her life like it was just a fact to simply say.

Cause you don't look all white.

And Olive feels small again.

She hears the older girl whisper first the taunt before sliding her freckled hand down across Olive's bare arm and then turning to wipe her fingertips along the skin of whoever stood close behind, the whole of the lunch line recoiling at the thought of contact with dirty little Olive, hysterical screeches gaining volume and velocity as they passed this gruesome contact to the furtherest student standing at the back.

Olive's germs on you!

Olive's germs.

And the schoolchildren passed her shame through the cafeteria, giggling and howling, *yuck*, reaching at each other in delight as they rid themselves of her germs. Olive, the tarriest one in line. There were other tarry children, a whole range of shade, a spectrum really, but they were not hated by this girl as Olive was hated. Bullies were just other girls back then. Olive feared them at the bus stop and missed the bus a lot.

Her grandmother yelling for her to leave earlier or this will keep happening.

The teacher that day finally grabbed the ringleader by her pale arm and shook her as Olive looked on in tears.

Mrs. Morris barking, you're no better than she is, little miss! You're no different!

Shaking the one girl Olive wanted to befriend but feared, until both girls were crying in the lunchroom before the whole student body. The smell of seven-layer dinner resting in their throats, gagging them both.

You say you're sorry right now, say you're sorry to Olive!

But the girl who started the hateful game would not say she was sorry.

I'm sorry.

The sound of regret in the man's voice brought Olive back to her adult-self.

Perhaps you are not supposed to ask that here.

No.

What?

I'm...not all white. Not really. Part Indian.

And that was the first time Olive had said it aloud to a stranger.

I didn't know you had Indians here.

We do.

So who are your relations?

I don't know.

And Olive is embarrassed because it's true. She doesn't know her relations. Some were accidentally lost, others mispronounced on purpose. Few could read the little paperwork they had to prove themselves before the flames came. Never was there a parish hall built permanent stone enough to protect against fortune's wood stove and a minister in his cups. St. John's burns down *encore* and all applaud the rebuild while Olive's forgotten place is blamed indefinitely for reckless kindling. The wealthy are permitted accidents, the poor found guilty.

Olive's once foreign brethren running from famine and feudal rule. Her native side stopped, stunned and suddenly steady, by the influx of men. The works of which settling for each other and the merchant's collar.

Olive is expected to magically untangle a hundred years of snarl for casual conversation.

Forget your relations. What's your name? What are *you* called?

And the man's voice was warm and she had always sought out warm places in others.

Olive.

My name is NaNomi but my friends call me Omi so you can call me that.

Olive smiled a little and then a lot at the thought of having a black friend called Omi. It made her feel beyond her circumstance and capable of moving further out of reach.

Omi finally hops out onto the sidewalk in a T-shirt and jeans. Sneakers. His footwear is insufficient for this dirty work. He is sweating. Great bands of sweat trench his face as if he has been weeping, though Olive knows it is sweat. She has seen him be accosted on a city bus without flinching. She has watched him lug a desk the length of Water Street a few feet at a time in the freezing rain. He is not a tearful man.

His perspiration will turn chilly in the mere moments he is exposed to the elements. He grabs up the bags and returns them to the porch in quick release. One snags on the brickwork and tears. Its slurpy contents slide out over the facade, and Olive feels bad for him as he hurries to scoop up the offending end and retie it tail to top. There is brownish liquid oozing from the plastic, and Olive knows Omi will have to carry his disgusting package across the whole dining room to reach the back door where the dumpsters are kept. She also knows that he has likely mopped already and wonders if he will mop again or spot clean to remedy the situation. There is a possibility that this will keep her on the curb longer as she is not allowed in while other staff members are staffing. She tucks herself in behind a car so he does not see her. He will insist she come in from the cold. This act of self-determination will anger the man who determines things around here. Besides, Olive does not want Omi to see her like this. She's a state.

Omi kicks snow toward the brick face while grumbling in English.

Olive wonders if he ever grumbles in his own words. She wonders what that would sound like. Olive doesn't even know her words. No one in her family taught them to her because no one in her family knew them. The act of not knowing was itself a mix of love and fear meant to conceal and protect from child collection back when they called it an orphanage.

Hush, Ollie, be a good girl or the booman will take you from Nanny.

Olive didn't know what kind of girl she was meant to be then and she certainly doesn't know now.

Olive's never been brown enough for brown girls.

Or white enough for white girls.

IRIS WAKES CLUTCHING her dead cellphone in an outstretched hand. Her arm has grown heavy and numb. She has to lift and shake it with her other hand to revive circulation.

It is insensate from the pressure of being her arm.

She had folded herself into the recovery position on the couch with her full weight upon the one free texting hand. She is wearing a coat and boots, apparently intent on going somewhere. She remembers. She had been upset. Been drinking through the storm. This had all been bad enough before he had come over. He had not been drunk of course.

He is almost never drunk when she is drunk.

Like the first time. Iris had been drinking cheap wine and sketching moose at home. It was a Wednesday evening. There had been no romantic lead-up to the encounter on that particular day. In fact, Iris had been weaning herself from her phone. There was a new guy a work who made her laugh and so she got to thinking that things could change if she changed them.

This night was back when Iris still believed men and women could just be friends.

She was busy being herself in her apartment. Listening to Destroyer records. Eating handfuls of dates from the open fridge. Sticky fingertips upon her brushes. Slow deliberate strokes. More dates. Another glass of Beaujolais. Fingerprints on vinyl. Antlers are tricky. They refuse to reveal themselves. But Iris was certain they would be hers. She was willing herself to see some pattern in her practice. She would keep after it into the night. This was her whole plan. And then...

I like smoking with you.

The little box on her phone told her and she smiled, of course. It is a statement meant for smiling. The intention is to curl a lip and maybe a toe or two, and Iris's lips and toes were still capable of curling then.

We could smoke cigarettes together in the snow.

She should have said no. She had drunk a bottle of

red on a half-empty stomach and she should have said no. That night and every night that followed. Last night, too. But Iris didn't want to seem shy or shitty or a silly girl. And he was so tall. Handsome. Smart. She had been, what was it, hopeful.

Though that hope is waning now.

She pulls herself from the sofa and lugs herself to the bathroom sink. The mirror. Soft pods of flesh hang from her sockets. Sobbing accelerates signs of ageing. Yesterday ticked off brutal behind her capillaries. She splashes cold water from the tap on her face and reads last night's opus while brushing her teeth. The insides of her thighs hurt and she vaguely remembers having sex. He had kept his shirt on. They had not gotten in the blankets. She had quiet cried after lying on top of the duvet. Before his phone sounded from his inside breast coat pocket. That muffled urgent notification signalling the night would turn sour. Even more sour. For Iris anyway.

And then there was yelling. She remembers clearly the yelling. Hands clenching the back of his coat from the floor after falling over wet footwear in the doorway. The deep shame of begging mixed with savage determination. Slapping her palms against the double pane as she watched him plough himself out of her driveway, rocking back and forth with the urgency of a caught animal in a shakeable cage.

In and out of her in less than an hour.

That's fucking shocking even for you, she messaged in an attempt to maim him.

The messages she sent in the throes of her bender are actually quite impressive given her level of intoxication.

Anger trumps everything. Even alcohol poisoning. Anger and desperation are twin crutches holding Iris up, and she is half grateful for even this unsustainable support.

Iris has seen grown women brought to their knees.

She too has been grounded in a slow miserable stagger. Suddenly scared and embarrassed when upright women attempt to assist her by pulling at her armpits, tugging at her damp hood, wiping back mangy fur-trim slick with puke against her wet face, to help her, they say. The erect urging a crumbling Iris to place her weight on them. The upstanding, having not a clue about the heft of their request, will email each other about the great horrible heaviness of her months later.

Their hurt for having borne her weight momentarily has been determined far greater than her hurt for having carried it nearly three decades.

They don't have a clue.

They've degrees in Earth Science and black-and-white photos of ancestors ages passed. They've been, for the most part, happy in a vertical world and hardly ever worried about accidental death. When they drink to drunkenness, it is in celebration; there is liveliness and bear-hugging and smoked salmon and chips.

Their faces hurt for very different reasons.

It would take them by great surprise to discover another quality of living. Their sweet brows, a deep furrow of concern and disbelief, as Iris labours to right herself so as to unburden them.

And like all buckled women, Iris is keenly aware that the shiny women are making themselves feel better for a time by helping her sickly self up when they've no real intention to give up their happy access to address the sleek slope that harms her.

Iris knows well enough.

She straddles shiny and sickly every day. Her mother is both, though never at the same time and never believably. Not like our Iris. It boggles Joanne's fucking mind how fluidly her best friend transitions from one to the other. The light and dark meat of her constantly on offer for those who aim to feast at the buffet.

Men. Men mostly. Mind you, straight men rarely slow to help her up.

The occasional homosexual will have sympathy enough to stop and steady Iris, but rarely straight men. Her stooped nature is a temptation that offends them when forced to face the conditions they've created in the wide open. Collateral damage consisting of women and children and dogs. The elderly. The ill.

Iris has overheard scientists discussing intergenerational trauma over lunch.

Shared memory, a kind of genetic recall of shame and hurt.

ACES, they called them. Adverse Childhood Experiences.

Iris has a pocket full of ACES.

Teachers always spoke to her in pitiful tones and never called home when a lunch was mislaid, assuming there was no food or no one awake to pack it. Doctors offered birth control to her while she was still in a training bra to curb what was expected of her scrawny body, claiming blemishes were of concern while facing a clear complexion. Meanwhile, dentists with rum on their twisted tongues urged older folk for full clearance, implying Iris's kin could not afford even the teeth in their heads.

There had never been an expectation of forefathers and there remains no expectation now.

Iris was meant to want nothing, demand less, not more. Her father's absence laying well the groundwork for the first one and then the next one and then John.

He had told her in honest afterglow that they were not even half a thing.

Not even half a thing, ringing on repeat in her head. One foot in front of the other through the slush on the downgrade toward The Hazel.

Not even half of something.

She has learned to abuse herself in a misguided attempt at thwarting expectation.

You don't deserve any better.

But very deep inside her body a tiny voice whispers into soft cupped hands...

...but you do.

Iris needs to get her paycheque and pay her phone bill before they disconnect her. She is determined to stay the course. She hauls the snarl of tangled dark hair from her eyes as she passes houses where she once attended parties. Iris used to be invited and beloved. But she can't bear to make eye contact with anyone anymore. Every party ends in tears. They will hate her for what she has done. What he has convinced her to do. She harshly counts and recounts her sins. Iris feels poorly.

Though riches, emotional and otherwise, have always made her uneasy.

Sure, even when she has money in her wallet a pervasive impoverishment runs through her. She can't get rid of it fast enough. It feels stolen. Not meant for her. She thinks someone will take it back. Or worse yet, call her out for being so bold as to expect to ever have money on her person. Who does she think she is? The Queen? No sir. Not Iris.

She played pretend-poorer as a child to lessen the bleakness by comparison. Her Fisher-Price dolls lived on farms far away from any ocean, this being the bleakest thing she could think up as a child. Feeding pigs. Harvesting grain. The thought of such dry vastness made the baygirl scratch an imaginary itch. She has always feared the great plains. She wouldn't make much of a farmer. Nothing fit to eat would grow. Gnarly vegetables. Self-disgust. And failure.

But baygirls make great waitresses.

They've the ideal upbringing for the whole undertaking. Efficiency bred out of necessity centuries ago, refined by capital and industry. Taking too long resulting in sickness and/or death.

Iris had better manage this time, it's the only time she'll get. Before she dies dead. Sure, she won't mind doing all of this. What with all her free time.

Young ones got a lot of time on their hands. That one over there. No youngsters or nothing. Still don't know how to relax.

Relax! What a waste of time, which is money Iris needs for food to live. Because she's hungry. So fucking hungry. But she's not to eat. Don't dare drop an extra drop in.

That is not for you, girl.

Let the men sit down first. Give your father the biggest pork chop if he's home.

Eat potato if you're starved. There are crackers in the cupboard. Iris will have the garden salad. No. A water. No. A steak. No. Nothing for her, thanks.

Because she's been so bad lately. Iris had been so bad. Is. So. Bad.

Her bread is mixed with molasses and guilt. Good women never eat more than a sliver.

Even if they've had so little. Nothin this whole time. Empty sure.

Iris has had to suck a peppermint knob and contempt to sustain herself.

Look've her, luh. Tits on that. Useless, useless as tits on a bull.

Hey misses! Hey girl! Hey Iris! Smile sure while you're at it.

Would it kill Iris to smile while she hands them their food?

Put on a dress, look pretty, eat nothing, have no feelings, never complain. What else can Iris do? Mississauga is calling. Welcome to the National Student Loan Service Centre —

Ring! Ring! When her phone is actually connected.

The government wants their money back now!

Newfoundland has run out of fish/wood/oil and patience, again. Where did it all go?

Spent on coke and hookers no doubt.

Iris robs light bulbs from the living room to brighten the bathroom. It's that or pissing in the dark.

Men yell at her from their massive trucks to get out of the jesus road.

Are you stupid, girl? Are you? Stupid!

She could talk back but has been socialized against it.

Instead, Iris sneezes into her sleeve as she sidesteps snow boulders pushed into her way. Sidewalks are for better people, she thinks, as she once again steps onto the slushy street to speed along the journey. Her gratitude for proper winter footwear swells despite her boots being purchased as an act of penance.

Not that boots could ever make up for ruining her life.

Iris dodges a side-view mirror which lies dormant after being snapped from a parked car by a snow-clearing crew full of contempt. Gashes of green municipal vehicle paint tag the driver's side of a dozen cars clinging to the crusty curb. But Iris cannot be dissuaded.

Her hangover has legs.

There's a clarity of purpose in its stride. A well-directed hangover, when gainfully rehearsed, will put the fear of god into those who have undone you. Iris can feel her filter falling away with each step. Sliding right off the back of her. What is left is a kind of self-preservation that would shock evolution into sitting up straight. Every man who has ever loved her has attempted to acclimatize themselves to this morning state of her, but no good will come of that.

She won't have it.

Iris, like every lady drinker before her, steels herself against it. It would be better, gentle man, to not have behaved like a manipulative prick from go. Iris will not feign innocence or blame the universe. The universe does not care for her atrocious decisions.

Iris Young is twenty-nine years old and that is old enough to know better.

She did what she did and will get what has always been coming to her. And then she will give it back.

Because some men deserve to be brought to their knees.

JOHN COULD HAVE lived fine never knowing how Iris moved through the world.

He felt confident he could have been okay had any one thing changed their impending course. All things could have remained the same had just one thing gone differently. Had she gotten the position at the gallery. Been accepted to graduate school. Received the residency in London or won that prize. Their lives would not have gotten smashed together had John not been lonely and her student loans overwhelming. Had they both been raised right maybe. Any other version would have cleared them of each other.

There was no reason for them ever meeting.

John would not have been tempted to tear into this fantasy world full of conceit. He would have resisted all romantic comedies and songs on the radio. He had prided himself on leaving those kinds of daydreams and melodramas to softer faces with disposable incomes and reliable parents. The privately schooled, near grown, pseudo-adult were at liberty to peacock through the concrete nature of their depression, but not John.

He secretly delighted in charging them great sums from their trust funds for a fish taco. They lacked the wherewithal to poach an egg and were incapable of providing themselves with basic sustenance. A nineteen-dollar hotdog was the cost of their privilege.

John's culinary comfort food was the equivalent of rich people stomach-slumming it.

Though this was not the macaroni and cheese some fisherman's kid would have ever eaten between skipping tides and copying pans. No Aunt Gert had ever poured this pasta from a box into a dipper on the stovetop while the wieners split themselves open on the boil alongside. This was not birthday party food served in the church basement where moms with stern looks half bragged that they could do nothing with their youngsters.

Hard ticket John is, can't do a thing with him.

The common pride of having the worst youngster in the pass-the-parcel circle.

Watch now he don't bite her, he been biting girls lately.

No. The macaroni and cheese John served in artisanal ceramics was covered in cod and laid atop wooden plates with logos of The Hazel burnt through. This was not food for children. There was gluten-free pasta and back bacon. Five locally produced and aged cheeses with names that referenced something other than their colour. Well beyond orange and white. This was real, dear holiday cheese you put out with toothpicks. Cocktail onions. Sausage discs. Food for guests.

Food John was never allowed.

The best of everything was saved for distant cousins visiting from the mainland, to prove they weren't poor. These same relations were allowed to sit in rooms of the house that John rarely entered. Virtual strangers fingered pillows that had not been touched since their delivery from Sears to prove that his father was a good man.

No Name spread and oily slices were the regular

cheese impersonators in John's kid sandwich. These frauds were shoved in the side of the fridge door, where the butter would be if they ate real butter.

So John learned to make miracles out of lies for lunch.

This culinary intuition bred out of necessity and a latchkey. John was often left unguarded. His only company the empty fridge and an undeniable sense that this was not how other children lived. His suspicions confirmed by television programs where women wore aprons to cut crusts and peel apples laid pretty on the plate. John's own mother would shriek that peels and crusts were good for you. That's where all the nutrients lived.

Stop talking big and eat your potato skins, we don't waste food around here.

So he learned early on he would have to make anything worth eating from his mother's mangy stores himself. And like all great magicians, John refused to reveal the tricks of it when asked the secret of his gnocchi by the well-heeled ladies. Their concentrated looks suggesting a belief they could recreate it at home.

It can't be that hard if you can do it, their newly lasered eyeballs declared.

These women wearing glittering watches with no care for time seemed not to like anyone or each other. They vied for every measure. They ordered steaks and salads but competed to eat the least, the winner being the thinnest, most hungry woman at the table who could afford to throw out the most food. John could always identify the newly rich by their cleared plates and compliments. They still appreciated taste.

Everything was delicious.

They are John's favourite guests. They married money, and these husbands often try to talk to John when he performs the required dining room appearance. The long-inherited well-off behave as though they are owed interaction. Some pretend that they are all friends going way back. Sometimes they ask John about his golf game.

John doesn't golf.

John thinks golf is the most fucking repugnant of all leisure sports. And these golfers are too informal in their banter. John lets their attempted endearments fall to the polished floor.

I am not your b'y, John wants very badly to say.

But doesn't.

He knows well enough there is an expectation of gratitude. They want him to be grateful they have chosen his kitchen to gorge themselves on tonight. But John cannot feel grateful.

Instead, he permits a sly smile. They assume something has landed and beam up at him with satisfaction. They will explain in exaggerated detail to everyone in the high towers tomorrow that John Fisher from the television laughed at their joke.

They don't know the truth behind John's smirk. Only a few people do.

Though he still believes, had things been marginally contrary, that there would have been no need for this degree of deceit. Or, at least, a lesser need for lesser deceit. He could have come to know Iris in the casual, roundabout sense. They could have respected one another as onlookers from the sidelines of their separate, yet parallel, lives.

They might have been introduced randomly at some

New Year's Eve party neither had wanted to attend. John imagines her simmering in annual hatred of an event attempting to dictate her mood. The holiday calendar cannot even force her will. John envisions admiring her brash consumption from across the cheese table. Delighting in watching her drink wine from mislaid bottles while swiping cigarettes from unsuspecting lips.

He could have learned to like her later as a person, over time, if she had been married.

He could have hung her artwork in the dining room, praised her use of evening light. He could have done so had he never seen the black sheen such light cast off her hair at dusk. John could have commented on the intensity of her lines, having never known the small, angled arch where her back met her upturned bum.

Perhaps he would have hung something in the living room. Oil on canvas.

Or, even, in the bedroom. Oil on linen.

John could have unknowingly owned pieces of her had he never seen her lean hard, palms pressing down upon the sink, to lift herself onto the balls of her feet while peering from a kitchen window. He could have begun and ended every day never having known the tiny tilt of her when she was consumed by a fast-forming idea. The slight cant of her hips when the secret thought arrived fully assembled and made contact with her resting body.

He could have retained some semblance of settled had he not witnessed feelings shake themselves shiver-like through her sharp parts.

You can't remember memories that you don't have.

You can't forget them, either.

CALV SHOULD HAVE never put Donna's fucking name on the house.

Amanda told him not to so he told her to mind her own jesus business. It showed Donna he loved her, didn't it? Was romantic or whatever. But Amanda says romanticism is for the emotionally crippled, sexually confused and teenagers.

Fucking sister always got to be right about everything.

He thinks this as he tiptoes around he's own bedroom looking for a pair of matching socks. Thank god Donna sleeps late. She don't hear him bump his heel off the footboard or the hushed swears escaping his mouth as he digs through the sock drawer. You would think she could roll his socks together. That's not asking a lot. Tuck one in the other. His mother irons underwear for fuck sakes. Not Donna. She just shoves everything into the drawer all the once and stray like. It feels reflective of her general demeanour toward him. Right haphazard and half-assed, quick to be done. Donna has yelled come or die at Calv in the middle of screwing.

He still came mind you.

Calv's buddy never put his misses on the house papers and got to keep the works when she left him. Told the courts she was his tenant. Calv should have done that too. Perhaps he'd have something to leverage for rolled together socks and a blow job if he'd have thought of it. Jesus. Can't even admit to anyone he's fucked now either.

She'll have everything you owns, know every move you makes, that's what Amanda said.

Calv hates it when Amanda is right. Hates it.

But that don't make her wrong. And there's no end to

Donna's demands now. Last night she was tormenting about some yoga trip. Said them parts he loves pawing after don't magically stay tight like that.

She also said Calv can get the fuck on if he plans on going back to the poorhouse.

She'll find a new man. And Calv knows she's as good as her word, too. That's how he got her himself. If Barry Coates had to of kept he's job offshore, she'd be shacked up with him still, but Barry went in the first round of lay-offs. He's own fault really for bouncing around between companies. Offshore. Alberta. Offshore. School. Sure, Barry never even bought a truck. What kind of young feller don't buy himself a truck when he's making the biggest kind of money like that?

Roger had a new one every second year. Never waited for the lease to be up. Go on to the dealership as soon as he was ashore and have another truck. That one time, in he's dirty coveralls, saying he's money was as good as the next feller's.

A shared hatred of Roger is the only thing Donna and Amanda got in common.

The pair of them would like to see Roger in the ground.

Amanda allows that he fingered her against her will one time in to he's cabin when she was only fourteen. She told everyone at school that Roger sexually assaulted her. She claims that Calvin's inability to even acknowledge this happened is further assaulting her. Which is revolting cause she's he's sister. Worse than that, he's twin sister. Ugh. And yes yes, he loves her, loves her more than any other human living or dead, but why she got to go saying Roger violated her.

That's the word she used when she told the English teacher from town.

Roger was after violating her when she was passed out drunk on the bunk. She said Deana Carter was playing. She said he hauled her snow pants down. She said she never took off her snow boots. She said he pushed her feet off the bunk cause he's mother would be mad if she got all the bedclothes wet and full of birch sap. She said that she was too sick to talk. That she threw up in a bread pan on the floor. Amanda said she stared into the blue plastic bread pan, into the remnants of her guts, kiwi coolers and BBQ, while Roger told her how much he always liked her.

And she said no, she said his name, and then no. No. Roger. No. Don't.

She could hear everyone racing ski-doos across the lake. Could remember thinking that Roger must have stayed behind especially for her cause racing ski-doos loaded drunk was his most favourite thing to be at. And she remembers thinking that he was going to pop her cherry right there in that bunk with a piece of wiener stuck to her face, and then on Monday everyone would call her a slut before home-room. Amanda said the only reason he stopped is cause she peed on his hand. All the talk was that she got piss loaded drunk but Amanda pissed on Roger so he would stop.

It was all she could think to do.

That's what she told Calv, and he wishes she never told him stuff like that. He wishes she was the same as every-one else. But Amanda reads too many books. Watches too many documentaries. She's right dramatic. Making a big deal out of getting fingered.

By Christ, Calv can't even think about how many

times he's hand been somewhere he wouldn't sure it was supposed to be. No one knew what they were at. They were only young sure.

Amanda never could take a joke. This other time Roger gave her a wedgie and tore the pants off her in the hallway. Grabbed her by the ass pockets and hauled her right off her legs. It was right alongside the girls' room. She could have went in there and changed into her gym clothes. No one needed to know, not really. But did Amanda do that? Course not. Stormed off down to the principal's office then holding her pants together.

Look what Roger Squires did to me!

She could have said she was on the rag and thrown the pants out. But that would have been too easy.

Easy for who, Calvin?

That's what Amanda would scream. And Calv knows she'd disown him if she ever found out what he was after getting caught into. She forever threatens to. It's like her favourite thing to say.

That's it, I'm done being your sister. You're a lost cause. Un-fucking-salvageable you are.

She guns her messages home to make sure Calv don't miss a single second of being shredded by her home-cut buckshot. She'd make some fine moose hunter if she still ate meat. Eats a bit of turkey at Christmas so she don't hurt Nan's feelings.

But do she try to spare her brother? No sir. Would sooner fire her hateful words at him in rapid succession. And nothing presses harder on her trigger than him going around with Roger. But what the fuck is Calv supposed to do? He can't not go.

Calv grabs up his buzzing cellphone. Roger is after sending a swarm of pussy gifs.

Coming? I'm coming. You coming?

Sometimes Calv thinks Roger got the emotional maturity of a baby cow.

A small bovine. Livestock in the middle of development. Something he accidentally seen on a Netflix factory farm program when he last fell asleep at his sister's.

He can't unsee that now, and it leaves him feeling right spoilt and conflicted.

Calv can't say no to hanging out with Roger but he can't feel good about saying yes either.

He peeps out the curtains and spots Roger drumming away on the steering wheel. He got the music up loud enough that Calv can hear it in the porch. The anxiety this creates makes Calv clear jump into his boots, almost sending himself head first into the closet door before catching himself on the door jamb.

And Roger got that Yamaha ski-doo jacket on again.

Lord thundering Jesus, Calv thinks it's a good thing Donna can't see it. She says Roger is worst than them digital billboards. Blinding. And Calv knows there's something to what she says. He used to wish Roger would just wear something normal.

This was back when he still cared if they stayed friends.

GEORGE WISHES SHE had not answered the phone.

She almost never answers unknown numbers. As a rule. She thought it might be the social worker so she picked it up. It wasn't, and now her day is ruined.

Why do they even have a landline? They're young, or at least, youthful. They've cellphones. And the internet. George would have happily entered middle age not knowing John was capable of this. Instead, here she is walking the dogs to The Hazel in a right huff.

John had left a note, he needed the car early for a supply run. His car was out of gas.

And for sure he has not done the run yet, she will have to do that, too.

Iris better have the liquor list ready. If she doesn't, George will call and wake her up. She is almost definitely sleeping. Iris sleeps in all the time. George wishes she knew how to sleep in. But she doesn't. Or more so, she can't. She has so many things to do. She wakes up at six and feels behind by nine, is totally overwhelmed by noon, and falls asleep with a book on her face before ten. This is best case scenario if she starts the day in North America. Things are even more hectic and tiresome if she's on a recruitment tour. George has priorities.

She is not so fancy-free as to stay in bed half the day sleeping off a hangover.

Her whole staff was trapped in some recovery loop. She would replace them with robots if it were up to her. Tidy, polite, moderate Japanese robots. Pay for themselves in a year, maybe less when you factor in spillage which is not even spillage. George has never once seen Ben spill a drop of draught or mix up a wrong drink order. He conducts himself with more competence than the rest of the serving staff combined. Which makes a fuck ton of sense considering George hired him, and Sarah hired the rest of these delinquents before fucking off to Korea.

Sarah didn't even respond to George's last email about the Thanksgiving decorations.

They were meant to be in a plastic container somewhere. A green storage tub full of wicker root vegetables. John said *ask Sarah*, like she was still sitting in the dining room drinking a cup of coffee. George wished she had gotten a chance to say goodbye. Or at least conduct an exit interview. She never did find the decorations.

George can't have Asian robots.

Customers want sweet undergrads with large chests and a hint of accent. Not too much, not straight from the Southern Shore or, heaven forbid, another one from the Northern Peninsula. Iris corrects George each time she forgets to say Great but George is pretty sure there is nothing Great about it. She would not have hired Iris. She is much too much of everything. Her feelings show right on her face. But the customers love her.

She's... authentic.

George is forced to accommodate her lying in for the sake of simple drawls and saucy drags. Linguistic laziness seeps into every inch of her core personality. She probably steals toilet paper from the restaurant. George knows none of them buy food anymore. Staff dinner, John calls it. They argue about this. George explains he does not need to make such a production out of feeding the staff. But John insists that it is important they taste the food and wine they are serving.

You cannot fake some things.

John thinks it is a bodily reaction. Uncontrollable. Impulsive. John wants diners to read pleasure on their faces when they talk about his food. He wants them to light up.

And George wants John to be happy so she lets it go. George lets things go.

He was weird when he picked her up from the airport last night.

She dismissed it because of the late hour, her own jet lag and the storm. But he was weird. Which makes perfect sense now considering what he has been hiding.

That man of hers is a sucker for punishment. If there are two ways, and one way is obviously the wrong way, John will pick that way every time. He is physically averse to the right way. He cannot see beyond the next step. His whole family is like that. Living in the reckless spot of time they exist in. Beholden to the island yet ready to swim ashore at a moment's notice. They make George anxious. She has to coax John's father into taking his coat off on the rare occasions he visits. John's mother insisting on wearing shoes in the house.

In case it burns down, she explained to her new daughter-in-law the first time.

Stunned, George ventured clarification. In case the house burns down?

John's mother lived her life in anticipation of walking over burnt-out broken glass in her naked feet. George had attempted to reason with her. Their home, which the elder John had commented was more house than two people needed, had smoke detectors that were wired to the grid.

I got no faith left in the grid.

Her mother-in-law's life was revolving cold load pickup. People dying in their beds after cooking in the garage. Sheets pinned up in the doorways. Dogs, cats and babies all hampered in the one room. Half froze and

33

bawling. Each story told more morbid and desperate.

These visits, thankfully, were not often. And rarely announced.

When given adequate prep time, John became agitated to a point of intolerability. Each day leading up to his parents' arrival would see his miserable pacing increase. The long list of past offences tossed out with unnerving contempt. John had been wronged, and he could not forgive the trespasses against him. Instead, he echoed it like an ancient bugler, setting off an internal battle cry each day until he faced the enemy who wore the same determined, wronged look upon the same intense face.

We don't all got a woman with money you know, Johnny!

Everything came back to having a woman with money.

Poor man/rich woman dichotomy being the barb to end all barbs before voices shot through the house and the front door was fired off the frame as John's father retreated to the camper for his evening's rage, knowing well enough the walls were merely covered cardboard.

The whole neighbourhood can hear him, John, George would plead.

The unsightly travel trailer embarrassing the entire street. Prowler indeed.

John's parents lived like immigrants. George did not understand them at all. Their inability to commit to even a dinnertime was mystifying. Maybe all baymen are like that. George doesn't know many of them beyond those she has met through John.

Which she realizes now are not many. A few men he skates with on Sunday nights, the couple they sometimes nod at while walking the dogs in Bowring Park. Not many. Sparse pickings.

George also realizes walking to The Hazel is a blessing. She needs the air more than the dogs. Air and an opportunity to simmer down before she sees John. She feels close to adequate now and is only halfway there. Forty more minutes will allow her to come up with a creative solution. Or a trap.

She will catch him in it. She will lay snares all about the place. She will make key chains with his severed bits for better luck next time. And as reminder to him that he properly stepped in it. She will hobble him for jeopardizing their family. And if he continues to deny it, she will use his own knives to skin him alive. This is George's current working plan. She will tweak it as she goes.

George is nothing if not adaptable. She is perfectly suited for this kind of thing.

RIS IS SO tired she can hardly lug herself down the last hill.

What doesn't kill you makes you stronger is bullshit.

Iris is convinced this kind of psychological drivel was spoon-fed to her as child to make her shitty parents feel less shitty. It did not make her stronger. It made her more likely to develop autoimmune diseases and cancer. What doesn't kill her now will kill her later.

It will cross her wires, and Iris is already wrong wired.

Jo has assured her that this can be undone. She has patiently explained that modern neuroscience confirms the brain's plasticity. You just need one constant person to always care.

And to sleep soundly.

But Iris has never slept soundly. She is a blanket thrasher. She is a pillow crusher. She mines the backside of her brain for clues when she should be sleeping. Iris is nightly running internal damage-control analysis. She lies awake mapping out ways to stop lying awake.

She remembers doing so since childhood. Her parents pretending little Iris was a heavy sleeper when little Iris was not.

What are you doing up?

I can't sleep.

Yes you can.

I'm hungry.

You're not though.

I need some water.

Remember the story about the boy who cried wolf.

But I'm not a boy crying about wolfs —

Wolves.

My belly hurts.

Iris, go back to bed before Dad gets mad.

Mom —

Iris, get back in the jesus bed before I puts you back in it!

So she never told them she was awake much. Instead, she willed herself to be a better sleeper. The best everything. Exceptional. Her debt accumulated at conception in the back seat of some car would have to be repaid.

Iris forever searching for change lost in the couch to make up enough. There was no orange juice because she had to have sneakers full of pumps. Glass figurines sailing into the canvas kitchen floor one after the other teaching Iris the true cost of wanting things.

Her mother crying from the hallway as the figurines that do not smash initially are fetched back up off the floor and re-fired at the wall. One stubborn dolphin pitched repeatedly until the tail end relented and came free.

Can't have nothing nice.

Iris silently repairing the figurines while seated next to her father starfished on the floor after having thrown the good right out of himself. Her mother having taken refuge in their bedroom long before the last sea mammal was split apart. Little Iris forever trying to crazy-glue back together what she did not pull apart.

Iris owed them for each moment of displeasure. Every hate they had for each other in those early days was shared about generously quick, loud and in full view of their five-year-old. Everyone said it would make her tough. And Iris needed toughening. The truth was she was all soft parts. Full to the brim with big feelings.

Though Iris still believes if she could get enough sleep to sustain herself everything could be corrected. She would be able to stand her parents, her painting, her phone. All things would right themselves if Iris could close her eyes and not find herself haunted by the feelings others did not have for her.

I'm taking that truck when I goes, the truck is mine.

What else in the cove is yours, Sid?

Knock it off I said.

Who else don't you take care of?

I takes care of me own.

She is the fucking spit of you.

Go on with your old foolishness!

I can't stand the sight of her in church.

Do you hear yourself?

You're after turning me into a bad person.

I dare say you was always a bad person.

I should have never moved down here.

I never said you had to.

You never says to do anything, though, do ya?

I said I never wanted youngsters.

But you always wants to screw.

Lord fuck, you got some long tongue Cynthia.

Mudder warned me your crowd was savage.

Listen, you better shut your mouth before I shuts it for you.

And then Iris's dad went to Alberta and stopped being her dad but Iris tries not to think on this before bed. Instead she bathes, drinks tea, swallows melatonin and watches nature programs. Sir David Attenborough narrates her dreams until the motion sensor is triggered by small steps along the path and a worrisome light floods her ground-floor apartment.

Iris listens for noise coming from Olive's.

She cannot remember a time before when things were different between them. Sometimes she smokes a cigarette as she waits for sounds next door. Other times she dials the emergency number ready to press send if a troubling sound wakes her again from her sleep. Most times she stands in the dark eating a banana over the open garbage can in silence. She never did this before they got to this place.

This is a new eating habit.

OLIVE CANNOT FEEL her toes.

Everyone will say it is her fault if she loses them as if every bad thing that happens to Olive is because she did not take care. But Olive has always taken care.

Regardless, bad things happen.

After her pop died, Olive was sent to live with a woman doctor in St. John's because her nan was grief-struck and bedridden.

The woman doctor lived in the university area with her husband who was in business. Olive never understood what kind of business but it required a lot of devices. The house was making a co-ordinated effort to be efficient in every way. The door required no key, a personal punch code sufficed. Olive had her own. It was her grandmother's telephone number.

Every time she entered the house, Olive envisioned the phone affixed to the wall in their kitchen, her nan winding the cord absent-mindedly around her doughy middle as she moved around the small space fetching frying pans and sauce pots mid-gossip with her sister over to Labrador.

Ollie says they got the biggest kind of homes with swimming pools and air conditioners.

It comforted Olive to imagine she was taking her grandmother with her through this urban doorway while she was recovering from the shock of it. This made Olive feel more new and less used. She thought her past would not matter in this large place where no one's past seemed to matter. Town knew nothing of her meagre means, her mother's reputation or her father's denial. It didn't ask what happened to her pop or if her nan got dressed that day. It cared not a lick about her origin story. At first.

And Olive's guilt for having left her nan did not outweigh her hope for something better.

There was a sunroom full of windows with plants on every sill. There were paintings hung in foyers and cut flowers on countertops. Picture books lay on coffee tables, lamps stood on three legs, there were bowls of nuts laid out for casual eating. The floors were warm and clean enough to walk across in your bare feet. And the woman doctor did so.

Every evening. She arrived home from her practice to at once pull off the trappings of her day. The refinished church pew held her fit frame as she unzipped her tall boots and unwound her scarf. Every article of clothing a neutral hue, with even reds appearing gently muted against her pale skin. Sometimes the woman doctor would roll her tights down right in the porch. She did so only when she thought no one else was watching but Olive saw her the one time.

Woman doctor laughing at her own impatience to be comfortable and curled up small in a lounge chair by the fireplace nibbling blocks of dark chocolate while reading of advances in modern medicine. Sometimes the cat sat atop the blanket on her lap. A weighted brown and beige knit patterned in Canadian woodland deer. Each family member had their own to throw over.

Olive's was peach.

She wore it over her shoulders like a cape while she watched YouTube videos with headphones bought for her by Businessman husband who opened bottles of wine that he didn't finish. He drank a glass with dinner, perhaps a beer while watching sports. He sometimes fell asleep before finishing even the single beer. Woman doctor would take a gulp as she passed en route to the kitchen or the bookshelf. They rarely drank to drunkenness or raised their voices. Instead, wordless music played in some unseen system in the ceiling. There was a glass pedestal case that held a cake though there was no birthday. Some people just had cake.

The woman doctor had a son.

And he knew Olive wanted him to like her. Her weak will quietly leaked her want into every conversation. Olive never had an opinion she thought worth sharing. She didn't care what movie they watched. She was fine just watching him play his guitar. She walked a step behind him on the trail. She never asked anything of him. Never started talking first. Never spoke above a whisper. Olive was eighteen months older than him but his sitting duck. He laid decoys out as well. To test his theory along the way.

His theory was: Olive would do anything to be his friend.

It did not happen all at once. It was a gradual warming. He made them cups of tea. Told her about his father's affair. Casually mentioned a favourite snack and waited for it to appear. He also ignored her for days. Too busy in his room playing his stolen car game to care. This too had the desired effect. A kind word after zero contact would leave her flushed.

One day he gave her a grey hooded sweatshirt. It became her new favourite thing.

Then once he said she had a pretty caramel complexion. And she felt sweet.

We'll keep each other's secrets, the doctor's son said another day.

And with each tiny confession, he forged them together. Olive thinking they were becoming close like real siblings. The kind she always wanted. Olive needed so desperately for someone to love her without expectation of her being smarter or prettier or funnier. Someone who might starve off the solitary feelings forming in her heart since her mother moved away. So when he asked to share her peach blanket, she let him.

He said his was in the wash.

But it wasn't.

Later, she would see his blanket draped over a chair in the formal living room. And she would make a confused, pleading kind of eye contact that he would return with a cold, defiant grin.

Because what was she going to do? Tell his mother that he had reached under her peach blanket and inside the waist of her tights? Describe over pancakes how she had let him tuck his fourteen-year-old hand into the furry part of her, then past it, until he was pressing his finger against the wet muscles inside? Carving small circles around the cavernous space before jabbing her in and out with some sweeping confidence. He had seen this move on the internet and believed Olive to be enjoying it as the women on the website had. He had not thought it pretend like a film or show on TV. He had not thought it make-believe for amusement like a board game or phone app. He had not thought to ask as the men in the clip had not asked. Everyone had liked it on the YouTube video. More than liked it.

They loved it.

Besides, his dad had said to practise on a girl he didn't like much first.

Never kiss the pretty girl right away, his dad said. Find a homely girl and try things out on her. Perfect your aim on a servant before you fire for the queen.

And wasn't Olive the best target? She was dying for his attention. And he thought it would make her happy. But it did not.

Not at all.

Instead, she felt like a great confusing excavation was underway. He was hollowing out more of her with each swirling, stabbing gesture. Olive felt a perplexing emptiness spread up through her stomach and refused to meet his sideways glances as he continued to insolently root in her cavity. She was suddenly grateful for not having eaten much. From this day forward, she would keep the pit of her on the slight side to discourage eruptions, because Olive was sure she would have thrown up on herself had she eaten more nachos.

Bits of Mexican pre-grated cheese mix and salsa would have come ejecting out her now defunct mouth-hole. It would have run down the front of her once prized blanket. It would have made everything impossible to pretend away. You can't feign ignorance when covered from chin to cunt in orange spew, the chunky glory of your former guts pooling in your crotch. This was not something easily seen or smelt away. Which Olive had decided early on. While he was mid-burrow. Olive would never tell anyone about this. Ever. She would will it out of existence. She would act like it had not happened. She would be more nice. Kinder. Better. Aware. Vigilant. Olive would never trust another man. Or even a boy.

They all just want to fuck you, Olive.

This, echoing, looping, bouncing and banging the inner sheeting of Olive's mind before she really understands the word fuck. Olive knows her body was built for fucking before she knows what fucking even means. How long had she known this?

The first time: an older cousin at her birthday party, him touching her chin to start, saying he wanted to feel her hiding bits. He told her she would like it, that it was what she wanted, he said he wouldn't hurt her squishy pieces. She had let him unwrap her ice cream sandwich after.

This meant what he did could not be yuck.

Each winter recess spent running through frozen fields or buried face down in the snow while hands weaseled around flush with the front of her snow pants. Classmates using the ground and gravity to assault her. Maybe she had known then. Maybe Olive had always known.

But knowing something and facing it is altogether different.

And facing it in the woman doctor's warm living room was harder still. Because Olive had let her guard down. She had been taken in by wool slippers lined up broadside in the front porch and an aquarium full of brightly coloured fish in the hallway. The tea cozy covered in crabapples had distracted her. Until that day on the couch. Under the peach blanket. Not her peach blanket anymore. She realized that it had only ever been conditionally hers. And conditions can shift. Weather conditions. Living conditions. Human conditions.

Even your name can go bad.

Olive Noseworthy was born with a bad name.

Any name that's not your father's name is a bad name.

And Olive's father refused to give her his name. So the only thing to be angry about at this point would be ever believing Calv's rides to the grocery store had meant he wanted her to have fruit because he liked her. Thinking too much on the one time he fixed her bathtub drain after she made mention of showering with water to her ankles was too much stupid thinking. Besides, watching the dirty run off herself to meet the tepid water slowly draining from her tub was what silly Olive deserved.

The landlord had asked over the phone if she had a man that could fix it. When she said no, he asked if she would have her rent on time. Or would it be like last time.

Olive didn't want it to be like last time. Last time she had bruises on her feet.

Poor feet.

She peers at them now before looking down Duckworth hoping to recognize someone. She tries to wiggle her toes inside her shoes.

Olive thinks they wiggled but she can't be sure.

JOHN DRIVES BY Iris's apartment on his way to work out of habit.

He had many times driven by her apartment on his way to work, a shovel thrown onto the back seat. He would push everything aside while she slept and she would awake to find that he cared. This act of service, a showcase of kindness, was another deed he could do to make up for not doing the deed. Occasionally it had already been cleared, which he assumed meant she was cared for by another. Of course men wanted to show her a kindness. He couldn't help doing do so himself. She was a sort of evolving argument for happiness, though he could not quite wrangle what kind of happiness or for whom.

She was amazing. John often felt amazed.

He tried to deduce the minor mysteries of her driveway, and when these endless deliberations yielded no satisfactory answer, John asked outright. Casually. He summoned a tone of offhand curiosity. A small-talk approach. Because any note of significance would have her squirrel it away to use against him later. They were all like that. Women.

So John lobbed things while she was preoccupied with repetitious acts, or, if necessary, he would sink her brain deep in hot places pre-emptively. She would tell anyone anything once brought to near boiling. Her loose lips would indeed sink ships as fucking over her navy didn't take much. John had her number from go. A light hand across the belly. Restful. Thumb atop the button of her. Over her blouse but close enough. Physical touch. Then a question, the question, whatever question suited him.

I shovelled it myself.

John would be overjoyed the dial was still in motion. Then gutted because he was pleased that she had shovelled the snowy walk. He pictured her in leggings and a parka, no bra, that little shovel, in the near dark alone.

He had told her to buy a scoop. Three or four runs of the walk would see it cleared. She could make things easier on herself. Easier on him. Make February less of a punishment for them both.

But Iris didn't listen. Not listening to each other being a common and shared practice.

I see you, you are there and speaking, her eyes read, but I am not taking in any of your words. I am hard listening, her body language sang, but I am filling in the blanks to suit my learned romantic language. Iris listens so hard that she hears words that aren't being said. She is constantly making it up in her colour by numbers, connect the dots, choose your own adventure mind. Her child's play approach to adult conversations was equal parts invigorating and infuriating.

He wanted to scream stop trying to figure me out! I can't even figure me out! I am an enigma!

Though John didn't scream this for fear of hurting her feelings. Or worse, getting through to her. Iris was a woman well-versed in hurt feelings, she could ignore them like laundry in the dryer, having to re-tumble repeatedly to get the same well-earned wrinkles out.

But getting through to her was something else.

She could turn a piece of unwanted information over constantly for days, months, years even. Explain it away. Hope for alternatives. Until the moment it caught hold, then she was off down the road. Gone in a puff of exhaustion. She would quit smoking in a day. Become a vegetarian overnight. So John never screamed for her to stop.

Sometimes he whispered it quietly while taking off his pants. And Iris laughed it all away.

You say you will love me from a distance as you drive to my house.

In those moments of clarity, he feels the pendulum crack. The snap steadies him to a stop and he feels like a prick. So he calculates and measures a means to feel less prickish. He would detour them far out of the way until she lost sight of her feelings. Then they could cross over onto another road. Any divergence could, would, should decrease the likelihood of circling back. John wishes after time travel to prevent him from ever seeing her cry or in need or sick or sad because of something he did. John would have been perfectly contented not knowing her had he not gotten to know her.

But there was no dialing back to that.

The first confession made in her ear: I don't think we would work and then you'd hate me.

Then there was really nothing else to be done. He wished it had gone a different way. He wished he had taken a different road. But John also wishes he didn't.

Wishing things were different would mean wishing she were different. Or wishing her away. And he couldn't do that. There was a pain that crossed his chest when he tried to whittle it down to nothing. A hurt that he couldn't explain, understand or ignore. He does not want those wishes. He pretends they were make-believe wishes until the tightness releases.

If wishes were fishes they wouldn't be in this fucking mess.

He wouldn't be sneaking into his own restaurant having slept three hours at most, having not moved a miserable inch, to appear restful. Confined to his own corpse-like state of perpetual worry so as not to disturb or engage.

John had grown convinced that certain beloved humans could hear his thoughts.

Sometimes he intentionally runs baseball scores, imagines changing the car filter or recites church hymns to square off what he is trying to deny. He will Minecraft his indecent proposals. Because, my god, they were growing indecent.

John is half the time throbbing like an insane person now.

John thinks this is what they mean when they say cunt-struck.

John constantly lies awake hating himself for his motionlessness but remains unable to execute any manoeuvre, knowing the slightest hint of repositioning would encourage discourse with one and intercourse with the other.

There is no safe place for sleeping.

John exhibits nine of the ten surprising effects of sleep deprivation. He recounts them to himself after midnight while lying stick straight. Sleepiness causes accidents: John had sliced the top of his forefinger off while dicing carrots, lost it momentarily amongst the tops and thought briefly the soup stock would have to be remade, considered not doing so due to lack of time and energy before celebrating the recovery of the lost tip, followed by a period of mourning.

His reaction time was stunted. Like cooking drunk. His vocabulary was impaired; sometimes he forgot the names of root vegetables. Couldn't recall a turnip. His heartbeat was certainly irregular, clip-clip-clipping away inside his cavity. And didn't his face look lacklustre, like his skin was being melted off by some secret radioactive toxic waste disposal strategy.

He was soft around the middle, indecisive and depressed. He was prone to high-risk situations and had the judgement capacity of a crackhead. John was hungry all the time. He wanted to eat and drink all the orange and yellow things. He wanted more than one Big Mary wrapped in bacon snuck into the restaurant through the side door. He would devour it over the sink. Three bites. The salt barely absorbing his sinking feelings before they sank low and heavy in his gut.

Someone is suddenly behind John touching his elbow as he slides his key into the lock.

He had grown distracted by his revolting thoughts and some kind of sick on the side windowpane, not noticing Olive as she timidly caught him by the elbow and off guard. This caused him to fall back long enough to warrant lurching forward. John is a reactionary sort. His whole life trajectory is a kind of chronic whiplash, with this morning's near takedown no different.

Olive had not intended to make him stumble.

He used the small woman's weight to right himself by pushing her swarthy body into the slushy ground. Any passerby witnessing the moment of bearing would assume John human garbage deserving of being hauled around back to the alley.

There was no spin he could put on that. So he was glad for the empty street and Olive's quiet nature. She didn't even cry out. A quick, soft intake of breath was barely audible within their communal personal space, and it occurred to John that Olive was a woman well-practised in silence. And this was a nauseating thought because John knew how women and girls went mute.

Jesus Christ, Olive.

Is Iris with you?

Why would Iris be with me?

Cause she's always—

You scared the shit out of me.

Her car is over there.

So?

I knocked on her door this morning.

Well, I guess she's not home.

Where is she?

How the fuck should I know?

John and Olive both know how the fuck he should.

I have cold feet.

Olive frequently wrapped requests in a statements so rejection would ricochet past her. Terse remarks repelled by the absence of a question. This magic cloak hung in John's closet, too. He tried it on for everyone.

I am making pasta for staff dinner. Rather than *would you like some pasta?*

I am going to smoke now. Rather than *I want you to join me.*

I am not leaving. Rather than *please let me stay.*

John holds the door ajar just long enough for Olive to meet his gaze and walk through to the bench. John had long since brought the dog blanket in from the car. It has lived at the bottom of the hostess station cupboard since the beginning of January when Olive started popping up randomly. Always on cold days. Always early. With a new bump or bruise. Refusing food until Iris arrives. She never goes farther than the bench for fear of George.

Omi peeps around the corner and spies them in the doorway. He immediately notices Olive's shoes. She is wearing ballet flats and wet socks. John hands Olive the blanket as Omi darts back into the kitchen. John is too preoccupied with his own hell freezing over at the moment to worry much on Olive's toes.

But Omi rushes back into the dining room. He has nuked a bag of peas and wrapped them in a red-and-white-checked tea towel. He lowers himself to the floor and wordlessly removes Olive's shoes and socks one at a time, wrapping his dark hands around the pads of her freezing right foot, the pink of his large palms glowing against the top of her tiny foot which has the beginning of a sheen like he has seen in nature documentaries.

Omi watched a lot of programming about the northern hemisphere to prepare himself mentally for the change in climate. It only marginally helped. Some days when the damp sets in, he is convinced no one is meant to live here. It is inhospitable. And Olive smiles through the pins and needles even though she is embarrassed because the gentle man is touching her naked foot and it is the single sweetest moment of her young life.

She wishes her toenails were painted some bright shade of pink.

John thinks this touching tableau is further proof he

is not a good man. He watches as Omi speaks tenderly to Olive and wishes he had thought to warm the peas. This would garner some forgiveness from Iris, maybe even buy a little reprieve. Last night's argument was a testament to her growing impatience.

That wild look having crossed Iris's face when he told her, yet again, that he was leaving.

Following him into the bathroom, watching him wash up, with that scary vacant stare, the look that said she was capable of great feats of destruction. The one that makes John fearful of her. And there is no telling her to calm down. She sparks back hot accusations before retiring to the bedroom to wrap herself and yell some more. She has been raging in her mind for the past eighteen months and each sentence shanks him.

She demands to know why he took up with her in the first place. He must not be paying attention to her at all. Because she did not pretend to be demure. No one in the history of the fucking world would refer to her as timid. Standing atop sheets soused in their mutual weak will, yelling, what in the fuck are you playing at, John? And then using his full name with senior-level authority though she is wearing nothing but a sheer navy thong.

And he loves her like this.

Even if he is the target of her vitriol, he still loves her ability to summon such outrage. Not yet thirty. Penniless. And naked. Yet roaring at him to grow the fuck up with the conviction of an ageless monarch. And she would rule him. He knows it. She denies it. It is discussed at great length. But John knows what kind of woman she will become yet. She would make a lowly petitioner out of him.

Last night, her yelling, finger pointed, eye trained down the line of it.

Your truth is not more fucking true than my truth.

And what was John supposed to say to that?

Nothing. He has no words to settle her. Instead, he grabbed the quilt and brought her down with it. Wrapped her in it and pulled her down onto the mattress. Like taking down a pissy gazelle in a half-damp blanket. John pressed himself around her. Pressure being something that calms her fits of rage. John often wonders if she is on the spectrum. Or if it is him. Perhaps he has lost his mind this time. He cannot recall a time before this when he felt more fucked up.

John is miserable. He loves her so much he cannot think straight. But he also loves his wife.

What is he doing? He has made so many mistakes. He cannot connect them in his mind in a coherent order so as to understand.

He must though. He must make himself understand before she puts a breach between them that will be impossible to cover. He will not have it end like that. He would like to put their rabid dog down kindly. Iris, though, is full of hurt. She intends to take it out back, tie it to a tree and shoot it in the fucking face.

She has told him. She has warned him. She has said the worst things she could ever imagine to put him off her. But nothing deterred him. Now she claims she has no other choice but to silence their mad barking. John knows this is his fault. In his heart, he knows it. John had foreseen this happening and then made it happen. He makes himself right. But now he just wants to stop the hurt that is being lavishly spread around. He wants everything resolved peacefully. He does not want to lose them both.

This kind of love cannot meet an easy end, John, Jesus Christ, grow up.

Last night he had told her about the boy. He hadn't wanted to. Had thought he had more time. That it would take years even. He had thought it would never happen. But George had called crying tears of relief.

He would be someone's dad before summer.

There had been a shift in him so Iris started asking her questions. This: one of her most reliable qualities. She will ask the very question you do not want to answer. She will unearth you.

You don't get to know what goes on in my marriage, Iris, John had said.

That had gassed her fire. And she exploded at him. He tried to make it so she could understand. He had promised he would never leave George. Shortly after that they had gotten the dogs. But the dogs were not the point. He got lost in the retelling. The promise was the point. He has promised to stay no matter what.

Your marriage is fucking ridiculous.

My marriage is none of your business.

You make it my business every time you fuck me!

Jesus, Iris.

You're un-fucking-believable, John.

John had tried explaining that it was different for her. She still had a young body and youthful ideas and could move about the world untethered. But he could not go with her. John's fantasies have always involved her far away from him. Upon first meeting, he took her in and at once anticipated an ocean between them. He calculated the immense, ravenous, ardent longing he would feel and thought best to avoid this at all costs. Whenever a less brutal alternative took hold in his imagination, he listed the many reasons he had been busy stacking against her while she fell in love. Sometimes he listed them aloud to her. And being as she was, as women are, she dismissed them out of hand. Or got angry. John hated her temper.

He burned his hand upon the stovetop of her every time he opened his jesus mouth.

D AMIAN IS ALREADY forty-five minutes late for his shift. He has been late for every shift since Dot was in the newspaper. He should not have read the comments section online. It had sent him into a spin. Damian was spiralling all over the downtown core. It was dangerous to cross the street under these conditions, under normal conditions even, but operating as he was currently would qualify as high-risk behaviour.

John would tear Damian a new asshole if his wasn't already torn asunder.

And he woke up somewhere in the Goulds. He knew it was the Goulds because he could hear dogs barking in the distance. A kennel or breeder or daycare or some shit. It's what farmers did now that no one had use for farms. Training expensive dogs had a greater market share than growing food in the current local economy. Doodles. They were mostly some kind of doodle. Even dogs not of the sketchy variety were mistaken for some appealing hybrid.

Queen Georgina complained people confused her poodles for doodles endlessly. She announced it to the dining room as if this were a real lifestyle indignity she was forced to endure. Dog breed ignorance being amongst the ever-growing list of things about St. John's she finds wanting. Knowing your English Springer from an American Cocker would win her admiration instantly. She was the Queen Bitch.

It seemed travelling made her grow increasingly discontent.

She wanted the same access as any world city. Like London or New York. She wanted Montreal bagels on Sunday mornings and smoked meat sandwiches on Friday afternoons. She wanted the *Globe and Mail* Pursuits section delivered to her door on a Saturday.

Queen Bitch wanted Denmark's public transit system, Iceland's heated sidewalks and all four seasons. Summer, fall, winter, spring, especially spring, and on time every year.

She wanted the impossible.

She wanted St. John's to be a different city, The Hazel to be a different restaurant and John to be a different man. She wanted all things bettered. She saw opportunities for improvement everywhere. She found breaches, attempted to cover them and was left scrambling on the rock face. She was solution-driven and goal-oriented.

Damian loathed her. They were all happier when she was out of town.

And she was without a doubt the reason he knew about dogs going to daycare. Which was rich indeed considering half of people living could not afford even childcare. His own sister was forced to stay home with her baby. Mel had failed to land a modern husband as those were still in short supply, and now she watched a lot of *Peppa Pig* and spoke of lorries and lifts. Not that it mattered who she married. Even the good ones were capable of shagging some young thing in the back of the bought brand new family minivan. Damian had been ridden on the back bench seat of a few Caravans himself.

So he knew a thing or ten about the state of domestication in his ragged town.

And what he didn't know, Queen Georgina was all too happy to share. Spooning the logistics of business operation down their throats at each staff meeting she attended. Educating them on the state of commercial income tax, rising overhead and gratitude. She wanted undying thanks for just above minimum wage serving jobs. She stood lecturing while a pair of thousand-dollar dogs slept at her feet, unaware of the contempt this bred in the staff.

The sharp whines and whimpers of some young bitch's litter had woken Damian. Hungry animals howling morbid songs for their supper. Or breakfast.

Damian didn't know how he got there really, he was just suddenly in a living room.

He was staring at a glass-top coffee table covered in short straws and empties. Through it still, underneath, he could see butts swimming in half-water-filled mugs, abandoned cellphones and a bycatch of Swedish fish. He could not remember eating candy but hoped he had.

He could not remember the last time he had eaten. Or had an appetite for food.

When Damian goes off nutrition, he really goes off nutrition. His mother said this was his way, every slight excused by his predisposition. She was not one to badger her son. Or pay him any mind at all. She had always had her private pastimes. And Damian was just like her. He never paid her any mind either or at all. He had intended to pursue their apathetic relationship through to the grave, hers or his, whichever came first was of little consequence.

Damian had fully intended to maintain the facade of being a loving, if not incredibly busy, son forever. His life did not allow for extended telephone calls beyond the obligatory birthday-Christmas-Mother's Day bullshit. In fact, sometimes, given the opportunity, he would avoid even those. Like on his birthday, he refused to answer her calls. Because he was tripping balls on acid, had believed quite readily there was a panda upstairs, and announced a great percentage of stuff in Campbell's soup was not worth eating before accidentally head-butting Tom, who had been leaning in to kiss him. Tom.

But it was his birthday, and you're meant to get what you want on your birthday.

Rather than be subjected, yet again, to another recounting of your actual birth where your mother implies indelicately that your sexual *deviance* is somehow a result of hard labour.

Tom said Damian's mother was an old hag sitting atop her son's chest.

Tom was convinced she said things like this to get herself off the hook for being absent and then a disaster. Tom had taken none of her passive aggressive humour.

Or, at least, he hadn't before he left. Tom left, too. And it was Damian's fault. Tom seated in the rocking chair, stroking their cat, shaking his head, voicing over and over his disbelief.

I can't believe you did nothing. I can't believe it.

But Damian can believe it. He is well aware of his capacity.

One time, in the beginning, long ago, when he first started doing all this, Damian cut lines on a framed family photo that had hung in his hallway. He was angry with his father for being his father and there was a sick twinge of satisfaction in his underbelly when he leaned over to see himself, straw in hand, snorting coke right from his dad's smiling face. They had been on vacation in Ontario. Some theme park. His sister liked the rides. His mother, the games of chance. Indicative maybe of the future.

The photograph had been handed around so all might enjoy the morose satisfaction of hauling lines from these friendly family faces. While they did so, Damian recalled, in a chilly, drippy way, that his father had yelled at him for pulling the bottom of his T-shirt up through the neck to cup his chest like his older sister. His dad had yelled that boys don't wear their fucking shirts like that. And mostly Damian wondered why no one seemed to mind Melanie's slim bits on display.

Or why this was somehow worse than taking his shirt right off. Because didn't his father also yell at him to swim shirtless when he tried to hide his soft middle under a Teenage Mutant Ninja Turtle T-shirt. Those nearly naked turtles were ripped and ate nothing but pizza. It was a dream. Fucking a Turtle: the sum total of pre-pubescent

Damian's ultimate fantasy. And everything became ninja. Bath ninja. Homework ninja. Breakfast ninja. He was totally aware of his inner ninja before that weak hip hop song ever became popular.

Jesus. You can't even dance to the likes of it.

And Damian is a dance god. He can do things with a glow stick that would blow a straight and sober man's mind, which was the whole point in the first place. Practising his moves along with the MuchMusic Video Countdown because he wasn't allowed to go to parties. He wasn't invited to parties but he wasn't allowed to go to them, either. Melanie went on, though. Apparently the possibility of her sucking dick in a downstairs half bathroom did not present the same moral dilemmas, so she was allowed her small sexual freedoms on the weekend while Damian was confined to an upstairs bedroom across the hall from his parents. And then, from his mother.

Because, you know, his dad left. Because, you know, dads can leave.

Though most did not leave like Damian's old man, who found a lawyer, got the papers signed and remarried in eighteen months.

Most men just went out west and got a secret girl-friend. Maybe a few secret kids.

But they maintained the facade. Iris's dad, who had never fully fucked off, still sent the occasional late birthday card with a twenty stuffed into it. There had been a Tarantino box set another time, a used Tim Hortons gift card taped to the side of some chocolates just recently. Iris and Damian had howled over the pitifulness to subvert the sting. Though her dad's partial fuck off seemed less appealing when Damian found himself caught rubbing the shoulders of a soft, weeping Iris after discovering her hiding behind the dumpsters.

Iris love, what's wrong?

Nothing. It's nothing.

You're chain-smoking behind a garbage can.

Maybe I'm getting my period.

Iris, my dick doesn't make me a moron. Or at least not all the time.

Damian—

Smile! That was a joke about me being a cock-hound. You love those!

I do.

You can tell me anything, you know? No matter what.

I just need a couple minutes to collect myself.

And Damian never has wise words to offer so he just checks on her tables during these collections.

Still, Damian thinks he would have preferred what her dad did. Gentle Jesus, ambiguity seemed kinder than his own dad, who was a definitive sort of man. Which is to say the only sort of man there could be that was deserving of respect. Any other way of being was childish. To be malleable was to be womanly. There was nothing worse than to be a woman or a child, be it girl or boy.

Damian was constantly negotiating being one or the other or both.

And his father, like fathers of the day, only took note when poor Damian stopped over onto some aspect of girlhood accidentally. Then it was all *wuss* and *pansy* and snot and bawling because Damian had no interest in bikes and skates and lakes and ponds. Eventually, he would cultivate an interest in these things, though no interest suitable for discussion with his father. Or any man in his family.

Moving to town where men studied sociology and were vegetarians without threats of violence was a great relief.

Eat that jesus Hamburger Helper and be thankful I don't put my fist in your forehead.

But Damian tries not to think on this. Instead, he never stops talking. Talks about nothing. Nothing anyone will remember later. And staying out all night proves he is still young. Lighting another cigarette is evidence of immortality. Age and death are lurking in the dark alcove next to Damian's mother's current address and Tom.

Don't stop on Tom. Think of anything else.

Melanie doe-eyed at the Miller Centre after getting vacuumed out the first time.

His mother sipping the same warm Pepsi on that same warm stool for six warm hours.

His father's second wife confidently carrying his little brother's cleats across the pitch in her small manicured hand.

His father's new mistress quietly crying in the cereal aisle grasping a box of oatmeal chocolate chip granola bars.

Even his dad the day he debated the way people were born, even that was a better train of thought to board. Anything was better than Tom. That would bring him down. Every night is but a fetus. Any night could be a babe. Given the correct assistance.

So Damian routinely opens his mouth and releases steady streams of bullshit words into lamplit rooms. Rooms just like the one he woke up in today. He does so with sufficient amounts of flare, befitting his handsome face.

He can think of nothing else to do.

IRIS IS FREEZING now.

She should have put some food in her body before setting out for The Hazel. But she never wants to eat anymore. She can remember the feeling of being hungry. The insatiable awareness of wanting breakfast. Bacon. Toast. An egg. The preparation of feeding herself being a tiny ritual that gave her a sense of joyous capability.

Now she just stands with the door ajar wondering if she will ever feel so inclined to keep herself upright. It is a chore now as she has no interest in consuming anything. She makes attempts with her favourite things. Green curry. Fish cakes.

But the banana bread spoils in the breadbox having just the one slice carved off.

A piece force-fed herself over the sink while still warm to make the time spent baking mean something. Though it is little time at all. Iris can make a coffee cake in twenty minutes. It's not much of a bother. John has taught her how to wash up as she goes, having just the mixer to wipe down when the loaves are in the oven. Her tiny apartment reeking of a happy home.

She will throw everyone off the scent.

Sometimes, on her days off, Iris sits on the kitchen

floor and lets the sun set over her by allowing its shiny beams to move upon her face. On these days, nothing seems worth celebrating. Enjoy your time off, they say.

But this is when time feels the most on. She wonders how widows in rocking chairs gather the will to survive. Perhaps they cannot reach the light fixture. Perhaps they've no rope. Iris, though, comes from a long line of resourceful stock. She thinks an extension cord would do in a pinch.

Her ability to rodeo the most heinous thinking has always made Jo uncomfortable.

They both pretend this kind of talk is a lark, but Jo confiscates the extension cords anyway.

Iris would certainly not off herself in any of the ways she has mentioned. That would be boring. Besides, she has lots of time to figure out something more original.

Iris used to fill whole days with tasks. Her life stretching out in front. So much to do. Clean the toilet. Hand wash her lace. Visit Jo. Call her mother. Endless was the potential for distraction. But there is nothing left now for that.

Fuck the toilet. No need for lace. Jo won't speak to her.

She makes her mother cry.

She has started watching every show and turned it off. Books are bought and then forgotten. Projects lie about in half steps as a laundry mountain grows steady on the couch. She foresees an eruption onto the floor, which is covered in salt. Iris hardly takes her boots off in the porch anymore. She drops her coat. Finds the remote. Lies down. Iris negotiates with herself regularly.

She will waste this day but not the next.

She will do all the things to make up for this indulgent self-loathing. She will shower. Dress herself. Clean. Paint. She will paint all day. It will make her feel alive. Remind her of who she is. But she has no confidence in it. She paints hundreds of seagulls.

She asked her father once why everyone hated gulls. They looked fine enough. Tidy and fit. Their colour palette rather conservative compared to birds on TV. Wasn't this something to be generally respected? Seagulls seemed to be birds who knew their place. Little flash. Few fancy feathers. They put on no airs. But her father and uncles did not appreciate these sensible outfits and used them for target practice when birding. Something to fire away at when turrs were elusive.

Seagulls were plentiful and therefore of little consequence.

A bit of sport in bouts of boredom. Hardly worth the bullet.

Her father said they were no good for nothing. Not fit to eat. Shoot one and another would appear. He felt plagued by them. Harassed by their constant screeching. He had made the mistake of feeding them scraps, but feeding gulls just attracts more gulls. Shooting them quietened his rage.

Iris paints their beaks spread wide. Eyes ravenous. Or at least she starts to. She can achieve the first step in her artistic process. And for a time, she thinks it will be all right. She can still do the thing she said she would do. The thing she did well once. Iris would do the thing her mother had sacrificed all her social currency to secure.

Iris almost did not get to do the thing because: they had no money.

She had laboured for months over her OCAD application in near secrecy for fear her cousins would laugh at her. Iris's want for acceptance was equal parts determined and fragile. One wrong word uttered about her portfolio would see it tossed in the stove. So she didn't speak of it to anyone. Her mother, though, took note of her quiet obsession, grateful her teenage daughter was scribbling away at the table.

She couldn't get knocked up in the kitchen.

Cynthia knew the time spent on drawing the best saltbox house, the deliberations undergone on a horizon, she clocked the investment Iris had made in herself. And when the letter came, it was her hands Iris grabbed up, the sheet of paper crumpled in their joined fists as young Iris bounced up and down blurting words: Toronto, art, downtown, school, painter. Her mother knew nothing of these words but she knew want. She could easily identify desire in this young woman she had made. Made all by herself really. The pride she felt stung every part of her. It echoed through to her fingertips. It scratched her eyelids in the nicest way.

But the initial student loan assessment said no to Iris, it said you do not get to do the thing.

On the grounds that her father made far too much money. Never mind that in reality they lived in a rickety trailer on some windy point. Never mind her mother pumped gas in the freezing rain and blowing snow. Or that they never saw a cent of the hundred and fifty grand the government said Sid was meant to share. The student loan people said no, and there was not enough time to debate, and that meant she could not go and would have to reapply, and the grief Iris felt was a teenage girl grief so massive and incomprehensible her mother could not bear it. Iris would go to art school. He owed her that. It was Iris's money after all.

And Cynthia, who had long since given up making demands on men, called her ex-husband and made some. And when he hung up on her, she called back and made some more. And when he hung up on her again, she made threats. When finally he refused to answer the phone, she called his sister next door. She said she would sue him for every red cent of back child support he owed if he did not pay for art school.

She did not give a rat's ass about his truck payments or how much he owed on the fishing licence he bought and never used. Gentle Jesus, what did he even want with a fishing licence, there was no fish left!

She said she had contacted a lawyer even though she knew no lawyers. She said she would tell everyone he never took care of his own, though she would never give the women over the road the satisfaction of admitting she knew the extent of who he did not take care of.

She said she would ruin him, she said a lot of stuff, some of it was even true.

Iris's mother made her full intentions known well and good, all the while aware that this display would result in social isolation. She would never again be invited over for Jiggs dinner or asked in to play cards on a Saturday night. Her former female in-laws would forget to tell her about ACW meetings over to the church basement. She would just see the cars parked there in the evening. They would not need another forward on the floor hockey team. She would go for walks by herself out the branch on full view of the cove. They would shun her right and proper for siphoning money out of their Sidney, who would boast that he was paying for Iris to learn painting in Toronto. After he filed for insolvency years later, he would give up the bragging for blaming. It was a tidy narrative that allowed the cove's continued grudge. They would hold Cynthia responsible for Sid losing his truck until Newfoundland men ceased driving trucks.

So basically, forever.

Her mother's ostracism was the cost of her big city education, and Cynthia was being poorly repaid for her investment. Iris was squandering her new start for a man who had told her he loved her on Christmas Day only to break her heart on New Year's.

In a text.

Her phone told her he loved her while she was at her mother's and pleaded she return.

I can't wait to see you, I need you, come back to me, please, her phone said.

And this was enough. Sadly, more than enough. He knew that, of course. He knew she would accept even less actually. Iris would accept so little. And she left her mother waving in her nightgown from the porch step to crawl back to town through a blizzard at barely seventy kilometres an hour. No snow tires. Hazard lights flashing half the way. Sleet and slush pushing against the bottom of her little Golf. All those cars lining up behind her.

Perhaps they thought her their fearless leader setting pace through the storm. Or perhaps they all hated her. She had angled the rear mirror to the car's ceiling because she didn't want to see what lay in her wake.

Iris only ever wanted someone to look forward to her.

On Boxing Day: he fucked her.

On New Year's Day: he fucked his wife.

George had been out of town for the holidays.

Iris feels so guilty and ashamed. Embarrassed and angry. Worse still, she is another stupid woman chasing after a man. A shit human and horrible daughter who abandons her mother to a cold trailer at Christmas, the windows rattling against the frames, every view of the ocean raging toward the road, gale force winds pushing the sea right to her door, into her mouth, suffocating her.

Iris let her mother down. Keeps letting her down.

Iris let herself down. Keeps letting herself down.

There is so far down to go.

But if she could still paint everything would be okay. This act of redemption would prove that some things remain intact after the heart is damaged. Her hands still move as they did before, her wrists are still fluent. Iris worried this learned skill had been destroyed. She had struggled to even shave her legs. Nicking and breaking the skin like a twelve-year-old sneaking a razor. That one time she shaved her arms.

That had been a bad idea dressed up as good one. Iris has a lot of those.

She thinks, if I do this, I will feel that and that will feel good.

But Iris has a crippled ticker. It is not ticking along

at optimum ticker speed. She constantly tries to figure out the exact moment it stopped keeping pace, but tired tickers wear down gradual. Iris has caught herself tapping her breastbone with her forefinger. She will rap on her sternum with a fully closed fist.

Sometimes she has sat naked on the tub's edge with the moisturizer in her hand, staring down at the dryness of her sheared self.

She would think, everything is cracking apart.

But she could not summon the will to press on, she could provide herself zero relief.

Iris with not even the energy to masturbate.

But hey, at least she's not day drinking.

Iris no longer feels feelings fully. She knew the red tulips inside the grocery store florist cage were her favourite. So she bought them, brought them home, trimmed and placed them in a clear glass vase atop the table and stared at them, knowing they held beauty but not feeling its presence. Cut flowers were a joy for her. She attempted to purchase this joy even though she could not afford it. But she had to have something to hold her in place.

A kind of experiment to gauge her ability to discern pleasure. She was testing her internal thermostat. The test did not yield encouraging results. The tulips were beautiful but they did not register. She could see them, touch them, smell them. She could not feel them in her belly. She photographed them with her phone. She looked at that picture. A sober second look. And it was true, they were pretty even against the dirty corners of the dingy room in a pixelated cellphone photo. Iris saved the picture. She would look again later and hope for a different effect.

She watched *The Princess Bride*, swam laps, drank cocoa, read a Chagall biography and went to the gallery. But there was nothing for it, nothing came. It was a worsening situation. She ran bubble baths but didn't sit in them. There was paint all over the living room dried in place. A younger artist sent along an e-invite to an exhibit at The Rooms. Iris did not attend.

On days when there is no change in illumination, people accidentally hurt themselves.

And there is no one to answer the phone because they have grown tired of listening to her say nothing about being nothing. But Iris did not always feel like nothing.

There were a few moments, clear and crystallized in her memory, when Iris felt very much something. And in those something moments she made promises to herself.

As a girl-child, Iris vowed to crawl inside her colouring books and clothe herself in a pretty palette. The cape of solitude she wore, while leaning hard over the coffee table examining her pencil leads, shielded her from the loud voices over her head.

Have another beer, b'y, go on have another, her mother sneered from the kitchen.

Colouring was like disappearing inside a nicer vantage point. It was like them not seeing her, and so she could not get shot up in the crossfire of their fight. Iris was a weapon for them to use against each other. There was no belt to hit above or below. There was no bell to ring. They were all in, all the time.

Sometimes, occasionally, when her father would storm from the wreckage, Iris's mother would colour alongside her. The warm presence of her welcome and unwanted in the same measure. Iris wanted attention paid but not like this, in the wake, where one would alarm at her allegiance to the other. And so she scolded her mother for colouring the elephant purple. She kicked off at the blue sun in the sky. Small Iris wanted things to be right.

Years later, in a restaurant, today in fact, she will realize in a caught something moment that her mother's colouring had gifted her the very best thing she knew. That her mother sighing those same sad words upon each reprimand had encoded her creative person.

I am colouring my feelings, Iris, these are the real colours of my feelings.

And those tiny tired something moments on their knees all bent over cheap black lined pages had made up Iris's good parts and bad parts. They were, together, the parts that eventually assembled like a surprising set of slowly appearing furniture to sit upon, and in this way, a gorgeous macabre room rose around her. She thinks she will paint this if she ever gets out of here. She will make something beautiful to prevent more wastage and as a memorial to her wounded self.

She will colour in a book all the surfaces of her house, the scratched tabletops, the dinged railings, the worn floorboards scuffed free of shine. Iris is a lived-in woman.

And maybe it is better to be lived-in than admired.

Iris's throat fills with bile at the sight of puke.

Someone has retched alongside the front door. It has frozen into a garish version of its former glory along the wall where the sickness took hold. Looks like lobster salad and sweet potato fries. Popular choices with skaters and suits alike. Their gullets don't differ in pedigree, and it all comes up after being chased down by a party favour or two. Iris doesn't understand why they even bother with lobster salad if they're going to get direct into the rips anyway. It would be better to rest their guts before the rot takes hold.

This, though, would mean acknowledgement. Iris's customers would have to plan to shit their legs off themselves and that would use up whole stores of self-awareness not yet cultivated.

Iris is almost nearing self-awareness. She's fortifying herself for a surge of epiphanies. When she leaves this res-taurant, she is going straight for Jo to share them with her.

And to apologize.

Iris kicks some snow on the brick hoping to hide the worst of it. This is not her job. Omi is meant to do it. But she's in early today. Maybe she has arrived ahead of him. Ahead of everyone, she hopes. But she smells the coffee as soon as she steps through the doorframe.

And Iris stops.

Lowers her body onto her haunches.

Coffee means he's here. Waiting for her.

DAMIAN CAN'T BELIEVE he's in the fucking Goulds.

Something smells strongly of horseshit and hairspray.

Or shoe polish.

It was shoe polish. The insides of his nostrils have a familiar wax and tallow to them. He pinched them with his thumb and forefinger to reduce the ache. This could only mean poppers.

Yes, Damian had brought the poppers to the party.

He can remember now the brown vial held aloft above his nose, delivered by a hairy back of the hand from behind, a deep inhale followed by a push. Momentary weakness, lying on beach, a disappearance. And then another...push. And another. Push.

Everything coming loose inside him. Weariness and worry. Like a suitcase handle slowly wrenching free after years of him minding to carry it upright through security or else everyone would witness the contents unleashed onto the daily-polished airport floor made shiny for visitors. Damian did not want to dirty up the place with his innards. His mother moaning, what will everyone think? That low, surging feeling back of his stomach that promised eventually it would all come out.

Because shit comes out. It just does.

And then alertness, cringing, a wounding, momentary regret and longing before the brown vial reappeared again to push the night onward against the edges of all those sad campaigns.

Stay alive long enough to buy new jeans, Damian.

That's what the economy wanted. Not for him to thrive. Find some kind of peace. Or gather up a fistful of happiness. It was not in the market's interest to keep him alive for the right reasons. And his human worth was sold back to him as such. Damian could sense it each second preceding the next push. Tonight. Another night. The nights that delivered him here were all a variation on this same theme.

He could never be comfortable wrapped in skin that was perpetually marked out. Marriage. Adoption.

Life-giving donation. What. Have. You. Mere distractions from the puzzle pieces that would never slide into place for Damian. The Board of Trade's campaign for wealth made all but a select island few feel increasingly worthless and act out in a reflection of their own self-loathing.

What odds if they all die? What odds? What are the odds? Really. That high?

Nothing is political and yet everything is political.

So Damian drank because Damian's people drink.

There had been a late-night after-hours party at a bar on Water Street. He had been dancing suggestively with the pool stick to nineties mixed hits. "Mr. Vain." Or "Rhythm Is a Dancer."

He could feel it everywhere when he woke up.

He touched his face, ran his open hands along his cheeks, down the back of his hair, along his skull, his neck, rested them for a second criss-crossed atop his collarbone, rubbing the thin nubs before examining his hands. Nothing. He practised clenching and unclenching his tight jaw, heard no remaining audible clicks, ran his tongue across his teeth. When was the last time he had brushed them? Saturday? He had showered before work on Saturday. He looked down now, recognizing himself. His still-black shirt read The Hazel. He had gone out after work. Work.

What day was it?

Damian became miraculously cognizant and adjusted to the reality of daylight seeping through the drawn, dirty blinds behind the curtains full of dart marks. Fingerprints clearly visible through the film of grime and nicotine. Evidence of an internal Peeping Tom likely waiting to be delivered once again by bottles retailed in the trunk of a cab. White or black only.

This is not the fucking NLC, the heavy man hurled back when Damian had requested brand name gin.

Not that it mattered at all what it was.

There wasn't a spirit in the world they wouldn't drink two days into a tear.

Damian's request for something better was just to keep up the appearance of standards so these other men—who were they again? he went to school with a handful of them—so these familiar strangers would think he was in charge of his faculties enough to still find him appealing. But Damian has no standards. He has shotgunned a jug of Carlo Rossi and chased it with Tylenol while watching *Queer As Folk* out of boredom.

Damian has drunk sticky cough syrup with curiosity because a decades-past rock god swore by its ability to ease. He has given a hand job for a bomb and gotten his dick sucked for a rip. One rip. Not even a set of wings to fly on. But it seemed like a decent enough arrangement at the time, he hadn't a clue what the cocksucker got out of it.

Damian just had to lean back. It was one of many unspoken agreements.

Everyone in their shit-bake circle agrees without discussion to outdo previously told narratives in delivery. It is a competition that no one can win, though added bonus points can be earned for displays of undeserved enthusiasm and startling volume.

Sound bites so sharp and loud as to snap all back together with a satisfying click!

Say it again louder, I can't hear, my grinding jawbone is speaking over you. Say it again louder still to ensure you will be heard by someone. Anyone. Again. Again. Again! Everyone is talking. Who is listening if everyone is talking? You will have to say it again from the beginning and for effect. You're a natural born storyteller. It is in your Newfoundland blood. Which is often complicated. And a part of our shared heritage. Except for that grad student over there in the wicker chair. He's from Alberta somewhere. Or the Yukon. They don't tell stories up north sure. Too cold. Freeze your cock off spinning yarns in the northern territories.

Anyway, what was I saying? What were you saying? What was said?

Yes, of course, telling tall tales is an island tradition. They made a commercial about it. They've made a commercial about every jesus thing now. Wipe your nose, b'y. Wipe your arse, b'y. You got a little something something. But come on. Come off it. Come down. Calm. Down. Sure. One more time, one more time, I'm listening now and again, one more time at maximum volume before your nose bleeds and/or the cops show up. Don't be like that. You might as well go to bed out of it if you're going to be like that. I won't remember tomorrow but tell me again and again and again why it is important we ravage ourselves like this.

Is it because of Oscar Wilde? The church? AIDS? How much Damian's father hated him? Or why his friend's father didn't? Is it the back seat of a hockey player's car? Or fucking his sister's friend at prom for cover? Is it never liking team sports but loving the change room? Or is it a haircut? The mere act of having one? Is it that?

Caring about how he looks when the world looks at him funny because he's less than deserving of the dick he's been born with based on a preference to house it somewhere slightly more compact? Or is it because he doesn't care to uphold the putrid fashionista cocksucker bullshit? What is it? Why is he here again? Still? Does he even like these people? Can he even tell? Can anyone remember how they came by all this cocaine in the first damn place? Was it given to them by an older boy at a party once? Did they seek it out after watching *Scarface*? Was he still high? Is this what being really nearly always high is like?

Bodies so conflicted by the presence of countering narcotics, all those beers will keep the gears even keel so no one appears lit up. Loneliness is the same as smoking twenty-six cigarettes a day so smoke 'em if you got 'em.

Damian remembers that a man, missing from the living room upon waking, had announced after some minor yet escalating skirmish that they were all on speaking terms now.

We are all friends here goddamnit!

The skirmish, if Damian was recalling correctly, revolved around an Aphex Twin video declared to be the most fucked up music video of all time ever.

Hyperbolic statements and flash arguments are fuck buddies without safe words on nights like these.

The missing man demanded they turn that shit off.

It's making me bones right edgy, he pleaded.

The fucking limo alone was enough to break a man's mind, let alone that flexible dancing fucker.

Turn it off, b'ys, he whimpered before changing tactics.

Once, just once, just once, I wishes that creepy fucker

would drive past them black girls, swerve broadside the player's car and blow the fucker up!

Why do we always have to watch this same jesus video? Missing Man demanded to know as he ran his forefinger along the neck of his shirt.

Back and forth, back and forth, with a friction so discernible, Damian could almost smell the sizzling rim of his hot collar.

Aphex Twin was melting Missing Man's brain, which, in all honesty, was the desired effect.

They were watching music videos made on drugs for watching while on drugs. It wasn't a complicated caper. They always ended up watching it because there was a clarity of pain inside it they could not themselves articulate. This was not happy people music and they were not happy people.

The doggie yelps had come into a dream Damian was having about being carjacked with a small knife held to his chest. Or snuck into his already waking thoughts about criminal activity. Or a conversation he'd been engaged in, perhaps. He can't be sure.

Suddenly, there was a vaguely familiar naked man sat on a fisherman's sofa chain-smoking. He was reading poetry from a wide-spine selected edition. Damian could not tell if the rendition was meant for him. He was unsure if he had requested this private reading or if he had arisen to it. He could not discern the words, their origin, the poet or the man. But he was handsome. At least the reader was good-looking. Worse to be the lone audience member for nude poems read aloud by some ugly fellow shrouded in a cloud of smoke.

Of this Damian was certain.

This is one thing he can feel confident about.

IRIS ENTERS THE Hazel listening. She can hear the radio deep in the bowels of the kitchen.

The Wilderness of Manitoba sound off amongst the clanging.

Iris thinks a comprehensive list must be made of all the songs that wound, catalogued and abolished en masse to prevent morning commuting mishaps. She envisions women from Calgary to Sault Ste. Marie weeping upon steering wheels as sour sentiments are sung to them before nine a.m. on a weekday morning.

Iris thinks the whole subverted pop song genre, with juxtaposed lyrics and melody, needs to be expunged from a shared mental landscape. As do greeting cards, surprise parties and poems about love. The latter likely more pressing than the former but considerably easier to avoid.

From far off she strains to hear the radio announcer recount a charming anecdote in his familiar brogue, and Iris suddenly wishes today would be a different day. Yesterday even. She wishes she could forget the things that had been said. Walk into the kitchen with a dime bag full of hope. Smile. Maybe still be a lovable woman. But lovable women don't say the ugly things Iris said. Says. Will say. Again.

Lovable women probably don't even think them.

Iris steps into the front dining room to take in a pair of bare heels dangling from her hostess bench. A horseshoe of reddened skin rings worn hooves. Damaged. Irreversible damage. This poor tenderfoot can only be Iris's shadow.

Olive: whose gentlemen callers are never gentle or men but dregs of former humans driving red pickups full of smoke. Their pumping cherries recalling every murder program ever viewed to warn, no, educate, no, remind, no, inform single women of the danger lurking just outside their double-locked doors, checked and rechecked and checked again for certainty.

Iris thinks she cannot be held responsible for Olive's starts and stops.

And she is poisoned at everyone who has left her to it as if she were capable.

Iris isn't even capable of managing herself, and they are both constantly thrown against the dash.

The first night the floodlights lit, Iris shot up upon hearing Olive crumple on the curb. Her shrill squeak followed by a thud and smash. She peeped to see Olive grab at the truck door in an attempt to alert the louse that she did not accept his stingy regard.

Iris watched on as he leaned through the cab, arm outstretched, and hauled closed the door on Olive's little frame, so fast that the wisp of her fell backward yet again before he thundered off. Her ball hat was tossed into the snow, and Iris's surging hatred for the man surprised even herself. She suspects Dirty Deeds is a regular track on his stagnant playlist. She wishes him found impotent.

Olive cried a bit over the loss as she attempted to recover her crushed half-case and cap from the gritty snow heaped atop the shared walkway. She sipped the one remaining bottle and smoked a cigarette before hearing Iris calling her.

Olive, Olive are you okay?

I'm great.

Who was that?

A friend from the bar.

A friend?

He broke my beer.

You don't need any more beer.

I wanted to drink them.

Fuck sakes.

Now, I have no beer.

Come here.

Do you have beer?

I'm not giving you a beer.

Are you mad at me? Maybe he's mad at me...

Come in the house.

I must have done something wrong.

You're loaded.

You're ugly.

Olive!

Iris!

It's freezing.

I feel nothing.

Come in the fucking house now!

You're not the boss of me!

I never said I was.

Who is the boss of me?

You are. Olive is the boss of Olive.

You said it would be better here.

I know.

It's not.

No.

It wasn't my fault...

I know.

Whose fault is it?

Iris reaches out to palm the bottoms of Olive's feet.

She wonders whose fault it was then and whose fault it is now.

The soles recoil at the warm, wet touch of Iris's sweaty mitten. Olive turns over to face Iris without uplifting herself. She doesn't say good morning or even hello but instead tucks her knees in close to her chest, making room on the bench. Iris sits atop Olive's feet. She feels the hot and cold shoot through her lining before bending to pull out her bootlaces. She mourns her red Sorels as they become slack around her ankles. She grieves the thick cream wool socks bought at a holiday fair. Both holding tightly memories of something that will soon cease.

Jo says it takes at least six weeks for new habits to form, which seems like a long time considering Iris hasn't started yet. She wonders why everything must be so horrible as she slides Olive's right foot out from under her bum. She pulls the still warm wool carefully over the foot, trying not to catch it on a toe. Iris has had cold feet before. She knows the misery of it. And Olive flinches but makes no noise or eye contact. She doesn't acknowledge the gesture. And Iris doesn't care as long as Olive keeps her toes. No one should lose pieces of themselves anymore. Iris is after sliding the second sock on when she hears real movement in the kitchen. She hurries along.

Sit up, Olive.

Olive follows instructions alarmingly well even when openly revolted. Iris convinces herself it is because Olive can forecast the boots will make her feet better but knows it is likely some other kind of worse thing. She slips Olive's feet into the Sorels and begins to fasten her in.

I need some money.

I don't have any money.

Ask for some.

He won't give me any.

He will.

I cannot believe you let your feet get this cold.

It was an accident.

You know better than this.

Ouch, they're too tight.

It's just your feet waking up.

They're too big.

You cannot go around in summer shoes.

I don't have other shoes.

What happened to your boots?

Lost them.

Well, don't lose these, they're the only pair we have between us.

I don't want your boots.

Just don't give them away.

Whatever.

Or trade them for pills.

I don't do that anymore!

Say you will give them back.

I'll give them back.

Olive, seriously —

Jesus, fuck. I'll give them back.

Olive swears repeatedly under her breath. She is so weak. Her feet burn. She wants the boots off. She wants to wrap her hands around her toes to take their temperature.

Iris.

Olive can see easy by the look on John's face now that the scene in the entryway displeases him. He has stopped mid-approach, halfway between the front door and the kitchen, holding a mug of steaming something in one hand and a soup spoon in the other.

What are you doing?

What does it look like I'm doing?

Giving away your boots.

Yes.

If you give away your boots you'll have no boots.

I'll drive home, my car is outside.

Of course it is.

Not now, John.

I gave you —

I know.

Iris.

John.

Be reasonable.

You're not supposed to be here.

Neither are you.

I'm just getting my cheque.

Iris.

Don't.

And he puts the soup down on the bar where Olive is meant to sit. The stool closest to the door for a fast getaway in case anyone arrives unannounced. He pulls back the stool and motions toward it without shifting his gaze. They, all three, stand-off. The memory of the boots is irrelevant now. It doesn't matter who walks out of here wearing them. The incision has been made. John and Iris could have a fake bicker about it but that would do little good. Besides, Iris isn't the least bit interested in indulging him anymore. Doing so isn't helping him anyway. It is harming him. Allowing him to meander through his life spewing confident superficial nonsense just encourages him to continue spewing confident superficial nonsense.

And, sure, she will admit to loving the sound of his voice no matter what cryptic bullshit is being spoken. Iris feels like she has won a prize in some accidental competition when John is in front of her. Even when they are like this, fully at odds and near implosion, she feels warmed at the sight of him. Iris wells up with grief when she considers the rest of it without him. Envisioning never knowing the movement of his days is too much for her, even though she knows it is what must happen.

Iris had just wanted to be near him, to live a quiet kind of life somewhere handy to his.

Sometimes, when she thinks of no longer knowing him, she regrets stepping outside for a cigarette with him that first time. Iris had been hired while John was away at Golden Plates. Sarah had been impressed by Iris's friendly demeanour and knowledge of wine. Supposed knowledge of wine.

But everyone lies on their resumé.

It's the only way to get a job in this town. That or know someone who can get you one. Iris knew no one. She had just gotten back from Toronto. She hadn't really kept in touch with anyone from home besides Olive. Jo is, or was, her only real friend. And that took a lot of doing.

Because being with others did not come naturally to Iris. She fakes it for money. Iris is a social tramp. Given the choice, she would not make idle chit-chat about bisque or debate the superiority of whole cream.

Sip your coffee. Snort your coke. Buy your cauliflower organic. Yada, yada, yada.

Iris knows she is getting paid to act kindly. She cannot even choose to be shy. The world is not ready-built for introverts.

There are great lists on the internet with tips for fabricating an outgoing nature. Being humorous will get you ahead. So Iris finely impersonates a confident well-adjusted human. Drinks. Goes home. And sleeps in her dress on the couch. It is all part of the persona she is projecting to keep the lights on.

She had no idea who John was. At first. The significance having been computed too late for Iris to change gears. She thought he was a cook. She thought he was single. She thought George was a man. Because George is a man's name!

This is why women should have more women friends, to ensure a thorough screening process.

Women could identify obstacles and warn Iris before her heart and pussy freeze out her brain. Her brain can get iced out of the control room in a matter of weeks depending on the frequency of contact. The manner of contact. That first time in the back alley he lit her smoke in his own mouth before handing it to her. The casual intimacy of it clocked.

Tick. Tick. Tick. Tock.

The long drag of him made her no longer care about

death. Some people just make you want to smoke. And there was nothing Jo could say after to persuade or prevent. She hadn't even seriously tried. She had never seen Iris so happy.

And then so sad. Then happy. Then sad. Then happy. Then sad. Loops and loops.

JOHN HAS RETREATED to the kitchen now.

Tuesday prep starts from scratch and the sous-chef has texted to say he has the flu. Party flu is more like it, John thinks, but he has no time to reprimand anyone today. Service is full. They've resos for deuces all through the room twice over. They will have to turn it out gracefully or pay the consequences. And John's mind is buzzing, the top of him full of piss and vinegar over last night's argument, and now the boots.

She is deliberating trying to ruin his life.

He searches the cold storage for available ingredients. He must deal with what remains of the weekend first and then go from there. The pork supplier will likely be late due to yesterday's weather, which means he will have to sort that during lunch service. No doubt Damian will be late, too. John promises himself he will fire that guy when he is less short-staffed. And now he will have to convince Iris to work a double even though she is openly seething at him. He's not sure how he is going to bring about a change in her. Fucking fuck. John wishes he could run away from home. Probably can't do that when you're forty. It's likely against some law.

They've laws against everything.

Olive sits sipping the soup as Iris tears apart the other side of the bar while quietly cursing under her breath. Iris grows incensed before throwing up her hands. There are only two ways this can go now.

Where is my goddamn paycheque?

John will not respond while she uses this tone. It would be like rewarding a yapping puppy. He will wait until she calms down and they can have a civil conversation. He will keep peeling carrots to settle her. He knows pulling strips off in tight self-assured motions is a gesture Iris finds appealing. And he's right.

Iris deeply approves of how he moves around his space so purposefully. She gets lost in watching him chop an onion. Just stands watching him do the thing as he had hoped to do. And that sharp pain preceding tears fires through her nostrils, up the centre of her face from her throat, perhaps originating farther down in her belly. Gaining momentum as it nears her eyes which she closes to regain composure. Sometimes seeing him as she has always seen him makes her forget the impossibility of it. Because she loves him and wants him to be well. Even now. Even still.

And the fact that these two notions cannot coexist is searing and incomprehensible. Her loving him and him being well don't seem to get on at all. This brings about a great sorrow. John has taken her for granted. He was reckless with her heart. She had tried to protect them. She had tried to prevent. But he refused to listen. Or acknowledge that she was his person. In every way but name, she had been his person. And now they would get nothing but ruination.

Where's my cheque?

Behind the bar.

No, it's not.

Nan must have moved it.

Don't call him that.

I'll call him whatever I want.

I hate it when you talk like that.

I know.

So why do it?

Can't help it.

That's not a reason to do something.

I do it cause I like it.

Your reasons for doing things are bad reasons.

Iris —

It's not even his name!

It's his nickname!

You can't just rename people.

Listen —

Don't listen me.

Iris had warned, begged, pleaded, tried everything repeatedly and to no end.

I do not agree to this.

She had implored and declared the obvious repeatedly.

I do not like this.

But her words mean nothing to him.

I cannot live like this, John.

Your words are not important words, Jo would say to her in desperation.

There are no important words to John aside from his own.

And then Jo would say he is a predator. The worst kind of man. A *faux-minist*. A liar. He made Iris believe in a falsehood. Fooled her. Groomed her. Identified the want in her and pretend-extended this back, though slightly out of reach of Iris's grasping hands. He kept her reaching and now she has been stretched beyond herself. No longer knowing her own mind.

Iris fits his pattern perfectly, Jo asserted whenever the conversation allowed her an opportunity to ladle out some tough love. Jo rhymed off the dispositions that made Iris an ideal candidate, hardly recognizing that one wouldn't say these things to a stranger let alone your newly broken best friend.

Never loved you. Never cared. Used you. Will use another after you.

And Iris feels like a plastic doll enshrined under coloured cellophane in a box high up and much sought after until handed down, unwrapped and found disappointing. The anticipation of her movable parts proving far more enticing than any joy found in moving them.

Jo did not mean to make Iris feel cheap, inanimate and replaceable, though this talk of her meaning nothing often resulted in the same sad feeling. Iris felt totally disposable. But Jo would not, could not, relent. She needed to focus Iris on the hate in it, for everyone's protection. Jo could not know that she had further traumatized her dear friend through her dogged effort to safeguard them until much later. Too much later.

You have just the right amount of damage to suit him, Iris. You are a bright open book.

Jo watched as John clearly read Iris's tender parts surging beneath the tough sinewy bits, and this scared her the most. Jo thinks Iris is a victim of a manipulative sex pest.

That man is not fit to lick your boot bottoms!

She made Iris take a "how to spot a sociopath" quiz with her morning cry and coffee while Harry played with Lego in the adjacent dining room. John was charming. Intense. Spontaneous and highly intelligent. John was very smart.

Iris loved how smart he was. She loved other things less.

John is dominating. Must win win. At all costs. If you're not with him, he's against you. And quick to aggression. John will flare up at mere mention of rebuke. A whiff of contempt raises up them eyebrows. Iris knows all this and loves him still.

Perhaps this means she loves a sociopath.

Perhaps this means she is one.

No, Jo has said. Because here is what splits you apart. Jo believes John is incapable of genuine shame, guilt, grief or love, while Iris marinates in the mixture. He is self-serving in all things. And Iris is not. She has no such drive. John is a delusional phony with a sexy gift for turning people's words inside out. He has riddled Iris so completely. Iris can't remember who she is or was before him.

John could tell Iris she was a duck and Iris would throw herself in a pond.

So Jo reminds her of her human self. You are a happy person. You like other people. You want them to be well. You have never watched this much television in your life. Turn that murder show off for fuck sakes. Take a walk. Read a book. Make a cup of tea. Or pick up your paintbrush, Iris, paint something, make something of your hurt. This is not you. You are not like this.

But Iris worries maybe she is like this, maybe this is what she is like now.

The last couple years have convinced Iris that she's probably not a good woman. Not a wholly good woman. Maybe, possibly, a bad woman even. And Jo had said, stop that.

That is him. Not you. You are not that. Everyone knows the difference, and anyone who doesn't is a fucking idiot. This will not make you happy, she had texted. He is not kind to you, she inboxed after midnight. Please stay away from him, she begged, standing forehead to forehead.

Jo is so mad. She is so friend-mad at him. She could kill John.

And it is true, Jo would kill him in her very own way if Iris would allow it.

Because Iris would crucify any man who treated Jo so appallingly.

Jo can see Iris deep beyond the treeline burying body parts in the woods. Hacking away at the frozen rocky earth with a Canadian Tire shovel stolen from a neighbour's step. Iris would break all the laws for Jo. She would battle cat for her only remaining friend. Iris wanted all the world made safe for the woman who hand-delivered single servings of won ton soup to keep her alive when things became disordered.

During the start, when Iris was pursuing a better path, she had awoken in the night to find Jo in bed beside her eating a bag of cheezies in the dark. Jo had taken to sleeping next to Iris again, confiscating keys, hiding the phone. Jo would keep vigil. She would sleep anywhere and say anything to starve off this man. Jo had shushed her like she shushes Harry, go back to sleep, back to sleep now, Iris.

But only after inquiring softly: Did you take off your bra? You shouldn't sleep in your bra, love. It's bad for your back.

The next morning Iris had woken up alone thinking it had been a drunken junk food induced mental episode before reaching between the bed and the wall to find the empty cheezie bag. So yeah, Iris would dig the hole for any man alive that dared say a harsh word to Joanne. Everyone deserves a Joanne. All women should have a Jo to ensure survival, though she knows friends like this are also in short supply. Iris is so lucky to have her. Was so lucky to have her.

But Iris had been weak-willed with their well-being. She had failed to protect them.

And she shifts in place, measuring the weight on each foot, focusing her attention on the balls first, and then the heels, then flat, then shift. She imagines the varicose veins seeping up toward the alabaster surface of her stretched-flat stomach skin.

You're so white, John says when he looks down at the rest of her in repose. Iris now suspects he says this to George. Iris now wonders if everything he has ever said is recycled. Perhaps she is a testing ground for new material. These thoughts feel wrong-minded and sinister as she gazes across the prep station while they both prepare themselves. She tries to give him more credit.

You never give me any credit. You discredit us with your imagination.

But Iris does not agree. This is the most generosity she is capable of under the maddening circumstances.

Where is my cheque?

Iris, listen to me —

I need my cheque.

Iris knows standing up to John like this in the restaurant is not in her best interests. He has punished her for less. Turning her mouth from his has garnered the cold shoulder for days. John will stonewall her if she even attempts to break free. He will defame her to her co-workers and cast her out of the kingdom. John will make food for staff dinner that she is allergic to on purpose and pretend that he forgot, even though everyone knows John never forgets. No one makes mention of it though. They just watch Iris eat something cold alone at the bar away from the cooked smell of John's rejection.

John can be right shitty when he wants to be.

Like right now. He is lucky she has not thrown a pot at his head for forcing this with her today. Last night, whispering in her ear, after urgently darting kisses all up and down her neck and face, he had said in painful tones: I love you but I won't leave her.

Not even can't. Won't.

Won't delivered with conflicting conviction through a held-fast hug. John is a fucking fabulist of the highest order. It is really rather rich to comment on the lily-white topcoat of her and then wipe her down with the concluded failings of her underbody in such affectionate rejection.

Because how else can a person feel when told you don't want them?

Iris's mind, along with the rest of her, has been truly

fucked this time. There have been other men who attempted to mind-fuck her. They have commented on many of the same aspects. Suspected her a vixen, this assumption based on some misplaced adolescent fantasy, childish song lyrics and porn. They have brought her milkshakes and completed her botany assignments. And she resisted them all in a fantastic fashion.

But John.

Fucking John, star alignment, proximity and poverty, has made this disaster possible. Commenting on how pale she is. What colour did he expect from the front of her? They live in fucking Newfoundland where it is perpetually almost summer until it is almost winter again. Though every man that has ever formed an affection for her had made this same discovery. You're so white, Iris.

Perhaps they are racists in their hearts. She considers this in as lengthy a manner as can be maintained. She does so to maximize the amount of time she can stand the pressure of her own impatience. She will speak first in this kitchen. They both know it. Iris has always been the one who says the things. John can wait her out. It's not even particularly challenging to do so.

Sometimes, he even enjoys watching the words simmering just beneath that loose lid of hers. She has an array of tells. John thinks she would make the worst poker player. She blushes like a teenager, refuses eye contact and fidgets. Occasionally she bites down hard on the right side of her lower lip like she is trying to clamp-hold the thoughts that are coming next. There is always something coming inside of Iris. But John really doesn't have time for this today. Or any day.

There is no love left in it.

How can Iris say the things she says and then still claim to love him? He cannot understand her duplicitous nature. All sharp edges and soft undersides. Angry words hove out on a wave of tears. This is not what he wants for them. Was never what he wanted. He was not entirely certain of what he wanted from one day to the next to be sure. But this was not it. Although he had hoped for some tidy alternative arrangement whereby everyone would be okay, unharmed and untethered.

He wanted something different.

Even though there is no obvious logical means to execute this that he can see, John keeps wanting it. John cannot help the want existing. He never could. His impulse-control issues are epic and astounding. It was unconscionable to think an actual adult man could be capable of such miserable choices. A legacy of barely believable misdeeds dismissed and forgiven.

Might I suggest —

No, you might not make suggestions.

It was not about —

You forfeited any right to make suggestions! We are broke up! You broke us up with your shit decisions so now you do not even get to know me. At all. It is not even fair, John. The hurt I feel now is not fair. So save your fucking suggestions for George, you and she can go on living how you like! What you are doing to me is wrong. What you did to me was wrong. I was so good to you and you broke my heart like it was nothing.

And seeing her hurt kills him. It does. It kills him. And he doesn't know how he keeps ending up at this same set of lights, blowing through her intersections, surveying the pileup in his stead. The carnage that he glimpses in the rear-view as he speeds away from the scene makes his stomach knot. He worries the police will find him out. He will be identified finally as a routine hit-and-run driver, cuffed and carted off to the clink where he will be forced to relive this roundabout series of crashes in his head endlessly. The loop of blame and guilt twisting his intestines until he is certain he will erupt. Implode. He can't think on it a second longer.

No. It must be Iris's fault.

It is her fault she is all the time crying at the drop of a hat. She has caused the flash flooding. It is Iris's fault alone she sits in a bathtub like a hobbled woman. Sometimes there's water. Sometimes there's not. Sometimes she takes pictures of her legs and sends them to John with harassing messages. And then, a couple beers later, about how much she loves him. This is the impetuous state of her.

Whiplash.

If I recall correctly, you were fucking me, too, dearie.

I was never *fucking* you!

And it's true.

That is a true statement they can both agree on in this kitchen in this restaurant in this city at this early hour. Her body was built for fucking but her heart was not. It was built for that other thing that eludes her. This is perhaps the great tragedy of her person. Her external structure does not elicit the desired internal response in men.

You are an oxytocin fiend, Jo would say. Hookups and Tinder are not your jam.

Jo tells Iris that she should not even engage in romantic notions because her romantic notions cloud her judgement so fiercely. And John knew this too. Iris had told him. She had accidentally mapped out a Go Guide to her wounded parts in an insufficient attempt to scare him off or encourage kindness.

Be careful with me, she pleaded when she still believed him to be a nice man.

But John is just a nice man on paper.

Iris had held out her heartstrings to him: the same few threads that still held her together, she had trusted that he would not haul on them. But instead, like an angry rival fisher from a long depleted bay, John started reeling in that trap line, hand over fist over hand over fist over hand over fist. It was only what he was owed. Others get what they want and so should John.

Even now, in this very moment, in defence of herself and her intentions, Iris has baited the skiver nail and John will have what is in that pot, too.

John knows how Iris feels about him. He always knew.

And so he places the knife down along the cutting board's edge and makes his way toward her. She recoils at his approach, shakes her head, places her palms against an invisible door to keep it closed tight. Every gesture is no. But she hasn't said it. She has never yet been able to find it in the back of her throat, this tiny tricky word that could save her has not found its way into her vocabulary. So John continues on his way toward a stone-still Iris. He slowly drops the full weight of himself onto his knees, palms upward, a too soon request for forgiveness. Please forgive me for this, everything, someday. And the first motion breaks through, he can see the glimmer in her, that little stir informs him she is malleable still, still his, they are still somehow together for this frame of time.

He starts forming words, inconsequential words, not intended to communicate anything with any sincerity, but rather merely sounds to distract from forming her own ceasefire words, a litany of soothing syllables to keep her focused on his steady lowly movement. The communication is in the forward motion as John crawls across this kitchen floor toward her on his hands and knees. Like a beggar. Presses his warm palms atop her stocking feet and pleads. And then kisses. Takes each foot in his hand to press against his face before sliding these same well-known hands up to the waistband of her tights, bold, gripping, taking all in one confident swipe, down now, holding her in place before pulling a foot wholly out, a breakage, a space. Iris watches from above, wordless, as the realization of what will come next forces her hard against the still warm dishwasher. The hot stainless steel steaming against her backside as John glides his head inside the hem of this A-line dress she has worn many times but will never wear again after.

The soup stock simmers atop the range.

Iris watches the bubbles bouncing up, and up, and up toward the rim as John runs his tongue through her, lapping her into a kind of fevered, quiet calm. And even in the surmounting scene, with her hands in his hair following intently as he moves his face along her very tip meant to please, Iris's eyes are trained on the delivery door. Though held hard and fast in her love-like state she is still aware that a burly denim-suited man is meant to bring the protein this morning. Pigs. Soon the pigs will come through that door and all will be skinned alive. Because they're meant to not do this, this thing they keep doing even though it will only hurt more. Hurt her more. But it doesn't hurt now. Now, there is only a kind of urgency. And inside this frantic moment that can't be happening, Iris reaches across to lower the heat surging beneath the soup stock. She must not let it burn on. Because they will need that later. Later.

But for now, she lets John pull her to the floor and push himself inside her until there is nowhere else left to go but down.

OLIVE IS ALWAYS surprised by the size of Iris's feet. Her boots are really too big. They hang heavy on Olive's feet. She feels childlike in the presence of these angry adults in the early morning hours. Iris is only three years older than Olive but she has an old rage about her.

Olive knows that, if kicked, Iris will kick back.

Olive lets her feet hang along the stool railing. She swings them a little but not so much as to make a sound. She is listening to the developing narrative in the kitchen as she sips her soup. She can feel it making contact with her stomach and pushing itself out through her veins and is buoyed by the conflicting chili and lime heat inside her middle parts as she eavesdrops. She has overheard variations of this argument before through Iris's low open bedroom window over the summer when it was hot. Olive had been outside smoking into an old plastic pop bottle full of butts when Iris's frustration came out flying through the curtains in fits. And then a different noise.

Some women were always fighting or fucking.

Olive can no longer hear the yelling from the kitchen. The vacant feeling she feels in moments of anxiety spreads quickly to her lungs, which have little air taking up residency. She has been mastering a shortness of breath since the first ice cream sandwich was unwrapped. This new technique of living is more a slight parting of lips, a modest tilt of the head, as some unseeable hand holds the nape of her neck up, barely discernible enough to spot as the smallest puff of oxygen is hauled in. Olive's mouth is a discontinued coin. Round. Forgotten.

The yelling in the kitchen has morphed into soft murmurs.

Olive readies herself for heading outside. She had hoped to stay a while longer but cannot stomach what is cooking back there. She wishes Omi were still here to stop it. This would not be happening if his lean dark body were still angled over the slick metal sink. Olive admires his frame when he brings the glassware into the dining room. She spies on him when she is supposed to be sleeping. He hangs the stemware so gracefully, sliding each glass along the line without clinking the next. It is soothing to behold. Olive, in secret, admires his forearms and imagines another place where they were formed. She would like to ask him how he is adjusting to the temperature difference but she finds herself too shy.

Her inside parts blush when he nods at her so she turns away from him.

She knew what would transpire when John sent Omi home before clearing the rack. She caught sight of him snatching up an envelope from behind the bar and tucking it in his apron as he wove the dishwasher away. Omi, confused at his dismissal, worried John was displeased by the mess on the facade. He apologized profusely for a thing John barely registered, because Omi needs this job. Omi needs all his jobs. All of Omi's shirts are second-hand shirts and all his leftovers are dinner. The necessary money from dishwashing was a lot so he begged John's forgiveness and expressed gratitude freely. It was the only free thing to do, but John waved it off like nothing and told him to come back early for dinner service.

John cannot be bothered with the dishwasher's feelings. He has too many feelings to be bothered with that aren't his own already. John cannot even see Omi. John can only see what concerns him.

Olive wants to give Omi a little hug or shake.

She wishes he would run away from here. But also that he would stay because the sight of him makes her feel lighter. But he has gone home for the daylight hours and she must flee now too. Her disgust with John and the act in general has been recently tested further. The whole concept of maleness has taken on a sour taste. She puckers at the thought.

Any romantic vessel that had been seeking safe harbour in a calm recess of Olive's inner cove has since perished. She has sunk all aboard that shitty battleship. She suspects the remains will be eaten by a shark. Thrashed by jaws so unforgiving and destructive as to devour everything that lies within fin stroke. Car engines, ship's hauls, great steel tower beams; the entire industrial revolution, best-intentioned recycling and the feminist wave are no match for the kind of shark coasting through Olive's imagination. This shark was murderous. Not even hateful for hunger. But murderous for pleasure. Sleek and efficient in ripping great muscles from the fine and fit.

Olive thinks John is just that kind of shark.

She has seen John present himself unkindly to Iris. Caught from the corner of her eye a ready sneer pointed at Iris's turned back. Iris has unknowingly been snarled at by this lover of hers. Olive has seen him roll his eyes at Iris's wet cheeks. Throw his hands up at her beseeching tone. Olive has seen John sigh as if it were Iris that caused *him* grief.

Olive wants out of his way.

She tries to visualize the remainder of her day. There are a lot of outside daylight hours to account for while she avoids her landlord, who will settle into his own couch after dark and then it will be safe to make her way back home. Olive imagines how the shower will warm her and hopes there is enough citrus-smelling shampoo left to scent her mangy mop.

Body Envy it's called, as even shampoo is marketed to make her feel inadequate.

Olive will add water to what shampoo rims the plastic seal to stretch it further. Olive is always shocked at the smell of blond women's hair. She finds herself thinking *your hair smells good* and sometimes saying it aloud each time she is near enough to the catch the scent. Even their hair has been trained to retain pleasant qualities. Even their hair. Each strand of it, regardless of quantity or quality, can hold fast appealing aromas. Fragrant bouquets. The herbal essence.

Olive's hair smelt often of sweat underneath a wool cap meant to keep out the wind. It was not so dirty-looking; the thick coarseness inherent in her family pedigree allowed for extended periods of drought. Her grandmother never washed her own hair more than once a week. She boasted regularly that it had not seen a drop of water in ten days.

Townies wash their hair too often, her grandmother says. But Olive's nan thinks everyone in there is wasteful, greedy and ungrateful. They want what they got and what she got and what everyone got. They want everything everywhere.

Olive grew up in a place where polar bears ate your dog. As did Iris.

They learned their letters on a coast where each day could be colder than the last, even in April when the brooks were meant to ease and the caribou were meant to move.

Olive was forever marching slowly backward to ward off temperatures threatening to assault her. Eyelashes iced over and held fast to let loose tiny pools of water down the trenches of cheeks. She would squeeze them shut to melt it clear before they'd freeze open. Squeeze them shut. Drain them. Let the drops run. Not teardrops. Just water atop your frozen lids. Olive knew better than to cry on the way to school. It was so far to the bus stop, her face would ice over.

Olive gathers up the things she will need; fills her pockets with paper napkins and candies before heading out into the elements. Iris's boots will take some getting used to. The heft of them weighs Olive down, each step landing

106

harder than the one before. But they are dry. Olive wiggles her toes again, which now wiggle just as toes should. She zips her coat and steps out onto the curb. She takes a long gaze down each sidewalk to scan for obstacles. She can't go back to her apartment without the rent.

She'd had hardly any money to speak of since she got fired from the bar. It was a yucky dive frequented by dancers who couldn't afford to drink at the peeler bar across the street, but easy enough money if you weren't scared of drunk people on drugs. Olive was, of course, but could mask her fear with jokes and swears, a lifetime of practice made perfect. Besides, being a cashier at Marie's Mini Mart was just as dangerous, and she had hated the sticky stink of Mary Brown's chicken grease on her clothes.

She sometimes cleaned Airbnbs in the summertime. This was her favourite job. She had loved every minute in the beautiful apartments. She would clean with the windows wide open, sometimes with views of the harbour, the sounds of boats and birds a comfort. There were often leftover fancy snacks from specialty stores, half-drunk bottles of white wine and imported beer. She would finish off the mystery cheese and tinned nuts as she tidied, collect up the soft fruit in a plastic bag and walk home with a little buzz in the afternoon sun. She had been saving to take her Traffic Control Person certification before Christmas. Olive would like to work outdoors in the summer.

Olive would usually rather be outside than inside.

Then everything had come loose. After, she had burned through her savings so quickly that it felt retroactively humiliating to have felt such pride over five hundred and fifty-three dollars. Olive's heart aches thinking about it. And her legs ache from the hard hostess bench. She wants to brush her teeth really bad.

She will ask Iris for a loan again after she finds her paycheque.

It is cold and wet and snowy outside. Typical day after storm stuff. The exact time eludes Olive, but it is before noon because The Hazel opens for lunch at noon and it is still closed. And it is Tuesday. And Tuesday mornings under these conditions are pretty dead.

Atlantic Place will be virtually deserted, which is a blessing as John's spicy soup is making a racket in Olive's gullet. John rarely takes into account the state of her diet. He brings out what he would want for himself and she eats it with an undiscerning hunger. Though, more often than not, the rich food does not agree with her nearly shocked-through system. The creams have not been properly introduced to Olive's guts. Like everything in her life, it is just thrust upon her, full-throttle assault, a foreign food bomb waiting to go off.

Olive does not have access to the proper defences to deal with the fallout. St. John's has notoriously few public bathrooms. This dignity is not a thing those in charge concern themselves with, so Olive stays handy to reliable spots. Atlantic Place is where she will go today. This will save her self-esteem. And her paper napkins. Out of the corner of her gaze she spots a small woman moving toward her from a distance with unmistakable determination and assurance.

And unmistakable dogs.

The dogs always give her away. It looks like they're wearing coats. Olive squints to discern the matching argyle coats or sweaters or scarves across the lot for what seems a long time as all three come into view, until their destination occurs to her and she is startled from her stare. They are headed for The Hazel. They mean to go to the restaurant. Which will cease to exist if they reach it in its current state of affairs. Olive must alert the kitchen or there will be no more soup and safe sleeping. She ducks her head back into the dining room. It is just as she left it.

Yet untouched by the fast-moving disaster.

So Olive, whose basic nature and learned behaviour has made her an expert in using so few words, must now find the right words to alert the louse and Iris. She must yell out. But this seems far beyond any stretch of imagination she can span, so instead she searches the room, eyes darting from the wet bar to the wine bar, antlers hung high overhead, along the length of the stemware rack wearing its glassware fringe, and each idea forming seems too much or not nearly enough. But she must must do something. This is not fair, she thinks as she grabs up her licked-clean soup bowl.

And fires it at the wall.

JOHN HAS BEEN letting that sketchy girl nap inside the door again.

George puts it together the moment she's through the entry. You would think he was trying to provoke divorce. Except he would likely claim this was her doing as well. Nothing is ever John's fault. He will claim her past over-reactions have made it impossible to confide in her for fear of retribution. But she always finds him out. He leaves clues around like a reckless bugger.

The dog blanket they keep in the car lies limp on the bench in front of the hostess station. There is a weirdly familiar odour. And the candy tray has been cleaned out. Again. Likely because misses is on drugs. That's a thing, right? Drug addicts need candy to curb their drug cravings. Meth-heads with pockmarks and poor teeth. Humans ageing so rapidly as to shock ex-lovers into committed lifelong sobriety upon sight. Yes, for sure, they mentioned it on *Breaking Bad*. And that was obviously a well-researched program.

No one wants to eat Sweet Sesame Duck surrounded by opioid addicts.

This kind of thing is definitely going to have to stop now, George thinks as she carefully folds the blanket away from herself. She will have Nan wash it separate from the linens before she puts it back in the car. She had a list going for him somewhere behind the bar.

George shuffles papers to one side trying to locate it before she forgets to add the task, careful to circle *separate* in sharpie. Nan would wash table napkins with bathroom towels to conserve time and water. It's not even his fault, really. They do things differently over there. It's not like he lets randoms nap in the porch. George knows this because she had accused him of doing so first off. Had fired him in fact.

This was before John confessed his private humanitarian project. George had felt ungenerous but whatever, she was still right. Poor people sleeping in doorways is not appetizing. It does not encourage hunger or the right kind of patrons: namely, any human that still has disposable income in this economy. It does not allow them the freedom to spend said income on soft cheese wrapped in prosciutto while drinking ten-dollar pints of craft brew from Ontario.

In fact, it makes them feel guilty and reconsider their spending habits. They go somewhere cheaper to discuss cooking meals as a family and donating non-perishables to the food bank. This year they will turn over leaves and be better people without telling anyone. But they won't. They never do. When they do occasionally support something, in even an indirect way, they take a photo of it for visible proof and post it immediately on Instagram so they can enjoy the full scale of their benevolence.

Some people do nice things just to be nice, but not George's people.

Sometimes they don't do nice things at all. They think they will and then forget. They're the kind of people that can forget without consequence. They don't know the fear that George knows.

Her mother grew up piss poor. But she had looks.

And so does George.

Beauty can make up a lot of lost ground quick.

But it can't make up for the contagion of beggary. This poor outlook, while not really looking so poor for George, makes spending two hundred dollars on a whim Wednesday dinner feel distasteful for some.

Her surname does not make her oblivious to the world, like John would think.

She knows the socialists are up the hill protesting with their children on their shoulders. She caught a whiff of the citrus scent in the air. Fantastic optimism always has a certain pungency. Throngs of SunnyD liberals hoping for an egalitarian utopian future imagined in the prologue to some science fiction book. George dated a sci-fi fan during her undergrad. She excused the D&D and *Star Trek* nonsense because he was so handsome.

His beauty had a wide footprint.

And she agrees with her rusty neighbours to some extent. But she agrees from her nicer house in her staunchly red dress. George has no desire to live surrounded by swarms of illiterate skeets either. She teems with envy every time a recruitment event lands her at a speaking engagement in the Halifax library.

That's a far stretch from letting alcoholics sleep in the porch.

Besides, she had never known John to concern himself with the plight of the underclass. John had never served in a soup kitchen or even donated time to charity. In fact, she has heard him suggest homeless people should get a job, like it was the easiest thing. Put them in the dish pit, he'd say at parties.

And truthfully, she preferred him that way. It was virtually the only subject in which he afforded her the position of good cop. Now, he is all the time shaping himself as some kind of community activist, which is not to say that she does not like it. John looks great on TV. She likes it. She does. But it was *her* thing. Not John's thing.

He could not tolerate any of it five minutes ago and now he is out of pocket preparing snow crab, crème fraîche, fennel consommé to fight poverty on a weeknight. He is giving television interviews in his whites discussing the need for a multi-layered approach with concrete and measurable community action. He is feeding some skinny girl out the front door and swiping sweaters from George's closet.

George is pretty sure she didn't marry this guy. Which is to say that she likes him well enough but finds the shift perplexing. She had attempted to discuss the change once in an inquisitive tone and he'd been hurt. Or was it insulted? Something got his back up. Regardless, a marred expression had darkened his face before he'd stated that of course he cared about poor people.

I thought you knew me, John said. You of all people should know me better than that.

Following it up with, come on, Georgina, you're the only person who truly does.

Playing the Georgina card, placing it down on the table with a toothless bay grannie's level of certainty, the kind that takes twenty years of card games in the church basement to curate, the kind that attests, without flash, that this hand is over, give up, give in. And she did. John knows the trumps are in her kitty and he's not afraid to call for them. John will play a blind hand. He'll suss out every trump she's got.

You know me better than that, don't you?

So she can't rightly inquire again as to his motivation even though she has a lingering feeling that John's new-found love of humanity is questionable.

Gretchen and Mol are both investigating the blanket area with some interest. It smells like them. And someone else. Their intrigue is tangible. The poms on their tails signalling their excitement. George wishes men had tails that worked in such a manner. Or, at least, visible tails. To wag their indecent thoughts. George envisions a world where men have tails that wag of conquest until it turns frantic. And she takes back her wish almost immediately. No one needs to see that. Revolting.

The weird smell is revolting too, and the girls are not acting very dignified.

Sometimes George barks *act dignified* at them when they behave improperly. Goosing people on the street, right in the ass. Or worse. Men and women alike spinning around to meet George's eyes. Responding, *you* act dignified! George apologizing, sorry, sorry, the dogs. My dogs did it. Men letting their eyes drip all over her, saying, sure, sure they did.

As if in any reality George would shove her hand in their ass on a busy downtown street, implying that she was a sexual predator using her dogs as a cover.

Gretchen and Mol want to search out the rank smell. They are pulling on their leads. Circling the doorway. Barking a little for the sport of it. Their confidence in their doggy prowess is amusing and unearned. They cower and yelp when the neighbour's cat makes physical contact. The dogs whimper and whine as George removes their tidy sweaters. They lick and pull at the clumps between their paw pads. The girls hate salted sidewalks, they hobble along in their dainty way. But now they too are revived, full curly coats now ablaze and unsheathed.

John prefers the dogs buck wild, messy, fussed. This is not a species-specific preference. It bleeds through the animal kingdom. If John had his way, everyone, man, woman, dog, otherwise, would be in a constant state of bedhead. Post-coitus would be the only blowout available in salons across the land. Not that hair alone is sufficient, the full-focus picture would have to capture a fine glaze of sweat, shiny across the upper lip, soaked through the torso, and then the flush. A glow. Or a fog. Call it what you like. And George can't even stay mad when she thinks of him this way. Kissing her eyelids as she rambles about renovations, food inspectors and the rising cost of protein. Her body in repose but her mind humming. Fully lit up.

John had been a surprise.

George had married the right guy the first time. The lawyer guy with the straight-striped suit and the gleaming brown oxfords. She had followed all the rules, had fashioned herself correctly, waited patiently for her ring and then planned accordingly with a keen eye and level head. She had not bridezilla'd, not even once, not even a little bit. There had been chalkboard doors, beeswax candles, patterned fabric triangle banners, hundreds of tiny paper cranes, full flocks. There were umbrellas and rubbers, big-top tents and baby-blue cotton candy, a fish taco truck, a sweet shop. Andrew had worn a polka-dot bowtie, her in fitted antique lace, it had been precious and heartwarming. They were featured in a free local lifestyle magazine as an example of how to live your life in style. They had celebrated their union through the streets of downtown behind a bagpiper.

They had been a parade.

George had actually started her victory lap the moment Andrew slid the pink-gold princess-cut over her finger. She had rejoiced. She was done standing broadside women in dresses she did not fancy. She had paid her bridesmaid tax each time she had received a notice of assessment. She had watched the sisters-of bicker over running order and stepped in only when threats of physical violence against fake eyelashes and hair extensions were issued. In those moments, George was happy to have no sisters, no siblings. She was not bothered. Everyone accused of wanting their own way. Of course everyone wanted their own way. What other way would you want? Someone else's way? That's preposterous.

There'd be no inside the clothing rubbing-up of Princess Georgina of Circular Road.

George would eventually learn to quickly tell what kind of fellow you were according to how you addressed her. Clear patterns emerged early on regarding intentions and perceptions of her based on chosen title. This carried on into adulthood through Andrew, who preferred Gina, to John, living strictly on Georgina, to her father, proclaiming their shared name repeatedly and with great significance. The serving staff at the restaurant rarely called her anything. Or at least not to her face.

She is sure they have a slew of stupid shitty names for her they dole out freely behind her back. She often wonders if John participates, hopes he doesn't, though thinks he probably does. John is the biggest kid of them all. The great irony of her second attempt is enough to wind her when it comes flashing through the daily grind of shit surefire shot her way.

John is her towering man-child.

George is still up front unaccompanied steering this bloody battleship as it rockets toward the sun. The call from CRA this morning verifies. It is undeniable. And

George had thought that they had gotten through, her and John.

She had thought the worst of it was over.

The endless ultrasounds, injections, legs over her head, hoping. It had not been sexy for Andrew and it was still not sexy for John. But he was her real guy so she believed it would be different. Andrew had been her starter marriage. The conception troubles were a blessing dressed up as a curse because if all had gone the way of the stork, she would now have children, a boy and a girl ideally, with that bastard. Andrew was her woman dues and now she was fully paid up. Overpaid. The universe owed her John. Beautiful John and his beautiful offspring.

Sometimes, though, sometimes George secretly grieved the first wedding photos. Never the first husband but the photos. Once, in a fit of drunken mourning, she had posted a profile picture of just her and Miranda in their wedding gear, Miranda clasping her pearls, young, gorgeous. But that was short-lived. Miranda demanding she remove all those photos because that raging asshole Andrew means nothing. It never happened, Miranda said. You were never married before.

Andrew is dead to us.

And so it was, because John was her real man, George had felt certain they would make a real baby. This time she would get her way because her way and John's way were the same way. He told her so the night of her divorce dinner. She and Miranda had ordered bottle after bottle of champagne in the finest dining room in town and then drank with the staff after service. There was a handsome sous-chef Miranda thought looked very capable of rebounding. She had leaned in nudging her cousin's sticky summer skin and whispered to George, what about that guy? That guy over there.

What *about* him? had been George's initial thought.

But as the night progressed into morning she became more about that guy over there. About fucking that guy. Andrew would not be the last man she slept with. This guy, whatever guy, could be the last guy. What did she care? Champagne!

The first night after John, George had called Miranda and gushed.

She had not known it could be like that. Her ass in the palms of his hands, held feet off the floor. George had not known. Did Miranda know? Did everyone know? Why had no one told her? Someone should have told her. Someone should have said. All that time with Andrew only to find out he had not been fucking her right.

George would have left had she known they had been doing it wrong all that time. And the morning after the rebound, George, now horrified, admitted that she would have continued on with Andrew like that forever had her father not found out. No tee time at the club, he had said.

George, that husband of yours has no tee time at the club this morning.

Miranda, in her concerned cousin voice, warning not to get attached. You are not ready for another relationship. And he's a cook. You don't want a cook.

Miranda then evoking her special incantation. Georgie, Georgie, newly divorced women are meant to bounce around now. You cannot date the first man you fuck.

But George was not the bouncing type.

And she didn't date him.

She married him.

George had tried to live quietly after Andrew had not teed off. She had taken a leave from work that turned into a leave from working. It was her father's idea. He said she should concentrate on herself. So she did. On what would have been their anniversary, she randomly walked into a salon and got a spontaneous Brazilian and a blond bob. There was no saving that day. It was ruined anyway.

She ate only spinach for a week even though she hated how it felt across her teeth. She put a gym-style treadmill together by herself. She would be entirely self-sustaining. She imagined all the things she would master in the stead of human interaction. Mandarin or Japanese. All of her friends spoke French. She signed up for diving classes, considered buying a horse. She would speak only to Miranda. She would not entertain the idle questions of women who pretended to care.

They were just pleased it was not their husband.

George had thought she would ease out of the world gradually and they would forget that it was her husband who was not the golfer she thought he was. Ex-husband. She always forgot the ex part. George had accidentally referred to Andrew as her husband so many times after the separation because the idea of having a husband was hard to quit. Or maybe it was the idea of being a wife. Regardless, her readjustment to the idea of single life was not smooth.

She often reminded herself of this for motivation. She'd make her second marriage work.

Their last blowout had been over John's smoking.

She was having needles shoved in her ass with a therm-ometer in her vagina and he couldn't manage to stay away from cigarettes. Perhaps he should get loaded in a hot tub while eating sticks of butter and shoot up before baking his knit tighty-whities in the oven to wear under brand-new too-small leather pants. Fucking idiot. George was ready to leave him on the spot. And he would get noth-ing. Nada. There was no cash-out option. Her daddy had been sure of that the second time round after lawyer boy did his gouging.

She would do it. Get out there and search for num-ber three. Fuck it. Relationships are hard. And everyone would forgive her this sexy little marriage.

But then John bought the patch and the gum and the book and the video to show her he was trying. And, truth-fully, she settled down cause maybe, maybe she didn't want this guy's baby either. Maybe she needed time to think about what she wanted.

It bothers her though when people ask if this is her family, pointing to the dogs. Or if she likes kids. Or why she didn't want them. These tiny barbs cut her through. And there were also comments from John. Minor asides about taking too many pictures of the dogs.

You will seem like one of those sad childless women.

This was a crushing blow. It made George feel pathetic and embarrassed. It had not occurred to her to be ashamed of her life. Certainly, it was different from the lives of her friends, but it was still the life she was leading. This was her husband. These were her dogs. Her experiences were not wholly traditional but they seemed to be worthwhile experiences.

That is until John suggested that posting another photo of Gretchen and Mol would make George appear foolish. This too was a brand new notion to George. Foolish not being a complaint ever lobbed at her. Andrew had said she was overly focused. Miranda encouraged her to relax. Her father remarked that she was much too stern.

Be like that if you want, my girl, but you will be alone.

So she softened. Made herself sweet. Wore pastels and said please.

She met John and things improved after they let a little air out of the tire. He had grown more independent in the last year. Pleasant at home, eager to go to work, excited about the business and the future. He even walked the dogs.

It will happen for you, love, if you stop trying and don't want it so bad.

That's the kind of passive nonsense they said to her in the frozen food section. The exact inactive advice that John devoured. If it's meant to be, John says, but that is just idle. And George is many things but she is not idle about her life. So she forges on doing the back-breaking emotional labour of two humans because one is busy making fancy custard that brings him great stores of admiration from strange women.

George regrets the restaurant. But it was that or have a husband who was a sous-chef alongside twenty-three-year-old skaters. No way. Not on. Off. That could fuck right off. What is worse still is she gives him credit for things he's nothing to do with, in order to make it seem all right and forward moving. The alternative would be to admit that she once again made a wrong-headed decision having learned no lessons from the first rather public undoing. She definitely, without a doubt, heard them refer to her as Mom once when she arrived ten minutes early to catch them shooting Jameson before dinner service.

B'ys, put that away, Mom's here.

Tears had stung the inside of her eyes and she had turned to take a pretend phone call because you never let the help see you cry.

And George disciplined them with a heavy hand. She had to because John refused. He said he needed to keep up morale in the kitchen. But that wasn't it. He just didn't want to, and John is not great at doing things he doesn't want to do. Miranda pointed this out regularly, being as close to a sister as George ever had, closer even, as they need not enter into any competition for resources.

Both George and Miranda were resource rich.

The dogs are licking at a broken soup bowl on the floor.

George shoos them away. That is all she needs, poodles with gashed up tongues. A massively annoying trip to the veterinarian who is never the same veterinarian. More useless antibiotics and stitches they can tear at with their paws. Bloody mouths and draggy red spit all around the house. Why is this happening to her? She is a good person. John. Where is John? John!

George thrusts the dogs' leashes into Iris's hands as she slides around the corner.

You stay!

Iris doesn't know if George is speaking to her or the dogs but stays and stares.

George moves on around the corner to the kitchen

where she finds John in the dish pit. She has grown furious again and needs to buy herself a moment to collect her thoughts. All the intrusive interviews and childproofing the house followed by years of silence. The countless emails concerning their application status that went unanswered. Children's parties and baptisms, every fucking holiday a reminder of her lonesomeness. George had almost given up. She was considering buying them a trip around the world as consolation. Until the phone rang and everything became new again. Now, John had put that all at risk. For nothing! Who doesn't pay their taxes? Poor people. And they are not poor people.

George vows to murder him if he has fucked this up for her but attempts to calm herself. She still needs him. Act dignified, she thinks.

What's wrong with Iris?

Iris?

She looks upset.

Having some man trouble, I think.

And George gathers up her snares in one sweep. Sets them. Souvenir key chains for all.

She's not the only one.

DAMIAN ENTERS THE HAZEL to find Iris on her knees wiping soup from the floor with leashes tied around both ankles, poodles pulling her feet toward the loud kitchen. This day that Damian is about to have is going to be a bad one. He mixes himself a fast Caesar while listening to the yelling. Shit is not right here this morning and they are about to open for lunch. And Damian hates his fucking job and this place and his mother and even Iris who is giving him a terrible look with them watery eyes of hers.

You smell like booze.

You smell like cock.

No, I don't!

Honey, believe me, I know what cock smells like.

LUNCH

· · · · ·

SOME YOUNG ONE LEADS Major David to an empty table in the centre of the room.

She obviously does not know who he is so he tells her. When she still doesn't address the appalling seating arrangement, he repeats it again slowly in case she's stoned.

I am the Mayor of St. John's.

But she just stands behind the chair opposite, arms criss-crossed atop her menus, over her breasts, of course.

This is a business lunch, he tries again.

Nothing. She just nods and continues staring at him with a blankness common in women her age.

There was a time when waitresses in this town knew to be warm. They smiled readily and wore lipstick during the day and said *sir* without contempt.

Not like now. Everything is ruined sure now. Just like lunch is being ruined by this skinny waitress.

Major David watches her scurry in and out of the kitchen. Nothing in her hands. Nothing on her person. She appears to be doing nothing at all. And she can hardly manage that from the look on her face. She is not in any kind of mood to be interacting with the public. Thank god there are no tourists around at this time of year. And look at the arms on her. Covered in fucking tattoos.

Sleeves they're called. Major David has learned this off the television. A lot of humans in need of intervention have sleeves. Major David bets his skinny waitress does drugs. She's certainly thin enough. Her hollowed-out eyeballs suggest something quick. Cocaine. Probably buys a ball of the coke and then complains about being paid minimum wage.

That's why Major David doesn't tip.

He will not have hard-earned money going up some server's nose. If his group is leaving a cash tip on the table, he'll have "no change." Or when he's using a machine, he'll make a "mistake" putting in the percentage.

No change and lots of mistakes.

If they call him a moron, he'll act like a moron.

They don't know what hard work is anyway. They should try teaching thirty-two fourteen-year-olds algebra. That is easily harder than pouring water into mason jars. And what's-her-chops hasn't even mastered this skill apparently. Major David has been sitting here water-less for what feels like eons. Alone. She has not even thought to bring him a newspaper or a magazine or even that hateful arts rag.

Major David needs a new table.

And this young one needs a cardigan with full-length sleeves. She probably doesn't even need sunblock in the summer. Can you get sun damage on top of skin damage?

Can't break what is broken. Surely the same would apply to damage already done.

There are a lot of commercials about undoing skin damage and Major David thinks this is a great swindle. But he can't stand Diane when she is feeling helpless so he lets her waste his money on pots of whipped chemicals and caffeine mist meant to tighten what already let loose years ago. He doesn't dare say that, though, cause she would be in the bathroom sobbing and then she would for sure look a fright. Diane has complicated feelings. Like all women. They've catacomb minds simultaneously working through a baker's dozen of emotions. Going to brunch is like eating waffles with a fleet of NASCAR drivers ready to take the steep angle at a moment's notice.

Major David sighs and peers out the window.

The harbour is still tight with slob ice packed in and piled against the dockside. The iron fence, now wrapped in a shiny coat of freezing drizzle, is right majestic looking. He pictures it adorned with welcome signs and balloons, hung heavy with banners of tiny flags from visiting nations delivered to their doorstep by modern and stately vessels. All those fine Europeans in linen suits walking the streets of his city taking photographs. And buying things. The retail experts claimed that the revenue generated from cruise ships was minimal and hard to measure but what the fuck do they know? Of course people would spend money. The shops just needed to sell better stuff.

He told them so. It was the shopkeepers' responsibility to sell what visitors wanted. In retrospect, he should have not used the word responsibility. That always sends the downtown crowd into a frenzy during the winter months. They become agitated and spit as they rant about sidewalks. Not like in summer.

Summer is best.

Never mind what the bearded hipster twerps say about the changing foliage or the crisp smell of autumn. It's decomposition they're happily hauling in through pierced nostrils.

Major David knew all about fall. Fall meant youngsters and germs and hormones.

Teenagers have the strongest stench of pheromones. Tangy and unpleasant. They're not yet smart enough to talk sense and they require a lot of praise for keeping themselves upright.

People in the service industry are like that, pseudo adults trapped in everlasting adolescence. Just muddling along whilst hating any authentic adult for embarrassing them by doing stuff and owning things.

Skinny waitress probably thinks the frown stretched broad across that lovely wide mouth of hers is somehow Major David's fault. She has no actual comprehension of what the world entails. No concept of what it means to contribute to community. Her notion of contribution is reaming off needless details about how food is cooked.

Sheer lunacy: the things young people believe.

They want food trucks and parades and music and art. Fish tacos and foreign films and bikes and espresso. Right there, on the road, where the cars go, all summer long. People-friendly. Stroller-accessible. Green space. In the downtown corridor. Preposterous.

Regardless, summer is still best, even if it does inspire outrageous thinking in youths.

Don't have to worry about that now. Months (months!) more of winter coats to go before any of that. Wet wool scarves full of tears and snot smelling of sour breath and neck musk. Women think men like scarves but they don't. When a man tells a woman he likes her scarf it is because he wants to tie her up and is pleased she has all the necessary equipment for the whole outfit.

Not that Major David could ever get away with that anymore either.

Too old. Past the point where women will allow him to wrangle them. And he mourns bondage as the skinny one re-approaches uncrossing and re-crossing her arms over her chest. It is a tease. But also a reminder. Peekaboo for the aged. Her body language proclaims that she has a beautiful rack, one she surely tips back in ecstasy; he can picture the curve of her neck, the underside of her chin, arched. But it's not for him.

Life is hardly worth living, Major David thinks as he takes a sip of finally poured water.

R OGER THINKS DRINKING without getting drunk is a waste of money.

And Calv got to agree with him, though he's not sure he should get drunk today.

Donna said not to bother coming back if he gets on the beer with Roger again.

She also said she'd sooner eat shit and die then hang out with the likes of Roger and whatever tramp he got rolling through he's rental apartment full of cheap Walmart furniture not fit to sit on.

Just sawdust glued together by little immigrant youngsters over to China somewhere!

Calv don't mention they're not immigrants if they still lives in their own country cause Donna would fly off the head asking him if he thinks he's funny, only to follow it up with the ever growing list of reasons why he wouldn't. He failed out of college, twice. He's father is a fishermen, still. He's mother can't read, even. And he's sister is a bitch.

Calv was soaked in the same utero juice so it's fairly likely that means he's stupid too.

Once Donna accidentally said stupid blood of a bitch and Calv hove a potted plant at her head, so she's after learning there are lines not to cross. Like, Calv don't say fuck all when Donna gets going about Amanda being a stuck-up cunt. He don't even register that kind of stuff anymore. People have been saying stuff about Amanda he's whole life. Calv is proper immune to it now.

But he won't have Donna calling his mother a bitch via Amanda's umbilical cord. That's over the line.

He never really meant to fire that houseplant at her. It was just handy to him, practically in his hand already. Then Donna was off making out like Calv was a brute and calling him a baywop. Donna gets right mean.

She's on a mission to prove to all of Newfoundland that Calv is a cultureless shit cause he grew up wrong side of the overpass.

And he supposes she's right about a fair hand of it. He would have bought the same furniture as Roger. What do he know about buying furniture? Looks good enough. But it's not good enough for Donna. You got to get that Amish furniture made of wood and everything. Some of it don't even have nails or screws or nothing. And Calv don't know how them men in their wagons is after getting he's sofa put together but by the Jesus, it's the best couch he ever had. Loves it. When he wakes up from a good couch nap and smells salt meat cooking, Calv thinks life is all right.

Truth is Calv been after Donna since that time he seen her at the Breezeway.

She was supposed to be getting her teaching certificate or degree or whatever they calls it. She was with some other feller then, too. Always with someone, Donna was. But that was never no concern to Calv, he was watching that window close on. And he was ready to haul himself through the moment it come clear. Or near clear, which was how it happened in the end. There was some overlap. What odds though, he's not prepared to let her go, not for nothing. Supposing he got to go to Africa for work. That's what she says to him some days, that she don't care if he got to go to Africa or the Middle East somewheres. Calv is scared shitless of them hot places. He got fair skin. There's bombs everywhere. And they throws acid at little girls over there. Real acid. Not like the kind you takes in a tent at Salmon Festival for a laugh.

But Calv would sooner get he's dick blown off than tell Donna she can't go yoga in Jamaica.

Can't lose Donna.

So he don't know how he's going to manage here today. Roger says they needs to talk about the thing that happened. Some fellers is having a hard time over it. Roger thinks him and Calv got to reassure them before they does something stupid like tell someone who wouldn't there and who wouldn't understand. Like a woman. Roger allows Calv only got to look to he's own sister for proof of women overreacting.

Roger says vile stuff about Amanda easy enough now that she's got a man.

But Calv knows Roger would change he's tune something fierce if Amanda suddenly decided he wouldn't the scum of the earth. But that'll never happen. Everyone ever lived handy to Trinity Bay knows she hates he's guts. Though it would do no one any good to remind the poor fucker that the reason he can't stand Calv's sister is cause she won't have him.

Instead, Calv just entertains Roger's reams of vicious bullshit.

He got little better to do now that they're all laid off.

Everything's after going to the dogs. Again. People abandoning campers, giving up their bikes, sleeping in their trucks. There was a man on the news can't afford to get his youngster's braces off. Roger's convinced everything will get sorted now the Americans got a better president.

Go on, b'y, Roger says, don't be so foolish. Guns'll fix that. Guns'll fix anything.

And Roger is steady looping the two streets that they considers downtown. There's a whole neighbourhood of colourful houses above it where Amanda lives but that's nothing to them cause they never goes there.

When Roger says downtown he means beer and food and music and women.

Roger's swearing now cause he can't find a parking spot cleared out enough to haul into so he's half poisoned. He hates parallel parking. Too embarrassing. Roger would sooner loop the same two or three blocks for better part of an hour than attempt to squeeze himself in somewhere.

Sometimes Calv insists that Roger just let him park the damn machine. They both knows Roger can't park with all this snow around but Calv don't mention it.

Roger will just get pissy. Pissier.

JOHN CAN TELL Ben hates working here now.

He can hear the bartender grumbling curse words as he preps his station. And it is true, Ben doesn't belong here. There are lots of other restaurants that would be better suited to his demeanour John thinks as he watches Ben slice the citrus.

Damian bumps Ben's arm as he carelessly reaches for a lemon, nearly causing the bartender to take a row of knuckles off as he slides his knife hand down. This would be no small injury given that the bending of his fingers is fairly integral to Ben making and shaking cocktails. He can't very well be doing so with gauze-wrapped hands. It would put the customers off their food and drink, which would put Ben off his food and drink.

John grins at the shiver of spite he sees run through Ben.

Maybe Ben will hit Damian. A fight would take some heat off of John today. And then he would have sure footing for firing Damian. He wouldn't fire Ben though. No, better to have him indebted.

But Ben's not the kind of man who fist fights. He was raised better than that.

And Ben knows his sustenance is held inside the tightly cinched leather clutches of the ladies eyeballing him. He needs his pretty face and all his fingers to gain entry past the clasp. The brightly coloured purse holders want no indication of Ben's anger or vulnerability. This would break the fourth wall they've got built up. Ruin the whole performance and threaten Ben's chances at paying his rent on time. Ben just scowls at Damian, sighs, and he says nothing.

He's too well-adjusted for a punch-up.

John is both impressed and a little disappointed. He could really use some entertainment. But Ben is right of course. There is no point. John has walked past Damian already only to haul in the heavy scent underneath his clean staff shirt. A clean that smells of Iris. Because Iris washes the staff shirts just in case of such occasions.

Lucky for Damian the linen closet has not borne the brunt of her melancholy.

There is absolutely no way Damian is not still drunk. He is basically rancid. Everything he has on should be burnt. Damian, who is a lost cause on any day, has outdone himself in the category of self-destruct this morning.

Today is a personal worst for the lot of them.

Though Damian may pull ahead of the pack, which is a genuine accomplishment given the commitment to annihilation they seem to share. Not even share, relish. They are mid-relishing their capacity to implode.

Damian is making merry in his own self-detonation. Even John can see that.

Ben has confided to John and Iris over drinks that he has never witnessed anything like Damian. Said he had lived in other places, more violent places with challenging demographics. Belfast. Atlanta. Winnipeg. Hung around locales engaged in active race wars where there were drive-by shootings and football beatings. Places that were brim full to bursting with people totally fucked up and abused. But not like Damian. His savagery was self-inflicted and sinister. Growing up in central Newfoundland had not prepared Ben for this particular breed of Gander Bay gay.

John had felt a smack of pride.

Iris remarked that her people were murderous.

But don't worry, you're a handsome white guy. You got a job and all your hair. Your dick is basically dipped in gold.

Around the bay, she said as she took a drag off John's cigarette, we are more keen on the murder-suicide.

Ben did not laugh at her joke because Ben was not sure it was one.

Iris had said he was handsome though so that was something.

This lineal instinct to implode was as concerning to Ben as it was clear to anyone looking around the dining room most evenings. Some mornings. This afternoon is particularly ominous. They're all wearing their worst masks. It is a hideous display.

Damian's eyes are saucers of self-loathing and shit.

He has the look of a person who has not been eating food recently. Ben hands him an OJ and ginger ale and everyone watches it disperse through his body like African rivers flooding the great plains after the seasonal drought. John can see the vitamins and minerals moving like emergency service providers dispatched at an accident scene. Ben is shaking his head in disapproval as he shines champagne flutes. Iris rolls her eyes as she grabs a stack of menus. Damian is not winning any popularity contests today. But he has not lost yet, either. There's a lot of today left to lose.

And even more of tonight.

Ben wants Iris to move to Montreal with him. John knows this because Iris told him because Iris tells him everything. She does so out of some devotion to honesty but also because she wants him to be jealous. Not for the sake of envy. But for the sake of progress. Iris wants to shake something loose. She doesn't seem to care what comes free as long as a shift occurs.

Besides, John can tease any secret out of her. He knows the right way to pull at her panties until they come off. And then she's all free-flowing info even though she feels guilty confessing Ben's failed attempts. Ben has only ever been nice to her.

John found this the most fun of all. He delighted in the news and suggested they all sit together at the staff party. Him, Iris, Ben and George. He said he wanted to rub her thigh under the table and talk about their holiday plans. He thought he would ask Ben what he wanted for Christmas and then squealed at the notion of it being Iris's pussy.

When Iris became angry at the joke, John declared he could not live without her and so she settled.

John has enjoyed playing with the bartender. He amuses himself toying with Ben's infatuation. Encouraged him to talk about Iris. In great detail. And Ben had done so willingly because he didn't know yet not to trust John. Besides, he wanted desperately to say her name to someone who knew her. It was like conjuring her. Or getting her out of his system so he could sleep. He had thought John was doing him a favour. He had felt like a plague going on and on about this woman he barely knew and had thanked John profusely for his patience and understanding.

I totally understand, John had said.

Ben did not know then that he totally understood.

Ben had thought he was referencing some past love. A crush from before he met his wife. College. High school even. It never fucking occurred to Ben that they were reminiscing about the same woman in real time. He had thought they were friends. He would brag about how lucky he was to have such an amazing boss because his boss was amazing. This guy, not that much older than him, who didn't feel the need to patronize his staff or bully them. In the service industry, this was an anomaly.

Ben had considered The Hazel home. He had felt he fit in with these weirdos: the roguish head chef, the intriguing hostess. He had even said this to his mom.

John had sat there across from Ben and listened intently as he explained how he felt when Iris walked into a room in a pencil skirt. Or when the cold left red circles on her cheeks. John had sat mesmerized as Ben drunkenly recalled how she applied lip balm, or folded napkins on her lap. John had exchanged stories about a mystery woman who had also snagged him up.

They had done shots over their shared misery.

Sometimes John had raced off so Ben had locked up after them. He did not know John was racing off to screw Iris after hearing on end how strongly Ben felt about her calves.

John thinks it is delicious knowing something others do not know, baiting them, tripping them up in their own words, in order to feel better than, to feel whole. John rubs his hands together over it like an old-time villain in a black-and-white film. It was half the fun. The other half being the knowledge that he is fucking a woman other men want to fuck.

This makes John giddy as shit.

It is clear Ben still cares about Iris. Even if he is mortified over it. He was disappointed that she had pretended to be single. Allowed him to flirt with her. Dismissed pass after pass.

Not dating, she said. Undateable.

She should have told him there was someone else but it's not her fault he got hurt.

John can sense Ben's embarrassment every time he speaks to him. Most days he looks like a man who wants to bury his head in the snow. Each time John touches Iris, Ben instantly relives the humiliation. John can see it rise to Ben's face so quick he thinks surely the poor fucker's nose will release under the pressure. He imagines blood squirting from Ben's eye sockets, dribbling from his ears. His grave marker would read Died of Embarrassment.

They would probably ask John to speak at the funeral.

Ben made a damn fool of himself and they both know it. But John will make it up to him.

John will give Ben what he wants. John will give him Iris.

Iris doesn't know this yet but she will go. Ben harbours residual romantic feelings for her against his own will, and while Ben has long since realized that you cannot make women have feelings that they don't have, you can still be there for them when they need you. And Iris is going to need someone when John finally finishes with her. It has gotten too tangly anyway. He's stressed right the fuck out over it. Someone is gonna get hurt.

Sometimes John looks around the restaurant and wonders who is in the most trouble.

He hedges bets in his mind. His wagers are constantly shifting depending on the nature of the day. Most often he thinks Damian because, Jesus, that guy is a wreck.

Another day, it's homicide. Iris blowing out the corners of their triangle.

Or George after having found out what she was paying for.

It would probably be George. It should be. She should shoot him in the cock.

No wonder half of women everywhere are screaming their heads off about being poorly treated. Some of them really, truly were. But also, John finds it hard to idle stand by and not defend himself in large groups of female chatter. It's not like he fucked himself. It's not like he raped her.

Maybe John will let Ben take Iris home tonight.

She won't want to go home alone. Ben will drunkenly kiss her. And that would be that. They would date for a bit. Move away. Then John could start over.

He would know what to expect from day to day even if his expectations involved some of his employees functioning at low levels. Like Damian looks like death warmed over out there. John wonders if this is a trial Damian is putting himself on for being a homosexual.

Poor sad fucker, John thinks. And now his mom's in jail. No wonder he's a state. John peeps out into the dining room again. He wonders if he can grab another smoke before the next order is up. Ben is wiping the bar down with wood cleaner, the pine smell cloaking Damian's rancid skin scent. John knows Ben will do this constantly. Everyone assists in the cover-up. Also, the ladies love it when he wipes down the bar.

Ben's the hot bartender. Maybe that is why he stays.

Ben shakes a plastic tub in John's direction and he eyes it, nodding. They are low on celery salt and Tabasco, which is unacceptable given the number of Caesars that will be ordered. Big George will be here any minute asking after things they don't have. Big George is the loudest silent partner in town.

John smokes his ninth cigarette of the day and promises himself he will quit after he finishes the pack.

Because he doesn't have cancer, yet. George doesn't know about Iris. His life is not over. It will go on. Starting tomorrow, he will be a better man. He will take such excellent care of himself. He will treat his body like a temple. The temple of John: bow down to his strength of character upon a moral reawakening. Fuck smokes. Mary Brown's won't see another fucking dollar from him. No more reality television. He will floss, eat salad, read. He will be ripped like no one's business. Like never before. He will be so good. They will love it. And his mind inadvertently leaps to scores of women, all the women, prostrate in front of him in prayer pose ready to worship his newly cleansed temple, and he has to shake it out fast-like before his plot thickens. Something is always thickening in John. Jesus Christ, not women. Just one woman.

Just one woman at a time, fuck.

George. He will dedicate his life to making her happy. Everything from now on will be an act of sacrifice to make this up to her. She never has to know what he has done, she will just be made happy by him every day until he dies. He will enslave himself to her contentment.

He will give up Iris because George is too good for him anyway. He never did deserve her, would not have gotten her if things had been different. She would not have even seen him, so lowly. Piss poor. It was nothing but luck that turned her head.

Luck. A divorce. And a lot of champagne.

And he knew it the very first night he pulled the lace off her trim ass, that this was his chance to be with a woman better than he was ever meant to have. He was so fortunate for George's unfortunate events. He would not fuck it up. That's what he had thought the whole while he ran his tongue over her smooth parts.

Don't fuck it up, John, don't fuck it up. Make her come.

And so he did. And he kept on doing. John never thought he would even get close to a woman like that. Lots of women threw themselves at him. Sent him drunk messages. Pretended to be interested in cooking. He did not want for choice.

But not women like George. She was the best woman. And Iris, sure, sweet Iris was, is, well, John cannot think on Iris just now because that would fuck up his resolve. This is his come to Jesus moment. He is having it right now, today, in this kitchen, and he can't let Iris interfere with his clarity of purpose.

Besides, she is young and will be fine and bounce back and, more importantly, is not his wife. His wife is the priority. He cannot lose his wife. Lose everything. Have to start over from nothing. From scratch for an itch. The punishment does not fit the crime. Why should John lose everything over a little bit of tail? No job. No house. No car. My fucking god, John is scaring himself just thinking in retrospect. He has been jeopardizing everything for a bit of extra pussy. Not that he thinks of Iris as extra pussy, not exactly, but fuck, what was he thinking?

He was perhaps thinking that he wouldn't get caught.

Or that he would.

But this morning was too close. Thinking what George would have seen had she arrived just ten minutes earlier cuts along the quick of him. John gets weak in the legs picturing the picture he almost painted for his wife. He'll stroke out at this rate. In an uncompromising position. John imagines himself dead, elbows deep in some forbidden pussy. And then abandoned because the woman could not even bring herself to call the ambulance. This is the alternative reality to the one he is living. Where George throws him out and Iris does away with him after realizing, finally, though he tells her all the time, that none of this is his.

It's all George, he tells Iris. But she doesn't listen to him, none of them do.

Iris says she believes in him because she does, because they always do.

John has got to learn to fuck in his own bed.

Or at least in his own house. Or on his own property. Or at least, just his own wife. Lord Jesus, John does not want to die somewhere seedy like a tramp. So he must give that kind of behaviour up now no matter how exciting it is. For self-preservation. Because seeing something like that would destroy George. And then: vengeance.

Women avenge themselves eventually.

Or at least the women John likes. He wonders if his penchant for spiteful women is sadistic. He courts the optically upright ones. George, so fierce and determined. Last night in the car, leaning back on her headrest, she had told him she was going to build a library. A library, she said. Like it was nothing. Like it was a greenhouse. Or a raised garden bed. This kind of feat, anything she could think of, seemingly a possibility. And he believes her, too. George can do anything. There is no one like her.

She told him about the beautiful libraries she had sat in on her trip and how it had filled her with such joy. The vaulted ceilings, the crown moulding, pillars and light. The rich hardwoods. She said it was such a clean feeling. The joy George feels surrounded by books is totally uncontaminated by the world. She found it refreshing. It made her feel new again, she said, and reached over to squeeze his knee as he navigated the slushy roads. And so he took her hand for a moment and raised it to his lips and kissed her fingers because he loves her.

John loves his wife.

He doesn't know what he would do without her. She makes his life possible. He wouldn't even know how to be in the world without her. When a love song comes on the radio, he thinks of her first. When he hears a funny joke, he wants to tell her so she'll laugh. When he feels worried or angry or paranoid or unpopular, she is the only one who makes him feel secure in his mind. It is only George for John. It could only ever be George. She calms him. Makes him feel like where he is and where he should be are the same place. And he has never felt that before. And he wants to always feel that. Which horrifies him more because it means there is a real something to lose here. She is a real person to lose.

He is so glad to see her hair on the pillow in the morning.

He had not thought she would get in. He had thought her flight would be delayed. She had texted him from Halifax saying they had turned back. They had gone back to Nova Scotia. So John had gone out and had cut it close. He keeps cutting it closer.

Last night he had thought he was trapped with Iris. The plough had covered the back end of his car. And Iris was throwing a fit about the adoption. And he couldn't think or leave because he couldn't very well hear above her bleating or abandon his car there overnight. And then George texted.

Made it! Landed! Come collect me!

All the delayed flights landing, the airport full of people, St. John's International in February, John in his panic had done the thing he had been able to avoid for the past eighteen months.

Where are you in the airport?

A text meant for his wife, sent to his girlfriend, who he knew was in her shabby apartment now crying and losing her mind. John had to turn his phone off before he found George by the luggage carousel. Iris was rapid-firing threats at him. Nineteen in the last three minutes.

Jesus, she has fast hands. John cannot get over the agility of her sometimes. Even in the middle of her temper tantrum, them fingers of hers are lightning through his cell, he's barely the time to react or absorb one before another appears. Slingshot. He did not even know people could text this fast. Teenagers maybe. But not grown women. Maybe it was all the painting. He should throw his jesus phone right in the harbour. It has only ever caused him grief. A lot of fun followed by a lot of grief.

Tell her, John.

Wandering around the airport, John felt his vision blurring, felt weight in his face, his cheeks full of anxiety. The gravity of what was befalling him was pulling his entire visage to the floor. These texts, these were bad texts.

Tell that woman the truth.

And he fired back that woman was his wife and begged Iris to wait, said he loved her, loved them both, needed more time, don't do anything stupid. He appealed to her heart. He said he would never speak to her again. He would never forgive her. He said George was innocent. They had done this to her. They had hurt an innocent person. But Iris shot back rippling replies with warfare hate in them dexterous fingers.

You're wasting time.

George had commented on his wet hair as she hugged him and ran her hand along the back of his head. He said it was snowing heavily outside when he left the house. Which was a lie.

The truth: fastest shower ever.

And to think he almost started to confess when she

came into the kitchen just now with that glassy look on her face. John thought he would have to move away. Change his name. Start over. He thought about who he knew out west. He could grill a steak. But he had let her talk first. Waited her out like his father had taught him to do years ago, before the trimmings, before the screaming, before estrangement.

Don't tell women nothing. Keep it to yourself, Johnny.

And John had held it in. He had busied himself with the soup, he had hurried around the kitchen popping food into his mouth, the rankest things within reach, to ward his wife off. It occurred to him her fury was a blessing. It would keep her from embracing him. A kiss would be out of the question, John thought, his stomach churning in response to rising self-disgust.

He would not kiss George with Iris on his face.

He resolved to push her back. He would shove his own wife as a kindness. There had to be a line. This was his. And he resented having to draw it.

What was she even doing here at this hour?

Jesus, women were unpredictable. Especially when angered. Angry women are like hungry dogs, they will lunge at anything. And George stalked him around the kitchen as he popped artichoke hearts into his mouth, letting a bit of the oil run down his chin while she yelled accusations and insults at him. George hated artichoke hearts. She said they were not hearty at all.

Good grief, John, wipe your face. You're gross.

And he had happily scrubbed his face in the sink with a bar of hand soap.

IRIS HANDS MAJOR DAVID a lunch menu and attempts to rhyme off the specials.

Why are there dogs in the porch?

Sorry?

You've dogs in your porch, it is against regulations.

They're the owner's dogs.

I'm meeting the owner.

John?

George.

His . . . wife?

George Copperfield!

Oh, Big George?

Do you call your employer Big George?

Um, no sir, because—

There it is again, Major David thinks, that shitty *sir*.

Then I suggest you not call him that to me.

Yes sir.

Shitty *sirs* abound as she starts in on the specials. Major David is incensed. The level of disrespect is breathtaking.

There is a toasted fennel-lemon cake—

You can save your breath, honey.

Excuse me?

You'll just have to say it all again when my party arrives.

Yes but you said—

Bring me a cup of coffee, will you? Or a beer.

What kind of beer?

Is it too early for a beer?

Sorry?

No, never mind. How would you know?

Umm . . .

Just bring me the coffee. Two milk, two sugar.

Of course. Right away, sir.

Major David knows she wouldn't wipe her ass with that *sir* but he can't prove it. He wishes he could prove it. He would have them fired for their fraudulent esteem.

He can barely swallow another bitchy *sir*.

But she's already half across the floor, clipping away from him, right pleased with herself for being saucy as a... Major David's mother used to finish that statement on the regular when he was a boy. There was even a time when he said it himself. He occasionally lets it slip now in certain company after a dram or ten of scotch.

But it makes Diane uncomfortable, and there are immigrants all about the place these days. Not just in the hospitals or over at the university either. Everywhere. Just walking down the street like they live here. Well, they do live here. But like they always lived here. Some of them are even white. You can't tell where they're from until they speak and then, bam, thick Russian accents. Where did all these Russians come from?

Well, Russia, Major David supposes. Or the Ukraine. The former Soviet Union somewhere.

But, but, what do they do for money, hey? Who do they hang out with? Other Russians? Are there so many that they have a social network here? This would certainly explain the mounting socialist movement. They're anti-development, anti-business, anti-progress, anti-cooking, watermelons, the lot of them. Terrible waitress is a watermelon for sure. Major David would bet the house on it!

Or the cabin.

He would probably bet the cabin that she's as green on the outside as she is red on the inside. Probably doesn't eat meat. Not even cause she loves animals. No. Because of her thousands of never-ceasing opinions. Listening to a young woman's opinion is like stepping on an ant-hill. Before you know it, opinions are surging up your leg toward your ball sack and there's no set of paws big enough in the world to protect you from the insurgence. And skinny waitress is glaring at him now as she elaborately sweetens his coffee one slow spoonful at a time in full view of the dining room staff.

She probably fucks Russians. Looks like a pussy riot.

Major David smacks his palm down on his own leg at the thought. He wishes someone were here to share that with. He must remember to say it again later. Maybe to George if he arrives first. If they do a handshake deal before the Heritage crowd arrives, he definitely will. If they drink on it, without a doubt. George is exactly the kind of company he should be keeping anyway.

Major David should have friends like George Copperfield who would comprehend the complexities of modern humour while recognizing a joke about pussy riots.

Anyone can be creative. It only took him a couple minutes to come up with pussy riot. No one gave him a grant. Major David could probably write stand-up routines if the weddings don't pick up. No one gets married these days but everyone needs a laugh. The waitress is not married. No ring anyway. Women like that don't believe in marriage.

Even if she were the marrying type, she wouldn't pay him to marry her.

One of her friends would get certified online and marry her to some barbershop owner.

Barbershop owner?

Major David's sugar must be getting dangerously low. That skinny one should really bring him some bread or something while he waits. Perhaps they don't serve bread here. He would have never agreed to eat here if George hadn't insisted. Here he is now half starved with not even so much as a peanut to gnaw on.

Not that they would serve any peanut he would eat.

Everything is chipotle honey-roasted ginger garlic drizzled with kosher salt served with lime wedges he never knows what to squeeze over.

Major David can never tell what they are going to put in front of him in places like this.

Gluten-free oven-seared crackers to break your bridge-work on, and a side of grey-beige middle eastern dip or spread or sauce or some such slop to soothe your wounded mouth after. That's what the kids want.

Or better yet, to slosh something around in just oil. That's the best one.

They serve grease in a little square dish. What a shill. The chef probably snickers from the kitchen as he watches everyone eat their raw unassembled food. Ingredients. It's just ingredients until you put it together. Though they've a fancy name for everything. Serving you the parts of your hamburger is called deconstructing it. It's a deconstruction burger site. Or something like that.

A pot of oil on the table with some vinegar in it is not restaurant food. He could do that himself. Pouring liquids into vessels and slicing things onto slabs may be the only two kitchen skills he has actually mastered.

He can barely disguise his disapproval when fellow diners order a charcuterie board.

The emperor wears no clothes is what Major David thinks. Meat and cheese on a piece of wood. Good grief. He could do that. Or Diane could for sure.

She loves that section of the grocery store. He practically has to drag her away from it. He tries to avoid the regular grocery store altogether. There is a pleasing and noticeable difference in savings when they buy all their food at Costco but Diane hates Costco. She says people behave like the unbelievable discounts will disappear and they will once again be forced to buy toilet paper at regular prices. Diane is certain there is no savings in fuel costs while idling in those lines. She squeaks this every time Major David discovers she has filled the gas tank at a local station. Then she is running off toward the bathroom.

Women and the bathroom.

RIS TRIED TO hand wash the insides of her thighs but it didn't help.

It just made her feel more yucky. The gold-gilt oversized mirror in The Hazel bathroom, while her idea, allowed her no space to escape the reflection of washing her genitalia with blue paper towel. She was grateful for the fibre quality and tried to wipe herself while looking away. But this room belongs to John too. Of course it does, he has fucked her everywhere. And for the first time, she wonders who else John has fucked in here.

Definitely George.

Of course he would have. When they first opened the restaurant, John's appetites would have had him fuck his wife on every solid surface and even those that shook. And she can smell John on her now. The warm water seems to have had an adverse effect. So she pumps expensive partridgeberry-mint hand soap onto the wet wad and thinks that this will most definitely give her some kind of yeast infection. But Iris cannot give a fuck about a yeast infection right now.

She has to serve tables all night with her boyfriend's wife.

It is much safer to smell of bog berries and nan gum than spend one more minute paranoid that George will smell John's cum off of her battered crotch. She has marks all over where he has been nipping at her. It is territorial, like a dog putting grooves in a bone. And Iris has told him the little bites make her feel unloved. She has said to John outright that she doesn't like the look of herself in a full-length mirror when she is a bruised peach. Though John finds this a turn-on.

You're my little whore, he whispers from just behind her ear.

And she told him not to say or do that because she didn't like either, but he did both anyway because John doesn't listen to Iris.

Because John doesn't listen to women.

She has been trapped at The Hazel since George came back with the spirits. George did not unload the spirits of course. That would mess up her outfit and wet them tidy whip-straight bangs down against her forehead into a limp kink. God forbid. No, instead George pulled up near the door and texted her employees to come and get it. Even Iris. This was her text. *All hands*, George had texted, *even Iris*.

So Iris went out into the slob snow to grab the boxes of booze in ballet flats. Now her feet hurt. But she can't complain to anyone. The only person who could give her comfort is too busy fawning over his wife. Not that he would give her comfort. He would give her grief over her boots first. An opportunity to regain positioning. Fuck that. Iris would sooner hobble home.

She should leave this place. It has degraded her beyond all recollection.

Iris had been this whole time slaving away at grunt work only to have George swoop in and save the day. One please, daddy, is all it will take from this woman who has always had a daddy who responded to the very first please. People fall over themselves to do things for George. They marvel at the opportunity to pay her a compliment. Favours are endlessly supplied. They boast on Twitter for having bought her a cupcake.

Iris doesn't know what it is like to be the favoured woman.

But she knows well what it is to envy after the space. Everything she has toiled over is Magic-Erasered away like her emotional sweat was nothing but more energy to sustain John while he tried desperately to maintain some ideal for his wife. Keeping George blissfully unaware of his human failings was far more important than what would ultimately undo Iris.

She is seeing this take shape as she moves around the dining room in a sort of fog. She catches them from the corner of her eye visiting the tables of couples they vaguely know. John picks up someone's baby and gives it a little nuzzle. Hearts bang wild against cavities, at least two. George is glowing now. She is embracing the opportunity to be their necessary messiah. John needs her, and this need makes her happy as she is reborn vital and shiny again. Her father will handle that business with Canada Revenue. All she has to do is ask.

John probably always knew that. He was exaggerating his anxiety to dip himself further into Iris's panties. For a bit of fun. Not even just for pleasure. There were far more pleasurable marks he could have made. Alabaster scratches so easily after all.

But this is not infatuation.

This is small game hunting at the local coward gun club.

And what is worse, as every stroke of recognition is finally fully delivered hard against Iris's hurt timepiece, is that all was lost the moment she opened the door and let him step across the threshold. He wanted her less from there.

Iris is for sacrificing.

She watches John return the baby before slipping his arm around George's waist as they chat casually with the young couple at table six. Near the window booth. Priority seating. George changed the reservation herself because they were middle school friends of hers. John pulls George toward him playfully while making some joke, it is a gesture he has done to Iris many times, in front of her co-workers, his staff. His hand resting on the small of a back.

Iris replays all the long drawn-out conversations where

she reassured John that it would be okay. The restaurant wouldn't fail. And if it did, maybe it would be a blessing to have it all fall apart. All those evenings turning tables and smiling and faux flirting to make a buck or earn a good review, another follower on the newer cooler social medias, a ding, a like, a bump, a fork, whatever it took to assuage him, Iris was fully there, invested in the daily domestic drudgery of partnership.

She pulled her weight without fanfare as if she was his person because he said so.

You are my family, John said.

And for a hint of happy, she had betrayed all her people.

Jo, Harry, her own mother, even Olive. No one was as important as John.

That day in the park, Iris had thought, this park is not my park, these people are not my people.

She remembers clearly spinning boys wearing ball hats around to face her, having no regard for their clothing, age or height because she had lost trust in herself. The passing moments had penetrated her remaining confidence. Each passing second conveying that she was no longer trustworthy. Maybe she never was.

She thought he was wearing a blue T-shirt covered in Minions. The joke: they are really earplugs. She thought he was four years old. Their belief: that everything changes at five. She thought he was three feet tall. The theory: drinking packets of vinegar will make you grow.

But then Iris didn't know what to think, because if she was right it meant he was not on the playground. Oh, despicable Iris. So she touched other people's children in the hopes that they might morph into him. She even turned around a little girl with a pixie cut. Her mother firing daggers.

Iris was a strange woman touching another woman's daughter in a park. She wasn't even searching for a little girl. She was searching for a little boy. Her best friend's only child.

She decided to never tell Joanne she lost him.

She had raced around the swings, shouting his name, nearing hysteria. Feeling the panic rise up. Her breathing had become short, she couldn't catch it. She thought she might choke on her own guilt. Quick little waves rolled against her breakwater. And Iris tried to brace herself for them. She was scaring all the children. And their parents. Iris was everyone's living nightmare in a blue dress and cardigan. Very large sunglasses hid her terrible eyes. Iris had almost looked like a responsible human. And this was worse because it suggested that even responsible humans could misplace children.

Harry. She yelled, has anyone seen Harry?

She remembers looking at her forearm where his hoodie hung only to realize she was gripping it with her other hand.

But those people hadn't known her Harry. Her favoured child. Iris loved all children but she loved this one the best. This is never spoken aloud but understood when he crawls into her lap while she ejects details of some new hurt to Jo in code. It was obvious when he ran his fingers upward through the back of her hair, pulling the short twists apart, that they were meant to always be friends. He had unfurled the curls while confessing his preschool secrets. He told her she was the best grown-up person. He whispered, even better than Mom.

Some children are just nicer children.

That day in the park, Iris thought, this will mark my life. And it did.

Every event to follow would be dated according to that moment. And the next moment.

And the next. She would always be trapped in a loop where she remembered what she was doing the day before she lost Harry, the week before, the month. Losing him would define her. She would think of nothing else. She would be that mad woman on repeat. People forever examining her past offences and deciding that every choice she had ever made in life suggested this would happen.

She had always expected to lose him. To lose them both.

Why? Maybe it was all the drowned fishermen where she grew up. Or the never-ceasing wind. Maybe it was living in constant fear of darkness. The empty cupboards every second week. The cut phone, or her worried mother on the couch. Canadian country music playing in the background. The soundtrack to her father's departure. Maybe it was that. Maybe it was everything.

Because Iris had never felt wholly deserving of Jo's friendship. Had been trying to make it up to her for a decade. Trying to pay her back. Trying to keep her. All of Iris's relationships ran that way. Impoverished at the core. Permitting it to fall to shit and rebuilding. Iris is not great at maintenance. She was always getting over something.

Jo says: you will get through it.

Life with Iris is a series of events to get through. She

speeds past herself like angry men in trucks. That day she had wondered if she would be okay before it is okay to wonder that. And then she had been wracked with guilt to show such concern for herself that way.

Iris thought, I am really an asshole.

And everyone in the park was suddenly a pedophile. She knew that this could not be true. Somewhere logic suggested that this was not possible but Iris was not logical. The man with the dog. The woman on the bench. The groom sneaking a secret smoke. The saddest young teenager in the world. They were all sexual predators. They had kidnapped him. They wanted to sell his organs to China. He was in a trunk somewhere.

My god, she thought, he could be halfway to the ferry by now. But her phone said otherwise. Iris knew how long she had been searching because she looked away when she got the texts. The sound of a construction worker's whistle.

How could she have looked away like that?

Iris threw up then, too. Heaved a little against the gate of the new pool house that the Peace-A-Chord crowd despised. They didn't feel it was meant for them. No one felt deserving of anything nice.

That's for people who grew up riding horses and drinking smoothies.

Iris can remember the smell of bile in her nostrils. It smelt of Sunday morning. Of finding her wallet in the mailbox, placed there while she searched frantically for her keys. Iris was always freezing on the steps of her imagination. Always falling off the subway platform. Swerving into oncoming traffic. It hadn't happened yet but her certainty of it persisted. It was even more likely to happen now that she had lost Harry. Her accidental death was imminent. The oceans would warm, the rich would grow richer, and Iris would die as a result of her own poor choices.

This: the reason she continued to smoke.

Jo and Iris had fallen out twice in life before that. The first time because Iris had improperly installed Harry's car seat. The whole rig just came forward. The second time because she had eaten all the salad greens.

Your selfishness is costly, Jo said, while she opened a tin of tuna.

Iris bought a better car seat and moved into her own apartment. But those were the fights.

Iris had caused them. This one would be on Iris too. Ultimately, she knows she is a bad human. There were tiny signs to support this. She would never adopt a rescue dog. Or help old ladies with their bags. Her apartment was visually clean but rotten on the inside. She still found black hair stuck to the back of the crisper eighteen months after moving in. There was a lingering cat smell left behind by previous tenants. Something Iris could not scrub out, no matter the time spent scrubbing. The knee-pads her mother bought were still in plastic in the linen closet because who needs knees if you expect to duck out before forty.

She had called Jo from the playground. Formed words. Put them together in different orders. She had mixed them into explanations. Built excuses. But Jo hadn't heard them. She couldn't because she was busy screaming that Iris better find him. Or else.

And that's when the saddest teenager in the world walked up to her, tugged her sleeve, called her ma'am, cause to him she was a ma'am. And she turned to this morose, sweaty creature as Jo yelled through the phone and she saw the Minion first. Secretly, an earplug. She saw him. He was in front of her. Harry: smiling.

But it was too late. She had already lost him.

Weeks later Jo would say all the things in a Facebook message. She could not hold on to them a moment longer. Jo dug into every gross piece of Iris with abandon. She skinned and flayed her alive with her own shame before demanding to know what the fuck Iris had been doing when she should have been watching her son? And Iris couldn't say but she didn't have to. Jo knew.

You'll have no one left, chasing some man who doesn't love you. John doesn't love you.

And Jo was probably right. He probably doesn't and Iris will likely end up in jail. Or dead in a ditch like every other silly woman who loved a bad guy.

Iris has done shameful things that she knows should go unspoken.

She has spoiled her gorgeous brushes so that she could blast her hurt and indignation through a handheld. The delicate sable set hewed to the chrome tabletop, a tangible reminder of her ability to destroy. Worse still was Jo arriving one evening with strawberries and a found-on-Kijiji easel to discover her well-researched birthday presents forsaken in the kitchen. Quietly taking in the pointed-round and angled-flat brushes rock hard against the acrylic palette. Speaking just above the appliance hum.

I spent a lot of time and money on those brushes.

They had been meant for future Iris, who quickly promised to replace them just as soon as she got paid. Jo had placed the strawberries atop the stove, it being the only clean surface, put the easel down on the floor where she stood and shaken her head as she left.

Be careful, Iris.

That was all before Iris mislaid Harry. Iris promises herself she will finish the painting of the dumpster gulls as soon as she gets new brushes. She will. Soon. She will give it to Jo and beg her forgiveness. She has to pay her phone bill first but after that, for sure she will beg. Iris thinks of her gallery rep when last they spoke.

I can't sell what you can't finish.

Iris sighs and tries hard to remember the moment she last felt just happiness.

Her whole life has been tinged with low-lying sorrow. She has never been able to count on just one side of a feeling. But this is the worst. The worst hand she has ever been dealt. There have been other unplayable hands: her father's alcoholism, her mother's depression, his leaving, her crying; each time Iris thought *this is the worst, no, this*. Abandoning Olive. Bad. Financial ruin. Worse. Drug addict ex-boyfriend. Worse than that. Eating disorders. Homelessness. Violence. Bad. Badder. Baddest.

But no. Iris was just being readied. Life was a rigorous training period. And then, so swift and accidental. Like a poisoning. Ba-bam. John.

Most days Iris feels like the cat her cousins found in the brook. A black stray so eager for affection, not feral at all even for her obvious abandonment. Everyone in the cove struck by its congenial nature. Her cousins took turns picking it up, passing it around, marvelling at the volume of its purring. And then, they threw it off the wharf.

To see if it could swim. To test its endurance.

And that half-starved, already wounded cat swam ashore. All were in awe: a magical cat.

How clever. Some cat. They ruminated on the amazing cat and praised its perseverance in the face of such struggle. They rubbed its ears, they held it close inside their coats. Its warm heart beating against them. Poor puss believing it had finally proven itself worthy of affection, convinced of its safety the whole way out the wharf, right up until the moment it was once again flung, air bound, flying as cats do, with its paws outstretched, preparing to land in the cold cove water.

Nevertheless, each time the cat would return for a caress. Wet and worn. Puss believing that this would soon be over. Someone would intervene.

And each time Iris's cousins hove it away and waited in amazement. Speculating on the quality of cat. What fine kittens their indestructible cat would breed. Later, having learned her lesson too late, poor puss struggled to escape them before being soothed.

Here kitty kitty. Sweet kitty. Lovable kitty. Pretty kitty. A favourite kitty.

And though the cat understood none of it, she warmed to their voices as she wanted nothing more than someone to care for her now that she was too hurt to care for herself. Not to feed her. She was a mouser. Not to shelter her. She would find a place. But to care for her. Press a face into her fine fur and say she was a good cat. But this never happened. Those boys threw puss off the wharf until she didn't swim back.

Iris feels like a drowning cat.

She scans herself for the reasons why this happened. Her dad drove off that day with his clothing thrown into the back of his truck. Sweatshirts and jeans liberating themselves from the pan. A wool sweater. His hockey coat she collected from the shoulder of the road. She was always picking up after men.

A curious sight: this twelve-year-old girl carrying a winter's worth of knitwear.

Iris thought she would be a hero when he returned. But Iris's dad did not come back that time. Or ever. The first time he called, she was too busy to talk for long. She had a math test. And a skating party. He had gotten annoyed and hung up.

Iris failed the math test. Never went to the skating party.

The next time he called she said there was a girl who looked like her. He didn't call again for months. When he did finally call again the conversation started with I'm sorry and Iris learned to forgive men she loved for disappointing her. Her father was teaching Iris everything wrong before she got a chance to learn anything right because he did not know what a girl child needed or wanted. He only knew what he needed and wanted.

He needed Iris to comfort him long distance. He wanted to be one of the good guys without doing the good guy work. Even in retrospect, his lack of care for her small self still makes her want to cry.

But everyone would see.

Major David is certainly eyeballing her every move around the dining room. Mutual loathing wafts off the pair of them and the tension line is pulled taut.

It seems most days that every decision made in council chambers is meant to further exaggerate how poorly and unessential single women like Iris are to Major David. She does not have a truck or even a Costco membership.

She stays close to her own driveway.

Once she ambitiously drove to the arena Dominion because Jo had said avocados were on sale for fifty cents. Limes too, Jo said. It will be like you're in Mexico! So Iris had tried because avocados were nice fat. The kind of fat you wanted that would make your skin recognizable and elastic again. Iris would look in the mirror on day three of avocado lunch and remember bright-eyed Iris.

But that person no longer exists. Iris killed her. She had a fair bit of help. But it was Iris who did the deed. Every time she lied that she was not mad. Every time she said her feelings didn't matter. Every time she says sorry when she knows she's done nothing wrong.

The times she has refused to say it when she knows she should.

All of this seems easier than the truth.

MAJOR DAVID TELLS the skinny waitress he has been waiting a shockingly uncongenial amount of time.

Iris says she's sorry.

He says he would not want to have to bring this up with management.

Sorry, sir, she says.

He says she should consider adjusting her attitude.

So sorry, sir, she says again.

Goddamn it on these young ones and their *sirs* and *sorrys*.

The skinny waitress retreats.

She is a bit of a muppet but most of them can't be bothered to comb out their hair these days. At least she's wearing a dress. Major David fondly remembers fitted skirts covered in colourful flowers. Before terse white collared blouses and straight black pants. Before militant-looking short hair and brazen bangs. Before he was the Mayor. Before the papers started calling him Major David. It had seemed a flattering moniker at first. He had fucked Diane like a hardened soldier the first time he read it in print. In charge of a great campaign. He had went at his wife with a conqueror's cock.

But the bastard journalists have turned it on him.

The woman in HR informs him, whenever given the chance, that his brand has been tarnished. That he desperately needs to resuscitate it. Otherwise, his time in public office is dead in the water. She casually lobs demise analogies in his face to spite him.

He calls her JoannA to vex her.

He drags out the last bit for emphasis. He hits that non-existent A because it is a non-existent A he can hit. You are no Joe. He needs her to know her name is not even pertinent enough for him to remember. And HR glares at him each time he pulls a mispronounce but she underestimates how he has grown used to stink eyes.

His days are full of mean looks from women he can't stand and shouldn't have to deal with.

But they're in the workforce now so he supposes he's stuck with them. He once made the mistake of mentioning this to a young clerk. HR had dressed buddy down for being late two days in a row even though he had said plainly enough he had all three kids while his wife was away. HR reminded him that she always had her kid and still arrived ten minutes early each morning.

Single mothers are terrible women to deal with at work.

Major David leaned in to lessen the poor fucker's embarrassment. He conveyed his sympathy for the dark-haired fellow and implied that the ladies were here now regardless of want. Gave the young feller a wink. Felt good. A little showcase of mentorship.

Then returned to his office to google the noises coming out of the washing machine.

It sounded ready to orbit into space when the spin cycle was spin cycling. Diane insisted they replace it for fear it would explode. But they couldn't merely replace it. Diane thought it was a good opportunity to redo the laundry room. Major David could not for the life of him understand why this was important. Better to redo the curb. Or add an additional bathroom.

Diane sighed they didn't need more bathrooms than people.

He should have known better than to trust that China-man. Or Korean. Aboriginal maybe. It was really hard to tell. People could be from anywhere. There was a time when being a Protestant from some distant lousy bay was the worst thing Major David could think of but not now. Women came from everywhere now. The young fellows met them in post-secondary where they were studying engineering or medicine or getting a doctorate in some nonsense.

Human dynamics. Sociology. Fucking linguistics.

Anyway, it doesn't matter. Major David was trying to be congenial. He didn't even say anything that bad. It was not like he had been sexual. Buddy didn't need to tattle on him to HR. And she wrote that down, too. She writes everything down.

Nothing worse than a woman who writes everything down.

HR is a virus infecting the female staff while they pee and fix their faces. Feminism, Lord in heaven, Major David can't even get a cup of coffee without her nattering on about some infraction against her person. The coffee-maker is an affront to her. She goes on regular tirades about it. It is not environmentally friendly to utilize individual plastic pods to brew one cup of coffee.

She goes on and on and on all the time about mass fish decline and ecosystem destruction as if he is somehow personally responsible for the extinction of bluefin tuna.

There is no point attempting to reason with women like HR. They really need sorting out on a nightly basis.

Out of frustration for her existence and in an effort to finish it with her, Major David once said he did not invent the coffeemaker, while biting into a honey cruller.

You know, JoannA, that I did not invent the Keurig, right? Though I wish I had.

And off she went pontificating about the coffin-maker not committing the crime.

Major David chewed down slowly while peering over

her shoulder for an exit. Had there not been a number of junior staffers in the kitchenette that day, he would have just walked away from her. Just stop listening was a tactic he regularly employed. He left conversations with his wife and daughters all the time. It was a vagina-proof strategy.

The coffin-maker, HR bleated, *chose* to use the nails. He *chose* that and is therefore implicated in the act of nailing the coffin lid no matter the number of times he claims to not be ultimately responsible for the death. He creates a demand.

You, HR said, while fingering him and then the coffee-maker and then him and then the coffeemaker, darting to and fro as she sputtered you and that, you, she said, *chose* to create a demand for that and that causes waste and that waste kills fish so you, you kill fish and that kills the planet so you kill the planet.

Major David shrugged and reached for another dough-nut, thinking, women are crazy.

HR was then off saying that compartmentalizing is so typical *for a man his age.*

Each word is candy coated in arsenic. She litters the boardroom, reception area and copy station, each and every adult conversation, with a poisonous *for a man your age* in case he forgets when he was born with a penis a long time ago.

She thinks he's a stupid old man.

She sometimes says as much in her level voice so as to keep inside the realm of congeniality, and he plots ways to make her lose her cool. He thinks of devil's advocate pro-life arguments. Once, just before sleep, he had revised an ingenious counter-argument for sweatshops. He was not particularly for sweatshops or child labour or anything quite so sinister but he knew it would provoke volume out of her.

One day out of mounting frustration, he asked if she thought herself smarter than he.

You think you're smarter than me?

He had been nearing rage as they argued over walkable cities. Pedestrian-only streets. Old people should ride the bus for free. Affordable housing. Clean energy. Wind farms. On and on and on she goes, where she stops . . . she never stops.

The rasp of her Scandinavia-loving pitch crawled in behind his sockets through deep holes drilled into the sides of his temples.

She pained him. He couldn't believe the nerve of her. He wished he could call her father. He wished he could give her the belt himself.

The curl of HR's lip seemed to imply that he did everything wrong.

He had not been prepared for HR's answer to his question. He was so struck down by it, in fact, that for moments between the question and the answer and the thereafter, he thought he was having an existential crisis.

Why wouldn't I be smarter than you?

And she had laughed at him.

Why would you assume yourself smarter than me?

Shook her head and laughed. Sighed. Good grief, David, she said and walked away.

He wanted to lay hands on her that day.

Would you prefer to move to a larger table at the back, sir?

The skinny waitress is lucky he doesn't tear a strip off her. Of course, he would prefer a better table! He has been saying that this whole jesus time. God damn it!

He doesn't know why young women are so determined to work. They don't seem at all good at working.

CALV STILL GOT Donna so he tries not to think on what life would be like if he never.

Because that might be he's future if he can't shake himself clear of Roger. And Roger's some wound up today. Says he spent yesterday's storm trapped in the house with no power and nothing to look at. Had to try reading a book to occupy his mind and Roger is right poisoned over it. He got to get the stink of house off, he says. Woman stink, Roger calls it.

Susie never liked Roger either. She thinks there's something wrong with him.

She don't understand why he can't leave her daughter alone because he for sure don't actually like her. Roger don't want Amanda to be herself at all which is some awful confusing cause he carries on like someone obsessed with her when really he wishes all them parts of Amanda weren't her parts.

And he's already lashing into Amanda before Calv has figured out where he wants to eat. He's mid-sentence. Amanda was on a public service announcement or YouTube video or some such thing speaking out against sexual assault. Roger says Amanda exaggerates.

I only ever wanted to be nice to her, stuck-up bitch.

And Calv, even though he don't want to get into it

today, suggests Roger shut up calling Amanda names.

She's still me fucking sister, ain't she?

Not that Calv sees her that much lately. No. She's beyond done, she said. Done was where she was ten years ago. She is ten years beyond that now. Amanda makes sure there's absolute certainty in what she's after saying. She's learned to be clear like this to establish boundaries.

Amanda spells things out outlandishly now so there is not even the potential for misunderstanding. She has been taught over her whole life that attempting to spare a man's feelings will get you outright ignored. Roger, for example, will take anything other than a threat to call the police as encouragement to wail at her.

Look at what you've done to me, Mandy, he will bawl if given an opportunity, I've lost me mind.

This is the kind of simplistic bullshit Roger fires at her whenever she is in-between boyfriends. Amanda was regularly furiously texting Calv to tell that fucking maniac to get off her landing or she would call the police and have him thrown in lock-up.

What will they say at home if I has your buddy thrown in jail?

Roger carries Amanda's grade ten picture around in his wallet. This is enough to creep her right the fuck out. She wonders how many photos of her he has saved to his phone. And Calv says, go on, go on, he's just got a thing for you.

This thing Roger has for Amanda makes her cry at Sunday dinner.

They never even really used to *have* each other, Susie says to Calv in disbelief.

Calv tells their mother not to worry because Amanda can handle herself.

You expects your sister to handle all the men, Susie screeches through the phone. Why can't you help her handle 'em?

I got me own stuff to look after sure, don't I?

She's the only sister you got.

I knows how many sisters I got, Mom, please.

Amanda been always looked after you even 'fore you was born.

But Calv is too fucked to worry about Amanda.

He has to go make more money than is honest so he can take Donna to see Meat Loaf.

The woman's favourite band is Meat Loaf, Amanda snarls in the direction of anyone at all.

Amanda hates that "Dashboard Light" song. She likes dashboard songs by better artists. She cannot even believe Calv's musical taste. Which is not really true because she can believe it. She can totally believe he still listens to that same shit from high school because it would be harder for him to figure out what the fuck he actually likes. Meat Loaf appeals to the tiny ritualistic side of his nature. Calv's girlfriends in high school believed that wearing identical socks would rebuild some gone forgotten tribe. Conformity and repetition makes Amanda innately suspicious. Not Calv though.

Calvin always sniffs his deodorant before rolling it onto his armpit.

He is every time delightfully surprised to find the pleasant manly scent in a tube of roll-on and certain he would smell unnaturally feminine if he were not persistent. He keeps his pit stick on the dresser in the spare bedroom with his other things. Donna doesn't like how he insists on always being able to see his toiletries spread out across a surface. He tries to explain to her how taking a quick visual inventory regularly reassures him. But Donna chalks it up to some poor outport fetish toward display.

And honestly, there is something to what she says.

Calv has often wondered why he wants everything out on the front yard. He hates stuff being out of sight behind cupboard doors. Even the dishes in the kitchen. He argued that open concept would be more efficient in the morning when reaching for a mug or bowl. But Donna was not into it. Donna said the kitchen would never feel clean and she would all the time be trying to make them tidy on the shelf. She accused Calv of being too lazy to close a cabinet door after bumping her temple the umpteenth time and cussed him out. Still, he tried to talk her around.

You're not taking the cupboard doors off, Calv, just fucking forget it.

There are a lot of things in the house that Calv can just fucking forget.

Calv couldn't help what he liked and what he liked was seeing everything. He has a serious urge to hang everything up on hooks on the front step, socks, caps, his tool belt. Calv would spread he's clothes out over the bed, exhibit every bought thing to prove that he works hard and can afford stuff. He understands the campers in pits along the highway, loads of heavy equipment right in the community, cardboard signs on land squealing a surname in cheap orange spray paint.

175

Amanda hardly got any stuff at all.

Calv don't understand what she spends her money on. Concerts and trips. Nothing to show for it except a few pictures. Not even very many cause Amanda hardly ever takes pictures, gets right annoyed with Donna who wants a picture of every outfit anyone wears for the Instagram. They will racket on Thanksgiving cause Donna is taking too many photos of potato salad. Amanda thinks everything about Donna is in poor taste. Roger, too.

Roger turns her guts.

And he's after turning sour since finally parking the truck. Roger hates it, hates it with a passion, when Calv tries to be better than him. He takes it as an affront and gets defensive when Calv talks about quitting smoking or joining a ball hockey league. Roger puts the fix in and quick when Calv gets any mighty ideas about self-improvement. Reminds him that they are the same kind of man, have always been and will always be no matter what happens. No matter what. Roger and Calv have always been like brothers but they's closer than brothers now.

Roger knows none of the women folk wants Calv going around with him.

Calv should never mind picking up for that jesus sister of his. It's not like she's gonna stand by him when she finds out what they're getting into. No. Calv only got Roger now and they both knows it.

Roger is going on about how he hates St. John's.

He wouldn't live here if he could convince everyone to move back home. Then he wouldn't have to find something fit to eat for lunch on a fucking Tuesday. He would eat whatever his mother had cooked. Macaroni stew with chicken hearts and a bit of bread probably. He would have had Amanda knocked up by now if there wouldn't all these styled-up come from aways sniffing around her skirts.

Roger blames it on cable.

No one even knew what was out there till they all got the cable. Now, there is nothing but dissatisfaction. Lord Jesus, Roger is dissatisfied and he's going to have to go offshore soon so he's not ready to waste this whole day being miserable. He's got Calv out of the house now, might as well make a go of it.

Few drinks will straighten them right up.

MAJOR DAVID ASKS the skinny one if this is the staff-favourite table.

There is a slight lift in her eyebrow. He catches sight of it before she can adjust. She doesn't like him. It's perceptible. That, or she's on her period. Probably both. He's heard that the serving staff, being primarily female, get synced up. He would like to see a study on that. Major David has heard they have periods for weeks now because of the new contraceptives. He's convinced, convinced, that all the estrogen they piss out into the harbour is why there are more homosexuals. When he was a young man there was hardly a queer in Newfoundland, and now they're everywhere. The fellow wiping the glassware for example. Gay. Those mannerisms. That haircut. Gay gay gay.

He don't mind gay people now, he just wishes they didn't all look so fit.

Diane watches the decorating shows in the evening and now he can't find a bag of chips or nary a cookie in the cupboards anywhere.

A granola bar is not a cookie.

Nothing like a cookie. Would be called a cookie if it were a cookie. But it's not. It's a granola bar. The cupboards are full of kid food again. Just like how the house is full of kids. Kids he didn't even make. He loves his grandchildren. They're his grandchildren so he loves them. But they're really very loud and dirty. They're stickier than he remembers children being.

Major David mentioned that Clare's children are abnormally sticky one evening at dinner.

Or suggested perhaps their own children had been especially clean. It was rather embarrassing walking downtown with greasy smears across your backside. He was attempting to communicate this to the woman he had met at an amusement park forty-three years ago. He needed her to understand his frustration with the sticky hands that weren't just sticky hands but a catalysis for his increasing triviality.

I can't go around with a dirty backside at my age, he moaned, they'll have me carted off to the mental.

The lefties were forever searching for signs of his dementia.

But Diane started to quietly weep into her plate. He was so taken aback that he thought better of mentioning it so instead just watched the tears fall into her food, until she finally said that she was very tired. That it was easier when she was younger and that now she was not very young. Diane said she was too old for more children.

And then Clare's eldest flew into the dining room yet again throwing a hairy fit because he had shoved a bit of baby carrot so far up his nostril that it could not be sussed out.

Children have no appreciation for food.

Major David had refused to eat with them after Clare's youngest spent nearly an hour raging out in his highchair. It had scared him. He felt certain his grandson was intentionally trying to hurt himself. His flailing was violent like nothing Major David had ever seen. The girls had not behaved like this when they were growing up. He would surely remember Clare trying to asphyxiate herself using nothing but sheer child rage and the belt of her highchair.

But Diane says yes indeed, the girls had sometimes behaved like this, though perhaps not as often in the presence of their father for fear of repercussions. So Major David had made threats to repercussion his grandson. This was not the right move. Clare was suddenly beyond herself at the table and Major David thought maybe these hysterics had indeed come from their side of the family rather than Clare's good for nothing ex-husband.

Apparently, apparently, Major David was not meant to speak to the children like that because they were being raised in a violence-free environment. Never mind this violence-free environment happened to be his very same environment. Clare was still ranting about adult relationships built on boundaries and respect as Major David rubbed his chin and stared at his wife. Surely Diane must see the hypocrisy in Clare's statements. Boundaries and respect could not exist within this framework whereby Clare lived within their boundaries without respect.

His adult daughter chose her adult moments.

Moments that did not include her being an adult revolved around any and all cooking and cleaning, which fell squarely to her mother while Clare grieved her failed marriage. Grieve was her word. Not Major David's. His words would be very different words indeed. Shirk. Shirk was a word that sprang readily to mind when he thought about Clare's failed marriage.

Regardless, he banned them all from the dining room during real dinner after the infuriating conversation about parenting. So when the tiniest terror ran in with a piece of produce jammed up his nose, Major David knew he was on his way to the Janeway yet again. And Diane's tears rang true as he sat in the waiting area surrounded by sick children and their ill-advised parents. They were too old for this.

Poppys aren't Daddys.

Not that he had flourished as a Daddy the first time. Clare claims she was raised in a household shrouded in fear. Yes. Shrouded.

You wouldn't know but Pine Bud Avenue was the Gaza Strip the way Clare talks.

Shrouded.

Like she was forced to every day cover her face or be met with lashings. Major David never did anything of the sort. And heaven knows Diane didn't. She lacks any knack for discipline. The couple times she attempted to do so very early on, perhaps while the girls were still in diapers, were absolute failures. To Major David's knowledge, she had not attempted to do so again thereafter, not even when he offered to teach her how. He had been very generous with his time early in their child-rearing, he had offered to demonstrate how to manage the girls. Obviously, he could not expect Diane to know, she'd little experience with children, while Major David's education had prepared him for every eventuality. But Diane had not been interested. Had said she would just leave that to him. Said that he could handle that since she had to handle everything else.

So Major David had been made the bad guy in the household. The girls called him Father when they wanted to put further distance between them. And he didn't exactly despise it. No. It was more that he couldn't place something else in it. A tinge of something in need of punishment.

Major David couldn't wait to be Poppy.

They would all love Poppy. Poppy would get it right. But Poppy was getting it wrong.

The casino would change that.

Big George thinks so too, even if young George has reservations. Big George has warned him that young George's politics don't run as easy as his own, and Major David understood well enough. The next generation is always contrary. But all the Georges can be brought around onside. They're old money and old money is always in need of an influx of new money.

Casinos are brim full with new money.

Major David has been promised a hand in it for dealing with the crimson-coloured tape ringing the harbour. Big George had been impressed.

Dave, you've really impressed me. If ever you need advice, Big George had said on the telephone.

So when the house backing onto their lot was put on the market, Major David called Big George for his advice. In the slowest, most clearly coded voice he could manage, he asked if he should go ahead and buy that house. Big George had said fuck yes so Major David has gone head-long to the bank and bought the fuck out of that back lot house.

He is going to build a gate between the yards so the children can come and go as they please. Diane is going to be so delighted when he tells her. And Clare can get on with it. Maybe she will meet someone new, maybe she won't. But it won't matter either way, they will want for nothing. She can raise the kids in their own house handy but not right on top of them. Everyone can go back to loving Poppy again.

And Poppy can't wait for that cause Poppy's tired, too.

He's not sure how much he'll get for his part in it because these are delicate matters, George has assured him. There can be no real contract or paper trail because that's how they get you. They can't access information that doesn't exist. So the handshake is how the bigwigs do it. Very old school. Very gentlemanly.

He can hardly wait for George to arrive. He wrings his hands in anticipation.

ROGER DON'T KNOW what Calv is thinking anymore.

Calv is thinking their server looks crazy familiar.

Calv never knew what Roger was thinking.

Roger is thinking misses would be hot with a bit of lipstick.

These two aren't even looking in the same directions at the same humans looking in other directions at the other humans, so could any of them know what feelings were being felt unless words were used to express them?

Roger and Calv were taught not to express and then taught that to women they dated. Now they find themselves frustrated daily not knowing how to make up the miles between what they are seeing and what they are saying.

Roger and Calv misses a lot in this grey area.

They can't find each other in the everlasting fog and mutual insecurity.

There last fall Roger thought they was done being friends. Calv and Donna was doing real good and Calv had stopped coming around. My god, Roger wanted Calv to break up with her some bad. So when Calv called cause Donna was going to Fogo for a girls' weekend, Roger was overjoyed. They went to a dive Roger liked especially. He said it had the coldest, cheapest beer downtown but Calv knew they went cause it was handy to a strip club with a steady gear supply.

Donna thinks I got Justin Trudeau money.

The weekend will probably cost you thousands of dollars, b'y.

Six. Six thousand dollars.

Jesus, you could go down south and drink your face off for that kind of money!

What do she want to go to Fogo Island for anyway?

You got to set her fucking straight before you ends up in the poorhouse.

She's always hating on the dirty bay but wants to go to Joe Batt's fucking Arm.

Polished turd is all that is.

Threw my pillows in the garbage, wants the same jesus cushions now!

Donna's crazy.

Mine was for free made by me own grandmother but that was no good to Donna.

Donna's cracked.

Said Nan wasn't an artisan. Jesus on the cross, who's an artisan?

I thought it was someone who made fancy bread...

She's gone off with me credit card now.

You're crazy to give that to her.

I gets right sick to me stomach thinking about it.

You needs to tell her she got to knock off spending and start earning.

Or what?

Or you'll get another woman.

Another woman.

Yes, b'y, there's lots around sure look.

Calv looked around cause communication between him and Roger was not good and he was loaded on $3.75 triple Appletons and Coke. He remembers the cooler light washing over the new bartender making it seem like she was glowing in the dark. Calv had been thinking she looked nice when Roger caught hold of his eye's direction.

She's cute.

Yeah, I suppose.

What's her name?

Don't know.

Hey misses, what's your name anyhow?

What's it to you?

In that moment, Calv had searched the little bartender's face trying desperately to place her before Roger broke up his thoughts.

You Chinese or something?

She had laughed and said, or something.

And that was Olive.

Later, in the same bar Roger would witness Calv handing Olive a stack of bills. She no longer stood erect on the boss side of the bar but sat sullen and worn on their same sad side.

What, are you giving her money now too?

It's a just a loan.

You're a sucker for punishment my man.

She'll pay me back.

I bet she will.

Oh, she will.

Really?

Sure, why not.

Go on, you dog.

You think what you wants to think.

I thinks you're worse than me sure.

I never said nothing.

Calv didn't have to say anything. Implication is near defence enough to save himself from Roger's forthcoming taunts about being pussy-whipped by every pussy handy to him. This was easier for Calv. Or so he thought. In the short term it was easier and that is the only term length Calv minds.

His full time-lapse is paycheque to paycheque and the space spent in between.

In this very moment, Calv is searching the skinny guy's face trying desperately to place him.

Who was he?

Calv knows he has marked this face out in his mind before and he is tracing back slowly through the muck, but it's tricky because he's been stressed about all of the things lately. But he can't stop looking at buddy who is right ashen in the face, like someone who smokes too much and doesn't drink enough water.

Calv worries that he is attracted to him due to his inability to break free of this gaze.

He tries to sneak glances but needs to fully turn and look. Perhaps he's after going queer. He'll probably have to march in parades now waving a rainbow flag, vote NDP and sing show tunes. Amanda would love that. Everything would be forgiven. She would explain away all of his transgressions and her grievances with a closet diagnosis. Her theatre friends would nod in recognition and make idle comments about being true to yourself and following your heart and dreams and shit. Because they believed everyone could follow their gorgeous dreams mapped out on delicate Japanese paper, half of them with theatre parents, the other half rich.

There was no explaining Amanda, though, who had neither. The token outsider they kept around for a bit of authenticity Calv figures. Why else would they keep talking to her? Sure, Amanda is a right pain in the ass. She was the only person he knew who seemed to actively want gay kids. Yes, the invitations would come furious in the mailbox if Calv were gay. My good grief, they'd want to be nice to him then. They would use him as an example of their worldliness. When accused of maintaining no rural friendships, they will quickly cite their bay twins. One is an artist, the other gay. Amanda's friends would fucking die over it.

But Calv don't feel any desire to get his dick out for the waiter.

It is more like his memory is saying there is a really real reason he should remember this reckless-looking homo. He had eaten at The Hazel with his sister half a dozen times at least. Amanda likes the Brussels sprouts here. She raves over the raw bar. Will eat anything that swims. Not feather or fur, Amanda says as she wilfully ignores the massive amounts of meat being consumed by everyone else in the dining room. Last time they were here, she frowned as Calv shredded her hypocrisy. He ordered onion rings battered in french fries and dipped in bacon coulis because it was a thing. Sausage-infused matzo sticks stacked atop a steak the size of a grown man's palm. When she begged him to eat something green, he ordered the beer-battered broccoli and then double-dipped it fingers deep in hot chili mayo. Calv would put salt on salt to spite his sister even if it burned the tastebuds off his fucking tongue and seared the roof of his mouth until wells of water gathered in his eyes. He would talk endlessly about his carnivorous tendencies and proclaim himself a great lover of all the woollies. They're delicious.

Calv would eat anything with eyes.

He knew this kind of talk bothered Amanda's heart. That was why he talked it. This didn't make him feel great. Not at all. But he couldn't really help himself. When he thought on it too long, it seemed like the feeling was very close to anger. And he could not clarify that angry feeling either. But it was related to her never fucking listening to anything he said. Asking opinions but not really listening is just wasting everyone's time.

I can't wait to hear what you thought of my show! Come tell me in the car.

So he would tell her exactly what he thought while smoking in the back seat of her old two-door Pontiac Sunfire.

Amanda drives a four-door AWD with a roof rack now. She doesn't ask for his opinions anymore. Probably asks Freddy.

Fuck Freddy's opinions though, they're just Amanda's regurgitated.

Before Amanda had a boyfriend with opinions, she would ask her brother for his.

And so he would pay really close attention to whatever she was doing and saying on stage as if getting tested later. And he would tell her, when she kneeled down was when she should have stood up, when she walked toward the other actor was when she should have backed away. Sometimes he even went again to the last night, the closing one, cause they would have a party and Amanda would be in a nice mood to be around now that it was done. Their parents would want them to all go for drinks or pizza to celebrate.

This was when Amanda still drank drinks and ate pizza. Still ate bread at all. Intolerant to bread now she says. Intolerant to a lot of things, Calv thinks, critical feedback and friendly advice included. There was never a time when she actually corrected her mistakes like he said. Amanda kneeled exactly when she wanted to kneel. If she didn't want to, well, then she didn't.

So why the fuck was he watching her show at all if she wasn't going to listen to him?

Then Calv would feel right poorly. Like she didn't think he was smart enough. Or understood it. And sometimes he would feel embarrassed that he had thought she cared about his opinions at all. He couldn't tell her cause she would accuse him of making everything about himself.

My play is not about you, stop behaving like an asshole.

But it wouldn't like that. Everything was always about her, about being nice to Amanda, watching her prance around, or listening to her every jesus thought on why fast food was not food and hydro projects was evil and oil was dirty and how everything and anything Calv was ever interested in or into was wrong, wrong, wrong. Amanda made Calv feel like he was destroying the fucking planet by his own self, but he was just doing what every other jesus human was doing. That's what he said to her.

That's not a good reason to do something, Calvin, Jesus!

So they kind of stopped talking about how Calv made money or what he fed himself when he was in charge of making money and feeding himself. He still went to see her act in stuff but he never said much afterward, and that hurt her feelings same as when he said too much. They agreed on a range of unmentionable topics to keep things congenial. Amanda claimed she just wanted to have a nice visit with her brother. Share a pleasant meal.

Somewhere they could both eat food in front of each other.

Though there was nowhere for them really to go or, at least, few places where there were actual options they would both agree to pay money for. The franchises Calv preferred on the harbourfront were non-starters. Amanda grumbled things about sending money Western Union to the richest men in America. Send them your little money fast, she would randomly blurt out after two cocktails she claimed not to like but drank in record time.

Women do that, Calv has noticed. Says they don't like a party or want to be there but then drink faster and talk more than any feller there. Donna does this all the time. Says she don't want to be at any parties where Roger's at but then is the first one drunk at the party. Don't make no sense to Calv. Don't look like a person not having a good time. And then the next day, Donna will tell him he don't know a fucking thing. Don't understand her at all. Sometimes she says he don't understand either woman alive. Not he's mother or sister or her. And the worst of it is, she's right. Calv don't.

He half the time don't know why they says what he wants to hear.

It don't seem to make anyone happy. Like when Amanda agrees to go to the restaurants he likes down by the water, he don't know why she agrees to it after already deciding she's going to hate everything later. Why not just say no? Not go? Go somewhere else?

Instead, she'll go and the whole time point out everything that she thinks is stupid. The only thing she would ever willingly eat was some salmon wrapped in phyllo pastry which she would mock the entire time for its *originality*. Making jokes about sending her food back to the nineties where children dressed like children and music was less rapey. Which, honestly, was not even stuff Calv thought about. Calv never noticed what little girls had on. That would be gross. And he never even registered the words in songs. And he tells Amanda to chill out when she brings up stuff like that.

Relax, maid, he sometimes says to her as she looks around the massive dining room with its high ceilings, in mid-rant about energy efficiency and what this place must pull from the grid.

Just relax, girl, Calv says, cause what does Amanda know about surplus capacity?

You never mind cold load pickup, he says to her with actual familial concern.

Amanda is going to give herself bad nerves worrying over shit she got no control over.

And she says that's his fault too. That he don't do his share of worrying over anything. None of them do, so all the women is left to worry their own worries and the worries of every man nearby who is too busy playing some fake game in a fantasy world.

Play real football, Amanda yells, at least then you wouldn't be fat!

Get off your ass, Calvin!

And that hurts his feelings something fierce cause Calv knows he's after putting on a few pounds especially since he got laid off. Can't fit into any of he's shirts from high school. Amanda didn't have to point that out to him right before he eats his dinner. It's still body shaming even if you're a man, ain't it?

191

Amanda would knife a person for saying something like that to a woman. A stranger woman. Any woman on the street, and she would be writing letters about it. But she says the likes of it to her own brother easy enough. Then she pretends she's worried over his health when really she's worried over how much it will cost to keep him alive in the future. And that makes Calv want to deep-fry a whole jesus cow the one time. Here she is being rude to him in public because they got the highest health care costs in the country, as if that's Calv's fault too. You wouldn't know but he invented diabetes. Sole cause of heart disease, Calv was, according to his sister.

Don't twist my words into bullshit, brother dear.

Oh, yes, they had some real pleasant meals before they called the truce. My god, Calv remembers it almost always ending in a drunken bicker at the corner of Adelaide and Water. Amanda waving in the direction of the fashion district, yelling loud enough for motorcycle gangs and homeless people to hear, that there were way better restaurants right there!

What's wrong with our own food? she'd demand. Why buy cheap food from elsewhere?

The truce consisted of a set of rules and regulations for emotionally rewarding family time.

That's what Amanda's counsellor recommended they do. Amanda is secretly resentful that she is the one got to go to a counsellor, too. That just seems like another thing she is responsible for that Calv is not. Her money and time are wasted trying to come up with further ingenious ways to get through to her brother so they can maintain some kind of relationship, when the problem is not even her!

She buys him copies of the books so they can read them together. But he never reads them because Calv don't really care if he has a relationship with his sister. That's what she believes when the books go unread. Once, upon discovering a well-worn, spine-cracked copy, she was briefly overjoyed that he had spent some time investigating his emotional health and well-being. She was optimistic. But it had been Donna that read the book in the bathtub. She found this out when Calv asked her not to bring any more of them kinds of books over.

I don't want you putting stuff in Donna's head, makes me life difficult.

And then they did not speak for months. Maybe six or seven. Whole seasons passed with them merely receiving second-hand information from their mother, who was very distressed over the situation indeed. Susie was in counselling over it. Kind of. She visited the local minister twice a week during the twins' estrangement. Not because she was particularly devout. No, she had little faith in the church, or any church. The religious ones was always feuding over one thing or another. That's all you ever heard tell of on the television, this crowd's god told them to blow up that other god's house. Yes sir, as if any spirit could be homeless.

As if burning down a building changed what was in people's hearts.

Never really did anything but caused a lot of unnecessary hurt and frustration. Susie was sick of seeing them bloody babies been hauled out from underneath piles of rocks. Little youngsters, like the way Amanda and Calvin was little once, covered in so much dust, deep trenches washed clear with tears and snot. Sin sure. Susie didn't believe into any of that old religion garbage anymore. She didn't tell everyone though. Her brothers would not know what to do. Also, she liked talking to the minister about her problems. He was educated into counselling same as a nurse or whatever, Susie figured. He was free of charge and also married, not expensive or a sex monster, so she went to see him over the twins.

Now, Calv and Amanda would find a neutral place that suited them both temporarily and meet there every second week for a meal. Until Amanda found out something that ran counter to her ideals and, by god, it was rather impossible to be a feminist vegetarian in this unrelenting town. It was rather tiresome to be her twin brother, too.

But here (!) but here (!) but here was this locally owned restaurant run by a lovely married couple who were community minded. There were vegetables on the menu. You could still hear your own thoughts over the music. There were homemade candles. They made their own candles and Amanda loved that.

And yes, she recognized that the burger was wrapped in maple bacon wrapped in blue cheese wrapped in more maple bacon but could Calv just let her have this one nice place where she could eat her tiny cabbages in peace, pretty please? Just a moment of contentment before it was ruined for her. Because Amanda still liked The Hazel. Sometimes, sometimes there were even dogs sleeping in the porch. She liked that. It reminded her of home. A favourite place. Whenever she went out to eat, she ate at The Hazel. Amanda is a creature of habit. Calv wondered if that was a woman thing or an actor thing or an Amanda thing. Regardless, she liked what she liked.

Which was another reason why him and Roger should get the fuck out of here soon.

DAMIAN KNOWS WHO they are as soon as they walk in. Of course he does, they only ruined his life. They had some help from his mother mind you, but they certainly were the impetus for the recent attempt at self-destruct.

Damian has been sneaking dressed-down Caesars all afternoon as he can't be caught drinking something so gussied up as Ben's king-prawn-styled concoction. Everyone would know he had a glow on. Damian is currently swilling a beverage dressed out of necessity. It is the mother on a school run of Caesars. The vodka and Clamato is the coat and cap his body needs to power through what he fully expects to be the worst evening service, so he feigns discretion.

Like everyone at drop-off, Damian is unwashed drawers underneath.

Queen Bitch is staying on to serve tables. She just assumes she will be good at serving which she most certainly will not. Iris looks like she will heave her guts up at any moment, and Omi is poisoned with him because Damian is after scraping food onto the floor already a half dozen times. Ben hates them all but is meeting their request for drinks anyway.

Damian takes a gulp of his domesticated Caesar and feels reassured.

He had seen the not entirely ugly guy in the restaurant before he ruined Damian's life. Lately though, the not entirely ugly guy sometimes eats with a pretty actress who rehearses just down the street. She smiles and says thank you a lot to compensate for life. Damian clocked them the first time they came in because he thought they were maybe the best example of why Tinder doesn't work.

Straight folks do hookup apps wrong.

Women got a hold of Tinder and agreed to change its purpose for existing without informing men. It's supposed to be a sex app. Or at least that was the point of Grindr. It was for cruising. And Grindr is Tinder's gay dad so Tinder should have followed in its father's footsteps. But oh no, oh no, that would be clearly too straightforward. If everyone agreed to use the thing the way it was designed to be used people might get what they want. Instead, girls who came over for one beer started moving pillows around and lining shoes up in the porch. The ladies were looking for love in all the wrong places.

Not that there is anything wrong with love. Damian has been in love. Is still in love.

Is it still in love if the other person has blocked you on all their devices?

That's what Tom did. Or tried to do. It's not like they don't have all the same friends. Damian signs in to social media under Jeremy's name at least once a day. He knows this is not a productive way to move on but he doesn't want to move on. He wants to move back in with Tom. He wants to live once again in their sweet apartment that smelt of bagels from the adjacent building. Damian thinks love smells like warm poppy seeds. Or heartache.

He guesses it's heartache now that these men have ruined his life.

Damian thinks his full life is over now that he is no longer a friend of Tom's on Facebook. Because Tom will add anyone on Facebook. People he barely knows. People he doesn't like. Tom would never throw shade over such a nothing thing as a social media.

But he deleted Damian.

And it was weeks, weeks before Damian realized Tom wasn't getting his texts. Texts he had agonized over. Damian had tried to find the correct combination of words to unlock Tom's forgiveness. He had spiralled from abject apology, to self-defence, to outright hostility, to begging. He was pleading last going off, which turned out to be going off to the middle of nowhere. Jeremy told him. He had been experiencing this range of emotional turmoil wholly on his own because Tom was not having it.

You're not who I thought you were, Tom had said finitely.

All this, everything, was that half-handsome fucktard's fault.

Damian knew he was bad news when he sauntered into the hotel that night just by the way he walked. Trying to seem confident. Acting like the little one with him was not with him. Beelined for the elevator, her easily three or four steps back. Everything about them screamed that something terrible was going to go down. The sheer distance between them, the disparity in their stride, he was so well out in front of her, she trying to keep up though uncertain of their proximity. Cautious of too closely closing the gap. The imbalance was striking. Even heteros would have seen it, even hetero guys, the body language was all wrong. The man in front was clearly too nervous, the woman tailing him was clearly too eager.

But like he said to Tom, what the fuck was he supposed to do about it?

Not let people go to their rooms? He was just the front desk guy. That was most of his then job. His responsibilities ended when he checked the first lot of shitheads in and, OMFG, they were shitheads, too. They couldn't contain their shitty heads even in the lobby. Pretending as if checking into hotels was something that wasn't well beyond their familial experience. Acting like their mothers could not count up the hotel beds they had laid with, like lovers, on both hands.

These men, so newly made in every way, needed everyone to know they were made men.

They bragged about how much money they owed. They did not yet know that owing money was not the same as having it. Damian has seen hundreds of them pass through airports. They were an easy mark. They talked too loud on their cellphones so everyone would know they had cellphones to talk on because they were important people worthy of love. Really they did not feel so important in large cities that did not care for them at all, let alone love them.

The group had arrived well before not entirely ugly guy and the girl.

Olive. Iris's Olive.

Damian had not known that then.

198

RIS'S SINGLE IS now a four top.

The Mayor has been joined by two middle-aged women and a forty-something-year-old man. He insists on keeping the chair across from him empty even when one of the women tries to seat herself in it. She shifts to the side without comment though it is an awkward exchange. The man with them has undeniably well-groomed facial hair. Either he is childless, divorced, and/or a dickhead, Iris thinks as she takes in his peach paisley-patterned collared shirt. He has spent a lot of time putting this look together. His attempt at approachable congeniality is so direct that all women in the vicinity should proceed with caution.

This is not the guy you ask for directions.

In St. John's, though, being not shitty is the same as being awesome.

Iris feels strongly that nice men don't try this strenuously to appear nice. They just *are*. It is just a thing they were forced to become by a single mother or frustrated sister. A stubborn enough sister will smack the cocksure right out of you.

The cocksure are cocksure for a reason, and that reason is unchecked practice.

They've been practising on the shy ones. Or better yet, the ones who feel unpretty. Girls like Iris who can't get away. They've got no pieces to move around the board or tokens to collect for extra mobility points. They persist, painfully unaware that the ringside seats are held for the emotionally well-off and purely ornamental.

Women like Iris hope to change hearts and minds by being good enough.

Sweet enough. Hot enough. Nice enough.

Nice girls cannot hear truth as they are so used to being lied to.

Iris can't even read between the lines in that rap song John sings in his car.

She has to act like he never told her because she can't hear the truth in what he says through his suffocating embrace.

Besides, if at first you don't succeed, try, try again, right?

And Iris is dogged. She has always been too eager for petting and therefore no one's pet.

Wait your turn, little miss, and Iris is waiting regardless of her placement in line.

You can unlearn this, Jo has said. If you know what to look for you can make it through the douchebag wasteland of ghosting guys blowing up the dating sites for their skin.

Iris hopes it won't matter that she got no game later because actual nice guys got no game either. They are a gameless lot and, therefore, her very best bet. Iris is gonna get herself a genuine nice guy if she gets through this day alive. Promise promise.

Iris and Jo strongly concur on this last point. Iris and Jo mostly agree, so much so that Iris becomes disappointed when they don't. She is forlorn when they don't laugh at the same jokes. Other things they don't agree on include pop music, Timbits and technology. They had been divided along parenting lines until Jo's own nice guy showed up on the scene and became the deciding factor. Iris has yet to decide where she stands on this man, though she currently has no recourse in the matter. Or any matter.

But there were theories that Jo and Iris had enthusiastically agreed on before Mr. Tiebreaker showed up in his full cycling gear. Reflectors and all. Iris has never been comfortable around men in Lycra. Spandex in any bright colour makes her sweat. Jo says that Iris is uncomfortable with men who take an active interest in anything other than ranting and drinking because of her father. Of this, Iris is aware. Jo has always been the exchequer of emotional currency, keeping track of accounts, in an attempt to keep them solvent.

They schemed in the early days how to manage the nicer ones while sitting on the kitchen floor listening to the dishwasher run through. The kind ones were easily spooked by quick replies to one side.

Keep your filthy shit to yourself at first, Iris, Jo suggested.

Nice guys can hardly manage themselves. Your filthy thoughts overwhelm them. Do not expect whole paragraphs about getting bent over a desk from any fit man with manners. Nice men don't randomly send strangers messages about hauling their dress up and licking their pussy.

Jo knows. She has gotten explicit Facebook messages from buddy two floors down next to accounting, but not in accounting, never *in* accounting. And while it was flattering and maybe made her panties damp, she did not respond because he was almost certainly not a nice man.

Because a nice man you barely know would not try to fuck you through your iPad during an information seminar on the building's new heating system. That is not appropriate correspondence. That is something else Jo said when it happened to her the first time.

Don't acclimatize. Resist this adaptation of thought.

And don't say explicit things to anyone you like before you see them naked, for fuck sakes, Iris, Jo had squealed as she tossed a dishtowel in her face.

He will probably blush and throw his phone down on the couch cushions in frustration when you nearly imply something something about eating cheesecake in your underwear while watching *The Godfather*. Because, goddamn it, he does not know what to do with that. He will have to think it over for days.

Jo thinks deliberation is best kind. It proves he is thinking. It proves thinking men still exist. She imagines them wandering from the forest eating custard cones. Perhaps they've fashioned a walking stick from forest floor debris, or picked wild berries now cupped in their free hand. Maybe they are with their dog or best friend.

Both.

Maybe two nice men and a hound emerge together from the thicket, sober and speaking to one another about their shared interests. Perhaps these first-contact men will be engaged in a conversation that they will actually remember later.

Genuine human interaction.

Iris fantasizes about men holding up one side of an honest conversation while she holds up the other and imagines them taking shelter together under this decent communication.

Iris's table is too busy to order drinks as they discuss with great enthusiasm their theories of place versus non-place.

All of Iris's places are non-places.

The linen closet. Smoking alley. A fast food franchise in a suburb.

Don't say he ever takes you anywhere nice because he doesn't, Jo has said.

Someone might see Iris, crying in a drive-through on her birthday when he says this will have to do because George came home early from her conference.

Iris had worn a summer dress that she thought would flatter her collarbone in a girlish way that made her feel light and appealing, though she was instead boiled down to broth logistics. Weak and unsatisfying. Just enough to tie John over while waiting for the main course. Trying to hold back deep sobs while holding a cheeseburger made Iris feel truly pathetic, and she promised herself she would not eat another birthday meal of any kind with this man who makes her feel less concentrated than a tin of off-brand soup stock you only use up when you've cleaned the cupboards before holidays. Something to be eaten on moving day. The last bit of sustenance in the house.

Iris has felt, feels now, today even, not deserving of a dipper. Pour her in a bowl and shove her in the micro-wave. She is just the quick fix. A pretend something is still nothing. An imitation thing.

Iris feels unreal.

This is why people are chasing their aces all over the poorest bays. Not because they've some genuine belief that they will catch the card. They can barely catch a break at all. A century of impoverishment and industry collapse, pillaging and recrimination, has taught them not to hope for much but a bit of fun when the cards are cut. So they pack themselves into their domestic cars and pickup trucks built tough to drive to the town hall two or ten towns away.

And the feeling they bask in feeling is sold to them by organizers as excitement for the draw when the feeling they are actually feeling is unity. They are together, experiencing an experience together. What they are delighting in is shared humanity. This euphoria they seek out in far-flung regions of the country is so they feel less far-flung.

Iris's people belong to this moment, this movement, this mania regardless of the worth of it.

And later, when there is nothing left to pay the bills or buy a pull ticket, they will once again be united in a feeling. From the wild fray and hysteria of calling cards, they will look up to find everyone struggling and wonder how it came to this again. They will ask people who seem in better positions how they have managed. And these same better-positioned people will turn to face them from their fully restored Victorian homes and ask how they have not managed their affairs more fairly.

Like the crowd at Iris's four top are casually wondering why all those bay kids flunk out of university. The Mayor is pontificating about rural Newfoundlanders' lack of ambition.

The Mayor is boasting to Iris that his friend is the head of Heritage NL though she hears how his tidy vowels betray him. Paisley Shirt originated in southern Ontario in some civilized-sized town named for some other civilized place as is the way everywhere in the new world. This attribute he shares with his co-workers. That and a shared preoccupation with community-building communities that were built many decades ago by families who still live in them.

Iris responds that her best friend works with him too. And the Mayor twitches slightly before asking who that might be, and then again when she tells him.

The world keeps getting smaller around The Hazel.

The Heritage diners have been diners here before. Iris has seated them herself, but the lunch crowd rarely recall her face. They're economical with their time and dollars and for the most part do not want to engage, but today Heritage NL via ON is buoyant. The table is bursting with theories on rural Newfoundland. They are animated while discussing a penchant for dumping old automobiles, cars and trucks, the occasional piece of heavy machinery even, into the pits, down over the beach, off the side of a cliff.

We even found an old cherry-red jeep driven into the forest!

Baymen, the Mayor says, giving them further permission to forge on.

The thinnest of the women wonders aloud if they've no pride of place. The other chirps that she is always amused by their inability to see natural beauty. The thin one claims her bay neighbour had not even noticed the flowers growing wild in the yard until she'd pointed them out one day.

The Mayor is astonished and all agree in their tight-lipped way that not knowing the wild flora and fauna's proper taxonomy suggests that Iris's people take everything for granted.

And Iris stands broadside pouring lemon waters, all

the while simmering because the implication around the table is very simply that the diners are smarter for having learned the correct names.

They were given more words to use, and their daily usage of them means they are obviously of superior intellect.

As if having more is reflective of being more.

And Iris wants to implode and feels she will if faced for the rest of living with this same oversimplified rhetoric, day in and day out and night on and night off.

Perhaps Iris could have had some kind of happiness if she hadn't read all those books while her mom was at work. All those books opened her up, and now here she stands, opened.

Why is the rural Newfoundlander [insert anything here]?

The answer is poverty.

Why is the rural Newfoundlander [insert anything here]?

Still poverty.

Why is the rural Newfoundlander [insert anything here]?

POVERTY. POVERTY. POVERTY. FUCK!

And Iris will not discuss the shit her people buy. Buying lots of shit is not an argument against the kind of poverty they face but proof positive that they face it.

Her table is wondering if the fish is fresh.

This is a question Iris must endure because they want to impress on her that they are seafood connoisseurs now they've pledged allegiance to the island. One pipes up in a giddy declarative fashion that she knew immediately upon stepping off her flight twenty years ago that *she* was *home*. It is the level of boast still alive in this woman that gives away her own heritage as much as her penchant for pronouncing all her consonant sounds. She sees nothing idiotic about inquiring after freshness in the middle of a February snow squall.

Fuck my life, Iris thinks, as the former mainlanders talk incessantly about the merits of flash-freezing and the ideal way to batter cod. She half shakes her head and concludes the world is gone ass up in every way. Just nod and pretend ignorance, baygirl.

Smile. Smile for your money. Or starve.

The conversation turns to winter trawling which Paisley Shirt suggests they should reinstate now the stocks are stabilizing. And Iris says, without warning, that winter fishing causes severe mental illness in fishing communities along all coasts. The table falls silent and stares when Iris utters the word suicide.

Because it is more dangerous than summer fishing, which is fucking dangerous enough.

The fact that she has to even say these words discourages her faith in humanity. These individuals, all likely reasonable people, cannot discern for themselves why other reasonable people would be anxious atop the fierce North Atlantic Ocean in the middle of a January gale.

Worse than a gale even.

A gusting.

It is the gusting that takes you off your path worse than a gale. The persistence of never-ceasing wind is something you can adjust to, plan for and abide. The unpredictable nature of a gusting, though, is not worth living through.

207

This aggressive gusting keeps all off-kilter. It is terrorism after every fashion. The most brutal aspect of it being that for a brief moment there is respite enough to once again manufacture some hope.

Iris is baffled that these people, with their great passionate joy for all things Newfoundland, have such a measly understanding of her stock. And the woman who first inquired after the freshness of this fish peers up at Iris through her purple-rimmed fashion glasses now with the expectant look of someone who often hears what she wants to hear because she can't handle being told otherwise.

So Iris gives her the recitation on the freshest seafood on hand, skilfully prepared by their very own culinary master whose well-versed paws would (and will) squeeze the last essence of liveliness out of any creature.

And the woman is grateful and says she will order the salmon. She was always going to, she just needed Iris to reaffirm all the preconceived, ill or otherwise, notions she had of this restaurant and the calibre of people working in it. That made her feel at ease which made her feel at home which made her feel that spending all this time was the correct choice and not a waste of her life.

Usually we spend our winters down south, the woman says by way of explanation for having had to request any information from her waitress at all. Iris wishes she could tell Jo. Wishes she could angry text about what she must entertain on the daily.

But she can't just text Jo anymore.

Not for this or anything. Not even in cases of actual emergencies is Iris meant to text, because Jo claims Iris doesn't know the difference anymore. Iris has lost her ability to tell a campfire from house fire.

The extended overtime conditions she has been playing under have spaced her benchmarks apart in an inconceivable way and her voice breaks sporadically without warning. She stops speaking in the middle of a conversation and stares off into space as if some invisible hook has slid into her conscience and caught her up. She will stop walking in the street, disappear into a bathroom stall, close her eyes so people cannot see her thinking her thoughts. This: the only way to hide her feelings from invaders. It is worrisome, disheartening. And rude.

It is fucking rude to Jo and Harry the way Iris gets on.

As if this asshole was her family, even though Jo and Harry have been her family this whole time. They have been eating pasta together and going to the playground and wrapping presents on the living room floor. That's what family does. A family overcooks the turkey and blows up balloons and uses napkins as band-aids because what kind of woman has fucking band-aids in her pockets anyway? A family naps all over the house on a rainy Sunday and spit washes the floor before company arrives on a Saturday night. Not for each other, for company. Jo and Iris don't even get dressed when they are together. They spend whole days and nights bra-less in soft clothing.

Harry yelling from the other side of the locked bathroom door for Iris to let him in because he needs to tell her something while she is in the bath.

No, it cannot wait, his feeble yet insistent voice echoes through the hollow door as he kicks at it.

The wobble wobble against the frame was annoying

and funny. Iris would sink herself under the water with just her face above the surface as she tried to negotiate with the tiny terrorist attempting to trespass on her private time. She had crossed her legs and covered her breasts on the off chance the cheap latch reinstalled poorly by the neighbourhood handyman gave way.

The neighbourhood handyman is not actually very handy. He is just a man that will fix things on the real cheap for single women around town. They all have him in their contacts under Mr. Fixit. They call him to turn off the water when a pipe bursts or relight the pilot light on the propane fireplace.

Why doesn't Santa come in the front door? Harry had yelled urgently.

Iris was a wiper of Harry's bum and is therefore a member of this particular slung together flock. So she is, was, patient when the boy child needed to tell her something while soaking in the tub because he doesn't understand when she says he's not allowed in because she's naked.

But you see me naked!

He does not understand the wrongness in seeing Iris naked because she sleeps over at his house and that's family. So when Iris had said she is nothing and has no one because this raging asshole is unkind to her, Jo wanted to scream that it is like saying her and Harry are nothing and no one. And they all know that is not what Iris meant, not now anyway, now that Jo has a boyfriend. It's changed now but not for the better.

Things keep changing for the worse, Iris says aloud disbelievingly.

In these moments, Iris surveys all the broken hearts laid in front of her. Those she breaks herself and those broken by someone else. It is a horrifying vantage point yet she cannot look away or find an alternate route. Just this one way forward, where she slips and falls face first into the carnage.

Iris can't manage to keep her feelings inside.

She stuffs them down with her fists, tucks her hand in, tries to edge these drawers closed. But they just won't latch. In the process, she harms herself. Closes it tight on her own thin wrists. She bumps herself against doorways and windowsills. You can always tell when Iris is getting over another something. There are the little bruises and minor marks.

John says, Jesus, Iris, watch where you're going.

Iris envisions herself swollen large, gigantic with his vicious treatment, each bruise present on the top layer surface. Underneath, the one before. Under that, further scar tissue, until each hard-healed layer stretches fully over the one belonging to her parents.

Iris's mother would cook dinner when she had a boyfriend.

There would be clean hair, curled and pulled back in a loose elastic at the nape of her neck, V-neck sweaters in sweet colours like rose or plum, and a tidy bathroom sink clear of toothpaste globs recounting each parental brushing. There were never wine glass rings on the nightstand or a lack of tea bags in the tea jar. Iris's mother would make elaborate meals like roast chicken and steamed vegetables for a man. She would peel sweet potatoes and slice carrots and jesus if she didn't marinate meat in orange juice and soy sauce which was the ultimate gesture of devotion. There would be lots of pork for whatever new fellow was holding the television remote while he fell asleep on the sofa.

Napping on the sofa being highly indicative of the status of their relationship and thus calming. Sleeping men couldn't walk away from you. Or, at least, not quickly.

Best to let them sleep on. Iris's mother had disturbed many naps in her first marriage and was taught her lessons accordingly. Never wake a sleeping man. Or he'll leave. And so Cynthia was the very best woman human version of herself for any Reg or Steve, but even this was not near enough or too much for the Regs and Steves so they would move on elsewhere to someone less needy. Iris then went back to eating pea soup from a can because it was the only thing in the cupboard.

Iris wanted a different kind of family than the kind of family she had. For a time, she had fastened an approximation together. Jo's ingenuity and Harry's lovability made it easy enough. Though she always knew that clock was ticking down. She could every day see how great they were and knew eventually some fellow would take her makeshift family from her.

And she was right. Chris did. But she could hardly hate on Chris for loving the same people she loved. If anything, he was a right smart dude. And it hurt a bunch that Jo was her person but she was no one's person, so she yelled at Jo to not say she meant nothing to John. Saying she means nothing gives her nowhere to go.

The Mayor orders a round of pints while they wait for

Big George, who is never in a hurry to meet anyone on time as a general rule of ruling importance. Iris orders the round off of Ben, who is trying to engage her in conversation. She whispers, don't waste your time, and he infers the diners are thirsty for their pints. Ben hurries on to make some little thing easier on her because she looks so like she has been beat. Iris imagines crying into the checked tea towel, she would like to hide her face in fabric, but instead she throws it over her shoulder in resignation.

Because Iris is a soldier still.

Some maniac sergeant, a composite of more men than one, had been running drills inside Iris's cortex. Land mines lay limp along the path, live wires from a previous onslaught swung and sparked overhead. Dangerous connections were being made in these instances of negligence. Iris's safety network had been compromised and Jo could not stand adjacent waiting for all to collapse under the weight of such a reckless surge.

No one would ever fault Jo for giving up.

Trying to revive Iris was like breathing life into a half-mannequin. Jo was just winding herself as air blew out the missing bottom. There was nothing to catch it, there was nowhere for it to go but out. Jo had tried sentiment but the ass is well and truly out of her best friend. She had even tried to manipulate Iris's own sense of loyalty, knowing well enough it was the same tactic the enemy was employing.

Dirty tricks left nothing for a person but more dirty tricks.

So Jo had powered through. Facebook posts. Text attachments. Emails with images imbedded. Iris pushing

Harry in his stroller. Reading Robert Munsch on the couch. Baking cookies in their pyjamas. All of them, half asleep every which way across the sofa on a snow day. Iris convinced she was bleeding to death and watching *The Princess Bride*. Harry hanging over the side of the tub trying to fill a hot-water bottle for Aunt Iris's bad belly. Each photo implored Iris to remember better.

Remember who we were before it was every day *John says John says John says* . . .

Remember yourself, Iris.

Jo had launched a re-education campaign running counter to the brainwashing onslaught of false memories and preferred realities chosen to suit John's own manipulative purpose. She had been determined not to let him convince Iris that this was as good as she'd get and all she deserved. Jo was certain Iris deserved more. Just like she is certain that Iris is beautiful, even though her friend refuses to make eye contact in photographs because she is so positive now of her own hideousness. John is a very bad man. Jo thinks he is the worst kind of human.

Iris had said that Jo would not feel this way toward John if things had been different.

And Jo nearly passes out in rage each time this or some semblance of this is uttered because of course she would feel differently about him if he had been different. But he had not been different! This was John Fisher! How John Fisher is in the real world! Jo judges his actual behaviour. Not his bullshit bullshit bullshit theories.

A nervous breakdown is a real concern, Jo had thought, as she watched Iris shrink further out of view. Barely in the frame at all.

All pictures of her these days are of a woman searching for something more promising out of shot. Jo detests this sideways view of Iris while John peers out confidently from newspapers commending him for feeding the homeless as if this was of his own inclination. As if John ever had a good idea in his life that wasn't in some manner executed by some smarter woman well pressed at the end of his thumb.

Pulse, pulse, pulse.

And this makes Jo crazy.

She yells at her laptop while surfing the interwebs during a Netflix marathon. A photo of them posed around the polished kitchen pops up in her newsfeed. Jo coughed and spat tea at the sight. It dribbled down her chin as she scrolled down to reveal Iris and George flanking John like unknowing sister wives. John with his hands on them both. Jo had called Iris, yelling.

Why are you in that fucking photo with them?

John will have Iris babysitting George's kids just as he already has her walking George's dogs. Jo is sure of it. He will have them all around the same table eating Sunday supper like some alternative family off the documentary channel.

It's not fucking polyamorous if no one has agreed to it, Jo wants to scream every time she is forced to be nice to John's face.

He will have Iris paired up with some meek fellow also in his employ who will be regularly sent out of town for every food festival and cooking show within reason. He will marry Iris off like a piece of cattle, for cover. He will discourage Iris's own family. He will talk about her commitment to art and the toll of kids on women's bodies.

Auntie Iris, sitting pretty at the back of the room for baptisms and graduations, would run a kind of concealed life so that John was never for a moment without a woman to tend to his every physical want and emotional need.

John needs a woman focused on him at all times for fear he will disappear. His loner status is a fake. A facade. Another unreal thing about him.

Jo can tell and so tried to tell Iris. But Iris could not hear her. And it only takes one call to Child, Youth and Family Services to ruin your life. Ruin their lives.

So Jo abdicated. Removed herself and Harry from the fucked up picture.

The last time Iris saw Harry was in a centre city grocery store. Not Jo's preferred grocery store in the east end with the better liquor and finer deli meat selection but a Sobeys brimming with welfare attire. Jo's carnivorous tendencies and preference for blended French wines did not typically bring her into the heart of town, where carts were well stocked with cases of Vienna sausages and canned pop.

Iris had spotted Harry at the other end of the bakery and so hovered amongst the proteins, staring blankly at a rack of ribs as if that were something she would conceivably eat.

He was so much taller. The last vestige of his baby fat was pulled tight along the lean and long limbs protruding through pants legs soaked through and salt stained on the bottom. One partially tucked into a boot, the other frayed and dragging along the floor. His coat was open because even as a child he despised the sticky feeling inherited from his mother, who could not wear certain colours or fabrics to a formal event due to nervous perspiration. But it was her Harry. Slightly dishevelled, cheeks flushed and sweating with his coat pulled back over his shoulders in that cool way kids do. He was wearing a hamburger backpack Iris despised for sheer ugliness though she knew Harry likely loved it because he would think it a great horrible joke to have a burger on his back. Such a funny kid.

And Iris had felt akin to a kidnapper without the courage to kidnap.

A man Iris had never seen before approached Harry, who did not look entirely sure or impressed with the interaction. And the man, mild enough looking, reached out and ruffled Harry's hair in a far too intimate manner for a man Iris did not recognize.

Who the fuck was this man touching the child she loved so much?

Iris had never felt such panic or helplessness.

Here was this child who she felt a great kindness toward being touched by a stranger. And there was nothing she could do. The full gravity of what had been taken from her bore down on Iris as she stood there holding a large box of tampons. Paper applicator because Jo claimed the world did not need more plastic in it.

Besides, Jo had added with a sternly raised eyebrow, a bit of cardboard is not the worst thing Iris is after putting in there, now is it?

So Iris had tried to discern Harry's relationship to the unknown person by body language alone until a woman approached them. The woman was familiar. Iris had searched her brain in earnest to place her. She was from Jo's work. She was a work friend.

And just like that she felt entirely foolish.

Jo had replaced her already. Someone far more suitable than Iris. Really, they had not been a good match. Iris was unfit for polite company. She always said the wrong thing. A regular line breacher. Not like this new woman friend who looked capable of navigating with ease the situations that brought Iris down. What was worse still was how dumb she felt because she had believed she had also been important, a special person in Jo and Harry's lives. She had been missing them so hard and assumed they were missing her in return.

But of course they didn't miss her.

Harry was just a little kid. Little kids don't care for the whereabouts of grown women. Friends of their mothers. What foolishness Iris had agonized over. Worrying that he would feel betrayed. Or abandoned. Worrying that he might think he had done something wrong. Or that she didn't like him. Had no time for him anymore. Because it was not true. Iris was not like that. She had always made time, found time, sorted it out. Before John had upended her life she had promised to never cause the same kind of harm her father had caused.

Iris breaks promises to herself.

Here she was, in and out of Harry's life, an unreliable actor on stage spewing bits of dialogue to make herself feel better. These things kept her awake on the nights John stayed home. She had been in anguish over Harry. But here he was, fine now. No worse for wear at all. Happy-looking. Life goes on. He is at the grocery store with his mom's new friend. Nothing to it. No big deal. How silly is Iris to concern herself with lost attachments.

And then Harry had seen her. And had run up to her calling her name. Wrapped his arms around her legs like it was any day and no time had passed.

Iris, Iris, you haven't seen me in a long while!

And Iris thought she would wail in pain like someone struck in the stomach, or maybe say the wrong thing like a person incapacitated, so she put her hands on his head and said nothing at all until the new friend caught up, saying they had to leave immediately.

But this is my friend Iris.

The woman saying she knew, knows, exactly who Iris is, was, this information a warning to Iris, before stating that Iris also knows, knew, why they had to go. A warning and a threat. Like Iris was someone not to be trusted. And Iris wanted to yell *back the fuck up, lady* but it had been years since she'd used adult language in front of Harry.

The last time in Jo's car, when he echoed *traffic was a bitch* from his car seat.

At first laughing, and then agreeing that his language acquisition had caught up with their dirty mouths. Not long after, Jo had stopped "taking out the garbage" during the day. And then taking it out at night. And then she only took out the garbage when she was loaded. And then not at all. She never drank on weeknights anymore or ate dirty food when she was hungover. She was rarely hungover because Harry had memory now. Harry will remember, Jo had told Iris, and she wanted what he remembered to be nice.

Iris still smokes.

Slowly. As if each inhale is an inadequate attempt to set a dumpster fire inside herself. This behaviour is most disturbing during times of high anxiety. Iris is convinced no one likes her anymore because of what she has done or allowed to happen. Women can be hard on each other and themselves. Jo's inability to forgive her has pushed her paranoia clear off the cliff. Jo has always forgiven her. Jo is the forgiveness gauge.

Iris has blackened Jo's freshly painted ceiling with a candle while having weird sex in her bed. Forgiven.

Iris has gotten them pulled over by the police for singing "The Sweater Song" out a moving car window. Forgiven.

She has thrown up lemon chicken in a bathtub and stolen children's toys from a party. She has taken acid before a formal dinner and swiped the host's nicer shoes from the front foyer after declaring she didn't even eat fucking lamb. Iris has puked in houseplants, insulted family members, lost a pet frog, one time she got into a screaming match at a wedding rehearsal. Forgiven. Forgiven. Forgiven. She was crazy hungover, possibly residually high, at Harry's birth. She maintained a safe distance from Jo's mother who insisted that it didn't matter if she stood on the other side of the jesus parkway.

You got eyes on you like a pair of dollar store snow globes, Iris Anne. I'm not stunned.

Iris was thinking of her long listed trespasses as Harry rambled at random over all the things that had happened since he had last seen her. The woman, Jo's friend from work, then handed a baguette to the man holding Five Alive as Iris knelt to zip Harry's coat. Harry knew not to inquire further as to what Iris knew that he did not. Children reared in conflict always know why someone has not been invited to their birthday party.

But he could not help but try another tactic so attempted sussing out promises. This was a decent strategy because Iris didn't say she would do things she had no intention of doing, so he fired at her all the options he could think including a Minecraft marathon or watching *Inside Out* again or playing cars or, or, or, which soon turned to bribery when he started suggesting things that Iris liked to do.

This meant he was desperate because he did not all the time like reading rhyming books or looking at the planets. New woman friend was tugging at his coat a little by the time he reached painting, which was the last ditch to fall in. Harry was tumbling quick when he suggested painting. We could paint pictures, he had said, or walk in the woods, or practise guitar, which was the most heartbreaking because Harry hated guitar. He wanted a drum kit. But he needed to know when he would see her again. Because kids like to know these kinds of things. But Iris couldn't say. She didn't know herself. She worried maybe never.

Maybe Jo would never forgive her.

I am just sick of listening to you. I don't fucking care if I ever hear John Fisher's fucking name ever again in my fucking life, Iris. And don't, don't tell me you can't get another job, you tried for what, like, three weeks. Any fucking job would be better than working with that manipulative dickhole every day. He is ruining everyone's life. He is a fucking life ruiner. And don't tell me you love him, or he loves you, or whatever bullshit excuse he has convinced you of this week because it is lies. You are lying. He has made a liar out of you. And that's the great fun for him, the appeal, the fantastic fucking trick. He makes good people into liars because it makes him feel powerful or smart or important or less like a raging sociopath. I just cannot listen to you talk about it anymore, I'm done, done! It is fucking torture, it is worse than torture, it is boring. I know what you are going to say before you even say it, and no, I don't want to read that jesus phone of yours full of riddles and nonsense, my good grief, he has made you fucking predictable. I mean, that's a jesus crime unto itself! Worse than the wreckage! Worse than the hurt! Talking to you is fucking tedious. You never have anything interesting to say anymore. I hate that guy. Hate. Him.

And Iris knows she should probably hate him too.

IRIS IS SO lost in her pitiful replay, she doesn't see Major David flagging her like she's the last illuminated cab at Mardi Gras.

The look of frustration on his face is not mayoral. The trifecta sitting with him seem thrilled. They are practically aroused at the thought of Iris receiving an earned tongue-lashing. She never came over to ask them if they needed anything else and they needed lots of things, including being asked regularly about their needs.

Iris had not thought to do so. She had not really thought at all. She just stood right there for everyone to witness her not serving them. Instead, they watched her quietly fold the same napkin repeatedly. Everything was taking forever. Not that they were in a big rush.

But still, they shouldn't have to wait.

Purple fashion glasses supposes Iris is body stoned. It is like a kind of paralysis, she explains to the others with a lot of confidence for a woman who hasn't smoked up in three decades.

The table seethes in anticipation. Maybe they would even get their lunch for free! Though the look of defeat spreading through Iris's body as she walks toward their table is deflating. And this makes them aggressive, too. She is ruining everything about their lunch. She is even ruining their desire to scold her.

Purple glasses thinks Iris is obviously fragile and probably has mental health issues. She should not be working with the public if she is so oversensitive. She should be doing something else away from people.

You shouldn't be a server.

I'm not.

Well...but you are.

No. I'm not.

My dear girl, you are serving us right now.

I am.

Which means you are a server.

No, it doesn't.

What do you mean no? What does she mean no?

Iris doesn't even know how she has come to serve.

Was it John? Or George? Her father? The past? Was it something lacking in herself?

Major David is blistering now, shifting in his chair, making a lot of eye contact with his table mates while they discuss Iris's behaviour as if she is not standing just alongside their table. They take turns firing off complaints as to how they have been personally let down. This is met with smiling now, totally out of context, which further aggrieves them. Major David's volume ratchets due to acute embarrassment.

He demands to know what Iris is smiling at.

But Iris doesn't answer because she can't hear him.

Iris has gone underwater.

Like a person on the bottom of a pool, Iris is held down by some unknowable force, looking up through the shimmering blue crest at a surface just beyond her reach. She kicks and stretches and struggles. She tries to retain breath yet it escapes her. She watches the bubbles break.

She can see people above pretending not to see her below.

They walk a little faster along the pool deck, they don't run as running is not permitted and these are people who follow the rules regardless of drowning girls.

So too the people seated in the dining room hurry along while she stands before them getting berated by the mayor of this town she is not from.

Though it hardly matters where she came from cause she can't hear him.

She is still underwater. His words are just roaring muffles. Waves of sound lap over her, in and out, the tide of authorial tone washes Iris. She is so wiped down by his disdain. She is wetted with everything he deems inadequate about her person.

Major David is lavish with his contempt. He lives for

an opportunity to display his impeccable standards and import.

Under normal circumstances, the four top being so upset would upset her.

But now, meh.

Iris's waterlogged brain can no longer summon the will to care, or react as if she does. She cannot recall the part she is meant to play in this scene. Iris cannot organize herself in the moment long enough to come up with a soothing solution.

She waits on the bottom of the pool for someone to come save her.

For a time, no one comes.

Until Major David shoves off and up as men do so he can lord right over her.

It has occurred to him, deep inside his own bad wiring, that the reason he cannot make this girl understand her wrongdoing is a matter of perspective. So he raises himself up, pushes his chair back, hoists his right arm and points a rigid human handgun right in Iris's face. He darts it at her with each offer he makes toward her. When a man moves his upper body at a woman like Major David is doing to Iris, he is offering to hit her in the face or worse.

Men are just bigger.

Major David tilts his head to the left in order to better train his eye on his target. These are movements Iris has seen a million billion trillion times. Iris had been exposed to many variations of this same rough stance before even reaching the full height of herself. She can spot it a mile off but can do little to stop it coming. She was long ago taught to suppress her own biological urge, which is just another example of how effectively wires can be manipulated.

Fight or flight, fight or flight, fight or flight.

But women aren't meant to do that anymore, Iris has learned.

Stay and suffer through.

Or lose your job, your house, your kids, your dog, your sanity, your self-respect, your life.

Stand and stay and suffer in what you've been trained to think is noble silence. This conceit, though it has served women poorly throughout history, is still wildly popular.

Hold that tongue of yours or we will spit scream in your face, Iris.

Just like now. Just like this. The Mayor steps inside her personal space because that space is not even hers.

She can smell sour coffee on his breath. There is a lingering fishy smell about him; likely he takes Omega 3 tablets and eats beef every day. She focuses on his neck, he has razor burn, the rough rash of the rub is ringed with tiny spores full of waiting white pus. This likely adds to his daily rage. His wife definitely buys the most expensive razors to no avail.

The best a man can get is way better than anything Iris will ever see.

Though this is still not good enough for the Mayor who she is afraid to look in the face. She can't look up. Her neck hinge has seized with tension. The muscle fibres where her neck meets her shoulders have decided to wrap themselves around each other for comfort. They knot themselves together to protect what is underneath from damage.

More damage.

And she wants to reach her hands behind herself to press the lumps out of her shoulders as a way of pressing the lump out of her throat. She thinks all these lumps are connected somehow and she's right. But she can't bear exposing her soft underarms because this too may be taken further as an affront.

Iris has been picked up by the armpits before, tight, mean hands gripping the web between her arms and breasts like handles to steer her up and into a wall. Not John but the one before him. John knows this. He has all the information about who has previously harmed her soft parts.

Iris stares into the Mayor's chest a bit, follows the citron on citron print of his tie with her eyes. Then repeat. Iris's mind is trying to distract her from pronouncements about her performance being the worst performance and an inference about her mother being incompetent. And though Iris can hardly argue with that, there is a little surge in her, a little fury not yet formed.

Because who the fuck does this guy think he is bringing up her mother?

She wants to rage at him about her childhood and her parents and this man who takes advantage and the man before him that did the same. She wants to scream her face off. But she doesn't.

Instead, she decides men are obsessed with paisley because it looks like dressy sperm.

This thought rushes to the front of her brain. She tries to fend it off but it persists. It keeps coming. No. Stop. She begs her sardonic sense of humour to shush.

Please, you will get me in more trouble.

But it is too late. Iris is picturing this brightly coloured textile homage to ejaculate quivering and pulsating. She has a visual back end. There are always silent picture shows running in the background of her brain. She holds in the laugh. But it makes that crunchy noise in the back of her throat as she tries to suck it back. The garbled air grasped at the last-second movement of her head brings her ever slightly closer to the cum tie which she is now thinking of as a cum tie. And the table catches hold of her snicker.

Do you think this is funny?

Iris doesn't think any of this is funny in the nourishing way a good belly laugh makes you feel. Or the comforting manner of an inside joked shared amongst friends. It is not funny like cutting satire is funny. Or so vulgar you cringe laugh until your vulva clenches up. But alas, some horrid sense of irony raps on all the funny bones that make up Iris's body and she is left once again pressing her face into her hands in an attempt to stifle her urges. Iris's urges are hard to stifle and the giggle can be seen rippling through her as tears squeeze from between her fingers and roll down the back of her hands.

Little bitch.

And there it is, the line.

The dining room had been watching the scene from the corner of each eye, glancing up occasionally to check in with its progress, unable to determine who is at fault, assuming the young waitress deserving. It was nobody's business until now.

But the b word is a throwdown. That one's easy. Even

Omi peeps around the corner rubbing dry his hands on the dishtowel hung over his shoulder.

All hands appear on deck and ready themselves for a punch-up.

O**LIVE HAS ALWAYS** found the bruises you can't see just as bad as the ones you can.

She feels especially poorly when she has a mark on her face. Once, she had a cigarette burn high up on her cheek after a man shoved her outside a bar. She had slipped on the ice as she rocked forward trying to remain upright, but the cherry on her hot smoke made contact just under her thin eyelid regardless of attempts made to erect herself.

He had yelled at her not to be so fucking clumsy.

He had told her it happened because she was a drunk.

Not because he had grabbed at her when she didn't answer him.

Stop ignoring me, he bawled.

Olive had not been ignoring him. She had been trying to calculate the correct way to answer when he had asked if she wanted to fuck.

Her mind had been mitigating the possible damage and attempting to locate the pitch-perfect tone that would not anger or offend the man further. Her brain was considering possible routes of escape, both literal and figurative. It was always doing that. She didn't realize yet that her tendency toward perpetual anxiety adversely impacted her odds of success. She wasn't ignoring his question. Opposite. She was so resolutely focused on it that she had completely forgotten about the smoke burning between her fingers.

She wishes she had a smoke now.

Though there's hardly a soul about the place to get one off, almost everything downtown has remained closed for the day. People, business owners and possible clientele have chosen to stay home with their loved ones in front of fireplaces and floors covered in puzzle pieces. Their children rush in from the yard with dogs wearing heavy snowballed coats. Olive used to walk through the jelly-bean rows on snow days just to listen to the children out of sight behind fences, explaining game rules in circles, heads thrown back to snuffle snot, all agreeing that blowing your nose was a waste of time.

Beep beep beep.

You can hear the fleet moving backward all throughout the city.

On these walks eastward, Olive has overheard neighbours discussing the most advantageous snow placement like it's a new problem instead of the same problem they had last year and every year since they moved home from the mainland.

We'll have to dump it in the harbour, says a woman in a brightly coloured vintage one-piece snowsuit clearly too tight for physical exertion. Really a promise of a future exchange to be made for her young husband's ready labour. This one knows the secret to a happy home. She keeps a nurse's uniform ironed and hung at the back of a spare bedroom closet in the event someone's sore shoulders need attending. There's a pink stethoscope and a white store-bought folded cap. Young wife will not be first wife. She understands well the appeal of a little costume. It has nothing to do with necessity.

Olive avoids the jellies today though. No one will give her a smoke up there.

Sure, they are mostly all quit now but for the occasional inebriated puff. There was a time cigarettes could be got up Gower but not so anymore. These days you'd have to wind the steep sides hoping to find a stubborn poet or former singer willing to save you even a drag. They're all mindful now. They have new kitchen cabinets with track lighting and half as many mice in autumn. A scatter little fucker still gets in though, and the whole household is in throes when an earwig is spotted crawling up the baby's fat arm. A long tail trail in the freshly fallen snow just beyond the double exterior glass doors will put the house up.

At school pickup, the young mothers who once shared an affinity for blowing brainers stroke out over the rat population which they believe is surging because of irresponsible development. Olive has heard them moaning that they will have to pay money now and forever after to pump water to the jesus neighbourhood no one wants, to shore up one man's insecure legacy.

How much attention does one asshole need? they all groan.

He is regarded as worse than Smallwood by the breastfeeding support group in Bannerman Park, who can see that Olive is sweeping the ground for bits of butts. Instinctively they hold their babies a little tighter and then feel alarmed and then ashamed for having done so. As a penance, they promise to go to all the social justice rallies. And they do.

The sight of Olive fills them up with guilt no matter what the season.

She refuses to make the young moms feel shame during the worst part of the winter by accidentally looking on her. Olive can't have anything else put on her. She is way too rough to look upon lately. The children think she's weird. Not good weird like their aunt who liberally and enthusiastically swears on the government. But dangerous weird like people on the evening news.

She doesn't take that path unless she's fully scrubbed up.

Besides, it is the path she takes when feeling most optimistic, which is not how she is feeling now. She has felt well enough at times to search out the bright-side of downtown. She has sought out the quiet residential streets and admired the colourful houses like a tourist off a large ship for the afternoon. Olive often wondered why they don't paint their houses up nice like this at home. Once she mentioned it to her care worker. The exercise was to list three things that made her feel happiness. Reliable things. But it felt like a test to Olive. She wanted to say Calv's single cab truck, the kiss in her grandmother's bread, the smell of a newly lit wood stove. But the care worker would have questions so she said the houses were pretty instead, which for her was like wishing her wish in code.

Olive felt so silly now for doing that. And she turns up by a shuttered dress shop once called a boutique to make her way along Duckworth back to The Hazel. Damian will be at work by now and he'll loan her smokes for life eternal. If not, she will make Iris give her one.

Service staff have woken up for the third time that

afternoon and are now attempting to venture past their doorsteps in search of Gatorade on their way to work. And the grief they feel hungover is exacerbated by the fact they almost did not see the day. The lot of them forever reminisce over their childhoods while watching shows in celebration of their generational arrested development. They still morning smoke inside with their fingers held high along faces to prevent tarring. They still think someone will love those hands later.

Olive used to hold cigarettes upright to prevent tarnish too.

Back then, Nan would tan her backside for smoking. Though no one worries much on that these days. A bit of maybe future lung cancer seems hardly pressing when faced with for sure everyday survival.

That night in St. Anthony, it was Iris's older cousin who yanked on Olive's sleeve and yelled at her as she cracked her head off the frozen gravel ground. She had started to confess the scene while they shared a cigarette in the walkway between their two apartments.

Iris had been leaning against the privacy fence tilted between them. She was deeply involved in explaining away a noise complaint someone had made about her and John on Old Christmas Day. They had gotten into a fight which of course Olive knew because everyone knew when Iris was yelling.

He gave me a set of steak knives, can you fucking believe it? Knives.

Iris had wanted Olive to share in the smoke and her aggravation but a casual remark about her notorious temper had snagged Olive up in the memory.

I swung my purse at him like he was a pickpocket.

Olive thinks John is a style of pickpocket from an ancient cobblestone city. Iris should wear her purse across her belly like an elderly tourist to ward him off.

I got right hairy, worse than Dad. Imagine. Disgraceful, I am.

Deon bawled at me once.

What?

Deon swore on me down to St. Anthony once.

What was you doing down there?

There was a hockey party.

You don't play hockey.

Everyone was going.

I dare say.

Deon tried to drag me off.

Fuck, Olive, what are you telling me stuff like that for?

You was talking about bad temper running in the family—

Yes but I don't want to hear that shit now, do I?

When then?

What?

When do you want to hear it?

Never I suppose.

But who am I supposed to tell?

No one.

But you're always telling stuff.

That's different.

Cause it's you.

Maybe you misunderstood him.

He said come we goes and has a screw.

Yuck.

He grabbed me and I fell and burnt my face.

That don't sound like Deon to me.

It was Deon.

Where was I when this happened?

In Toronto.

Fuck sakes, you have got to stop putting yourself in harm's way.

What way is that?

Every way.

Right.

Look, Deon didn't know better.

That don't make it any less gross.

What do you want me to do about it now?

Just let me say it and know that it happened!

Okay, fine, you said it happened and now I know.

It sucked.

It did.

It does.

Deon is an idiot when he drinks, we all are.

It left a mark on my cheek.

I got marks everywhere too.

Then we're both marked up.

Anyway.

Anyway.

Did you have a good Christmas after?

A good Christmas?

Yeah.

You fucked off on me.

Something came up.

Someone came up.

Olive.

No, I never had a good Christmas.

You know you can't hardly see that mark on your cheek anymore.

Marks are never as worrisome as what could have happened if Olive had not already known or had been too drunk to manage. What is worse haunts Olive long after marks fade. She thinks about it a lot when she is walking. In public. In bed. Anywhere.

Everywhere Olive is, she is thinking about the worse things that could happen to her.

She imagines how men will react if she laughs or cries out in the wrong moment. If she wells up or moans when things are not right. She imagines what they would do to prevent it from happening. Or to punish her for any kind of noise determined unbecoming of their preferred sexual fantasy. Olive spends great amounts of time scaring herself so she will be more vigilant. This was her very first social worker word. Vigilant.

Olive held vigil over herself.

The fact that she would probably not be able to cope without sight has always been a very real concern and she often imagines herself even now with just the one good eye.

Men would not like her with less than two working eyes.

This kind of thinking makes her want to hide away inside somewhere and never go out again. Not just inside, but farther inside, as far inside as she can go, under the blankets, down into the cushions, deep inside the springs of the couch. Olive wishes she could honey-shrink-her-body-down which feels bigger and more repulsive when there are bruises on her topcoat turning a little bit purple a little bit blue. She does not want to be awake to feel the bruises come out and then go back in again. She curls into the couch.

Olive's body is familiar with this recovery position.

Allowing a semi-conscious state, the fluid transition of wakefulness to deep sleep with no start or end, just approximations of time, morning, mid day, night, mid night, morning. Olive never turns the lamp in the living room off during these changing states. She sleeps in full light, waking to look around the room repeatedly during the darkest parts to keep her mind's monsters in her mind. Olive would perhaps sleep with an overhead light on if there was one. But there isn't. Just the one floor lamp from Walmart that seems to go through a lot of light bulbs. More than is normal. And Olive knows it probably has something to do with surges in electricity.

Power is unreliable for Olive.

She often hears a little pop when she flips the switch. A connection connecting with a tiny sizzle. She has told the landlord but he doesn't care. He asks her what does she expect him to do? And does he look like someone made of money? The answers: *fix it* and *yes* are never uttered. He barks at her about what odds because heat and light are included in her rent. But that is not what Olive is talking about.

Olive is talking about fire. There is a soot ring around the light fixture in the hallway. It is like the ceiling is warning her that it is hiding something hot. So she asked her landlord to inspect for safety and he walked into her space like he owns it because he does. He owns all her space. And what space he doesn't own is owned by another.

They refuse to acknowledge Olive's claim.

Silly half-something baygirl from a non-existent bay believes herself deserving of her own safe space. Acknowledging any part of her would undo the whole setup, and so Olive's person goes unacknowledged. Her landlord is only following a precedent previously set. One time he brought over a torn green leather recliner he needed to store somewhere until his new cabin was finished. He told her not to sit in it so Olive never does.

Not that she wanted to sit in his ugly fucking chair anyway.

She mostly sticks to the couch. She does not go sleep in her bed when she feels poorly, which is often. A bed is too good for her. She doesn't want this Olive sleeping in her bed. If it were warmer, she would sleep on the floor. But it is always dead cold and drafty on this city floor even though she rolls towels against every doorway to trap the little baseboard heat in, the rectangle tops speckled in many different shades of beige paint. Nothing colours flicked over by decades of tenants hoping it would cheer the place along. Never being permitted to have real colours. Vibrancy is for homeowners. Beige is for the poor. Olive has tried to apply more appetizing words to the colour in an attempt to shift her thoughts. The apartment is biscuit. But it's not. Oatmeal. Wheat. Nope. Neither.

This is just a trick; people love to trick themselves. But hey...

If you can believe your brown nan is white, you can believe anything.

Olive constantly gets tangled up in her own rebrand. She's some part Indigenous, rural Newfoundlander, former foster child from a single-parent home now. Before that she was some dark-skinned young one whose mother ran off and left her. Later on they called her a piece of jackytar ass. Someone's unclaimed youngster. Father unknown or wanting nothing at all to do with her. Sometimes whore and squaw are thrown in the mix as added seasoning to keep the slurry call-down fresh and tasty.

Iris had to tell Olive it was wrong to call herself tarry.

Don't say that, it's racist.

It's not racist if I says it about my ownself.

It's like calling yourself a Newfie.

What's wrong with being a Newfie?

There is nothing wrong being anything.

Then why not say New—

Just don't say it, okay?

Nan says it.

That's cause your nan can't read and don't know any better.

What am I supposed to call myself?

Nothing.

You don't call yourself nothing.

Baygirl then.

But there's no bay where we're from.

Everything that isn't town is bay.

We're not even girls anymore.

Women are always girls in Newfoundland, Olive, Jesus.

Olive thinks that the apartment/unit/suite/single is the sad house version of herself.

The dividing walls are barely sturdy enough to divide. They never saw enough plaster, the webbing clearly visible underneath the thinnest layer of paint. Olive has overheard her landlord telling John, while he shovels Iris's driveway, that he has no intentions of sinking another penny into "that" house. He winks at John and makes a comment about having her scald.

Olive wonders who he's got scald and worries about finding herself in hot water.

She is especially quiet when her landlord is around. She tries to have little or no contact at all now that she has learned what kind of fellow he is. Even before the pipes had burst under the kitchen sink. Even before that, she learned not to interact. The pipes burst under the kitchen sink on New Year's Day. Olive's landlord claimed it was because she didn't keep a sufficient amount of heat on in her unit. She tried to defend herself. That was as much heat as she could pull off the grid. The heaters were trying their best but the door in the kitchen led directly to the back path. There was no porch or weatherstripping. There was no way to keep the warm in. She had a sheet hung up but he had barked at her about the sheet's appearance.

What would the neighbours think?

And Olive thought: nothing, because they never see it.

But the landlord knew it was there and this was really about what he thought of himself.

Worse than gypsies, he growled as he pulled the sheet down with a tug of his hairy wrist. All the thumbtacks came free and scattered around like little hidden daggers waiting to catch themselves on the underside of Olive's feet. It had taken her ages to get the sheet up with those tacks.

Olive spent most of the Christmas season half froze in the fetal position holding herself between her legs. The pulse in her hands reverberating the pulse in her vagina. Pushing the throbs back inside, a barrier against their escape, Olive was attempting to hold herself together though her mind was all in pieces. The pressure slightly eased her, it made her feel like she was doing something to comfort her ailing parts. It was the smallest gesture toward forgiveness she could bring herself to make. Olive knows she needs to forgive herself. Has always known. But knowing something and doing it are two very polar notions.

Sometimes she would wake up having already drained her face through the night. Olive checked and rechecked to see if the pain was still there by pressing down lightly on her big bone. The little shot of hurt would send a nauseous feeling to her belly. She needed to pee the entire twelve days. The tiny tingle feeling niggling away at her, reminding her of what had occurred to her body physical when Olive emotional was not there to take care, making it hard to sit still or concentrate or ignore. She would sit on the toilet and sob as the little dribble of urine ignited the splits along her soft folds.

These little rips in her private fabric hurt more than the toonie-sized welt on her chin that was yellow like a banana only fit for bread. Olive tried not to pee that often. There was so little of it left, and she had no desire to put liquid in. This: another fake out by her jokester brain which reasoned that less hydration would equal less grief. And she hadn't the stomach for more grief. So she poured just enough water down to keep her flower from fully wilting. Besides, the pain far exceeded output. She thought if she held herself in place, barely moving, hardly breathing, then her insides would forget that they were trying to get outside. But there was a constant sting where the moisture of her hurt body tried to repair itself. Olive's swollen vagina fought to soothe the small gashes because Olive's body had tried to tell the other bodies that it was not ready and willing for them. Olive's body had not given consent in the way that bodies sometimes do.

And the attempt to communicate for Olive, who could not communicate anymore, just got her poor body further hurt as the stark unyielding entry was forced upon. Now it too felt guilt for having been pliable. Regretting even the blood it let loose after it had torn. That same blood meant to scare had proven to rally the remaining who found the little opening more manageable when wet.

She really wants it now, b'ys, one had said, then after, yelling that the bitch had bled all over him. The others disgusted at the sight of proof upon the sheets. A horror show, one said.

But not for Olive, laid out on her belly with both hands over her eyes, for the room.

The concern was mostly for the linens themselves because this one yelling man had put his credit card down for the damage deposit. Deposits had occurred beyond any expectation and now he would have to pay. He announced to the room that they would all have to chip in for this state. A declaration not unlike the one he had made hours earlier when the hard drugs came out.

Oh no, he said when noses were upturned, we're all going to do it together.

She had only agreed to go because Calv had started texting her again after weeks of silence. She had no idea why he had vanished. They had messaged each other for months and then suddenly nothing. No response to her banal question which was merely a polite reply to his initial banal question.

How are things going?

She had answered cheerfully and asked the same in turn. And then nothing. He didn't even look at her message for eight days. He was the only reason she kept Messenger on her phone. The main reason her phone was a priority over food. It was the only way he contacted her.

Olive obsessed over her message in those eight days because silence hurts girls like Olive.

Silence encourages paranoia that can't be fended off because the battalion is busy defending other fronts. Olive had thought how it had not even been the truth.

She had never been *great*.

But she had wanted to appear pleasant and uncomplicated. Someone worthy of Calv's time. And lying about herself took on the shape of betrayal in those eight days because she had tried to sugarcoat her sourcoat for this person who did not even care enough to fake say he was fine too.

He refused to open Olive's little pleading request for interaction as if she was not deserving of polite niceties. A *fine* was too good for her. Four letters took too long to type. And she felt so silly for having thought Calv had liked her. Iris warned her not to catch feelings.

You're not important to him if he doesn't want to eat dinner with you.

And sure as shit Iris knew how that felt, but Calv had eaten dinner with her. Taken her to diners outside of the city where he said they served the best turkey soup. Better than your nan's, Calv had said.

Olive didn't pay Iris any mind cause she didn't have feelings to catch anymore. Hadn't had them since the doctor hauled her out into the porch calling her a whore. Dirty little whore, she'd said. The doctor really meant it. Not in the way older girls at the centre or her foster brother meant it. Or even the way men sometimes yelled it from their cars. No. The doctor was convinced that Olive was a whore. It was not her son's fault. Her son was a good boy. He had to be because she had made him and if he wasn't good then she wasn't good.

So it must be Olive. She must be a whore.

The victim-blaming Olive perpetrated against Olive was far worse than any external victim-blaming. This was a never-ceasing internal narrative that confirmed repeatedly that Olive was disgusting. So when Calv stopped responding, she did not demand to know why or even say anything at all.

She missed the little kindnesses though.

Still, her body felt it had betrayed Olive. And it had and it hadn't. Because Olive was not really there when the blood came. Olive was gone. She had woken up to find the blood. But it wasn't really her body's fault. She knew that. It was hers. So she held herself on the couch for an added layer of protection.

And Olive thought, poor body, a sin for you, body.

In her couch dreams, which are many and sometimes awful, she is back home at Grandmother's but Grandmother is not there. Olive is in charge of bringing in the dogs when the temperature dips toward danger. In the dream she has not done so and cannot bear to go out and search for the dogs in the snow. She knows they will be pressed up against each other against the house. Mounds of snow all around the perimeter. Everyone in the cove can see what she has failed to do and so done. They've more sympathy for dogs than Olive.

She wakes from this dream feeling like the worst person.

She had once tried to explain to her case worker that it doesn't matter if she is the worst. It doesn't matter if that is for real the situation because she feels like it and so she may as well be. Her case worker would ask her a series of questions meant to refute the thinking error but Olive often just felt worse.

Other dreams, the better ones, are of riding in the family wood sleigh with her cousins, playing clapping games to entertain themselves under the heavy quilts Grandmother used to break the wind overhead. Pulled by snowmobiles because it made better sense in the country trails, their dogs then running wild abreast the wooden box and all exploding out onto the lake surface after having to hamper along at a frustratingly patient pace while going through the narrow tree path humped with ridges. Everyone still knew how to get into the camps on the lake back then. The smallest girl child still had a sense of which pond was which even though their names in any language did not lend themselves to easy navigation. Big pond, little pond, inside pond, outside pond, all the ponds in relation to the great body where the water ran south freely.

They were always digging a tunnel while never digging a tunnel.

Grandfather driving the tow ski-doo, Grandmother riding in the sleigh.

She despised the fumy snowmobiles, thought it unnatural to ride long distances spread-eagle and forbade pregnant women from doing so. Grandmother thought it was worse still to ignore obvious danger. So she always chose to ride in the sleigh with the children, claiming to be providing supervision, but really it was just more pleasant and suited her principles. Sometimes, after a stretch of particularly fine weather allowed the snow surface to settle down, Grandmother would even nap in the moving box. Napping outside being one of her very favoured things. A trait Olive acquired from her natural as a child. Grandmother would parcel out handfuls of raisins frozen hard together and tell them stories of all their relations. She would explain how they had been spread out but remained connected to each other.

Great-Grandmother Decker could cast out the real bad fever with her potions.

Her open face tight and turned a little from the wind and sun as she matter-of-fact told stories of spells and hard feelings, the booman and mothers lost in childbearing.

Grandmother never wore sunscreen. In the country, she did not mind a bit of colour. It didn't matter if you were marginally darker cause no one would judge you for it inside. The animals did not care about the shade of you.

The wind in the trees did not whisper harshly about your russet nature. Later on, it would come in style, a wholly confusing mix of tanning beyond this or that pond.

But Olive's dreams remain in the woods.

The freedom Grandmother felt in the country radiated from her as she confided the best way to jig whitefish through an augered hole after informing them, repeatedly, of her fondness for the auger. They had to chip chip chip the ice away when she was a girl and this greatly restricted where you could fish. Grandmother has since become convinced that the best spots were always out of reach. A tin of kippers helps, too, she would say with a wink. Toss a can of kippers down the hole and haul them up hand over fist now they've got that brilliant blue auger.

There were new tools she appreciated more than others.

But her eyes are always kind and shiny on trips in the country, this feature further illuminated by the absence of tint around them where her snowmobile goggles had shaded spaces from sunshine reflected off the frozen earth. Grandmother releasing her happy laugh at the childish raccoon jokes heaved her way. Her cheeks plump, perfect hearts lifting themselves up when she grinned, and Olive could never resist poking her finger in the dimple until Grandmother cooed to be kind to her. Children rounded up, cousins all, cupping these precious apple cheeks in their palms, always amazed when they fit perfect into hands.

The littlest cousin, looking back expectantly with upturned almond eyes, head to toe in OshKosh B'gosh handed down the line to her. Everyone clucked OshKosh

B'gosh like a clutch of chickens. This was before expect-ations were perverted by the world's weary divisions. Before they knew of accents or rural or poor.

They lived innocent and oblivious until Grandfather's accident that others said was no accident, after which Grandmother took to her bed for weeks at a stretch unable to bear the new condition of her life. Olive was sent to town then, and suddenly they knew everything all at once like a swamping.

Olive still dreams of Grandmother sitting on the kitchen table chair rocking herself to and fro after learn-ing Grandfather's body had been dredged up by a drag-ger boat. In Olive's reliving, Grandmother murmurs her broken heart into the room like an incantation while pulling one hand along the other from her wrists. She softly peeled away at the thin skin like these hands of hers were dirty gloves she had forgotten to remove and now must discreetly be rid of before found out. Grandmother has always stared searching at her hands when she feels unease. This motion: her unravelling.

He done it out on the water so no one would have to clean it up after him, sweet man.

Grandmother would air her epiphanies like winter wool on the line regardless of who was in age range or understanding. And so Olive and her cousins quick learned the logistics of chosen loss. They regularly recounted to each other where they were when they learned Pop died, this small conjuring a ritual, a game.

I was over on the slipway.

I was catching minnows in the brook.

I was waiting for a new couch set ordered from Sears.

Olive longs for the before hands when Grandmother wished aloud, as she does now given an audience and opportunity, that she could keep all her lovely grand-babies in that sleigh box eating cold raisins and napping as her lovely tidy man pulled them through the woods atop the fallen snow.

But she could not.

She was old now and no one cares for an old woman's concern. Olive's only grandmother.

When she dies, Olive will have no grandmother, she warns to prepare her but also to focus her admiration. Which was only true because her father's mother knew nothing of her, or did and couldn't say.

Grandmother's voice always pitching up and down as they were tossed like little balls of dough in too much clothing. Pleading to shed a layer in the sleigh while they went through the thick trees. But no, she would insist, the wind off the lake would cool the sweat on their bodies and the chill would sit on their shoulders like a cloak or get in their bones like disease.

Back then she would tell Olive and her cousins stories of themselves to distract.

Grandmother would account for the shifting terrain and space out her especially favourite parts of storytelling for the flat bit where the dogs running alongside were quiet and it was just the ski-doos' revving engines to compete with. Up and over the ridges they would travel, with daylight laying on the blankets casting different colours over them depending on where they sat. Olive preferred to sit under a blue blanket and pretend it was like swimming in open air as they all coasted across the lake surfaces, occasionally peeping out through the box slats to check on their progress toward the deep interior where the poaching camp sat.

You can't poach what you owns be rights, Grandmother would wink.

All of Olive's best memories are from before her grandfather died and her mother moved away. She remembers that bouncing along the ridges in the forest path was like being bounced on a person's foot but better because there was no person or foot involved. This foot bouncing game has always troubled Olive. The same adults repeatedly wanted to play it and would look too intently into your face as they popped you up and down on their skin boot.

You can wear skin boots in town again now.

First when Olive arrived in town, you could not. The doctor had frowned down at her tapped boots and warned that people were sensitive about seals. This, of course, made no sense. Olive was fond of her boots. They were good boots. But the doctor said the sensitive people would become angry and yell and throw paint and bought her a pair of real Canadian premium leather boots made in China. Olive tried to defend her boots. She said they were made by a person she knew. She had seen the skins stretched on a frame by Aunt Jessie's house knowing they would make her own boots. She had sat eating strawberry sugar wafer cookies while Grandmother and Aunt Jessie brushed the fur free, commenting on the beautiful tobacco colour the boots would be when they were finished.

This was before that fellow the Bannerman Park moms disliked began parading the streets in his coat.

Before he declared the seal hunt a point of pride. Before it was decided popular and fashionable by his wealthy friends, Olive was made to feel ashamed of her beastly boots.

But all leather boots are beastly by nature.

This whole debate discouraged Olive from wearing her mother's coat as well. Because she would feel miserable if someone threw red paint on her beloved coat that was a little too short in the sleeves and a little too wide in the waist. Before she went into care, Grandmother had re-trimmed the hood with a foxtail tip in the centre. She kept a blue Tupperware container of fur pieces overhead for just this kind of thing. It was how she showed her love. Grandmother felt responsible for all the hurt though she had never laid a hand on any of her grandbabies.

Olive lost her mother's coat.

And the remorse she feels over losing that coat is like being homesick for a home that doesn't exist anymore. There is no way to answer it back when it calls out to you just after dark. It is overwhelming grief. And so dumb. It is so dumb for her to grieve a coat so aggressively when she has lost so much more than a coat in her short lifetime. But this coat with the foxtail tip made her feel all at once like things might be okay until she woke up one day without it. She searched every inch of the grimy flat and found worse than her coat. She found a different woman's coat. A mistake. Another one. Maybe that was the start of this new downhill slide.

Nothing nice had happened to her since.

BEFORE THE **B** word was flung in full-fledged ancient hate, an argument could have been made in the Mayor's defence.

Damian approaches the scene reluctantly and hyper-aware of the booze his body is focused on metabolizing. He places his man mask on as that is the only mask acceptable in this particular circumstance. He will play the only privilege card he has and so demands to know what is going on here before he spots John coming out of the kitchen. He knows now this will escalate fast.

John is in hard checkmate today. His father-in-law will be here any minute and Iris remains shamed and shocked to a full standstill. She will be embarrassed by her lack of action later. Damian has heard her replay similar scenes. Always with the same forlorn disappointment in herself. Always with the same desire to be a better woman.

I'm a bad woman, she says to no one after service, head hung, picking at her cuticles.

Damian did not think her any worse a woman than he was a gay guy. He most of the time let himself pass as hetero because it was his right to do so and none of anyone's business. This made his sister angry. Melanie said that he was ashamed of himself when he had nothing to be ashamed of, and Damian would quip that he had lots to be ashamed of but it wasn't sucking dick. Sometimes Melanie buys him packs of fresh socks with patterns on them because new socks are a little nice thing that she thinks Damian deserves. Damian knows he doesn't but he wears them anyway cause the rest are dirty on the floor.

Damian hasn't seen the floor in his bedroom for months.

Sometimes he pushes all to the side, up against the wall, in an attempt to reclaim some space, but it is temporary. The next time he needs a shirt he will swan dive into the heap until he locates something passable. Everything smells vaguely of the gym. His one fitted sheet has been off the right-hand corner for ages. He could easily pull it over the edge again but he never does. Tom would line-dry the laundry. Damian would press his face into the pillowcase and breathe as deeply as his worn lungs would allow. He always slept soundly in those sheets.

John is amongst them, pushing his sleeves up to his armpits, the webbing of his hands running up and down his biceps. Every gesture is as purposeful as a warm-up. John is dying to evict someone. His body language screams welcome to my gun club. Damian would burst out laughing. Or into tears if he felt the freedom to do so. But the dining room is much too ramped up to allow emotional liberties. All stand in position, rank and file behind John, who is speaking in his slow voice.

I cannot allow you to speak to her like that.

A quiver of hope runs through Iris. Maybe he does love her. Surely.

Though what John means is I am the only man who is allowed to speak to her like that.

The Mayor is recounting his grievances, there is a debate in his timeline, the others cannot attest to Iris's behaviour before their arrival and so wash their hands of the whole conflict. But the Mayor persists. He has always found it hard to locate his off switch. A total lack of accountability has moved his shutdown out of reach. Besides, he has already invested too much bravado to back down. He applies sunk cost to all aspects of his life and so forges on, degrading the young waitress who did not know her place.

Which is the only truth in this exchange.

Iris does not know where she stands.

The temperature of the room grows steady hotter.

Major David and John are both playing at alpha until the true alpha walks in an easy hour late for lunch. The mere appearance of Big George takes the wind out of them all. It is nearly like the heavenly father has appeared while the holy conclave was in upheaval pronouncing a new heavenly father.

Everyone's legs are gone.

They share in the mortification as the dining room goes quiet. The hum of the coolers can be heard over the wind outside. The hush of hard breathing is interrupted by the ice maker making ice. Big George has long ago harnessed instrumental automation. The human machines in his employ are far less manageable.

What seems to be the problem here?

No one speaks because you never raise your hand when the teacher asks a question.

John?

Do not speak until spoken to.

I am trying to discern that myself.

Wait for others to get it wrong.

David?

Only after the process of elimination has eliminated wrong answers should you come forward.

The waitress was conducting herself in a very unprofessional manner.

Lay blame immediately to deflect responsibility.

Is that so?

She said you were fat.

Make it personal.

Excuse me, what?

I never.

Yes, yes, she insulted you.

Always always stick to your story.

Iris, what happened?

And just like that an arm has breached the surface, grabbed hold of her nearly drowned frame and hauled her up on the deck. She sputters to speak, she has swallowed so many words, they come out in bursts; like a choking child, the urge to cross her hands atop her larynx overwhelms her until she finally coughs out the word *bitch*.

Well, I am sure you misunderstood his meaning.

It turns out the man who pulled her from the pool is also the man who built it.

But but but.

Iris has a mouth full of conjunctions, they are being shook up inside her, she is carbonated self-defence, the pressure released with the smallest hissing sound out of her nostrils. John has heard this sound before and has memorized the signs preceding implosion.

He has memorized a lot of things about her.

But but but.

John would never admit to being the cause of the hissing for fear of retribution. He is a lowly lifeguard. He threw her in so he might save her later and be deemed a hero.

Why don't you just say you're sorry to the Mayor so we can all get back to our places.

And Iris says she's sorry. And everyone resumes their places. Like it is nothing to be called a bitch. At your place of work. In front of all your co-workers. And your lover. And his wife.

Big George orders a bottle of wine that is not on the wine list as the four, now a five top, is seated. He requests that John return with it himself. Big George claims to not typically drink during the day though everyone knows he does. The sommeliers love to see him coming. They purchase bottles just for such occasions. Everyone at the table pretends that this is not the case. They laugh in their good-natured way like betas bowing. John offers up an edgy chortle when he returns with the bottle. The barb does not escape his father-in-law, who makes a production of having him explain the wine as he pours. John's ignorance is aptly marked. Of course he has not a clue about it and calls Iris over, claiming she is prepping for a level two test.

The practice will be good for her.

And Iris's brain buzzes with pertinent and not so pertinent information.

She says, this is a 1989 Brovia Barolo Monprivato.

She thinks, your daughter and I share this man.

She says, it is from a traditional hillside village in northwest Italy.

She thinks, he has tripped us up in some triangle.

She says, the grape, Nebbiolo, is often described as tar and roses.

She thinks, please stop him before we are all worse hurt.

Big George eyes the thin waitress as she continues on. Tar and roses is right.

He can see the appeal in her. He cannot tell if she is better-looking than his George, though, because he cannot see his daughter as appealing. He can just see her as his daughter. Her lean teenage limbs stretched across the floral sofa in the formal living room with a heavy quilt around her shoulders like a shawl reading some heaving Brontë novel while weeping into her tea.

Sometimes she would call out at night for him to turn off her lamplight. Often she would be reading some thriller novel and too full of fear to move. He would be down the hall working late, or drinking late, awake anyway, and hearing her call him convinced him this was the real reason he was up. He would huff from whatever seated position and plod down the hallway, up the staircase, down another hallway, a miracle really that he could hear her, and pick up the book as he gave her a little peck on the forehead. Always the same request not to dog-ear the corner, his great lover of books. Big George would pull a receipt from his pocket and tuck it inside while shaking his head.

I don't know why you read books that scare you. This was a little bedtime bit they did. They both knew she was not really scared while he was awake, which was partially why he was awake. He could not refuse her these quiet hours of reading. He longed for her to stay forever quietly reading tucked in bed. Or propped up on pillows in front of a fireplace. The fire lighting the raw feelings flickering across her engrossed features. His George had a pensive look to her. She was so utterly focused. Big George has no such desire to see raw feelings on his baby's face now. Because that is how he thinks on her when she cries. His baby. His hurt girl.

And his desire to take John by the throat surges. He has to clench his fists to quell the violence inside himself. They have given this man everything and this is how he thinks to repay them. Fucking the help. George will see him hung up for this. He would gladly kick the chair out himself. One swift boot to the bucket and down John comes, twitching.

ALL THAT COW'S milk is after making Iris's feet too big for her body.

That's what Olive's nan would say. Not like her Olive, who was perfect proportioned in Grandmother's eyes because she had been reared on pap and country food. Olive still tears white bread apart and pours milk overtop of it when she has an upset belly. She eats it from a mug with a spoon while standing in the dark kitchenette. The light bulb overhead having blown out ages ago is not even thought on. The pap provides her comfort and then Olive sleeps. Grandmother never trusted Old MacDonald and his fast-food farmed friends. She said he transported sad pigs in dark trucks through the night so rich people did not have to see the disrespected animals.

Everyone knows what's wrong in their heart, Grandmother says, it is their brains that don't know stuff anymore.

Grandmother said a lot of things before Olive went into care. In the short weeks leading up to Olive's departure, Grandmother tried to rally, remember and then say all the things she thought that Olive would ever need to know.

Eating and drinking unreal food in an unreal place makes people feel unreal.

They would not be able to tell the difference after their guts had been turned. They would not know what the truth was if the only thing they put inside was lie after lie after lie. She begged Olive not to eat lies. Olive thought maybe Grandmother's mind was going to pieces because of being old and lonely and sad.

But Olive cannot believe a lot of what happens will happen until it does.

That night in the hotel, she could not believe anything. She could not believe how quickly she hated the man wearing the shiny gold dragon shirt. The gold dragon lit the man's fat face like a cheap flashlight. This man she had met at the bar some months before getting hired, Rog they called him, was already sweaty with energy drink and vodka. He was clearly obsessed with flight and spoke constantly about wings.

Red Bull gave him wings, you can't fly on one wing, he was on the wing, winging it, she was a little bird, come here, Tweety. Sufferin' succotash, he said as he leered at her, each time shaking his head from side to side like a dog with something in its teeth.

The others laughing and saying go on, Rog b'y, leave her alone.

Rog rubbing the spittle from his bottom lip with the inside of his thumb and forefinger like someone thinking thoughts she would rather not know about but was sure he would share eventually. He made her nervous like the men who wanted to give her a pony ride over their sock. She drained her first drink to dampen the regret rising in her. All that fear handed down through all those stories in the sleigh.

Olive had immediately regretted her red tights.

She had bought them in a fleeting moment of merriment.

They had felt festive and sexy under Iris's black dress deemed too faded for dinner service. That's what Iris had said. It wasn't dark enough anymore. And Olive thought it a funny thing to say considering half the world worried about being too dark. But she had not objected because she wanted the dress Iris held in her hands.

I'll probably never wear it again, Iris had said.

Olive stayed quiet because Iris looked very near tears. If she broke the moment, the dress might be reclaimed or reconsidered. And it was a real pretty dress. It had a lacy black collar with matching lace cuffs and trim just above the knee. There were tiny skull buttons down the chest to a neat, smaller lace trim just below the bust, and Olive really wanted to wear that dress to Calv's Christmas party. The one he had mentioned in his text. Calv would remember why he liked her when he saw her in that dress. He would not let weeks go without saying hello again.

Olive knew now that the dress you wear is of little consequence.

A dress can't make a man fall in love with you. Perhaps, that is how the dress came to her in the first place. Perhaps, that dress was cursed. Had she asked Iris she would have found a contrary voodoo at work. Iris would no longer wear it because it had been her lucky dress, the one she had worn the first night John had kissed her.

In retrospect, Iris had decided that it was not any kind of luck she wanted.

That kind of luck would see you quick to the grave. She probably should have destroyed it rather than give it to Olive. But Iris could not bring herself to do so. No more than she could bring herself to clear her kitchen of John's little gadgets and gifts. John wanted to have everything he needed within reach wherever he was so he had supplied Iris with all the same small appliances he regularly used. He had even brought over dishes for the dogs and placed them under the table while confessing that he felt bad when she watered them from her own bowls. Iris would wonder what about this made him feel bad exactly. Everything was open to interpretation. And the dishes remained. But the little black dress with its girlish lace had to go, and as she turned away from Olive on the walkway, Iris had called over her shoulder, through a sob, that she always wore it with coloured tights.

Iris doesn't wear coloured tights anymore either.

Olive had settled on the red ones after a prolonged internal debate.

There had been green ones there at the grocery store as well. She had wanted them both but she could only afford the one pair. Couldn't afford those really but would spare no expense for Calv. This was what Olive was like, she didn't know any other way to be.

Everything was very immediate for her. Her immediate needs were the most pressing needs. And she needed to look pretty. Calv had texted that he'd had a shit time. He was telling her about his troubles so that must mean something. He was turning to her. He said he needed to have some fun. Actually, he said, the b'ys really needed to have some fun. They had all gotten laid off and right before the holidays, too, which only made everything worse. Most of them had already bought stuff they couldn't return. That is to say, they could return it, but they would not under any circumstances. So they were having a party at a hotel. Everyone was bringing someone. Did she want to go?

Olive wanted to go anywhere with Calv as his someone.

The Canadian Tire in Mount Pearl was a desirable destination if she was with Calv. She would happily wander the aisles while he shopped for premium motor oil and a mixer for his mother. Calv did not buy a gift for his girlfriend so Olive hoped that meant she was not his girlfriend anymore. Calv told her about playing 120s as a kid on Christmas Eve and eating eggy French toast in the morning and all this made her feel part of his family and holiday preparation. She would gladly listen to him complain about his sister's boyfriend and muse about going back to school. One day he wanted to be a cabinetmaker, a mason the next. He wanted to do something with his hands, he said. Calv told quiet Olive that he would like to make things. His sister made things. Plays and shows and songs and stuff. His mother and father beamed with pride at Amanda's creations. Because they made her and she made something and everyone liked it. He wanted his mother to feel that same way about him.

The red tights had won out because she could wear them again later.

In Olive's reforming fantasy of her future with Calv,

she had more than one occasion to wear coloured tights. She had decided that this was the first holiday party. There would be others. She took her time getting clean, shaved all of her important parts which were all of them, and dried her hair on a low setting. Its diesel colour not nearly oily slick as she remembered and isn't that just the way, she thought. As a child she had despised the dark sheen that set her apart from the blond-headed ones, now she grieves after it. Not that Calv cared about the colour of her hair.

But Olive had worried his friends would.

Lots of Newfoundlanders did, but Olive assured herself Calv's friends would not be like that. Or at least not all of them. And even if they were, they wouldn't bother with Olive because she was nobody to them. It was just a party. Calv said after they might even go dancing.

Just us, he had texted, just us will maybe go dancing, Olive.

And imagining them an us made Olive breathe faster which made her slow down her external self. Don't panic and mess it up. She got ready so slowly it was painful. She started getting ready at six o'clock even though Calv would not be by to get her until after nine. She force-fed herself two apples. It was all she could eat, though she had very little else to choose from. Olive thought maybe there would be cheese and crackers at the party.

People love cheese and crackers at their holiday parties and Olive still thought she was going to a holiday party. An auspicious one sure, but a holiday party none the less. Olive was not at the party very long before realizing this would not be an eating party.

She was the only woman. Or girl. Iris was right. Olive would always only ever be a girl.

This happens sometimes when people are mistreated like Olive was mistreated.

They cannot grow out of it. They remain stuck in their first hurt. And the frustration felt is further amplified by the world's insistence they do the thing they are struggling to do. Grow up. Get on with it. Sort yourself out. Get your shit together.

Occasionally, Olive searched about the place for her shit to gather together only to discover she didn't have the shit they were speaking of. No one ever gave it to her. She received her fair share of shit now mind, but not the kind anyone would willingly collect. When Olive thought on it like this, she wished after some record of it as proof to show those who grew impatient.

A museum exhibit to walk through recounting all the unkindness shown her recklessly and randomly by people who determined her value less.

A monster book of pain to read safely in bed handy to someone who loved you. A dog even. At the very least, a cat.

Before Olive had language to communicate, her issues were already well forming. Mother left. Came back. Left. And came back again until she didn't. Still in Alberta somewhere. Before going last off, she had raged so hard at Olive for approaching Brian on the wharf. Screaming. Wailing. Olive wasn't allowed over to the wharf. Or handy to any of the Youngs.

Her mother was full on horrified at history's tendency to repeat itself.

If Olive had been home, or not out alone, or ever alone, nothing could have happened. But the reality is Olive was often alone because, well, that's how her mother left her. And then being alone was made easier and easier because being not alone often resulted in a bad memory. Olive felt no feelings about her whereabouts.

Now Olive makes bad attachments out of loneliness. She cannot help herself. She cannot help it.

There will be another study but it is no great mystery.

They will have her entertain it all over again on the news. Papers will be published one hundred times over recounting the concurrent issues that contributed to Olive's inability to discern a positive attachment from the alternative. But the truth of her person is that Olive had no parents because her parents didn't want to be her parents. Or themselves. They did not want to *be*.

She was her mother's living rejection. Her father's secret lark. She had tried to make them parent her. She had demanded their attention when she was only little. She had even attempted with her extended family. Her grandmother had shushed her out of concern.

My dollie, don't want for people who don't want for you.

She had been punched in the mouth upon confessing her paternity.

I think your dad is my dad.

The blood running down her gashed lip as the older girl cried in the principal's office.

Make her stop saying that!

Her beautiful mother sighing as she left once again for the mainland.

Men around here only want pretty women for one thing.

The tights had been an attempt at being pretty and Olive gravely regretted her less than smart choice upon entering that hotel room. Five men were sitting across the two double beds facing off without touching. They were all holding red plastic cups. One man held two. Another man sat on a chair by the window, he held a green frozen mug that was significantly thawed already from his hand sweat. He brought a special drinking cup. Rog fancied himself the head of this wolf pack, mangy as they were, this was apparent upon first glance. He spoke as if men lived in the forest and required ritual and regular hunts.

He acknowledged them as they entered, commenting on everything he had heard about Olive. Things she had never heard about herself, and she looked to Calv for clarification, wondering if she had told him about her landlord. Olive was certain that she had not.

This was the man she wanted to like her.

Calv countered almost immediately that it wasn't like that and that he thought everyone was bringing a friend to the party. Top dog said that no one else had friends like Olive. Calv must have misunderstood. They argued the point momentarily like two people familiar with the act of arguing moot points. Calv let it drop away as quickly as it was picked up. Olive wondered how many such topics Calv dropped, and felt uneasy. In hindsight, this is where Olive knows now she should have fled. Should have turned on her heel or reversed out of that room. Because Rog had a snarl about him she had seen many times before. Rog ended lots of sentences by informing people that he had intended humour.

Just joking with ya, b'y.

He said this readily in an unmistakable smirking way. But everyone knew he was never just joking. Not even a little bit joking. The claim provided him cover to make asinine remarks at everyone. He cloaked himself in a facade sense of humour cape, draped it over his own shoulders and across his face with every barb he sent into the world. If shots were not met with uncomfortable laughter, Rog advised any human hurt to get a sense of humour. Like his. This was just another coded way of saying once again that the hurt man, any hurt man, was like a woman.

Blow that whistle he did.

Our jokester felt certain being like a woman was the worst way to be and slandered them all female. The shortest man seated closest to the night table alarm clock seemed to be a particular favourite target. His height made him an easy mark.

The short guy had a sour disposition and a snotty nose. Not currently, or at least not yet, but as a child his nose had been runny and his attitude poor. This is not the first time Rog has brought this up in the company of these men. It is clear to Olive that he brings it up every single time they congregate, to agitate the short guy, who wears sunglasses on his peaked cap as if a sunshine emergency might overtake him at any second. He must be prepared to shield his eyes at a moment's notice in the darkest city in North America on the darkest night of the year. Olive should have gone home.

But instead she drank from the red cup Rog handed her, claiming he knew Olive wanted a drink just from the look of her.

Rog teased her in that way men do about how much she could pound back, like Olive was a dummy unaware of innuendo. She did not acknowledge because women can't, so she made the required quizzical facial expressions that made the joke good. Even better. Rog had counted on her going along. So he forged further with it. He said he was sure she'd had a load in her in the past and Calv told him to fuck off with his foolishness.

But the other men were laughing. Because it was a great joke.

They liked it as much now as they did the first time they had heard it in high school. And while the jokes were geared to Olive, they were safe from the unfolding comedy. The short one chimed in wholeheartedly. He especially did not want Roger to tire of this new direction. So he made insinuation after insinuation about what they did up in cold places to keep warm. Their animal appetites must be right savage up there. He wanted to know if Olive was savage too. She looked it, he said. And Olive's little eyes darted toward Calv, darted toward the door, hoping to go dancing, to go anywhere.

Rog, upon determining that this turn would ruin the fun he had planned, steered it back toward the purely recreational. He pulled a bag out of his inside breast pocket and started cutting fat rails up on the back of the black room service folder. Welcome to Hollywood, he exclaimed. It was a call to which the men all responded, what's your dream?

And then all the men, Calv included, recited together in surging volume.

Some dreams come true, some don't!

Room service was passed around, with each dipping and pulling twice. Olive had never seen this much cocaine at one time. Thick powdery lines bigger than minigolf score tally pencils. Longer. Wider. Larger than a cigarette. And disappearing faster than one as well. Followed by ritual shakes of the head, throat clearing, chests puffed, necks stretching. It was all preparation. They were, the lot of them, preparing for going out. Even Calv. So Olive did it too when it was handed to her because she did not want to be removed from Calv. She did not want there to be space between them. She wanted Calv to see them as alike. Kindred. Look, Calv, she felt like saying, all your friends like me, this is how easy it would be to fit me into your life. Olive would take up so little space. Calv would hardly notice her there at all.

Cocaine makes everyone do a lot of hurried drinking.

Not the kind of drinking you can feel in your gut. Not even the kind of drinking you can catch up to. This is drinking in an urgent thirsty way found unnerving by level-headed people or even the socially intoxicated. The drunkest man in the establishment, having gotten normal drunk by drinking, will start to take an inventory of the reasons why he is unable to keep pace. Should have eaten more carbs. Too much coffee, not enough water. Got up last night with the baby. Walked the dog after supper. These are all possible reasons why his buddies from university seem to still be able to drink him under the table.

269

No one tells him that it's actually because the works of them are on drugs.

Everyone in the hotel room had been pre-emptively refilling their glasses as if worried they might find themselves suddenly and surprisingly out of alcohol. Rog was topping Olive's glass up after topping Olive's glass up. She was never near empty. It sloshed around on the rim each time a man stood from the bed to make his point more aggressively or take a piss. There was a lot of pissing. Their kidneys were well aware of the rate at which they were expected to work. The constant up and down had at first concerned her as the boozy mixture slopped against the sides of her cup. They were going to make her spill it on herself. Ruin her whole outfit. But her dress was black and her tights were red and you couldn't see the proof of it. The concoction dried in to match the mixture. And no one would see that in a bar, Olive assured herself. The start of the evening was what people remembered and used as reference material later. No one mentioned last going off. Or most didn't. It was an unspoken agreement. The nerves that had initially plagued her subsided for a time.

There was a brief window ledge where she sat between sober and flattened.

From it, she looked about the party she was attending because she was at this party. Not just at the party. She was a part of the party. Not just a part of it. She was the party girl at the party. This had taken on prestige while she sat in the transitional window dividing feeling too much from feeling too little. Here in the window, she felt the right amount of whatever feeling it was, and that allowed her to feel a little at ease. The coke helped. At first, coke helps.

How many times could Olive have gone home? One hundred? One thousand? How many times did her body alarm at the prospect of teetering out the window? How many times did Olive ignore it? The only answer is: many.

The other question always posed is why stay under the circumstances that other women would call problematic at best? Dangerous at worse. Those other women, all of them with someone to go home to, are the first women to discount the reasons why Olive stayed. Because to stay there and let what happened happen is not something they can understand. They had rarely felt the kind of loneliness that Olive feels and so cannot comprehend how being alone would be a scarier option.

Suddenly alone and drunk after the evening going polar to all expectation and hope, that was Olive's real worry when Calv grew restless and reached for his coat. She would be left to reconcile it with herself. The truth of what had transpired would be really very painful.

And it was quick, Calv's determination to leave, it came from the side. It was a periphery decision made immediate that she barely caught at all. He would have left without saying goodbye had she been in the bathroom. Even saying goodbye to her would be admitting that she was somehow there with him, which he could not admit because then he might be culpable in some way for this evening.

He needed to not be there.

Something about Rog touching the lace hem of Olive's dress had set an alarm off in him.

Calv had without warning grabbed up and pulled on his coat. The zipping sound had ribbed tremendous inside Olive's ears. The outer layer had startled her. Olive had tried to readjust. She had tried to ask questions now of this man she had never asked questions of. Unasked questions could not go unanswered. This was a lesson Olive had been taught long ago. She almost never makes requests. She hates asking for help. Or clarification. Hates it. But she tried. She stood though Rog pulled her back to sitting. She asked where Calv was going. She had hoped for an inviting answer but Calv said he was going home. He was suddenly not in the mood for this. He said he could drop her off. Saying that he could drop her off implied that she was not going with him to his final destination. Later he would tell himself that she wouldn't leave. This would absolve him. He had asked her.

What was he supposed to do, drag her out of there?

But the truth is, he didn't try very hard. Because he suddenly didn't want to be in charge of Olive who he didn't want to be in this room with even though he had brought her here. He was distant. Shifting in desire. Already stepping out of this evolving disaster.

In his mind, he had moved on to never speaking to her again. He would pretend he did not know her altogether if he walked by her on the street. Or any of the b'ys. Especially Roger. Amanda and Donna were right about him. Keeping company with the likes of Roger Squires was why Calv couldn't get ahead in life. Why he thought it acceptable to keep company with some slutty young thing he met in a dive bar. Bring her to a party. Do a swarm of blow.

None of this was right or good and Calv wanted no more of it.

So when Olive asked if he wanted to hang out at her apartment for a bit, he snapped vicious at her. She had said this right pathetically and in front of all the guys, too. Like they were friends who hung out at her apartment. Like they were on the go.

And it was barely words that came from her, a mew of desperation. He was repulsed and afraid of the need. She might need someone. That someone might be him. The realization made Calv panic.

No, he was not going to hang out, he was going the fuck home out of it, wasn't he? That's what he said, didn't he? Home to Donna. His girlfriend. He would get the cab to drop her off if she didn't want to stay but she had to come on right the fuck now. Right now. This instant. It was a super-fast proposition made just to have said he had made it. Olive knew a real offer when she heard one and this was no real offer. It was barely an appeasement. Olive would not appease him. And so she didn't go. But she should have.

The whole discussion about leaving took less than five minutes.

From the moment Calv picked up his coat, to Olive alone in the room with these strange men, four minutes had passed by her. She could see the night table alarm clock flick its numbers over. Slightly deviating strokes making their way toward the future. Bringing it into being. She could see them now and then forever. The digital red stick figures slowly turning all through the holidays, ushering her into the new year, every time she stepped into a hotel room or spotted a cheap clock in a discount department store, this kind of technology would mark her passage through the world. Olive wished away her bargain time. This time and each time. With each new person. Wanting it all to be over and done with. But being home alone high during the holidays was the scariest thing Olive could think of when Calv said he was leaving. Worse than being there with those men. So she chose to stay.

Olive does not make her best choices in an altered state.

And not long after Calv's departure a harder fault shifted. It was introduced by the television, which was as expected as it was unexpected. The fifteen-dollar movie with its cascading volume occasionally cresting the human chatter of the coked-up group of laid-off riggers advanced a strident tone. The woman's moans knocking the wind out of Olive as she examined the grey-green carpeted floor that might lead her out of here. The rutting from the actor bounced off the wall sconces and back into Olive's face. She felt anxious and ill. Trapped. Well and truly caught up in this version of a holiday party that was like no Christmas movie she had ever seen on CBC. This would not be deemed appropriate viewing by the public broadcaster, which found a lot of everything to just be too much.

That's much too much of everything. She's really just too much.

And yes, it hurts to look at Olive here with these men not unlike her own family. Uncles, cousins, ordinary men who would just as easy pump a strange woman's gas during a downpour. But it's not right to selectively see only certain people in focus. Our own people is a thing and it is not a thing.

Because Olive is our people, too. We are all the same people.

And baby it was cold outside. And there were no cabs. No one to wait with her on the side of the icy street. No way to cross town in the snow. Olive, Olive, Olive, her mind ran her name through its paces in her head, the accusations coming even before the deed. Why did you leave the house? Why can't you just stay home? What will happen to you now?

This was the internal line of questioning taking shape as Olive interrogated herself pre-emptively. No one was as hard on Olive as Olive was on Olive. She knew all the right triggers to step on. Knew all of the buttons to wordlessly push and so she wordlessly pushed them. Though the vocalized line of questioning had become directed at her tastes and experience.

You likes that, don't you, Olive? You're into that kind of stuff, hey? Aren't ya?

And they snickered and declared it another great joke when she stood to move away from the bed. The short guy pushing her casually back down to sitting. Joking. Just joking. Olive's head a hive of bees buzzing in her mind. Her cheeks tingled. Her hands began to shake. At some point during the evening she had taken off her coat and shoes. She attempted to locate them around the room. Visually locate them. She didn't want to alarm anyone. She wasn't even sure if there was reason to cause alarm. Perhaps, this was how it was in the world for her.

Perhaps, Olive needed to get used to it. Embrace it. That would likely be better than the constant unrelenting disappointment. And there was a great grief inside Olive for the momentary fantasy she had been harbouring. Even though she claimed to have relinquished them long ago, Olive still had romantic notions.

Up to the porno, she had still hoped there might be something better in store for her.

She pretended that she had no hope but that was to divert the pity of others. Olive didn't want people to think her pitiful. No woman did. A lot of men don't seem to mind it much, they repackage it into attractive anguish. But most women had become rather averse to being cast as a damsel in distress. Being hopeless and hard seemed a preferable option. And wasn't that what all across the kingdom wanted from the hurt and soft-hearted? Toughen up. Take it better. Thicken that skin of yours so you might rub raw less quickly.

She remembers readjusting her eyes to a hand on her thigh like focusing a camera lens on her own limb.

She could not see well while she could see everything. The others were watching too. She wondered what they could see. Could they see Rog kiss her? Could they see him push her onto her back? She was removed from the room already. Could they see that? Did they care? Her absenting was a pre-emptive measure taken by her mind. Her mind decided to abscond from what was unfolding. As it was waving goodbye, it whispered encouragement in the form of options.

It will be okay, you will be okay, we can forget this later.

Her mind put a fair bit of distance between it and Olive's body so they might not be broken together. Her mind's suggestions were fading as Rog pulled Olive's Christmas tights down. Not right off though. Just off the one leg. They would stay like that the whole time. No one would think to remove the dangling tights hanging off her foot because it did not interfere with their comfort and their comfort was all they concerned themselves with. Mind kept track of their whereabouts, these special tights. Mind thought this was an important detail to focus itself on as it hid out of view.

You still have your tights. Your dress is still on.

You're not naked. You are not naked, Olive's mind said reassuringly.

But Olive's dress had been pulled up over her waist. Rog had ripped the lace hem in the process. Later, as he walked out the door, he would say sorry I tore your dress, as if that was what he tore. As if the dress were the thing he had ruined in that room. The statement thrown over his shoulder had made her want to scream. But she had no power left for that. The sight of herself was the horror show. There seemed a lot of reasons for yelling. There were instances where she clearly thought to scream. But no scream came. Or she thought to run. But her legs didn't move. They just didn't move. No sound came. People say that she is a consenting adult now. Her childhood has no bearing on her age. It's all about numbers for people who've always controlled the numbers. Olive knows this somewhere.

And she wants it to change. She just doesn't know how to change it.

So she just let Rog pull her panties down. They matched her bra. She had taken such care. She had tried. And she could hear them remark on her shaved pussy like there was proof in it. Her shaved pussy emboldened them. She wanted this to happen. She wanted it. Them. Olive tried to snap herself again into motion. But the short one held her hands. Another reached around and rubbed her nipple through her dress. He asked her if she liked it, repeatedly, you like that don't you? You like that, hey? Say you like it. Say it. And so she did. She pretended she liked it because objecting did not seem a realistic course of action. This is why Calv had brought her here. This is what she was here for.

Olive's body was built for fucking.

So Rog fucked her. He was the leader of this gang after all so he fucked her first. The animation in the room crested and broke when Olive cried out. It was not like the noise from the TV. It was recognizably different and it terrified the room. The room examined itself. The room dropped. The bottom fell out of her. The only sound was Rog finishing what he started. Then he turned the movie back on. Louder, and they argued. There was an exchange of information taking place over Olive. Rog would not be the only one. They had all agreed. Agreed. There was no backing out now. They had just watched him. And he was going to pay her, wasn't he? It's why she came. Get it? She's just a little fucked. Ha ha. Give her a hand, b'y. And so on and so forth until the cartoonishness of the gathering returned to carry them through.

Rog cut out more Hollywoods and gave one to Olive off the end of a car key. And she took it. Of course she did.

Everything hurt and she wanted the hurt to go away. She wanted to go away. Does this make it more or less her fault? Is what came after more or less her fault, too? When she made noises to encourage the ending for the youngest one who couldn't manage to complete, did that make her more wrong? Or when she raised her bum up slightly to ease the encounter as the short one hauled her by the hips in and out, did that mean she was to blame? When they told her to touch herself, and she touched herself, or opened her mouth, or called for one to come, did that make her deserving of being treated like a prop in a fifteen-dollar film?

When the fat one looked down to remark on the blood in his lap, was it her fault for not pronouncing the presence of it when she felt it run? The fat one having moments ago declared himself the one who fucked her best because she was so wet, now horrified that the wet way her pussy let loose was not what he had thought. But Olive welcomed the blood, it had temporarily hurt less. And then they were concerned about the damage deposit on the room. It had been put on a credit card. And the movie too. And buddy's wife looks at everything on the computer. It would come up. All that shit comes up now. And he would have to go home and change his shirt before they went out. Cause she had started her rag all over him. Fuck. His. Life.

How unlucky was he to get period all over his shirt, he said as he pulled his pants on.

That's what they told themselves, that it was period blood on the bottom front of their friend's shirt which he went home to change before meeting them at the big dance bar.

Too bad too, he loved that shirt. His mom brought it home from Florida.

A skirmish would break out amongst the gang when they were ready to go prowl around further. Because Olive was just the primer after all. They've stomach for more than this. The world owed it to them. The self-pity they felt over their unemployment would excuse any behaviour at all. And at Christmas, too, got laid off at Christmas, what a sin, no wonder they wanted to blow off some steam, their nans and aunts would say if ever they were found out.

The defence of their choices would be vicious.

Wives would force daughters to carry signs defending fathers. Defending their men. They would call Olive every style of vulgar word. They would make up new ways to verbally hate on her. They would get racist after saying repeatedly that they were not racist. When asked plainly by reporters what racism was, they would say they knew what racism was and then say more racist stuff. These same seemly white women with not nearly white enough grandmothers would now say the worst things they could think of to defend the men in the parade. Slutty jackytar is just a starting point. A warm-up. The first few laps around the gym before you take your hoodie off.

In the Legions, Lions Clubs, at a Rotary or two, they would verbally place their own hands over Olive's mouth if ever she got ideas about opening it. The women would stifle her better out of fear of the details Olive might share, which were likely horrid. They all know it because they know these men. Or men like them.

If they knew exactly how Rog had flipped her over

and pressed his hand on the back of her head, it would be hard to make small talk with him at darts. If they knew how she had bit down on the pillow to manage the pain while the youngest said repeatedly in a panicked voice that he didn't think he could come with people watching, it would make seeing him at Costco really awkward. Or if they knew that the snotty short one shot back hurry on cause the bars would soon be closing, it would make talking to his mother at church some uncomfortable. All the summer BBQs would be ruined, sure ruined, if Olive told on them. Really told on them. The well-versed and well-respected would take to the streets, to the halls, to the newspaper, to prevent the details. They would write a letter to the editor explaining their truth. Which would make it better for everyone but the victim. They would brutalize her further out of a twisted fear for their own safety.

They would remind everyone that women lie.

As if the world were not already working under the pretence that all words uttered by vulnerable women were lies anyway. If necessary, the female defenders would take it to the internet, or at least, the ones who knew where on the internet they could take it would. If Olive at any point fancied telling a medical professional or counsellor or even a friend that she thought maybe something very bad had happened to her, the mothers and sisters, fuck, even random women who liked a member of the gang for a time once, would cry out against harming their male reputations.

They went on a boat ride once, he made them laugh, be careful of his good name.

The men themselves won't even have to defend themselves. Not that they wanted to. Not unless the camera and recorder was sharp focused on their pain. To wade in with the women folk would be very near emotional labour, which they have spent their lives avoiding. They are not an emotionally energetic lot. Half of them don't know what the youngsters got for their birthday. The ones who do know, know because of what it cost them in money.

Not that they were all the same. No. There were, there are, lovely fellows about the place.

Dads that watch girl *Ghostbusters* with little boys without acknowledging that the heroes are women, knowing in their hearts that this will probably make their sons better people. Men who snow-blow driveways for elderly strangers and hardly ever steal parking spots at the mall. There are beautiful courageous Newfoundland men cooking Sunday dinner while their wives read books on the couch. Or just fix stuff. See that it is broken and just fix it.

No one is suggesting that these men don't exist.

But that's not who was in that hotel room with Olive.

The other kind of existing men, the brutally abled, will quieten for a time as the undebatable hateful thing temporarily silences their easy speaking. Some of their mothers will even tell them that they must shut the fuck up for now. They've said enough. Let Mom call the radio station for you. It's better coming from a woman. The best shield for a bad man is a good woman after all. Some mothers will even offer up cash rewards to people who can prove an innocence. It's a good strategy that has been effectively employed in the past. There is no financial harm in it. They'll never have to pay out the reward because there could never be any proof positive that their sons didn't do it cause, well, they did.

They did do that to Olive.

Everyone in this cove and that cove knows everything about everyone.

Except for when they know nothing.

Those same people who know nothing would encourage Olive to self-harm across all platforms. Directly and indirectly. If she could gather up her remaining confidence and defend herself, other women would recount tales of generosity and moments of joy to offset the sour imbalance of Olive's experience. Post pictures of a son holding a teddy bear, a kindergarten graduation cap and gown, a tux on his wedding day.

Look! He is loved because we love him and therefore he is good and not bad.

Because the lady folk could not handle more shitty men. If the ones believed good are also shitty, then it is indeed possible that they're all shitty. And what can they do with such a lonely hypothesis? Instead they will spout hyperbole. Good right down to his soul. Nicest man I've ever met. Can't believe a bad word about him. Never hurt a fly.

And of course, the best one, the cliché trotted out the most because it's the best/worst one of all, uttered at every girl before any training bra — ready, set, go: boys will be boys.

But really, rightly, that statement should be disputed every time it is used to dismiss the very genuine and deserved complaint from girls just trying to survive as girls in spaces where even mothers are used against them. Mothers must stop competing with their daughters. Daughters do not make men mistreat them. It is not right or fair to punish daughters further out of envy. Keeping the dangerous path dangerous will not make them better women but hurt them still in the same sad ways. The makeup on Olive's face does not mean she is a whore. It means she feels prettier wearing makeup. It means someone has made her feel less pretty without it. Peel it back. Remember the feeling.

Do not wish it on Olive. Olive did not do this to herself. No woman ever would.

Though some still maintain the line. They will hold a possible shitty man even higher in this regard. It is not their fault. This was how women were trained before Olive pulled on her red tights. Which would be used against her. Her wearing red tights. Obviously slutty. Obviously asking for it.

Obviously. Obviously. Obviously.

If Olive told, there would be long drawn-out conversations over cigarettes on front porches about the logistics of Olive's guilt. They would list the things Olive had done that support the argument they want to shape against her. Her going there is evidence. Drinking. Drugging. Staying. All this proves she wanted it. There need to be better processes in place to protect men from women like Olive, they will say.

They will act as if any woman in the history of the fucking world ever wanted to be treated mercilessly by a group of men, one after the other, coming inside her until she is light-headed from bleeding. As if that was a thing any woman would want.

Olive knew this, and so she didn't make a sound during or even ever.

Olive had seen it a thousand times before. The muscles in her body remembered it well.

Though there are rare instances where this behaviour is changed. The way behaviour changes. A little at a time. Someone draws a new line.

That line is: this is not okay for half of humans living.

Not nearly good enough. True accountability is knowing those who harm Olive will be held accountable. Knowing the details would mean women on the courthouse steps yelling.

Someone has done this vulgar shit to Olive. Argued over who banged her best. Kept time for the duration. A reverse racing score. Later, all participated in the skirmish about removing her from the room. Contemplated folding her into a torn dress, blood all down the insides, so she could be moved outside while they partied on. In case she beats it up the room, they said. Concerned for the potential damage deposited. This: the numbered value of the hundred-and-fifteen-pound twenty-six-year-old passed out belly down on the dirty bed.

On top of the covers. No one got in the blankets. This wasn't fucking lovemaking.

This was a gang bang.

DINNER

· · · · ·

THIS WAS WHAT ROGER had wanted. Him and Calv out day drinking like real good buddies.

He has always wanted Calv to play along but Calv ain't got the stomach for the unorthodox stuff. His porn choices always ran soft core. Girl on girl. Vaginal penetration. His Google searches never got weird. Never featured anal. Or anything handy to illegal. He won't hardly tell anything about what Donna is like in bed even when asked directly. Sometimes he lies about it. Roger thinks this can only mean Calv wants to marry her. Maybe Calv even wants Donna to have his youngsters. And Roger knows that youngsters would mean the end of their friendship. Calv was not the kind of man that would ever lose custody of his youngsters.

No sir, Calv's mother would have him skinned alive so fast it would be criminal.

Roger shivers when he thinks of Susie. He is sure they would have strung her up in the olden days for witchcraft or disobedience or whatever laws they had to make women like that shut up talking. My god, her and

Amanda hates him. But Donna might hate him the most of them all. Him and Donna screwed when Calv was offshore that one time he gave her a ride home. They had too much to drink. It was a mistake. Roger regretted it sure didn't he. He told Donna he was sorry. Jesus, what more did she want from him?

Wants him gone from the earth is what she wants.

Or at least from her and Calv's earth. Roger thought if he could get Calv out on the tear a little there before Christmas, then he might forget that Donna was after forbidding they hang out. Maybe he'd meet a new woman. Give up beating around with some little piece from up Northern Pen way. Lord reeving, women gets right over Calv. He is right susceptible. It's cause he got a silly mother and soft father no doubt.

But Calv had left before the party even got started. And now Roger had to deal with peeving from the b'ys. All up in a snarl. The youngest of them going around all Christmas asking people if they thought you could rape a hooker. Said rape! My good god, that stunned fucker would have them all locked up. They should have never brought him along. He had too many questions about it right from the start. You knows you can't discuss that kind of shit in advance, that got to unfold naturally or it starts to feel weird and sinister.

They never raped that girl. It was a bit rough sure, but sex can be rough sometimes, loads of women wanted to be slapped and bitten, the works of it. Sure, they loves them books. Some of them even liked a little bit of friendly strangulation or being called bad names. You never knew what you were going to get by. Could be great fun or pissy as a sick cat the morning after hooking up. You never knew. Could never know.

And he's trying to explain it to Calv that what's-her-chops is fine. It's the boys that's not fine.

They're convinced Calv is after turning on them cause he never returns texts and nobody has seen him since that night. Calv rhymes off a number of reasons why he hasn't been out much. Him and Donna made up and now she's after cinching up his leash tight around her hand. And he don't really enjoy bars anymore so it don't hardly seem worth getting into the biggest kind of racket with Donna to go out drinking. Which he can't afford on employment insurance cause he's flat broke now, ain't he? Nare cent. Besides, who wants to go out in the jesus winter? It's cold enough to freeze the cock off ya. Calv motions to the picture window he has spent most of the afternoon looking out, longing for escape.

Just look at it out now sure, shouldn't even be out in it, not fit.

And it wasn't fit. Nothing was fit. They were all unfit. If fit were a choice, they would all choose it.

Iris, Olive, John, George, Calv, Damian, Ben, even Major David would choose to be fit over unfit. But there is no such option. Like defining normal: a definition applied by fools with a penchant for oversimplified points of view. People can no more be normal than winter can be unified and made the same every year.

The couples have already started to trickle in. The young women pulling off their parkas to reveal their carefully chosen clothes. Frocks fingered because tonight might be the night. A few ladies in their thirties pull concealed pumps from their purses. These fine New-foundland women are prepared for happiness. They got everything you'd need hove in a bag they wear across their body. Not even over their shoulder, over their bodies so both hands are free in case they need to haul happiness up over the side of a cliff. It is the most reliable conversation topic. They do not applaud each other's accomplishments with the same degree of intensity as one would celebrate a nice man.

Knowing Calv's luck his sister would show up for sure.

He don't have a clue how long they been here. Too long, he thinks as he pulls out his phone to discover not one but four texts from Donna. Four is not a great number. Two would have been sensible since last time he checked but four is escalating. Four means that the escalator has already carried Donna up to the hairy floor housing all her favourite angry stores. She is thrashing about up there now, running up a tab and jesus only knows what it will cost Calv to buy his way out of this. Around-the-world trips in a pair of new Lululemon pants every day for the rest of her life while she drinks unlimited non-fat smoothies made of fairy dust and Calv's own tears sucked directly from his long-abandoned cock by this goddamn waiter he can't stop looking at.

Who the fuck is that guy?

Damian knows buddy can't place him.

He looks like a puppy waking from a nap to find all of the furniture moved. But Damian will never forget his pitiful mug. He will likely be forever haunted by the sight of Olive leaving that lobby many hours later. Well after the party had moved on to the street.

Damian had been watching British panel shows on his iPhone when she emerged.

Secretly, he supposed, he had been waiting for her to come out of the room. Needing her to come out of the room after having clocked not entirely ugly guy leaving without her much much earlier. And then the rest, rowdy and gross, yelling and shoving each other as they hurried away to harass other suspecting and unsuspecting women. No one stopped at the desk to check in or out with him. And the girl he met weeks later called Olive was not with them. Damian had been watching. Raising his head each time the sliding door buzzer sounded in either direction. First glancing toward the sound before glancing hopefully toward the elevator. Toward the stairwell.

When the group finally appeared he was relieved. He wanted them all to be gone and his shift to end before their return. They would be someone else's problem then. But his relief had been premature he realized as he watched them slurring and swearing at each other like rival sports teams from neighbouring high schools. There could have been a hundred of them, the volume impossibly misleading. The roar that came from their departure was tremendous because of the space it left in their stead. Through the sniffing and snorting back, Damian had heard one guy gallantly remark that she'd be fine after she slept it off.

So the girl was sleeping something off.

Finally the elevator made to move up again.

She did not step from the elevator the first time the doors opened.

They closed but the elevator stopped steady. The

second time the doors opened, Damian was sure he heard a small whimper and a woolly whoosh from inside. And before the doors slid shut, there clearly came the sound of a woman muttering low comforts to herself as she smacked the open-door button weakly. Then she emerged. Olive emerged. And it was an emergence, too.

So troubled looking, so plainly not right. Her peacoat not even done up correctly. It was a no-hearted attempt at closing the wrong-looking coat. Just the one toggle looped at the centre looking to be under too much pressure, having been given too much responsibility. The lonely toggle rebelling against having to hold a whole woman in with just the one frayed loop. All that suffering buried in a coat she hadn't bought for herself. Because it didn't look like a coat that she would buy or wouldn't buy, merely a coat belonging elsewhere to a different person. Someone who had the time and wherewithal to deliberately toggle each flimsy loop. The kind of person who had no need for zipped-up escapes.

It was something to aspire to, but Olive was nowhere near that fastening point.

She had held her arms over her chest while holding her collar together in her hands. She tucked her chin tightly into the perfectly pointed basin where her knuckles met. She kept her eyes concentrated on the floor in a manner that suggested she believed an invisible string of sight buoyed her upright. Not her body. Or gravity. But her eyes intensely trained on the path was what attached her to this world and not some other. She was a young thing folding in on herself in an improperly secured peacoat. She looked drained even of despair with her carefully applied makeup now wiped clear. She had all the facial markings of a woman who had recently tried to steady herself by cold washing her face with tap water and a cheap white cloth.

No kind of place you could find comfort in was the ever increasing irony of Olive's life.

And the bathroom cleaning products had not left her feeling more clean but less so. The tiny bottles with their travel-sized tops were impossible for her shaking paws to manage. She had wanted to wash up. But she just could not manage to remember the steps. And she thought of the cold at home. And her grandmother boasting of never having to wash her hair.

Smell it, go on smell it, fresh like the country.

And try as she might, which she did, try, she sent those slippery little soaps flying into the waiting sink as the thick tears quietly fell onto the synthetic solid surface like vegetable oil onto a hot pan. And Olive thought, as she had thought before, that nothing around her was made real anymore. Not this bathroom. Or this hotel. Not the people who brought her here. Everything was counterfeit and therefore fit no counter. She could not even get the shampoos to work because of their manufactured size. And in the desperate state of waking with your dress hauled over your bra which is hauled down to your waist, the whole everything seemed unreal and unnatural. Like looking into one's own house from the street after having left the lights on accidentally. The effect of which is mighty out-of-body making and Olive was left to wonder if her body was something just on loan to her. She felt this all the more acutely staring at her borrowed face in a mirror holding the wall precariously with four screws busy impersonating seashells.

Olive found herself to be a squatter inside skin owned by some other.

This is the only explanation going when someone barges in like Olive has been barged in on. She had mistakenly taken up residence in this long ago abandoned life thinking it was her own. The previous owner in charge of upkeep had not even been her mother. Her mom could not hold title over any life because she had no grasp on her self-own property.

They were all squatting to some degree, though that degree was rather further far afield for the foundations of maternity.

If you searched the interior of Olive you would find one hundred years of lady kin worrying desperately over eviction. Always wear pants to bed and get a boyfriend or they'll have at her.

But Olive had not been mindful of herself. She had not worn pants or got a boyfriend.

They had at her.

That night it was confirmed that the rightful owners of Olive's body could return whenever they required refuge and so took refuge in her no matter the boobytraps left to warn them off. Bobbles to distract. Even ugly-smelling things to turn their guts inside out.

Olive had tried many different strategies tried by many different girls.

She sheared herself when the utmost scared. That hair of hers sometimes got real short short. She wore mean-looking shirts. Always with the hood high up. She spat and swore and stole time which was her way of proclaiming herself a boy. Because boys seemed safer. Not safe. There was no such seeming thing. But safer.

So Olive would present herself as a boy. She would grow muscles, become strong, fast and ready to sprint at first notice of invasion. Like a warrior prepping for battle. She would be appropriately groomed.

But it never took because she was not hard and cruel and singular. She was not a boy. She was a girl. And as she pulled the cloth across her face, Olive promised to lock her girlhood down, it was not serving her well. She would seal herself against it, airtight, there would be no entry. She would make herself impassable.

And the steady, heavy, greasy grief had oozed out of her as she tried to turn the warm water tap for some sort of relief. She had used the little cream-coloured waxy rectangle on her face. Wiser women knew not to do that but there were never wiser woman around to advise Olive when she most needed advising. So she had hard lathered bar soap directly onto her face, which only made her feel worse off, and so gave up in a panic because she had to get out of there before they came back.

Olive ran out of that hotel room without her mittens like so many kittens before her.

Olive's abandoned attempt at recovery had resulted in the opposite effect, which was glaringly visible as she walked finally forward into the dingy lobby where the overhead lighting magnified the rubbed raw nature of her cheeks. Her puffy eyes had been scoured of makeup but there remained residual lines that would not come free.

Crying lines are always the last to let go.

And Damian wanted her to leave. Just go home. Any-where. Not here.

That's all he could think. He wanted desperately for this little woman (girl?) walking out of the hotel to def-initely definitely not tell him what happened to her. He did not want to know that. Damian could always claim to have not noticed her leaving if she did not direct address him, and so he had kept his head down fixed hypnotically on his tiny black mirror as Jimmy Carr made quips about not paying taxes.

Oh how absolutely droll for the oft-praised, openly applauded, previously charmed to shirk tossing a few cop-pers into the poor pot. Funny stuff indeed.

And Damian knew there was something foul in that but also knew his most favoured comedy men (and the occasional woman) had their feet lit at Cambridge. There was nothing particularly hardscrabble about it and they all had a great laugh at their agreeable good fortune. God-damn it though, they were clever. Damian could have proceeded admiring their aptitude for satire if only he had not looked up as Olive passed by the desk.

What had made him look up? Curiosity? Guilt? Sheer stupidity? But it had been something about her gait that he could detect even while pretend-focused on his phone.

She was teetering.

Human instinct made Damian look toward a person perceived to be falling.

And then there was something about her tights. He could not look away from them. They were incorrect. They were inconsistently coloured. Stained on the inside which was not typical for stains. And try as he might to override all his wiring, Damian watched Olive make her wobbled way toward the glass door. He could not help it. Perhaps it was all those years with a sister. Or growing up gay. Perhaps it was feeling evermore vulnerable. Some coddled combination. Whatever the reason, Damian could not sober look away for fear she would collapse. And as he looked on, the brain in his head did what brains do and took in the qualities of the stain, noticed the red that was a darker drying red reaching down the inside of her thin thighs.

The sight of her would be indiscernible on the other side of the automatic sliding doors.

No one would be able to tell from where she sat in a cab or, god forbid, the side of the street if she had to in fact walk to her destination. Which she did of course. Of course she walked home. Roger said he was going to pay her for the time she had unknowingly agreed to provide. But he didn't because he didn't have enough cash on him just then. He was going to, though. This is a sticking point he would get stuck on for the rest of his life. Roger was going to pay her but he forgot. But he was going to because she sometimes was paid for sex, wasn't she? That's what Calv had led him to believe, and Roger was certain that this information pardoned him. He was going to pay her. Was going to but didn't.

Would Olive taking his money make this more or less worse?

Regardless, there was no money for Olive to agonize over, and so she walked home after having spent the last of her dollar dollar bills on these sad tights. The street lights would not downcast enough light for random passersby to see the ruination of them. Damian knew, as Olive knew, that the cameras wouldn't really spot the stains and thus there would be no kind of proof. It was just the moment passing between the two of them that they would have to contend with later.

This moment was a pivot.

Olive, familiar with the feeling of men's eyes on her backside, knew the hotel clerk was seeing how her holiday tights clung but chose not to acknowledge. She knew well the feeling of a man's gaze desperately hoping she would not look up to meet it. So Olive just walked across the shiny floor reflecting the overhead ceiling lights she counted to track her progress. She caught a slight glimpse of herself in the golden arch of a baggage cart as she neared the door, and her reflection's ghastly nature moved her forward faster out of the hotel where she had awoken forty minutes earlier.

A quick cry. A gathering. And then an escape.

She didn't even have to look for her tights because they were still hanging from her foot.

And she had pulled herself into them like packing a bloody sausage into its casing. Damian would not, could not know that Olive could, would feel those parts grow cold as she walked the whole way home like leftovers tossed in the freezer. He would not, could not know that she could, would eventually run a putrid bath in her dirty tub to soak in fully clothed. Damian would not, could not know that Olive could, would fall asleep in that tub water until waking to find herself in an even colder position. That, without thought of mind, she could, would pull everything from the back of the bathroom door down into the tub with her. Used towels. A sweatshirt. A handed down robe. The lightest pink bra, a gift from a fading Iris, even her old belt.

Olive would pull it all down into the cold water bath with her and attempt to cocoon herself in some kind of comfort only to wake again hours later colder still. There was never enough hot water. Not enough hot water in the world. And Olive would pickle in this wet mix while watching a fat earwig make its way onto first her foot and then her leg.

Once upon a time, Olive would have gasped at the magnitude of it. Crushed it under a wad of toilet tissue before dropping it in the bowl. Though, that day, because it was the day when she awoke in a mushy tub, she just watched it crawl over her, thinking it was full up with baby earwigs that would perhaps flood free and wiggle into the holes of her not yet sealed up parts. And she thought on worse things that could get inside while witnessing the plump shiny candelabra bug move off her arm back onto the tub's lip. Perhaps it could sense she was not an ideal place for a pincer princess to burrow. It went behind the cheap tub kit to born its brood.

Olive wished she could crawl in behind the tub kit, too.

D AMIAN WOULD NEVER, could never know the worst of it so he would never, could never tell these parts to Tom.

The only parts he would tell, could tell Tom were the parts he knew for sure and that was parts enough.

Because Tom would not, could not believe Damian let that girl walk out of there without trying to help her.

Didn't even ask if she was okay. Didn't even call her a cab.

Instead, Damian had gone drinking after his shift ended without even a text. Had shown up the next morning ranting unintelligibly about some girl in bloody tights.

Though Damian was quick to defend himself because he was taught, long before he understood the implication, to perpetually feel deservedly under attack. When bombs rained from the sky to destroy the little life comforts Damian had constructed for himself, he knew that these bombs were made special for him. The stocked artillery that floated in the acid cloud above him became apparent to him long before his vocabulary could produce retorts.

Damian knew he was made wrong before his father confirmed it. He knew he was a loser before any girl, and then any guy, chose not to talk to him. There was not one single moment that he could pinpoint to attribute this knowledge. When he searched through his recess, he only found an elementary generalized understanding of self-disgust.

The games he liked on Nintendo were the same as his little sister and that was not normal.

This notion of normal was readily adhered to by his normal mother who would go on to steal thousands of normal dollars from her normal job.

Dot had prided herself as ordinary. Upstanding in all aspects of her womanhood. Even when her husband left, especially then, she storyboarded her reaction as normal.

It set her apart from her horrible ex-husband and his much too young new wife who were for sure abnormal. Dot needed so desperately for that to be true. It kept her in her life. She insisted that Anthony was exceptionally deceitful because to suppose that he was in fact the normal one and that these situations were actually ordinary was more than she could bear.

It belittled Dot's experience. It dismissed her heartache. And it suggested it could happen to her again and again. So she sketched out a villain in her ex-husband who also happened to be Damian's father.

It was not hard. Tony was sort of a dickhead.

Not to his second family. He was very present in the lives of his younger daughters, which totally supported Dot's case because he was not at all present in her children's lives. Dot could not accept that this was how it was, she reviled Tony endlessly for the rest of her life. Every time her children received Christmas presents at Easter, she reiterated the same sorry story about his exceptional idiocy. Her friends thought her exceptionally bitter. Her friends' husbands said she needed a good screw. Dot was not a popular character but she characterized her reaction, even to this, as very innately normal. While half of people were preoccupied with adding an extra to their ordinary, Dot was passing out her regular card like someone simply obsessed.

Nothing to see here.

But theft and fraud over five thousand is the same as theft and fraud over five hundred thousand.

That's what was printed constantly in the press coverage, alongside the information regarding the charges and then the court case and then the sentence and now incarceration. Over five thousand. They never said under ten thousand because that would make the bad guy in the tale less bad. Namely Dot. The satisfaction felt by all for nabbing a thief would be diluted if they knew she in fact stole so little. Not even enough to purchase herself a proper car. Dot still drove the same ageing beige Camry.

Damian's mother was found guilty, because of course she was found guilty, because she was guilty, of forging documents and breach of trust. Selling fictional family homes to fantasy families. This was Dot's great skill. Creating imaginary standard families with reasonable incomes purchasing starter homes at probable prices in banal centre city neighbourhoods all along the downtown fringe. Nothing fantastical to see here. Nothing that would alarm the underwriters in Toronto. Two working parents, teachers, nurses, two kids, preferably school-aged to allow for more income, one car, four-door Civic was good, believable, etc., etc., until the turnaround and a real family could be found. Dot had no intention of a full fake out. That would be wrong. This was just a grift grafted on her by her wealthy boss who lived in a house designed specific by an architect from Nova Scotia who designed similar houses up and down the coast of New England.

Not old England. New England. America: home of greatest grift. Wall Street.

This all trickled down to Dot when her boss suggested she could do better.

St. John's was a housing market mecca for the housing market mecca makers and they went with the inflate like marketers after politicians. There was a feeding frenzy like something off Discovery. Everyone watching the rapture coming like it was written by a staff writer rather than the real actual housing market eating its own tail. Dot was not even really playing. She was barely participating at all. Kings were building kingdoms in wetlands up the hill. Dot was not imperial. She was just pre-empting the truth. A little advance sale here to cover the *waps* on the weekend. It was that or staying home. And home was so quiet.

Melanie and Damian were grown up and gone and set on never returning.

Dot watched programs on Hidden Homes in Wales and Latina virgins. It was all a lot of hooey to pass the time. She gave up on cleanliness as there was no one to admire it. Sometimes she put dirty dishes in the oven and forgot them until they smelt foul. Dot's own mother would have been appalled but Dot's own mother was dead. She had never lived alone. Dot's mother had lived with Dot's father and then Dot's aunt and then thankfully died.

Dot did not like eating every meal on her lonesome but she preferred it to the prospect of eating with her own mother, who had continuously wondered aloud why Tony had left.

Dot was glad she died.

It was painless. In her sleep after complaining of indigestion. Dot hoped to go before collections caught up to her, though debtors' prison was not the one that got her in the end. Dot has since realized all prisons are debtors' prisons full up with people who found themselves insufficient. Before this move toward bankruptcy,

Dot been had blissfully unaware. She did not know who would pay for stuff after her death and did not care. No one talked to her. Melanie was always claiming to be depressed which was a popular excuse for women her age. And Damian was gay.

So Dot gambled. She didn't decide to gamble. Not really. It just sort of happened that way.

One Sunday she was at Shoppers Drug Mart during the supper hour. She was buying stamps. The post service was not even open and she did not even need them. But it was something to be at. It was a thing to report on Monday. When her co-workers asked her how she spent her weekend, Dot would say running errands and it would be true. Not like when she said running errands when really she had been looking through old photo albums and not getting dressed for two days. When everyone was delighted about hunkering down for a storm with a bag of potato chips, Dot pretended she too was anticipating this event rather than admit that every day was storm chip day. Or just chip day. Or just eating.

So she sometimes made up arbitrary errands to fill the time and ward off her never-ceasing boredom. Going to the pharmacy during Sunday supper started like that: an excuse to get out of the house. Dot knew most people were having family dinner, half napping on sofas, packing school lunches for the week. She knew this because she had lived this, but that was not her life anymore. Browsing or having a little shop was something Dot did to kill time. Her daughter despised it. Would bark that Costco was not a place to go unintentionally or without purpose. But Dot ignored Melanie's insistence she get a hobby or Damian chastising about unnecessary clutter. Her children did not know what she needed or enjoyed.

And besides, Dot loved pharmacies. Especially the ones in Bay Roberts or Carbonear. Everything was cheaper out there. Bay women would never pay tag price for a lipstick when they could wait and get it half off later on. The Shoppers in town were not as good but still better than her living room on a Sunday.

Dot didn't expect it to be full of people at that hour. That came as a surprise.

She had started going to this Shoppers by a set of lights and then another one on a big road. They were full of people on Sundays, whole families getting their court-appointed serving of suboxone which everyone now agreed was superior to methadone.

Methadone was yesterday's answer to Capitalism.

It was at Shoppers that Dot had first observed the women her age buying tickets. A swarm of tickets. All brightly coloured and glossy like bridal magazines she would never need buy because Melanie was dreary and Damian was, well, gay.

And Dot knew men could marry men but even if Damian ever found a man to marry, he would not need bridal magazines cause he would already know all about all of that because he was, well, gay. Dot had watched the women scratch their games the first few weeks. She stood holding discount nail polish or nuts or stamps. Dot liked to buy stamps. They felt like a normal thing to buy.

Dot would stand there empty-handed staring at the stamps in the same case as the tickets, and soon she was staring at the tickets because the moms and grannies had time to spare too. They were waiting on the rest of their crowd to get their medicine before they all got into a cab to travel a distance Dot would never travel in a cab. Dot had at first been greatly annoyed with the scratchy women until that annoyance turned into admiration. They made everyone wait. They made the whole place wait on them. Perhaps the only time they could extend such control. So Dot tried it. And then she tried it every time. And then she went there on purpose to do so. She would never see anyone she knew. And she always bought stamps as cover.

But then the need grew as needs do and Dot needed something more.

Dot needed to take up more space than just counter space.

Which was how she was delivered to those machines.

This was the other tidbit the press insisted on including in every article discussing the fiasco. Not that Dot had been a volunteer Girl Guide leader for the better part of her life. Or that she walked shelter dogs on the weekends. They neglected to include her love of musical theatre and her annual monetary donation to the Food Sharing Association. Not one reporter thought it appropriate to report why she had felt the need to embezzle money to support a recreational habit recently discovered in a checkout line. Or to ask after her plans upon release for recovery.

No one even asked Dot if she was afraid to go to jail. If they had, Dot would have said yes without hesitation. She was definitely without a doubt afraid of the other women. Nothing about jail was ordinary to Dot and therefore it was all in contrast with her perception of herself. She was very concerned about the sleeping arrangements. Her lower back is very delicate.

And she had worried endlessly about what kind of food they would serve.

Dot's digestion was constantly plaguing her and she feared her irritable bowel would start up again. Where would she poo? In stalls? Next to criminals? Would the other women listen to her poo? Dot was overcome. She was very scared of the young women she passed in the halls of the courthouse. They gave her dirty looks. She suspected they would give her more than dirty looks when they got her alone in the basement. That's what Dot found on the google. Assaults happened in basements and hallways where the blind spots lived. How did everyone know about these blind spots? Trial and error. The irony was not lost on Dot.

If the *Telegram* reporter had asked her outright or even hinted at it, Dot would have said she felt there was a very real need for adult undergarments because she felt confident that she would wet herself if a skinny twenty-something from the blocks offered at her. But the *Telegram* reporter did not ask her because the *Telegram* reporter hadn't the time or word count to get into it. Long-form journalism was on its way out, her new boss said. Get it in the headline, he said.

All Dot gets: one line.

The paywall, while merely a dollar for the first month, priced a lot of people out. They hadn't the credit to afford the card to get the news about why they were so very poorly.

Access to everything denied, b'y.

The people in charge, having allowed most, many, okay, more than before, the privilege of literacy, had now deemed having an educated citizenship a right hassle so were marking it up in a hurry, man. If motivation could overcome the hesitation and apathy long enough to scale that wall, people still would know that Dot was scared and full of remorse. Her sorry was not noteworthy enough, though, so the media, all media, mentioned repeatedly the bits about addiction. Behind the deadlines and hashtags, every tarp marked "pressure," the reporters knew there was something called context, but thinking on it just illuminated dissatisfaction.

So they presented bare and basic facts when they could get the space for that and those facts.

Dot was a slot jockey riding the games at hotel bars with a highball glass of cranberry and tonic bought with money "re-appropriated" from work, which was an alternative way of saying stolen, which would be closer to the truth.

Ah, yes, truth. Yee-fucking-haw.

Dot didn't drink. She wasn't a drinker. Tony's new wife was, and Dot was super careful to be everything she wasn't. They could share nothing. Except of course a bit of DNA in their respective four children. So Dot put a lot of space between them. She was the antithesis to her husband's wife. In her mind he would always be her husband. Or at least until she got a new husband which was increasingly unlikely given Dot's current lodgings. She stopped saying husband publicly though to suit her children, who said it made her sound crazy and desperate.

Dot wants to scream that she feels crazy and desperate.

Her Majesty's was not built with ladies in mind.

The powder rooms were virtually spotless of powder spare the meth snuck in by guards in need of a rim job on the side. Not all of the guards brought in drugs and not all of the drugs were brought in by guards, but the job certainly took its toll on one's moral compass.

The inmates were going to get it somewhere anyway was the reasoning and so they took turns augmenting their take-home pay with a take-in powder. The jig required all to act vocally insulted if searches were requested and so there was a quiet complicit nature to the little drug deals that led to pool sticks across the face and shanks in a thigh.

The stone-walled structure was never intended to house humans humanely.

The idea nearly two hundred years back was pure punishment.

It is a hard, purposeful word representing an even harsher, more intentional concept. Dot thought on it a lot while she tidied her cell. It was the prisoners' responsibility to maintain their personal living quarters. This was the freedom permitted them to a degree.

Attempting to communicate to her neighbour how unneighbourly it was to live in squalor was generally frowned upon, though Dot could easily smell the young woman in the cell alongside. Dot was taught as a girl to never mind what your neighbour got but Dot did not think that applied if your neighbour was right full of the head lice.

It was a miserable existence over there. The smelly one spent all day lying in the bunk scratching herself.

She rarely spoke full sentences even when questioned by the guards whom she seemed to despise equally. Though not as much as she hated the shower. Getting undressed undid her. She would cry the whole day after.

Dot could make little sense of it. She did not think misses was in danger of being assaulted. Not with the size of her. She was so large and foul that Dot never feared for the smelly one's safety. The sobbing would surely warn off anyone, Dot thought. She tried to talk to her about it but the smelly one called Dot a bad name so she ceased trying to be friends, even though she was sure a hot shower would make her feel better.

The smelly one died in the shower so Dot opted to be moved to the men's prison in town.

Nowhere was safe, but Dot thought being closer to home would make her feel better. Make the time passing less tiresome. She thought people would visit her there. Dot had not received many visitors in Clarenville. Melanie had come once but refused to bring her daughter.

Babies don't belong in jail, Mel had said.

Dot had attempted to voice an objection. Her retort circled babies having no concept of place, but Mel had returned it with a hard and fast quip about trying to be a good mother so Dot had backed off. She later ruminated on this in her cell for days and concluded her daughter cold for having thrown such a barb when Dot was in no position to defend herself. She said nothing, though, because she needed the contact. Damian had visited a number of times in the fall, bringing Tom.

Or rather Tom had visited a number of times in the fall, bringing Damian.

And Dot was grateful despite thinking Tom disrespectful and full of himself. Tom was always telling her she wasn't supposed to speak to her children the way she did. Stressing a need for boundaries. Tom thought he was too good for them. But Dot still said nothing because she needed the contact. When the opportunity to shift back into town presented itself, Dot lunged at it. Sure, it was a men's prison, but Dot reassured herself they would not put women somewhere that was unsafe. More unsafe.

Dot was operating under the misguided notion that she was still a white woman.

And while she was indeed that, she had recently become other things that trumped that.

Now, she was a criminal. She was a prisoner. She was unemployed. Homeless. Poor.

Though none of these things had made themselves readily apparent while she served time in Clarenville. Dot was just serving a little time. Just a wee bit of time. A pinch. Nothing to get worked up about. She had planned to use it wisely. Made reading lists and outlined a workout regimen.

She would read Jane Austen novels and strengthen her core while getting rehabilitated.

Dot hoped she might be able to hear the races from her cell but she could not.

DAMIAN'S MOTHER MADE it easy for Tom to play righteous. He grew up on a sandy beach island with a warm coastline suited for shorts and castle building in the sunshine. Their great claim to fame was a ginger-haired orphan who just happened to be adored by her foster parents and the town hunk. It was quaint and hardly ever rained. Their great exports were potatoes and holiday memories.

Tom had supportive parents who were actually still married to each other on purpose.

Not because they lacked self-esteem or money to divorce. Not even because they were religious or felt particularly attuned to societal pressures. No. Nope. Not even because they fucking loved each other which, of course, they did in a totally sweet and mature way.

No, Tom's parents still voluntarily lived in the same rural Prince Edward Island farmhouse passed down through generations because they preferred each other's company over the television. Cooked favourite meals that were not their own favourite meals. Painted rooms preferred colours that were not their own preferred colours. Travelled to cities that interested the other rather than travelling to the city that interested them.

And this formula was a decent working formula because they both got what they wanted without having to place demands or meet demands for themselves. Tom inherited these traits naturally and behaved in kind toward Damian. This easy manner of loving was fostered over a hundred years of gentle summer winds and evenings spent walking along the coast in one's naked feet.

The nerve of some people.

Damian had once tried to explain to Tom that he had none of these effortless instincts. The winds on his island had been murderous and naked feet would end in bloody amputation.

He just did not have the same tools, he just did not have them.

Damian confessed his useless nature and declared Tom could do better regularly.

He proved this every time he did not do the thing Tom would have him do. Damian did not casually purchase Tom's favourite cut flowers and place them in a green glass vase on the windowsill or think to paint the kitchen cabinets a glossy buttercream yellow. Damian never once in his whole life thought to bake cherry pound cakes for their friends or grow spider plants for their elderly neighbours.

Damian did not do the right things because he did not know the right things to do.

It was like resenting him for not speaking a second language. No one taught him fucking French. Like punishing a raccoon for pissing in the house when really it was raccooning the only way it knew how to raccoon. Tom found this argument amusing. At first. And then disturbing. Because Damian was not an mid-sized urban rodent. Tom did not think of him as a pest, and it worried Tom that Damian thought this of himself.

And as with all new love, the red flags flapped overhead but Tom refused to look up.

Until he could not refuse it because the overhead noise was thunderous and unavoidable.

Obviously, Tom now found it fast and easy to judge Damian poorly for not having helped Olive. It was a despicable way to fully fail them both, fail them all. Tom finally recognized his complicity in choosing not to acknowledge who Damian was these past three years.

Tom had ignored all the fabric flying just above him.

He had made excuses to excuse and covered up things in need of covering. But not this time. This time Tom hauled those red flags down from poles and strung Damian up in them and left. Said he was leaving and left. Allowed Damian just enough time to beseech him knowing that it was useless, though also knowing that Damian prostrating himself in such a pitiful way would help dissolve the last relationship bonds. Damian's wild proclamations and cascade of tears from the passenger seat did nothing to dilute Tom's will to escape to safety.

Please don't leave me. Please don't give up on me.

Leaving comes fast when nice people finally recognize they've been tricked.

Tom's desire to flee was large and overwhelming. It consumed the course as each step further from the fraud was more space to wonder what he was well and truly capable of. Tom found a sublet and ruminated on alternative endings that were even worse than the actual end. Tom's imagination ran away with him now that he had decided his decision.

And then they were all awful. The whole family. Tony was a bad guy. Deadbeat dad, cheating husband, cliché. Dot was miserably unsound. Emotionally manipulative, thieving mother. Melanie, it was a sin about Melanie, with her abusive boyfriend who would never marry her or help her with their daughter ever. No, my goodness, Tom could see his mistake with space and time. He had thought Damian different from his tortured clan but that was the blinders placed on his face upon glimpsing Damian's beautiful backside covered in tattoos.

Good head is really very distracting.

Tom vowed never to let Damian anywhere near his belt buckle again.

And so it was that Tom quit Damian just as Damian forecasted he would, which was of little comfort though Damian reminded anyone who would listen because it was as near to being right about Tom as he could get. And being near to being right about Tom was still in some sense being near to Tom. Being a wreck continued to explore the central conflict at Damian's core. He listened to Sufjan Stevens while sitting in the hallway coat closet weeping all over himself and into a bottle of old Pimm's Tom's brother had bought over the holidays.

Broken hearts know not of dignified breaking.

He resigned to being undignified now that lovely Tom had left him. How Damian referred to Tom was a clean and clear marker of intoxication. Tom became less lovely as the liquor levels fluctuated. The bottle measure is down but Damian is shot up until it is fuck Tom, that entitled Anne of Green Gables fucker.

Tom has never known what it is like to live in constant fear that you won't make it through the winter. Tom expects to make it through every winter. Knows that spring will return. Plans for the summer. This is the great difference in the two of them. Tom plans for the future because he never doubts that there will be one, while Damian feels he has robbed each day like an unworthy street thief. And though he understood well why Tom was so angry and disappointed, he still bawled accusations at his ex-boyfriend who would never fucking understand what it was like to be gay here.

But I am gay here!

But you're not made here!

Which was why Damian had been attracted to Tom in the first place. Tommy was sunny. Tommy was new. He talked to his siblings regularly and had not fucked all the same men Damian had fucked. Damian wanted to pat him on the head like a large-breed puppy. What a goofball. Damian loved him to bits.

Tom made him want to stay on the planet.

So Damian watered the houseplants and put money into an RRSP. He had googled trade schools and visited a mortgage broker cause he would need a real job and somewhere to live now that he had met Tom.

Damian started noticing children at the park. He looked into their little faces and then the faces of their parents, searching for resemblance. He had never done that before because he was a strange gay man in a public place. He was sure of his strangeness and gayness as much as he was sure that they would not want him looking at their youngsters. But not Tom. Everyone liked Tom. A PEI Popsicle. Refreshing and welcome at the party.

It was the hideous way Damian lashed about that made Tom leave.

That's what Tom said. He could have gotten over what happened. They could have addressed it. Sure, Damian had walked out of his job like it was nothing and never went back, but Tom could excuse that because of trauma. He was clearly in shock. And when Damian confessed that the reason he did not intervene was out of fear, well, Tom would have eventually forgiven that, too.

Or so he thought. They could never know now.

Because Damian had spun out all over the apartment saying vicious things about Tom's privilege showing. Or his ignorance showing. Or naivety. Damian said Tom was gullible enough to believe everyone was good and nice because it had always been that way for him. But it wasn't like that for all of us, Damian yelled through snot and a little fit of barfing brought on by hysterical sobbing.

It wasn't fucking like that for Damian.

And maybe Tom should have gone to Damian. Comforted him. Helped him.

Maybe. But he could not out of horror. Damian was way more afflicted than Tom had known, and his survival instincts kicked in before Damian had the chance to hide himself away again.

Tom was ordering things for his departure because this human that he loved needed a lot more support than Tom was able to give. Tom had thought this whole time that Damian was shedding the last vestige of his party boy ways. He thought this because that was what he was told and Tom, like others handy about the place, believed what he was told. He had been taught that was how language worked. You asked a question. The other person answered.

Damian had said he wasn't quite ready to give it all up just yet. He was just having one last good time, blowing off residual steam, sowing oats and the lot of clichés relied upon when presenting the alternative to truth. Tom had believed it though because he was in love and it was something to believe that allowed him to stay. Damian would grow out of it. Everyone was wild in their twenties.

But they're not in their twenties anymore and Damian is still wild.

Though the concept of being wild is not the sharp edge Tom ultimately nicked himself on.

No, it was the concept of coping that drew blood as he watched Damian weep uncontrollably against the side of the tub. This is how Damian coped with everything. Everything was an excuse to initiate a bender. It hardly mattered the occasion.

Damian would use the birth of his first niece as reason enough to celebrate. This on its face seemed rational enough, but as Tom stood there watching the cat sniff his partner's pants leg, he remembered how that night had ended. Damian taking ketamine in the back of a shuttered bar and then convincing Tom to do so.

Or it could go easily the other way.

Damian would use the arrest of his own mother as reason enough to mourn. Again, on its face this seems a rational enough response. Anyone would understand the inclination for a stiff drink to comfort, but as Tom stood there watching Damian wipe his vomit-stained mouth on the bathroom floor mat, he remembered how that night ended. Damian buying an eight-ball with an ex-boyfriend Tom did not approve of and then accusing Tom of jealousy.

All things—good, bad, celebratory, tragic—were reasons for Damian to go on a tear.

This: the moment a very real possibility of something snapped together for soft Tom.

Tom's human brain, powerful and fascinating as it was, was trying to form a hypothesis and present it for peer review. The peer in question was for sure Tom's heart, who had for the most part been ignoring the evidence supporting the specific notion suggested ages ago and frequently by mutual friends, Tom's family, even Melanie. Even Damian's own sister said Damian was not thriving.

But Tom really didn't want Damian to be that way.

He wanted it to be a phase. Something to laugh about later. He dismissed it with a shake of his head and posted another charming picture of them together on Instagram. The summer evening they drank old-fashioneds from mason jars overlooking Trinity Bay. Damian napping on a daybed in the wallpapered kitchen of an old saltbox house rented for a long weekend. Standing next to their first wine kit surrounded by two dozen label-free green glass bottles.

This was the reality Tom was willing to look at.

Warmth and laughter, vitality and joy. Tom was an affectionate sort. He was always touching Damian. A hand on his elbow. A leg tossed over a leg. He wanted oak wood fires and sweet tea with bourbon. Grins in the freshly fallen snow. He wanted a female Newfoundland dog called Rex Murphy. Delighted himself with jokes about how he might train that bitch to listen.

Tom nurtured these wants like carefully dropped seeds. He sprinkled them everywhere. Sure, Damian carried many off to the smelly bars on his heels knowing rightly that nothing vibrant could truly root in the places he inhabited, but that was no matter because Tom tossed down so many.

Like an illustrated character in a Little Golden Book, Tom the gardener was generous.

Happiness would grow on Damian.

This is what Tom convinced himself of, poor sweet

man, a spade in one hand, a pair of patterned gardening gloves in the other, contrasting yet well matched to his plaid cargo shorts, so ready was Tom. He pruned carefully to ensure the pretty bits faced forward. He deadheaded all the deadhead blooms.

Damian took advantage of this generosity in Tom because that is what he does.

Like even right now, in this instant, as his booze-soaked mind salivates over the details of his relationship demise, Damian knows he is taking advantage of the circumstances at The Hazel. He knows fucking well that John wants to fire him. John didn't even want to hire him. It was Iris who had gotten him the job after a drunken, cocaine-fuelled heart-to-heart at a New Year's Eve do on Bond Street neither of them could remember going to. Iris had been crying in the downstairs bathroom. Damian had been kind to her. Brought her a glass of water. Given her a bump. Listened to her ramble about some man who hurt her. Damian had been hurt too. Their broken bits bonded over the wreckage. She said she could get him a job. And she could. And she did.

Then one day in January the girl showed up looking for Iris at the restaurant.

Who was that?

Olive Noseworthy.

How do you know her?

We grew up together.

She okay?

Is anyone?

Suppose not.

Are you?

Not really.

People around home used to say her crowd is half witch.

What the fuck does that mean?

That people are shitty.

It's easy to be shitty.

Probably easier to not be shitty in the long run.

Who wants to go for the long run, though?

Her pop had bad nerves.

That's hard.

He drowned after his TAGS ran out.

TAGS?

Welfare for fishermen.

We never really had that out our way.

Everyone had it back home.

Fuck.

They said he threw himself overboard.

Who said that?

Everyone.

That's dark, Iris.

I heard worse.

Don't make it right.

Seemed normal at the time.

Jesus, I'm sorry.

Don't apologize to me.

I mean—

Just be nice to Olive, okay?

Of course.

Of course. Of course now he said of course. Of course.

Damian tosses those of courses atop the heaps of burning secrets and throws another dose of booze down to quash them. He should slow down to keep his lies intact but he doesn't because he also knows that John wants to keep all sides of his triangle sound. John is alt-j and Damian is riding this awesome wave ashore for as long as he can, goddamn it.

He has got John by the cock. Iris has got John by the cock. George has got John by the cock. Everyone has John by his penis! It is all hands on John's dick! It is amazing. Damian has never seen anything like it before. And he is after getting himself into some right fuck ups. But not like old Johnny boy over here with his wife and mistress currently dropping tea lights into candle-holders side by side while discussing the wine pairings quietly under their breath. And Damian can see that Iris is straining to educate George on how this show is run, and the abject horribleness of it is fucking delightful.

John is definitely a worse person than he, and Damian finds that truly delicious.

He feels like storming into the kitchen and thanking John for being a malicious fucker cause at least Damian is a better guy than that guy. John deserves a hug but, alas, there is always a lineup of plump chests heaving to press themselves up against John's. All of them, even the ones at the back of the queue, seem to know intuitively to patiently wait until he turns to them.

Damian thinks it must suck really hard to be John's secret girlfriend.

It certainly looks like it sucks. It looks like Iris has once again given up on eating entirely only to haul back hard on a chain of cancer sticks. Damian is going to smoke two darts on his break, he can't wait, maybe three, he doesn't give a fuck about smelling of nicotine in the dining room. Queen Bitch will have her hands full trying to turn over tables and also manage Iris who looks to be on the verge of homicide. Damian has heard her say repeatedly that she is not supposed to be here.

I have to go pay my phone bill, she has said half-heartedly to the universe.

Queen Bitch replied she must wait and the lights flickered over the bar as Iris spun a wine glass in her hand, catching a flash of something sinister. The word wait is a shot that goes through Iris's body from her hips to her jaw as if she will Hulk out on the wine glass. Or hit someone. For a fading moment, it looks like Iris might get revolutionary on behalf of all other women everywhere.

But she doesn't.

Instead, she just slides the glass along the rack overhead, and Damian thinks he should instead gift his hug to her if she'll let him handy to her after his insinuating she smelt of genitalia. Iris holding the clean staff shirt to her chest and speaking softly into her own fists.

I don't know why you would be mean to me today.

Saying again as she raises her face to his that she has only ever been nice to him.

I have only ever tried to be nice to everyone.

And it was true, and he did feel regret, but more than anything he wanted to pull the clean shirt she held over his head because the smell of his own body sweat was making him ill.

Damian recognizes his admiration for John is gross. He does and it is, but how can you not admire the nerve of him? It is fully insane the way he conducts himself.

Damian takes the women in again and thinks they might have been friends under different circumstances.

They would have probably liked each other.

But not now. Now there will be a riot. He catches Iris light up at some insinuation over the candles. Damian cannot believe Iris is going along with this. It is not a fit way to live. Even Damian can see that, and he's pretty damn sure he snorted Ritalin off some stranger's ass in the last twelve hours.

John keeps sticking his head out of the kitchen. He has the fear of god in him.

Damian wonders if ever there was a time, before the minute hand coursed toward John's pants, that some woman did not have his balls in her mouth ready to snap. Probably not. John has definitely always been face and eyes deep in pussy, and this comforts Damian. By all accounts, John is a respected human. Which means there is still hope for Damian yet. He just needs to get through this night, and then February, and then winter. He should probably move away. He would if he could think of somewhere to go.

But Damian hates everywhere.

Lately he has hated home the most though. Since even before Tom left. Lately Damian has wondered if people are meant to live here at all. Everyone seems right shabby. Going to the grocery store during off hours, because that's the only hours he keeps, means he sees a lot of sad-looking people buying out the centre store. They don't even pretend to take a quick spin around the circumference under the pretence that they might purchase food that was recently living.

They skip right on over to the boxy core where everything is gift-wrapped so it feels like eating is a small present you are giving yourself. It is a tiny surprise, a singular joy, shiny like childhood. The manufacturers have made eating feel like something that is not eating.

Instead, it feels like pass the parcel at a kid's birthday party, and not at all necessary for survival or adulting like cooking food. Preparing food without wrappers and mascots feels very nearly like unpaid labour and everyone is unpaid or underpaid enough as it is.

And while Damian knows that they are poor, he still hates them in his way. Their raw lust for something gross feels akin to his own raw lust and he does not want to be of them. They are worn and unappealing and soft-looking and Damian does not want to be viewed as such.

He would rather death than the lack of glamour associated with that lot.

IRIS HAS BEEN seeing spots ever since George insisted she serve all day.

Now Iris is trapped in here with their saviour who has worked out what she will do about the CRA payment between lunch and dinner. One conversation with her father will vanquish all of John's problems. Abracadabra. Alakazam. Presto fucking magic. Her Royal Highness of Circular Road arrived on a cloud of glitter and adoration to wield her magnanimous rule over the peasants. Yay for them. They are so goddamn lucky to know her. Iris would like to shove her sceptre up her ass.

Iris has lost control over the internal dialogue.

John would say, don't be like that, you're better than that.

But Iris is not better than that. Not anymore anyway. Iris is worse. Besides, expressing disappointment in her is just another way to quieten her. John would shame her into submission and silence because it's rewarding when he shoots up half her triggers in a sentence or two and then shushes her in less. Sometimes a mere forefinger to his lips or stern look over the dinner plates stacked along the serving station will do. He's resourceful. Growing up poor makes you a different breed of clever. John can make a meal out of nothing. An onion, a bit of carcass, sure that's soup. And John loves soup. Loves it.

Mind you, he's not above gathering up his necessary devices.

This is the future. And didn't Iris encourage him to join the future. A well-crafted text message sent in the early hours of a Saturday morning to greet Iris upon wakening would bring about a hunger for reconciliation. A love-song link sent straight through to her Facebook page would break down any security inside a pre-planned hangover.

Adele must want everyone to fucking kill themselves.

But Iris gets it. She is starving for relief as well.

John is aware of this and so ladles great heaping servings of grief to Iris and watches as she forces it down. He would tilt his head nearly touching a shoulder and frown at her before proclaiming how discouraged he was that she would behave so crassly toward George who was, after all, innocent in all of this and well above ever saying any of the things Iris says.

John claims George would never even think those things.

George is pure. It was they who had made her life untrue. It was their sin, not George's. If there was a spirit in the sky, then George was going on up to him, while Iris remains in the shit with John. He did not make her do any of this. She chose it.

He had encouraged her to dress a certain way, eat certain food, read certain books.

But he had not made her.

She had done so with what she thought was her own free will because she believed this was what you did when you loved someone unconditionally. You tried to make them happy. And if happiness was wearing a black V-neck dress while eating a Cobb salad and reading a Coetzee novel, then she could do that. It didn't bother her much what neckline she wore or that eggs upset her stomach. She tried to pretend that the book with the skinny dog on the cover did not disturb her to the point of waking nightmares. She tried to convince herself that John was not like that.

When he clearly was.

Still she tried to be easy. Casual. Uncomplicated. Iris did the things John wanted her to do because she didn't even understand that these were not the things she wanted to do because, in all honesty, they were. Kind of. The thing Iris wanted to do was please John. Though she preferred boat necks with sleeves, salads with nuts, and magic realism, she refused to admit his exuberance for teaching her was worrisome.

But when John asked to see her new paintings, Iris refused.

She suspected John would try to colonize every aspect of her character so that he could accredit himself with anything worthwhile later. Early on, before the truly horrid had happened, Iris was concerned that John could not care less what she was really like as long as this impersonation woman he preferred to her was believable.

And it doesn't all happen in one go. That motion would never get carried.

This grade of conditioning needs time to ripen and so John gives it space. Had he walked in that very first day with a long shopping list of subtle changes he intended to bring about in her, she would have fled the scene. She would have declared him controlling and harmful. But John knows better than to show his cards too early by now. He has got ACES up his sleeves, under his shirt, even in his pants legs. They are well-concealed because boyhood does its very best to teach half-feral boy children to swallow all of that.

It is a wary culture that tells boy children not to cry when they are hurt, and John was a boy child once.

Iris could wax on poetic about the feelings that were harmed and harnessed early on that led him frankly down this road but she's past that. At some point, this point here now, why is irrelevant. At some point one must stop asking altogether. Why John does this doesn't fucking matter anymore. It just matters that he does. And he shouldn't. And it has to end.

But endings are hard.

Because Iris has got to find some kind of truth in a mistake before packing it up and putting it away. Check the pockets for change. Shove dryer sheets in the sleeves.

Take it down to her mind's furnace room and hang it in the storage closet until she can figure out what to do with it. Until she is ready, years later, to admit, after seeing it hanging there again while searching for her skates or snowshoes, that it never really fit.

Then the work comes.

The slow process of acknowledging to your real people, with great regret, that you were wrong that time and the time before that, too. That truly you've been wrong every time so far and maybe you have no idea what you are looking for cause it didn't ever make sense, did it? It didn't suit her, not really. Every time she tried it on, she was dissatisfied.

Left feeling ugly and gross.

Browsing the photographic evidence and murmuring under her breath, what was I thinking? She wonders if one day far from today she will be full of remorse. Right now there is only fear. Iris is afraid to try on anything else because her closets are full of skeletons and she obviously cannot trust herself. This style she had long thought her style is just not working. And to sort through the dregs will require facing all the mismatched socks thrown in, the tights she meant to mend, all the would-have-fit pieces if only she had bought the right size to begin with.

Besides, this would require self-awareness, and John would cry atop her womb when she attempted autonomy of thought. She knows John will throw the taps open if found out. You bet he will. And he will mean it, too. Just like he means he is sorry when he says so. But ask for clarification and John will find himself adrift as he tries to find the correct lie. Lying is all John knows.

His life is built on carefully crafted self-deception.

John's cottage restaurant is not really a cottage restaurant. It just looks that way. There is a real cottage restaurant just over the road so it is not that John does not know the difference. Or that his customers are not readily aware. Everyone knows that the tin ceiling is not a real tin ceiling. Or that the hardwood floor is not real hardwood. The animal hides and heads hung all about the place were purchased at HomeSense with money that was not even John's. It's a facsimile they all tolerate for the sake of convenience and cost.

The real thing requires legit effort and John could not summon legitimacy.

John took no issue with appropriating identity. It suited him. He saw himself as a horse to stud. Not a real horse like a workhorse or a racehorse. But a beast built to insert a foreign quality. And if John is a stud horse, then George is his show pony. What good stock.

And Iris his little grey donkey in a Mexican hammock. So cute. But not any kind of horse. Not even the best close-on horse like a zebra or gazelle. Iris is a pack animal from an underdeveloped nation. Sweet. Amusing even. Gets the job done but certainly not deserving of John's serious consideration.

Sometimes the truth is as sad as it is simple.

He had told her as much from the beginning. So she had accepted the statement as true and refrained from expectation. But then he said there were doubts about his marriage. George, he said, really wanted something he could not give her. Which was unfair because George deserves to get everything, and more than that, he would say calmly, as he rubbed circles in the small of Iris's damp back, tracing the sharp upturn toward her bum. A ski jump, he said. Then, you've got a young body. And then, turn over, Iris. And then, give me your face.

Look into my eyes when you come. Say my name. Tell me you love me.

So she adjusted expectation to meet changing information hand-delivered in a sex storm. Jesus, Jesus, the roads were basically impassable. But she would forge on in unfit weather for John. If there was an opening for the position of John's person, then Iris would readily fill that staffing gap. She was already doing so on a part-time, on-call, contractual basis. He had told her he probably, likely, almost definitely would not leave his wife.

But then he asked her to describe the wedding she'd imagined for herself as a girl.

Then he asked her to describe how that image had changed. And then he asked her to imagine him in this new image. And then he said he imagined himself in that image too.

Then he said he was already married.

Loops and loops of ready-whipped turmoil sprayed aerosol-style all over her before running his finger up over her belly and inside her.

But he told her he was an asshole. He had said.

This is logic men like John prefer to lean on. He had not forced her, she had kissed him back, got in the car, gone for a smoke, opened the door. Every time she had opened the door.

It's not like I beat her door down.

No. It's not like that. Not exactly.

Here is what it is like: John would regularly drunk text Iris from his car.

Unlock. Your. Door.

Iris, asleep in bed, would shoot up at the sight of the illuminated box on the nightstand. Look around the room. Wonder how close he was. How much time she had. Disoriented and confused, she would jet out of her bed at the sound of banging a few walls away.

This way John could pretend Iris was an accident that kept happening.

Certainly not the plan he had been planning every time he left his house since the first time he left his house. Never make plans because this seems intentional. Very nearly a relationship progressing naturally. Which could not be the case because John was already progressing over here with his wife.

No, it had to be scapegoated on circumstance and definitely not because Iris was the person he needed to see. Don't give her any ideas about her value.

Instead, John would fire a warning shot in the air mere moments before he arrived at her door. Sometimes while seated in his parked car just up on the curb where he would watch her lamp light. And then the hall light. And then the kitchen light. The little one over the stovetop she reaches for first because she is afraid of the dark. Afraid of living alone.

Afraid and alone.

John could imagine her stumbling slowly through her space as he approached. He knew her way so well. Each step hardening him against her as they grew nearer to each other until they could see each other through the frosted frame in the double pane. John resting his brow against it in a gesture he well knew would break her soft heart.

Because she loved him and he knew that well, too.

It was not real for John but it was real for Iris. It was Iris's real life and John used that against her. Maybe, perhaps, at some point, John even believed he cared for her. Say he did, or thought he did. Give him more benefit of the doubt than he deserves.

Pretend he's convinced he loves her.

Then why show up in the middle of the night and wake her from her sleep when he knows this will scare her? Why do that repeatedly and at random? Is that how John loves women? Is that what his love is like? Reckless. Hurried. Guilty. Horrifying.

Let me in, Iris.

Bellowed across the threshold. Echoing down the street. Threatening to wake the neighbours. Alert Olive. Annoy the couple living upstairs, their Yorkie barking barking. John exposing them both as he stands fists up, banging weakly for Iris to let him in. In the snow. The rain. Before dusk. After dawn. Holding cookbooks or a tool kit under his arm. Gatorade for tomorrow. The shambled facade. A pretence of friendship. Chatting up the elderly fellow across the street while holding a shovel.

Hard winter, b'y. Hard ol' winter.

Drinking a beer on the cement stoop leading down to her door. Or leaned against her shitty Golf as she stares up at him out of frame. Smoking a cigarette. Or sharpening his knives.

Actually, literally, sharpening knives bought especially

for Iris, who ate bananas when she ate anything at all. What the fuck would she cut with commercial grade kitchen knives? She doesn't even slice bread. She doesn't even eat it. John ignored every pixel that did not suit his picture of her. She was just a piece of skin to sear through. Something to envelop a bit of hunger. *Thank you for the sex, Iris* met with a shake of her head as she stood in the dark porch to see him out and up over the icy steps. She never had salt.

You can't fall up, she said. Thighs still wet.

John tut tutting at her oblivion. Of course you can fall up.

Stop pretending we're just fucking, John.

Sometimes uttered in exhaustion. Sometimes spoken with hands on his face. Into his mouth moments before a kiss. Attempting to breathe comprehension into his reluctant body. Because he has to know that this is not how the world works for Iris. She is not going to struggle in this snare indefinitely; she would sooner gnaw her own foot off and hop through a new world worse injured than before.

Life is not a fucking pop song. Jesus Christ, love, learn to adult.

But John lives his life in a mid-career Ryan Gosling movie. He fucking dies over forbidden groping in warm summer rain. Hair wet against a face in desperate need for him to reach out and tuck it behind an ear. Collars that crave quiet repositioning. A tag requiring tucking. John likes touching women without their permission. He stands behind Iris, puts his hands on her hips, presses his face into the nape of her in a public place and whispers.

The possibility of discovery is too tempting for him.

John's a wolf. Iris his Little Red Riding Hood. He must have whatever is in her basket.

The whole notion that he cannot stay clear of Iris is his most favoured notion. It places all the blame on her. It's a physical thing. He can't help himself. Men just can't help themselves. She knows what she does, little vixen, little minx. She moves her body like that on purpose. John has long been planting these ideas in her head. She's a lot of trouble, he has said knowingly to a customer with a wink.

Wink wink motherfuckers.

They've complimented him on his hostess and John has said that she really is something. That he is lucky to have her. Everyone should have an Iris, John has said. To any human willing to stop steady for five seconds, John has said veiled affectionate things to amuse himself.

Later he will undo them. They both know that he will take it all back.

He will drag out his hesitation in that long implying way. Others will nod in recognition for fear of seeming daft. John will say that he doesn't know if he'd go so far as to say Iris was great or gorgeous or a genius. She's okay. She's not bad-looking. She's kind of talented for a baygirl.

He will steal back from her every compliment as if everything about her was a gift he had bestowed. He will take everything back so he can give to another.

He will do so slowly so as not to draw suspicion.

And it stings Iris to watch John across the dining room listening intently to his wife, who has become increasingly animated in a discouraging way. George's apparent joy does not make Iris feel well.

The fact that this woman's pleasure brings about such discontent is wrong too. Iris knows.

JOHN THINKS HE'S having a stroke. He is actually stroking out this time.

This is the most time John has spent out on the floor in his whole career and he hates it out here, but he can't very well leave his wife and his girlfriend out here alone.

On fucking Valentine's Day.

The strained feeling across his chest he sometimes gets when he thinks on things returned when the dinner service playlist started. In the confusion of the day, he had forgotten making it. And now he hears the first few lovely soft bars of *High Violet* coasting through to the dining room and he knows he is fucked.

Tonight he is well and truly fucked.

He had thought many times in the past that his order was up but it hadn't been. Tonight, though, will be glorious. They are going to destroy him. And he deserves it. It will almost be a relief.

But he has to at least try to save himself.

John had poked his head out the kitchen door when the opening bars played. He had scanned the dining room for them and found them standing shoulder to shoulder, deep in conversation. He tried to take the temperature of the room, attempting to judge their body language, searching every ounce of physical knowledge to determine if the playlist had registered.

George was swaying softly. She loves this album. She doesn't know. She is still fine.

Iris was not swaying softly. She loves this album too. She does know. She is not fine.

It never occurred to him not to listen to the same music with them. Albums came out and everyone listened to them. That was how music worked. And of course they like the same music. They like the same man. It was easy. Simple even. He memorized the one hymn book and sang from it. Women love it when men serenade them. They think it's romantic.

It's not, though, not really, it's a lot of plagiarism.

John plagiarizes feelings of songwriters with record deals and sound studios. John fucks them both to the same sad songs. Thank god he can't play any instruments.

If John was in a band, he'd be dangerous.

John is dangerous enough just looking like someone who might play music. John looks like someone who might do a lot of things. But he doesn't. He's a critic. He has a lot of strong opinions on those that actually do the things. He's an armchair centre, a back seat driver, a closed door politico. He would never be caught out doing or saying things that would shatter the perfected image he has of being a man who does and says things. John is insubstantial and therefore unsubstantiated.

Which is how he fucking likes it.

He should have kept himself scarce. But oh no. George said why be a cook when you can be the chef? Iris said why feed the wealthy when you can feed the poor? And now his life will be ruined in one go because of a melancholy indie band from Parkdale or Williamsburg or some other jesus hipster place.

What's more, he's a little annoyed with himself for not

thinking of it. He had covered so many bases, was fully in the splits when this flew by him. He had not foreseen them caught together under a sound cloud of his own hormonal devising.

He had thought George would be out of town. He had thought it would make Iris happy.

Now each song feels like it's ushering in his own demise. This terrible love is his funeral march and he's the fucking spider. Of course he is. But even spiders have the drive to live. It's physiological. So John barks at Ben to turn it off. Put something else on, anything, he snaps. Maybe something a little more upbeat. Alternative or rock. Ben looked at him perplexed.

You want to play rock music in the dining room on Valentine's Day?

Yes, Jesus yes, electronic music, house even, make it rave for fuck sakes, John said in hushed and hurried tones. He didn't care if Ben put on fucking death metal right now as long as they did not continue through this particular melodic nightmare. God knows what Iris would do if they got to the end.

John vows that he will not call the cops on her if she attacks him. Never.

Or maybe. He might have to. It depends on how savage she gets.

If that broken bird starts to sing, John will have it caged.

He will say that she is emotionally unstable. A good person in a bad situation who misread the signs. He will say that some women are incapable of having male friends. He will suggest Iris is not fit for mixed company.

In need of extensive counselling. If it comes to it, he will insinuate that the last violent asshole was not really a violent asshole, to discredit her. He will use question marks to poke holes in her well-documented domestic abuse. He will imply that she is the liar. He will declare her crazy.

Bitches be crazy.

If it really comes to it, if he feels trapped and can see no other way, he will claim poor mental health. That he fucked her, and kept fucking her this whole time, to keep her from self-harming. Oh yes, he will say all this and more. He's got a script ready-made in his head. He's even tried the material out. On Iris.

These are the exact things he has said to her about George this past year to keep her compliant. And now, he will say these untrue things about her to whomever will listen. Even to people who don't know the circumstances of their impending rift. He will pre-emptively and discreetly slander Iris as a means to make her words less meaningful. And John knows he has the upper hand in any blame game willingly entered into.

Because Iris is a party girl and no one believes a party girl. Ever.

Better than a party girl even. A very good girl with a wild streak. Iris is ninety percent weak milky tea and ten percent two hundred proof moonshine. This manifestation of her character makes her no bother to defame. Everyone has seen her drunk and in tears at the back of Bar None. Never mind John is the reason why. John will confide in a whisper, as if it pains him to do so, that everyone knows Iris drinks.

John has maybe, likely, driven Iris mad.

He can see it in her and it scares the bejesus out of him. Across the dining room, she stands, some half-feral thing focused on him like a nearly caught serial killer looking for one last homicide before life imprisonment. He should have stayed in bed. Kept the restaurant closed all day. He could have blamed it on the storm. Made the weather an accomplice to his crimes.

Forget blame it on the rain, blame it on the snow.

Everyone lies for extra time in the bunk. John sure as fuck does. And he could have easily stayed in bed today. But there were the reservations. And food going off. And Iris.

There was Iris. He had been thinking about her, too. He meant to calm her down after their disagreement, if you could call her tantrums disagreements. He wanted to make her understand his position before she went off her head, telling all and sundry what they've been up to.

You need to talk to someone that is not me.

Who?

You must have someone.

My friends would never speak to me again.

They'll forgive you if you're honest.

They won't and I can't.

A doctor then.

I don't have a doctor.

Your wife.

Don't be so cruel.

Cruel?

You know that's fucking horrible.

My best friend won't speak to me anymore!

I told you not to tell her.

I used to be a different person. Nicer. Open.

You're the same person.

But I'm not, John, this has changed me.

You're going to tell everyone, I know it.

I might.

John catches a glimpse of Iris with an idle look on her face which means she's already drunk. It didn't take much. John realizes he hasn't seen her eat anything all day. And he reassures himself he will sort George and Iris out after dinner service.

Had to have the both of them, didn't you, you fucking asshole.

No one hates John more than John hates John.

Clock that, it's vital.

John can hear his team struggling to get the orders up in the kitchen. They are short-staffed and stressed. Half of them are hung because of rolling sessions of storm roulette these last few days. He is certain at least one of them is drunk now, but he can't be bothered to pinpoint the smell because the whole space reeks of steaming lobster and he's, well, John is experiencing higher than average levels of emotional distress. He is certain his bowels are going to come loose or he will burst into tears.

Ben finally finishes mixing highballs and changes the music to New Order which is a fucking amazing choice. John hates new wave! He never listened to it with anyone ever! Not even high school girlfriends!

John smooths out his whites. He raises and lowers his eyebrows a bunch to release some tension. He stretches out his mouth and says vowels to calm himself before going back into the heat. He can hear them yelling to the dish pit for pots and pans and Nan is flat out. Thank god he is long in the limbs, John thinks to himself as he catches a flash of black forearm grabbing up a frying pan and dunking it into the sink. There is never enough and John is always found lacking.

When John was a younger man, he wanted to achieve much. He wanted to win all the awards and go on the shows. John made a lot of notes in the margins of cookbooks, sketched out menus on napkins, spent hours alone at markets smelling things, wandering over the bog tasting bits of berries. He memorized edible flora and fauna. He believed that he could do this thing he was setting out to do. He knew it in his belly.

He would be a success.

When Georgina had come in yelling this morning he'd thought his goose was cooked.

John thinks solely in cliché food metaphors when he feels overwhelmed. The tackiness of the language is soothing. John has always sought out comfort in the tacky. He likes the way the word smacks together and sticks between his fingers.

This unfortunate path passed down from his father whose snarky voice narrates John's thoughts while punctuating the worst of them with a hard hacking smoker's cough.

Georgina brings home the bacon.

George is the big cheese.

Gigi's the breadwinner.

John's meal ticket.

John does not want to be his father's son in any way. He's a goddamn man. Not exactly his own man. But he is not his father's fucking son anymore at least. John wonders what it would feel like to belong to himself. He has thought about nothing else since last night when he got those hateful texts from Iris. Since the first day he saw her John thought, oh for fuck sakes, let her be a lesbian.

Iris was definitely not a lesbian.

But John has been fucking his life up since before he met Iris. He is used to feeling the pain of worry surging through his body. He feels less alive without it. The state of perpetual dread is what drew him to the kitchen. Every day of his life is a battle where John dies in his imagination constantly because he can't keep his hands to himself.

He has fucked Iris while Big George held court in the dining room. He took Iris out back to discuss the pairings before service had even finished. She knew damn well what pairings he meant but followed him anyway, and as he finished from behind her, hands on her steering-wheel hips, he caught a glimpse of an old overhead fan hood George had been nagging him to take to the dump and promised himself as he came that he would do that for her now. John's guilt made him a better husband.

Bad behaviours don't just miraculously disappear. They are but rearranged.

He tried to solidify an alternative arrangement. This was regularly punctuated by the sound of broken glass. Iris had learned long ago how to fire breakable things. Once she hauled a pot of boiling pasta off the stove and whipped it at the wall beyond him. And he yelled you could have hurt me and she yelled you hurt me all the time! And he said stop yelling at me and she said stop fucking your wife! And he said I can't and she said then let me go.

Iris sobbed, please, John, you have to let me go. Please, I feel like I'm going to die.

But John would not let Iris go.

He did not rightly know how. Instead, he continued to share his trauma around like orange slices. One for you. One for you. One for me. In this way he still retained the entire piece of fruit harboured inside bodies he inhabited. He needed to be near both of them to ensure his life had meaning. He would be a noteworthy addition to their Wikipedia pages. George would probably be the mayor and Iris some famous painter. And while John cannot sure summon greatness himself, he can lap it up from another source. Crack a coconut open shirtless and pour that milk into his mouth from a high extended right hand.

John has watched enough soft porn to know what the ladies like.

In the bedroom and the kitchen, he is in control in a way that brings about clear results.

He feels a sense of accomplishment every time a clean plate comes back. Each compliment paid the kitchen gratifies him. Bolsters him. He needed their feedback to go on. Constant and clear continuous approval. Going without, even for the smallest amount of time, was a punishment he could not stand.

And every day he thinks they may not come. They may not like it. Or they may not come again. John has to put out better than before. Combine things differently. In a way that no one has thought to do. Make something totally new out of these same parts until they can think of no better way to eat. Or be eaten.

Clap clap, round of applause, standing ovations for King John.

This is the level of swerving self-loathing, introspection and grandiose fantasy John routinely indulges in while claiming to be a simple cook who just wants to feed people. John has practised his Michelin Star speech to the point of obsession. He'll start up on growing up poor, everyone loves a make good story. Then he'll talk nonsense about making gorgeous food that connects with people. They'll die for that. Then he will drop in some general references about beauty and love while looking pensive. Women will be wet for miles. Food Network. Netflix. Vice. The new Anthony Bourdain. John thinks he is definitely better looking.

See how far out of field John can go. John is far flung.

A woman's voice rises from the dining room to cut into the kitchen. John abandons the beet mash so quickly the bowl spins on the shiny slick surface. The sous take note. Even Omi hears the wonk wonk rotation as he turns the water off. They all contemplate future employment at the sight of their employer running into the dining room. There is nothing cool about this place anymore.

But it is not John's wife or John's girlfriend doing the screaming.

It has nothing to do with him! John thinks it is a miracle and is momentarily overjoyed until realizing, my god, of course it does, this is still his restaurant. And he calmly approaches the table to investigate.

A beautiful young woman in a red dress is screaming at a man with similar features.

SHOULD FUCKING PHONE Mom on you.

Amanda is yelling that she should inform their mother that her only son is drunk and high in a restaurant on Valentine's Day with the piece of shit that sexually assaulted his own sister.

The red bow belt across Amanda's middle is peering directly in Calv's face as she slides out of her snow boots into the fine pink pumps she has brought for dinner. Calv clocks the matching nails and pumps. He knows what he says next will escalate the situation further but he is drunk and high with Roger accidentally. He has little recourse.

Jesus, look at you, you're not going to the fucking ball, my dear.

This line gets him nowhere because Amanda knew she wasn't going to the fucking ball.

She was going somewhere better.

Right up to getting dressed a couple hours ago, Amanda had thought she would spend the evening sitting in a beautiful dining room with high vaulted ceilings and thick embossed velvet wallpaper. She had planned on sipping ridiculously expensive wine that perfectly matched her pink gold watch looking better than a Renaissance painting across from her man on this manufactured holiday celebrating love. Amanda intending to be fucking breathtaking in all pink and red right down to her lacy underwear.

She had waxed every inch of her goddamn body for this night.

She had done so after finding a receipt from the Golden Tulip jewellery store in Freddy's coat pocket while looking for matches to light a scented candle in the bathroom.

But the storm meant the better restaurant had decided to remain closed because it was not safe for people on the roads. While Amanda agreed with this decision in principle, she did not agree in actuality because she had not bought groceries. Amanda refused to eat pre-bagged salad and nacho chips while getting proposed to. No goddamn way. This was going to happen tonight.

She had not waxed her fucking arms for nothing.

And so she thought, okay, The Hazel. They ate there all the time. That could be okay. Named for a nan instead of a pop. There was charm in that. Something reminiscent of the bay. They could still drink fine champagne. The Hazel had better spirits than the food half the time anyway. And they made these little beeswax candles she liked, and there would be fresh snow to walk home in. Freddy would take her arm in his protective way and it would be sweet and thoughtful. Amanda thought the whole thing might be salvaged and proceeded to dress accordingly.

But here is her idiot twin brother strung out before eight with her most loathed human.

For the love of Christ, Calvin, what the fuck is wrong with you?

And she is whispering now as she leans in to her brother's face that she's not gone on Donna but she hopes Donna gives him the back of her jesus boot for this.

I hopes she tears you a new asshole.

Amanda goes full bay when she is angry at Calv. She

also goes full bay when she is about to come but that's not pertinent currently. Just a reflection of Amanda's inescapable linguistic heritage that even four years of theatre school and a thousand hours of voice coaching could not master. Passions cannot be coaxed out of Amanda, and that's fine because Frederick is wholly enamoured of the gibberish talk Amanda mouths moments before she sleeps. Amanda sometimes finds it a weird frustration that the man who loves her loves her just as she is, because it means she wasted a lot of time trying to change for shitty men she had mistaken for being not shitty.

Though some men you can't even mistake for not shitty as they are so clearly the worst.

Like Roger. And maybe, and this bit makes Amanda very sad, and maybe her brother.

Both men clock the lack of conjugation in Amanda's speech.

Amanda no longer fully in control of her faculties and capable of telling tales.

How long did it take you to get right into the blow? she cracks so loud that Calv darts his eyes around the room to see who has overheard.

I mean, my god, Roger has got a half gram hanging out of his nose. Why do you beat around with him? He is so fucking gross, Calvin! Cocaine is so fucking gross! It's not even real fucking feelings you're feeling. It's not even real fucking coke. It is probably cut to shit. And how do you even have the money to be at it? You got no job. You are unemployed, idiot. Lord fucking reeving, if I finds out you're after borrowing money from Mom for blow I will string you up worse than what they does to them poor Peruvian farmers you exploits for your fake jesus good time with that raging asshat.

The verbal onslaught that Amanda is bombarding Calv with now looks to be giving him an aneurysm. He's rubbing his head and face every which way. The pressure upon him is leaving red blotchy marks on his skin. Though it could also be the food and drinks he has ingested. Amanda has seen Calvin eat five different kinds of meat before two p.m. They call it Sunday dinner though it is usually Calvin's Sunday breakfast as the first meal he eats after waking up hungover.

Calvin plays his Saturday card wrong every week.

He also regularly plays his Thursday and Friday card wrong. Donna has confiscated his Monday, Tuesday and Wednesday cards and Sunday he is just too full of meat to play. At least when he's home for a visit. That's what Susie says when Amanda gets worked up about the heavy drinking. That he's only home for a visit sure.

You don't even know where that coke comes from? Or what it actually costs humanity for you and fucknuts to get on the rips? No, you know nothing and your ignorance hurts people, Calvin. Bolivian teenagers found in the woods with their heads cut off, all those black boys shot in the street, women made mules to get gear across the border so you can snort shit coke in some townie restaurant on a Tuesday night. On fucking Valentine's Day! But you don't care about those people, do you? You don't care about anyone. Not even yourself. You are a careless man. I mean, my god, don't you read the news? Or watch it on that way too fucking big television you got? There's

351

fentanyl in that now, you fucking moron. You are going to end up in jail or dead!

The thought of Calvin dead breaks Amanda's spirit a little and she softens beneath her own words. She is sick of being mad at her brother. She is tired of screaming at him. Yelling at him to read a fucking book never results in him reading a fucking book.

She doesn't know why she bothers. He doesn't appear to want anything more from being alive so why hound him? It only upsets her mother and father to see them so separate. Susie forever reminiscing over them as babes in the bassinet rubbing each other's backs. The first time Amanda was sent home from school for fighting. Having to turn the truck around as soon as they was in through the door to go get Calvie. Both sent home for defending the other. And Susie never minded at all that they got suspended. Little nippers they were, too small to fight fair so resorted to using their teeth. Susie gave them the appropriate talking to but she was actually proud as plum pie that they was looking after each other.

Roger stirs at the remark about jail.

Roger is like a bluebottle come to in the windowsill after spring sunshine has warmed the ledge. Though dormant for all of this due to the conditions of his mind, he is suddenly in a frenzy, darting like a mad thing off the glass wall of words Amanda has hauled shut in front of them. Roger cannot handle the thought of jail even hypothetically.

Amanda is going on about things in the hypothetical now and this is not a word he understands. They all blames him for his ignorance. Laughs at him for not knowing the things they failed to teach him. Somehow it was Roger's fault he never knew how World War II started. Roger only knew what they taught in the movies. And it's not that he never passed. He wrote the notes off the chalkboard just like everyone else in World Geography. But it was just words. Didn't mean fuck all to him then and it don't mean fuck all to him now.

They was just words. Meaningless.

So he don't clearly know what is being said around him half the time which has always made him uneasy. Amanda does that every time she sees him on purpose, he allows. She throws words he don't recognize at him which makes him feel all the more worthless and undeserving of her attention. Because he does think she looks pretty in her red dress with her loose curls hauled back like that to the one side. Roger is always filled with a desire to hug Amanda when she wears her hair curly. He don't care much for her straight hair especially when she got it cut short. He has told her it makes her look like a dyke and she has told him to fuck off worrying about her. She has barked across a church basement during the Christmas carol service that Roger Squires can never mind her hair cause he was never getting handy to it. And people would look at Roger waiting for him to say something, which he always did.

He never had the right words in he's head so he said the wrong ones.

Roger's knows Amanda's hair is only caught out curly when it gets wet. He knows that it falls in ringlets round her face as it dries. Springing twists you could put your finger through if you didn't have right sausage hands like he's own. And this evening's snow had settled in her hair nice and she had looked like some kind of angel when she pulled off her purse and coat in that way she does without even looking around first to see who is looking at her cause she don't care anyhow. And even though they ain't never been boyfriend and girlfriend, Roger has always thought on her as his Mandy. Ever since they was little.

He don't care if Freddy Fuck Face is stood up behind her to help peel off her coat, she's still his, but he makes a note to himself: help women take off their coat cause they likes that.

Roger has to make a lot of these notes. Because just like wars and words, he don't know the basic stuff about women neither cause no one taught him when he was young. Don't knock any one up. That's what he was told. Don't get anyone pregnant, said like it was the only important piece of information worth knowing. Wrap it up. Pull it out. Don't, repeat, do not come inside her even if she says she's on the pill.

This was what Roger knew about girls: don't leave anything behind in them.

You needs to watch yourself, Mandy.

Fuck you, Roger.

You should shut up before someone shuts you up.

Rog, knock that off.

Excuse me, sir, you can't speak like that in here.

She talking all loose like I'm afraid of her but I'm not.

Rog, what did I tell you earlier about leaving my sister alone?

Sir, you need to stop yelling.

Me? She's the one who started yelling!

You're so high, you can't even hear yourself.

Let's all just settle down.

She come in here looking for a racket.

Yes, that's why I go to restaurants on Valentine's Day —

She's crazy —

I go to restaurants on Valentine's to bawl at you.

—I'll give you something to bawl about if you're not careful.

I would love nothing more than to call the cops on you!

You're such a slut, Mandy.

My name is Amanda!

Really, sir, you can't talk like that in here.

Who are the fuck are you anyway?

See Calvin, see what kind of company you keep?

I knows your fucking face, don't I?

I think you should leave.

Me? I been here throwing down money all day.

Yes, and now it's time you go.

And it's time for you to stop being a faggot.

And John is there beside Damian with his hand on the back of Roger's shirt collar and Roger is up and out of his chair, and John is almost grateful for the physical motion he is required to perform in order to correct this situation as the woman in the red dress starts to cry a little now.

Coat, Damian. Now.

And Damian grabs the ski-doo jacket off of the back of the chair where it has spent almost all afternoon, and even as John rushes Roger through the restaurant toward the door he's explaining in cool tones that the customer is not always right in his restaurant.

He is always right in his restaurant.

And no one calls a member of his wait staff a faggot, least of all a skeet with rock hanging out of his face. And John is giving a small speech on respecting human dignity as he moves past Iris.

She could not fucking roll her eyes back in her head farther.

GEORGE IS CHARMED by the scene.

She had stood horrified over by the linen vestibule holding folded cloth napkins in a stack between both palms. Transfixed by the language. The man's sharp descriptors came as no surprise. His nature held firm to everything George presupposed about the class of people that caused scenes such as this in dining rooms such as these.

Raw skeet, she had thought when she walked past the table hours earlier.

The actress's partner was wiping her eyes with his shirt sleeve as the other man gathered up phones and keys and things before heading out the door. The scorned-looking one did not make eye contact with the lady in red, who begged feebly for him to please not be mad at her as he walked toward the hostess station.

This too made no sense to George at all.

Why in heaven's name would this sober, sensible-looking woman request forgiveness from the wastage that was nearly too cockeyed to manoeuvre around the other seated diners? Clearly it was he who should be ashamed of himself. And yet it was the sister who was repenting. Absurd.

The evening could be saved, though. The energy in the room could be righted with a little change in music. So George returned the music to the previous playlist, which was much more appropriate anyway. Ben knew nothing about setting the mood. No wonder he was still single. "Anyone's Ghost" settled the room and people returned to eating before their food got cold.

John had behaved right gallant, which made George feel vindicated for the day.

It had been hard to give up her library. But her father had assured her it was the only way to recoup the loss while saving face. He and the Mayor would announce the casino development and the new restaurant in the same breath. No one would ever have to know that John had run The Hazel into the ground. They would say they were closing up for renovations and repay the debt to Canada Revenue while claiming transition.

The whole of town would be consumed by the heritage houses coming down.

No one would notice that The Hazel did not reopen. Then they would call the casino resto Georgina's and people would love the feeling of rolling the word over their tongues. It would make them feel at home and comfortable but also brand new and young again. It wouldn't matter in the least that it was inside of a warehouse of gambling where once history stood. They were rewriting history.

It would be a destination, Big George said, and the Mayor agreed after attempting to disagree.

Big George had steadied Major David's opinions with a quick reference to having bought a house one could not afford. There would be no disputes from City Hall. So it was that the riddle fence admired for a century on a hilly heritage plot went from becoming a restored Victorian library from George's dreamy vantage to a casino of her father's magisterial design. George felt shortchanged even with her dad's rebranding.

But she still had John. And she would have a family, so her happiness remained visible.

Iris hates how happy George looks watching John deal with the drunken man.

It is not a right feeling to have. To hate another person's pride. Loathe their joy. Everyone knows that these are not right feelings even while having them. But you cannot help them. Iris looks down at herself. The little white half-pinafore George insists she wear has a strawberry stain on it from leaning against the bar to reach up for the wine glasses. George doesn't wear a pinny. Iris examines her dress underneath. She will always think of it as her emancipation dress. She wished she had known this upon dressing herself this morning. She would have chosen something more flattering to leave him. But she did not know she would end up here today. She is not even supposed to be here.

She was only meant to be going to the bank to pay her cellphone bill. Which she has not done. She reaches into her purse and is comforted by the little glow before recollecting that this is no kind of insurance against disconnection. She has to call someone to see if the call will make its way through the network. But she doesn't even know who to call. She calls Ben. Ben won't mind. Ben is a nice man. When women call him, he answers his phone.

But he will not receive any calls from Iris tonight because her call has been rerouted to her network provider so she hangs up.

There is no point in begging them to turn her phone back on until her debt is paid, and she has no way to do that. Her credit cards are at home. And maxed out. Iris looks down at this tiny hurt monster that has been used to harness her and vows to never turn it back on. She will start over. Get a different number. This is what women do, right? When men don't respect their boundaries. They set up roadblocks. Wall themselves in. Access denied.

Iris is mesmerized watching Ben cut more citrus and wishing she liked him. Wishing it had not been John that she had liked. Maybe John would have left her be if she had been dating Ben. Or maybe if she wore hideous clothing. Or maybe or maybe…

Or maybe nothing.

John would fuck forbidden fruit wrapped in a soiled liquor store bag. In all instances, in every scenario, what a woman wears is irrelevant.

What Iris got on don't matter at all. At all. And Iris knows this, but the words John whispers into her ears have lodged themselves in her brain and she worries she will have to scrape herself of every syllable crusted onto her box lid. Each and every one delivered like naughty take-away from John Fisher's handsome mouth. John knows well what manipulates her.

Though sometimes when John cries, Iris softly thinks, fuck your crocodile tears, buddy.

This time. The next time. Whenever George is out of town. Sometimes when she isn't. Ouch. That stings.

Overlap is upsetting. It makes everyone feel yucky. But who is gross? Is it grosser for Iris who knows? Or George who doesn't? Or is it maybe, just maybe, grosser for the man who moves between bodies like there is nothing a quick shower and shampoo can't fix? Made new again every time he runs his head under the warm tap. Shakes the water clear, towels his abs off and wipes the stream from the mirror to survey his stance.

A few side flexes. To the right. The left. Everything is okay. He is still hot. John will be fine.

They may not be, all the ones in his wake, but John manages to get up and go go go.

And yes, Iris opened the door. Continued to open the door. Stood in the dim hallway light in her nightdress. A girl-woman wearing a light pink knee-length gown with white piping around the collar. This nightdress will go missing later. But this night, this night she remembers now during her new reckoning where she watches John's wife watch John, on this night she was wearing it and panties covered in light gold stars.

You're a star, Iris. You're a fucking star, you are.

John wants nothing to do with real girl-woman Iris. He wants the picture he painted in his head earlier while listening to Ben confess his feelings over pints of local lager that John will mark as spillage later and blame on the staff. Doesn't matter which. Iris is a good candidate. His wife believes she's an alcoholic anyway. George will believe anything. John has mixed half-truths with bold-faced lies deliciously. And now there is nothing he couldn't tell her. John can convince women what they're seeing is not what they're seeing. He is that good at lying.

He has had so much practice. He will put whomever in whatever place he wants. And some nights it was Iris he wanted to put in place.

Go put on my shirt, he said.

And she had. The blue one hanging on her door atop her matching dress. Under his favourite tie. Left hanging there since they had attended the Restaurant Association party months before. Left hanging there because they both liked to wake up and see it hanging there. Or at least Iris did. It shone out at her blue when she opened her eyes. A beacon of reality proclaiming that she wasn't crazy. Look, here on the door is tangible textile proof that this is happening. She was not crazy. Is not crazy. Or blind.

Iris is seeing things now.

George is counting the candles on the bar again. She told Iris earlier there were not enough to turn the tables over thrice. Iris, who had been manning the book as the cancellations rang in, said they would likely not need as many candles as anticipated. Iris had motioned at the corner picture window that had long gone white.

Because of the storm, she said. There was no chance they would have walk-ins enough to make up the cancellations. To which George responded that it was possible. Nothing else was open. But, but there's a blizzard, Iris tried again. We shouldn't even be here.

You don't decide that though, do you?

And she was right. Iris didn't decide that or anything. They all just fucking acted upon her. And she had searched the room for Damian's eyes. He owed her. He would rescue her from this conversation. But Damian was busy recovering from the baymen who had been clearly doing cocaine in the bathroom all evening. They had reeked of bathroom adhesive. Everyone could tell they were high. They had a peculiar look about them. Rabid and speedy. Overly suspicious of Damian.

Are you paying attention to me, Iris? I asked you a question.

And Iris had not been paying attention to George then but she sure as hell was paying attention to her now. This was gory stuff and Iris wished a man with a chainsaw would finally saw her in half.

George had wanted to know what her plan had been if there hadn't been a storm.

They would have needed the not nearly enough candles then. She was insisting that Iris should have made more. She was questioning Iris's lack of forethought. And Iris wanted so badly to say how sorry she was that there aren't enough candles. George advised them to burn the candles to the wicks to preserve ambience. They were only wasting wax the way they burned them now, barely half burned out. And Iris tried to caution it was because the glass jars purchased in bulk from the dollar store did not hold up to the heat. But George did not heed her and said it would be fine to burn them down tonight. So Iris let it be as she had no fight left in her for atmospheric lightness.

Iris cannot even tell George something to her face.

George is here this evening to fix everything and Iris is so fucking angry at this woman. She blames George. She looks across the dining room and she blames her. It is George's fault. She let this happen. She keeps letting this happen. John can do whatever he likes to Iris while everyone pretends he is doing nothing to her. Even his wife. And trying to not cry at work is every woman's nightmare since women entered the workforce.

Iris bites down on the whole of her bottom lip and wills herself to not remember.

That night Iris had turned on her heels, walked back into her bedroom, pulled the pink nightgown warm with sleep over her head before pulling John's blue shirt down over her. She felt small in this much larger shirt. She didn't think about what she was doing. She just did as she was told. In fact, she liked doing what she was told. It was a relief. And she walked out into that pool of dim hallway light dressed in John's fantasy and stood in front of him as he looked her top to tail smacking his drunken lips like a shipwrecked sailor finally ashore. And he stepped toward her, mere steps, and placed one arm around her neck, sweeping her curls into his large left hand while he placed the whole of his right hand over her pubis, cupping her pussy entirely, his four fingers curved against the curve of her before hooking her up onto her tiptoes and whispering into her right ear, so close she could feel the moist word on her lobe.

Mine.

Just that. Up. Higher on her toes.

Mine.

Give that some space while Iris tries to keep her feet on the ground.

Mine.

Not I love you.

Mine.

Not I was thinking of you.

Mine.

Not even I wanted to see you.

Mine.

John forgot all the trappings of romantic relationship he had used to wrap Iris up in pretend love feelings.

You're ruined now for other men.

In that moment a fissure cracked through and formed inside her as his hand hook lifted her high up by the cunt.

I've ruined you.

He told her this again and repeatedly just after she climaxed when there were no border guards standing to deflect his whispered assault and so the words just snuck in, took up residence in her heart.

Ruined. Ruined, she thought with sweat still in the small of her back.

Iris would never sleep soundly next to him again. And that night, after he had satiated himself, Iris would pick up that same phone that John used to harass her and point it at that door still housing that dress and that tie. The shirt now a wrecked victim on the floor. She will point that phone of hers at this sight that she sees every day and she will take another photograph. Iris will text that photograph to Jo in the middle of the night and these new photos that come in after dark will exist as an unspoken dialogue between the two estranged women consisting of one word: insurance.

That is the sinister admission no one was ready to voice.

Iris knows then, already, very early on, that there is something seriously wrong going on and she is unsure if she will make it out okay. Even after they've stopped speaking to each other, Iris adds to the conversation in photos because she knows she is in trouble. John and George are older and wealthier, a powerful couple with influential friends. Iris is young and poor, a single nobody with very little and no one now that she has alienated everyone who cared for her. John and George can't even take Iris's power because she has none.

Some women have so little power, it is laughable.

John would laugh at her while saying her name. Iris, Iris, Iris don't cry.

He would laugh when she burned his cookbooks, page by page, in the sink.

He would laugh when she cut up his whites to scrub the bile-covered bathroom floor.

He would laugh at her because aren't women funny? Not funny intentionally like a good comedian. But you know, funny. John would offer this malicious nonsense unsolicited to further solidify Iris's failings as a woman and a human. Because the implication, effectively implied, is that Iris is guilty. If George was innocent of all and everything, then that means Iris is guilty. Though there is a small feeling in the grimy pit of Iris, well beyond the excavators and heavy machinery, that this is not wholly true bedrock John is slyly propping her on.

Feeling the ground shift within her made Iris feel thoroughly groundless.

This was what fuelled John further and helped him poison Iris against herself in piecemeal. What was worse than this was the uneasy fact that Iris was well aware of what she was ingesting daily. There is nothing so tragic as a woman aware a man is filling her full of toxins while remaining powerless to stop it. It is a grotesque poisoning.

John loves Iris best when she is sick and bleeding. He cannot resist fucking an open wound. It was titillating to screw her through a fever. Or when she had drunk herself slurry.

I don't want to be with you this way. You have to respect my boundaries. Stop making excuses for your shitty behaviour. This is not fair. It is not right. Fine. Go be with your wife. Just be with her then if you want to be with her. Leave me alone. You have to just leave me alone. I don't want to be treated like this anymore. You will always treat me this way. Please leave. Never come back. Don't try to contact me. Respect what I am saying. I don't accept your apology. Stop saying you're sorry. Just be a better man. Make better choices. Jesus, John. Just leave it. Leave it be. Just leave me alone.

But John would take a run at Iris always and forever until she made it impossible for him to ever do so again. And she knew it. She fucking well knew it all along but had hoped against hope that she might be wrong. That it might be prevented. But John would not be put off Iris. Or the next Iris. Or the one after that. John is a fuck collector. And Iris recognized herself for the bit of tail he thinks her to be and it makes her very angry.

Despite all her rage she is still just a rat in this cage.

But she is still raging.

She has not given in or given up on the rage. It persists. Her rage is not a new story. Not even for our Iris. But the ending must change so Iris decides she will change it. Expecting otherwise is just fucking foolish. Iris wants to stop lying to herself. She wants everyone to stop lying to themselves.

And she wants to gnaw John's cock off as a matter of public safety.

Iris thinks she really needs to find someone else to make her come. Or burn down this jesus restaurant. She should set this fucking place on fire. She recognizes this is not sensible or generous or even feasible but Iris is tired and hungry and hurt. She didn't eat family dinner with the rest of the staff today because George has been here all afternoon lording over her like she has nothing to offer. Maybe she doesn't.

To John, Iris has nothing. Is nothing.

She's nothing to me, he will say soon. Very soon he will start saying Iris meant nothing to him and say it as often as he feels it is necessary to clear his name and a way forward.

But Iris is not nothing.

She's a person.

BEN HAS SERVED the red dress and her boyfriend a complimentary cocktail with cherry pieces ringed up by maple sugar to calm them. They are starting to settle into the sweet warmth when Damian approaches the pair. He does not want to. He has told Queen Bitch it is a bad idea to do so. But Queen Bitch is buoyed by some formidable mystery win and tells him to question the young woman about the drunken men who have been removed from the building.

Someone should pay their bill. And that someone should be her.

Damian has reiterated that the bill is rather steep given that they had been downing drinks with recreational assistance for the better part of the day and evening, but Queen Bitch doesn't mind that much.

Not my problem, she says. Tell the sister, she says.

So Damian is asking Amanda if she can contact her brother who never actually intended to leave without paying. Calvin is all kinds of things but bold is not one of them. Dine-and-ditch would be well beyond his level of initiative. To do so without first clearing the whole process with Roger was unthinkable. And Roger had been thrown out by the owner so that conversation had certainly not occurred. Calvin had just followed Roger without thinking through the consequences, because that is what Calvin does.

He follows Roger. He is a follower.

And Damian can see how much it pains Amanda to say this about her brother. He reaches out and puts his hand on her shoulder. The boat neck shows off her fine collarbone and he compliments her on the dress. She says she ordered it from a favourite shop in Belfast and Damian knows this is noteworthy. Amanda is wearing a special occasion dress, and Damian frowns. Not at her but at the evening in general. The very need of it grieves him. He wonders where Tom is tonight. He hopes he is home alone somewhere with their cat. The cat. Tom's cat now, he supposes. In Damian's mind, he hopes Tom is missing him, wondering if he is also alone. Tom probably knows exactly where he is. So it's not like Damian can even pretend Tom might be trying to reach him. Tom could reach him every way a human can be reached. Damian didn't even ask for the house key back. He didn't even change the locks.

He should not have yelled at Olive.

He was outside chain-smoking during staff dinner. He could not sit there with them and pretend Queen Bitch was not sitting in Iris's chair. John laughing and eating too much to hide his repulsiveness. Shovelling food in everyone's direction. Food fucking them into silence while Iris was folding table linens in the vestibule.

Not hungry, she said when the sous asked her to join them. Already ate, she said when Ben urged her to sit next to him. But they knew well enough that she had not. They had all been held hostage in the building together since lunch. And she was here when they mostly arrived so it was impossible for her to have eaten earlier. Maybe breakfast.

But you were supposed to eat more than once a day.

Not that Damian is excelling exactly in eating but he knows you're supposed to eat. He had tried. Sat down with the coconut green curry soup anticipating the warm hit to his belly. But he couldn't get through it. It was too awful. Queen Bitch praising the curry, commenting on the lime, suggesting John make it at home or more often. She cannot remember having it. Ben piping in, as if unable to resist, how that was odd because John made it at work all the time, at least once a week.

Because it was Iris's favourite.

And the barely discernible twinge is clocked before Queen Bitch decides to shrug it off and carry on complimenting her husband's cooking. Shrug it off by launching into a detailed recounting of the first time John cooked for her, while Iris sits on the floor in the vestibule guarded by the fine French doors pulled close around her. Damian can tell she is a little bit crying as she folds the napkins into bunny ears and small swans. Delicate romantic gestures come naturally to Iris. What a waste.

Queen Bitch is speaking loud enough for the anecdote to carry across the dining room and it is rather hurtful that she has to on purpose remind Iris that John is her husband. Everyone is well aware. Now anyway.

So Damian does not eat the curry, as a show of solidarity. He looks down at the ice shrimp floating amongst the water chestnuts and thinks that he will wish later he had eaten it. Later when he is trudging through the snow without even a slice of Sal's to sustain him. Later when he is drunkenly opening and closing cabinets that house old crackers and an abandoned bag of almond slices. Later when he is spooning just salsa into his mouth because he has not properly eaten food in days, Damian will remember the citrus soup with fresh cilantro and wish he had eaten it.

But now he is still loyal to some notion of friendship and he does not even clear his place.

He just gets up after having a spoonful and goes outside to smoke. This will enrage John. Any perceived slight is enough to send him over the edge. He freaks when customers add salt. John's father always adds salt without tasting as if John's mother was not even deserving of the pretence that she had adequately cooked anything in her life. His father just dumps salt in, remarking on how he *knows* it is too fresh. After, he may even remark that he wasn't fussy on whatever had once sat atop of a plate he just wiped clean with the heel of bread. John's mother taking it all as John simmered and seared at the other end of the table. Just to hear a patron request salt and pepper shakers sends John into an unholy frenzy, blurting that it was already perfectly seasoned as he paces around the kitchen. John thinks his way is the right way. He does not allow much for personal taste. Everything contrary to him is shit.

Leaving the table to smoke makes John crazy.

But he won't say fuck all about it today. Damian knows it. He's probably not working here for much longer anyhow so he is taking some liberties. Besides, he is half cut and has no appetite for curry. Jesus, of course that's what John made for Valentine's lunch. Gross, b'y.

And them fuckers from the hotel had stuck around. As if Damian didn't have enough to deal with. The right ugly one kept asking if they knew each other. Asked if Damian ever played any Triple A hockey. Blew through his food like a missioned man. His risky-mission-almost-definitely-possible was in one of the too many pockets on the sleeve of his stupid snowmobile jacket, Damian figured. And it wasn't long after dessert that the two of them started their steady tag-team trips to and from the bathroom. Handing off like no one in the dining room had eyes.

Everything had made Damian snap at Olive when she came around looking for a smoke.

That, and fear.

He had bawled at her when she came around the corner to ask for a cigarette. He laced into her about sneaking up on him. Bitched her out for being places where she wasn't supposed to be all the time. Told her off about taking Iris's boots and complained that he only had three smokes left for the whole night. Damian had said everything he could think to get her to leave before the men saw her. Or she saw them. Who knew what they might do? Maybe rape her again! That's what rapists do, right? Rape.

So he tried to scram her off like a stray dog. Get on. Go. Get.

But Olive just looked further hurt. Beyond her normal regular agony. And so Damian gave her his last twenty and told her to get her own jesus smokes.

Get a whole deck, he said. Smoke yourself silly. Smoke yourself to death sure, girl.

Damian had been mean to her face. The exchange had confused Olive, though she decided Damian was obviously on drugs and went off in search of an open store in the storm. She was actually delighted. She had change enough in her pocket to buy them a deck apiece! She would bring Damian's back to him because he was stuck at the restaurant. With John. Ugh. Damian could probably definitely use cigarettes and it would be like she had done something to earn hers. Iris might even give her a ride home because John's real wife was here so Iris would be going home on her own.

The last Damian saw, Olive had turned to walk toward the gas station that stays open late.

Now, the red dress and her bow are once again rightfully twisted. Amanda is attempting to call her brother on the phone. She has already sent him a number of increasingly threatening texts concerning not paying for his fucking bender.

CALV HASN'T HAD a chance to deal with the mounting notifications on his phone yet.

He hasn't even thought to look at it. Each little red flag flies a warning about his life but he is too busy chasing Roger from bar to bar on a fiendish hunt for more blow. Roger says he needs to find another gram in order to drive his truck home. Roger says he can't leave it downtown in the storm. It will be destroyed if he does so. The skeets will have at it.

Roger tells a story about waking up in the back of a parked Corolla years ago. He was after snapping the side-view mirrors off himself and bringing them in the car with him. He woke up with one held tight to he's chest. Calv can barely hear the words what for the blowing snow but he is pretty sure Roger says he pissed in the driver's seat and slept in the passenger's seat.

And Calv is yelling, what do you mean you pissed in the driver's seat? Like in a pop bottle or something, right?

But Roger is after moving on to a new topic. He's zipping between stories.

Calv suggested calling a cab to double them home and they tried for a time but there are hardly any cars on the road. Snow in combination with any holiday means you are walking the streets in your finest duds like a streel. Roger says it's not fucking dignified. He thinks walking is beneath him. They stop into the Celtic Hearth to warm their hands by the dryer in the men's room. Roger gums the baggie before tossing it in the urinal. Not enough to straighten up a pixie sure, he says, before heading upstairs to ask the bartender if he knows where they can find some party favours.

Roger does not wash his hands.

The twenty-two-year-old bartender looks Roger over and says she don't know where *he* can find party favours. Roger don't hear her hit the *you* hard but Calv clocks it and gets them out of Celtic Hearth before buddy b'y taps in to her disdain. Them young ones is right provocative. They're doubling back toward The Hazel again. Roger says he knows this shitbox where they can for sure get blow. Calv cautions to maybe not call the place a shitbox while they are there. He doesn't think the regulars will be enamoured with them even if they know it's true. It's like he can call Amanda a bitch but nobody else can. And then he suggests maybe not announce they are looking for blow real loud like he did in the grimy wine bar that smelt of sewer. One woman sitting at the bar actually thought they were narcs cause of Roger's lack of propriety. Her friend agreed that it was a pretty heatbag move even for such obvious assholes. No one else would make eye contact. So Calv is preaching discretion which is pretty rich considering the fucking state of the two of them.

Roger is saying, yeah yeah, I got this, I got this, Calvy.

But it don't seem like he actually got fuck all when they gets inside the shitbox. Seems like he just looks at the three people sitting at the bar and says *yayo* in a variety of ways. Like this:

Yay oh.

Ya yo.

Yayo!

Yah yo...

Ya yoh.

Yayo?

Yayo yayo!

It is like listening to a bay baby seal beg for cocaine in the coldest dive yet. They are looking at Roger like he is someone out on a day pass they are considering sacrificing for media coverage. This is not a friendly room. They are right hostile in here. Calv thinks they should not be here at all. Some dives will accept anyone with cash but the bartender is in no hurry to pour the round of shots Roger has ordered for the works of them.

One for yourself, too, Roger says, oblivious.

Whatever you wants, he says. I got lots of dough, he says.

Calv thinks he is going to get them killed. He takes in the room. There are two skinny guys and one woman. It is the woman he thinks they might have to worry about in this instance. She looks very capable of throwing lighter fluid. Might even have a pocket knife. For protection.

And the bartender looks to a dark-haired woman who raises her eyebrows in permission.

He mixes lemon drops as Roger makes his case for an eight-ball. He says he'll share with the works of them. Or a gram if it's dry around. Or whatever they got on them is where Roger lands after the shots hit their stomachs. They've been shooting booze while on this campaign trail. Roger claims it is so they can leave right away but Calv knows it is because Roger thinks it makes him look tough. That, and he's not got a lot more space for tossing rum and Cokes into himself. The burps coming from him are a wild mixture of food, pop and blow. And something worse.

Rot. Calv thinks Roger might be rotten inside.

All pretence of sobriety, once maintained with the assistance of their good friend Charlie, has been abandoned and Roger barely turns his face away to release wind. He has his hand across his belly like a man in distress and the dark-haired one looks at her companions and questions Roger's reality. Is this guy for fucking real? she asks no one and everyone at the same time before looking straight at Calv, who is honestly kind of scared of her. He is not at full life force just now and she looks like someone who might self-identify as a feminist.

These women have always worried him. Amanda says if he's not a feminist then he's a fucktard, but Calv thinks he'd rather be a fucktard if these are the only two available options. Roger has downgraded his request to a rip because can't they see he's in punishment here. He says, c'mon, b'y, ate too much. And the dark-haired one stands before saying he looks like a person who does a lot of everything too much.

But she tells them to come the fuck on so he will shut up begging and heads toward the toilet.

Roger thinks he can drive again now. He says he got a window open where they can get the truck home. Calv tried to convince him that the dark-haired one was into him but even Roger's not stunned enough to fall for that. Or not openly. He secretly grabbed at her in the ladies' while Calv was having a smoke in the men's, but she gave him an elbow to the side of the face and said the word *never* very slowly to make him comprehend. And they was outnumbered so Roger bawled that it was time to go to Calv, who came out the men's with a smoke in his maw. Time to go when you're outnumbered but Roger never mentioned that bit. He just called misses a dyke as they walked up the road and continued rambling about getting the truck back to her own driveway.

He tries to bribe Roger into a cab with promises of a bottle and dope he got hid in the shed. But Roger don't fall for it. He knows Calv will fuck off in the house when the cab pulls up and it's not like Donna is going to let them sit to the table and drink peacefully. Donna is going to go wild as soon as Calv gets through the door. Roger thinks it is better to keep on drinking or get right sobered up for that.

More blow is the only way Roger can see them going forward.

Everything about this sounds crazy but also very rational to Calv, who's too drunk and high to formulate a better strategy. Roger cannot drive, though. Don't let Roger drive. This is all Calv got by way of common sense right now as he trudges through the drifting snow behind the man who first explained to him that one day a girl would put her mouth over his penis.

Right over it, Roger explained to twelve-year-old Calv. She ain't going to puff air over on it neither. She was going to put it right in her face and suck on it and lick it and stuff.

This was the very same man who once coached him not to panic when this happened because the girl wasn't going to hurt him. The man who advised young Calv to just put his hands on her head and help her out if she was doing it wrong. Just move her head around for her if she's not doing it right. She won't care.

That man. That is the man Calv is following through the snow tonight. There had been no other man to follow.

His dad never told him the difference. He couldn't ask Amanda. He tried to ask her once when they were sixteen. He asked her how to make girls come because he didn't know and it embarrassed him to think he was doing it wrong.

She had said yuck, b'y, I'm your sister.

This had made Calv feel dirty and too handy to incest to ever ask her again.

If Amanda had her time back she would've been honest and said she didn't know but would tell him when she found out so he wouldn't spend his whole life listening to Roger.

Honesty would get everyone out of some lot of scrapes.

Roger hasn't even bothered to zip up the front of his coat. There is snow all down his neck everywhere, clumps of it in his beard, around his eyelashes. Calv has never noticed what long eyelashes Roger has before. Like a girl's. Pretty and perfectly curled back toward his sockets. Calv almost makes mention of it but stops cause Roger is liable to take anything the wrong way right about now. He looks like a man apt to strike his own granny. And then, as they're almost back to the truck, the world changes again.

For a minute, Calv thinks he is after blacking out.

But he's not blacked out. He is still upright. He can feel the weight of his body on his knees. The strength of the wind against his chest as he leans into it. His eyes are still open and adjusting to the new vantage. He can tell he is still cogent by the headlights turning up Prescott. The snow has turned to a sleet mixture. He sees it shimmer in the light. For a moment he feels trapped inside a comic book movie. Why do they call it black and white when everything is throwing shade? Nothing is called as it should be called. Calv catches a glimpse of the dark street lights swinging.

He misses when the colours were friendly. Already misses them. He knows they're only just gone but he feels how dreary it will be for the rest of his life without them. Two large hands have finally got hold of Calv by the shirt and he is being shook to his boot bottoms. He feels his guts churning out bile and gas. His discomfort grows as a small voice inside his head says, look, b'y, look at what you've done, the only colour you're left now with is yellow, cause that's the colour of your jesus heart.

Little yellow heart.

And he brought this on himself. Calv is growing numb here stopped steady on the corner peering around this miserable intersection. You used to be able to see the mouth of the harbour. But they stacked capsules like Lego atop each other to block the view. And it occurs to Calv that there is something really not right about cobbling together such blankness at the very start of where they all begin. Calv feels like he is losing hold of something. Someone. Everyone. Or that he is just now realizing a loss has already occurred and it is singing on the inside of his ears as he strains to recall the voices he has many times wished away. He can't hear their warm words but he can still remember what they sound like in full revolt. Colourful language, disaster and delight. And then, vision and volume return momentarily to remind him he is utterly lost.

Donna in her purple yoga pants grinning about a new bikini that he will just love.

Amanda giggling and blowing dish soap bubbles with a straw, get em, Calvy, get em!

His mother holding a Dream Whip–covered whisk out to him after taking one quick lick.

All of them smiling in his direction. These women shining love through to his heart this whole time, the brightest amongst them the first who loves him so steady and hard that he feels heavy how the truth of him will break her.

He hears her say knock yourself out kid as she hands him the whisk and runs her hands through his hair.

And he knows his mother's love has the strength of ten thousand wood stoves stoked and blazing against every shitty remark ever aimed at him for having an accent or a crooked nose or being shy. Calv had felt less cold around her broiling affection and wanted to always stand on that sunny side of the street where she thought he was the best one. Her favourite boy. The captain of her cherry heart. Flushed and full. Calv was always just waiting for her to turn toward him so he could tell her all the things he couldn't tell other people about his feelings. He had been envious of the time she spent turned toward his sister. He did not understand then.

But he understands now and feels this first painful surge of grief. Maybe he will be sick. The balloon of shame sickens him as it rises through his abdomen to his throat. He was so wrongfully jealous of Amanda who loved him second only to and seamlessly just like their mother. Amanda had just needed more of everything when they were little cause girlhood is maybe harder. Calv should not have begrudged her the extra hand she was given, he should have helped pull her up. If he could go back to there, he would be a better brother. That's all Susie ever wanted for him anyway.

I wants you to be a kind man when you grows up, Calvy.

I wants you to be nice to the girls and be good to your sister.

That's the most important thing, Calvin, I wants you to always be good to your sister.

Promise.

Listening to him practise his comedy for the variety show. Laughing. You're a talent, my boy, a natural talent. His mother, rearranging her life to go watch his wrestling, watching it even though she hated it. Worried that every smack would bang up her boy. Come now, what about softball, what about cross country skiing, they got swimming lessons to the community pool now. Saying she would drive him even though the community pool was almost an hour away and she was nervous driving after dark. Whispering in the kitchen to his father that she can't hardly watch him down on the mats. Cause she's scared to death he's going to make a mistake and get hurt. Or hurt someone else. That would be worse. She never wanted that to happen either. Cause she knows her boy and hurting someone else would be worse for him. He wouldn't be able to live with himself.

She is going to be so mad at him. Susie won't hold Calv up into that kind of stuff at all. She will not call the open line to defend her son. Susie will wipe her wet eyes in her dirty apron, sit on the floor and mourn what he has done even if he didn't totally do it.

She will be so disappointed in him for bringing that young one to that place.

It will totally defeat her because she had tried very hard to make him kind. All this time, she was outnumbered and overwhelmed by the meanness everywhere, but she still tried. And Calv feels his mother's confidence shatter for what has happened. He knows she will replay every moment of his childhood trying to identify some pattern of behaviour she might have run off course. Susie will ignore outright the random nature of Calv's choices that brought him to this dark place, because the inability to prevent an outcome makes her feel powerless.

Calv stands watching the dark street light lamps swing on their hooks and feels the same.

They look like any moment all might come free and crashing down. He thinks on the many times he has driven upon the same scene and watched the lights swing before racing through them to avert disaster. He had always felt relieved that he had got through, but not now. Now, he stands and waits, wishing he could take it back. This night. That night before Christmas. Every night he was mean to a woman before now. There are so many nights, and Calv is so sorry for them all in this one moment.

But sorry is as sorry does and Calvin is one sorry fucker.

THE MAN AHEAD of Olive is giving her a hard time in the blackout.

Is you some kind of mute?

He made a joke when the power flicked off and Olive did not respond.

She is too aware that she is in a dark gas station in dirty weather with three strange men.

After Olive's pop died, she was sent to stay with an aunt and uncle. Olive lived there until she did not live there because sometimes the uncle wasn't really an uncle but boyfriend of an aunt. Sometimes not even boyfriend. Sometimes just a man Olive is made to call uncle.

Then she lived with her mother's cousin for a time. And then a single mother who had small twins with asthma. These were not ideal living conditions. Her stomach couldn't adjust to the shifting dinner plates. She found it all hard to digest. And this made school a bother. Olive couldn't think to learn.

Every teacher from town soon became convinced Olive was deaf. There must be something wrong with her ears, they said in pencil skirts bought at outlets in Orlando. These trips: proclaimed rewards for having taught up North. Not real North but northern. Even Olive's north was found insufficient.

Everyone muttering it could be worse, instead of it could be better.

Halfway through the freeze, frustrated young teachers would hand Olive off to eager new social workers fresh from accreditation, who would then in turn usher Olive to a foreign doctor.

But it wasn't her ears. Her ears were fine. Unfortunately. It would be easier if her ears were broken. They knew how to fix ears. Bewilderment, concern and disappointment from all as Olive caused them to fail more.

She brought out the worst in grown-ups. They could not teach her. Counsel her. Or doctor her. She was impenetrable to their years of education, skill and practice. A child pretending the world did not exist with hands on her small face cupping the sockets of her tiny eyes. Later squeezing them shut when her hands were not available.

Conversations happened over her head like she wasn't there.

Well, there must be something wrong, they would say through arms crossed. There must be something wrong with Olive. Because if there was nothing wrong with Olive, it would mean there was something wrong with them. Something much bigger than one mixed-up baygirl who did not see when a teacher stood in front of her. Olive just tuning them out, turning away, sometimes with her head, later with her body. Olive did not blink. Would not. Refused. She registered no expression on her face.

There must be something wrong with her brain then surely, they would say in the staff room before planning Friday supper. Might be slow, someone would offer. Pizza Delight, another would suggest. Then, over cheese fingers lacking in cheese and garlic bread lacking in garlic, they would wonder how could she possibly not feel the feelings they told her to feel.

Another time, it was her tongue. Olive's tongue was the culprit. Or what lay beyond her tongue. Perhaps her cords were in need of repair. Could be her tonsils required removing. Because the child barely spoke.

Which was not normal, the educated professionals who had only read about suicide agreed. They felt confident they knew more about being Olive than she did and so tried to advise her even though their advice seemed like something from another place. Sometimes she tried to inform them of their wrong ways.

My home is a hard home. There are moose. Black bears. A lot of dead rabbits on the road.

Sometimes your pop dies by suicide when the fish plant closes and they send you away because your nan is too sad to cook. Your dad pretends he's not your dad and everyone laughs at your immaculate conception. Your cousin tries to fuck you at a party and your mother leaves. No one says it is okay to feel hurt. No one says anything. Everyone just goes on living. We all go on living until we lose more of each other. And then we are made lesser.

But they could not hear Olive's words through her ragged accent. They didn't even want to hear them. They wanted Olive to play pretend all white, play pretend all happy, play pretend they had all fixed her.

But actually fixing anything or anyone would mean a lot of work. And a lot less money. More work and less money was not what anyone in charge was striving for, so couldn't Olive just speak up in a way everyone could ignore? They were just trying to pay back their student loans so they could get married, buy houses and have kids. That's all they were doing when they were teaching Olive math and trying to get her to speak the Queen's English.

Her silence bothered them.

They knew nothing of the hurt in having a crippled tongue. Olive's tongue had been hobbled generations ago.

So it doesn't matter if men yell at Olive anymore.

It doesn't matter if Damian yells at her for being so slow with the smokes. Or if the men ahead of her in line at the gas station taunt her now in the dark. Olive has been made ready for them all. Every reaching, grasping, clawing embrace has prepared her for the moment she opens the truck door and climbs in, answers the Tinder message and goes out, takes the draw and forgets again, swallows the pills and feels numb.

Olive doesn't want to be a woman anymore if this is what being a woman is like.

IRIS REGISTERS the sound of the wind first.

The power loss has created a vacuum seal temporarily absent of human sound. The first wave of shock cascaded over them but now everyone is held in place willing the music to return. They can suddenly and properly hear the storm surge against the corner picture windows. It is swirling and unpredictable. Great arms of it feel hauled up by a Precambrian grudge as if the weather patterns themselves were trying to break the place even further apart to right an ancient wrong. A great shoulder of air heaves itself against the door and blows it open. The candles near the entry fall victim to the gale and the whole front of house falls into complete darkness as Ben dashes out from behind the bar to push closed the door again. Shuttering them all in here together. Everyone can hear things being picked up outside and thrown down.

Don't want that. Don't want that either. Don't want none of this.

Tossed against the neighbouring buildings. Slapping surrounding signage. Rejected by mother nature. Shovels accidentally forgotten. Garbage can lids not tied on. A sandwich board pulled out in general pervasive denial. Blue recycling bags holding one-time remnants are tossed around in defiance. Everything gets swept up. The internal consistency of the swiping and slamming cannot be clarified. The noise that thrashes them violently is all things at once.

Snow changing to rain changing to hail changing to sleet changing to snow.

The noise against the window suggests they are all barrelling toward undoing as if all progress made has always been futile. And then, against the grain of glass, they silently witness the storm whipping itself into a further frenzy as each swipe like a large hand throws great fistfuls of rock salt in everyone's face.

More. No. More than that. No. Stop. No. Even more. The storm cannot be satiated.

There will be no respite from it because someone made up an arbitrary day to waste paper.

The storm does not care for beautiful lies. It rages on. Killing in the name of not listening. Because this storm does not humour liars. It knows only facts. Recognizes reality for what it is. A blizzard is a blizzard. That bad guy is a bad guy. Believe him when he tells you. Iris looks toward the window again. Hopeful it will clear. But it won't.

This here is a whiteout.

The diners gasp and murmurs break through the register. Iris takes a headcount of the tables low-lit by candles made with her own gentle hands. She wonders if Olive is out in this and then feels guilty for not thinking this before and then feels guilty for every time she has not thought on Olive because she was much much too busy obsessing over a man ignoring her. The whole mess of her and Olive's relationship brought on by another man ages ago ignoring them both.

I asked your Uncle Brian once if he was my fadder?

What? Why?

Nan told someone on the phone my fadder was over on the wharf again talking big when I never had school supplies.

Uncle Brian used to fish with Dad.

Scared the shit out of him.

What did he say?

He asked me who my mother was.

GEORGE HURRIES TO the front to relight the tables that had gotten caught out in the gust.

She is attempting to make merriment even while her mind searches for solutions to this unexpected payment problem. No one carries cash. There is no way anyone in here is carrying enough cash to pay for their dinner. They all knew this was a possibility but forged ahead anyway.

Why? Why was it so important to open the restaurant today?

They could be home in front of the fireplace with the dogs.

Oh god, she hopes the dogs are okay. The dogs are probably okay. George doesn't know what she would do if something happened to them. Sometimes they feel like all she has. She knows this is not true. She has Miranda. And her father. And John. Of course, she has John. But sometimes she thinks that she would not recover from losing the dogs. Because it was what got her through losing the babies. They weren't babies, of course. Embryos would likely be more accurate. Not even fetuses.

But she thought of them as babies that her body lost.

And then after, John had given her the dogs, and that hurt too because it meant he had given up. But then it didn't hurt as much. And then it only hurt sometimes. And now, she mostly feels okay. George mostly feels like she'll be okay no matter whose baby they get. She hopes the dogs aren't scared in the dark. She hopes the alarms are not going off in the house. She checks the blackouts on her phone.

Apparently, they are rolling.

Good grief. George needs to get these people to pay for their dinners and leave.

She needs to get them cabs or cars or a snowplough. Something. Are there emergency evacuation procedures for this kind of thing? How will she get the power turned back on? How will she get them to pay for their food? Can they send her their money with their phones or does she have to go around taking names and call them up individually like a collections agency? Holy lord fuck. George does not want to do that. But she also does not want to buy dinner for all of these randoms. Iris. Iris will know what to do. And George looks up from lighting the last candle to search for Iris, who is already looking at her.

Waiting. And they just stand there looking at each other in the near darkness.

There is a building commentary throughout the room climaxing with exasperated exclamations of expectation.

Of course the power went. Of course they've no surplus capacity. Of course.

And everyone in the dining room, from Amanda in her pre-packed pumps to Ben behind the bar, feels ashamed for having hoped for some improved-upon outcome. They feel liable too for having left dreary posts unattended. Romantic fools, what were they thinking? That something nice might happen? That it could work out? Well, Jesus Christ on the cross, that kind of optimistic thinking practically willed this into fruition. It really is everyone's fault for expecting a Crown-owned utility company to keep the bloody lights on.

All hands are thrown up and arms are crossed as backs are hard pressed in frustration against chairs in a fluid motion denoting, of course, I fucking well knew this, of course.

And George knew too. Of course she knew. But she is not ready to know it yet.

She can't know it yet. So when John comes out and sees these two women staring across the dining room at each other, he makes a choice. He strides over to his wife and takes her into the kitchen. He needs to talk to her, he says, he needs her. Iris watches this motion and panic overtakes her. But the table closest to her is trying to discuss the situation. They will leave their credit card. Or a driver's licence. Would that do? They're not trying to shirk the bill but they cannot wait for the lights to come back on. It might be ages. Their babysitter is only fifteen. They should go home soon. In case their kids wake up in the dark asking for them. We're going to call a cab now.

Miss? Iris. Iris, right? Iris, we have to leave now. Can you bring us the bill? Iris?

And Iris is helping people. Because that's what Iris does. She's writing down their information and tracking who is in line for cabs. She is weeding through coats, all black and pea. This one? No. This one? No. What does the collar look like? Do you have anything in the pockets?

She is watching the kitchen door. They've not come back out. They're still back there.

What are they doing back there? What colour were your gloves? What could they be doing? Were they in the sleeves? Arguing? Red ones? Not arguing? Here. Worse? Here they are.

And the people are jostling about to see through the front window. They are discussing the wine and the amount of snow. Will there be a snow day tomorrow? The kids' daycare will definitely remain closed. Some men, drunk now, nuzzle their wives, whispering things that make the women giggle and playfully tug on a toque.

Because there are nice couples in St. John's. There are men and women who love each other in Newfoundland. There is warmth and happiness, in the clear and understood. Some people just go for dinner and laugh in a lovely good-natured way about what they will do later in the dark. And it is not wrong or gross or naughty. It is joyful fucking.

Or lovemaking. Some people still make love around here.

And maybe that is what John thinks he is doing with his wife now. Or what he did with Iris in the same small space twelve hours ago. But it is not. And it is sad that John

391

cannot tell the difference. That is John's great shame. A pity, really.

But Iris knows the difference now. That might be a pity too.

When the coats are handed out to the last customers, Iris stands with her face in John's. Inhales his smell. Her coat is there as well. And George's. They are left hung together surrounded by empty wooden hangers that George insisted on. And Iris agreed. Wooden hangers were better. The real thing is always better. There are other jackets too. Ben's responsible coat. He probably wears long johns under his jeans. The thick wool hat peeking from his pocket. Damian's coat still with a tinge of sweat, sour with tobacco smoke. Omi's much too big coat, a gift from the sous-chef after he got a new one. Iris runs her hands over all their winter wear.

There are other staff coats that she barely recognizes because fucking the boss means you don't get invited to many parties or have time to attend them. Besides, the other servers don't like her much anymore. They think she's a slut. Or a whore. It's probably a whore when his wife pays your salary. Regardless, no one wants Iris at the potluck. You can't say anything around Iris. She'll tell her boss.

They cackled—the other wait staff, everyone on the line, their friends in the industry.

Imagining threesomes distracted them from their own fucked up lives. All the while Iris was alone and paranoid in her dark basement apartment. Afraid that everyone knew or would find out. Worried she would be shunned. Outcast. A misfit. Nobody's business until found in the tub. Maybe they'll paint her picture and hang it at City Hall.

No.

No.

She doesn't want that.

No.

FUCK THAT.

Iris pushes herself off the coats.

She really should have eaten more. Drunk less. There is a little waver in her wobble. But no. No. Fuck that she thinks again and she crosses the dining room. Ben calling Iris. Damian saying leave her to it. And she knocks each painting off the wall onto the floor as she proceeds. She'll announce herself. I'm coming, John. I'm coming to get you! But John can't hear her. Never could. Cause John doesn't listen to women he's fucking.

And the lights come up, and the alarms beep, and the music gives her headway, and Iris turns the corner and through the warming trays, the sliver slits, she can see John fucking George on the salad station. You've got to hand it to him, he's got some stamina. When John commits to ruination, he fully commits to it.

What the fuck, John?

At the sound of his girlfriend's breaking voice, John pulls out of his wife like a man caught. And he is. And maybe he wanted to be. Maybe that was the whole point.

Iris! Iris, wait! I'm sorry.

George, spread-eagle, takes in the sight of it. John pinning himself into his pants, tripping around the warming

trays as they move, bread rolls falling onto the floor, Iris
shoving one down before turning, screaming, screaming,
screaming worse than she ever heard on the wharf. All
those cruel words built up in the back of her throat moving
forward, barely dammed enough to start, breaking free,
all the hurt and hate and disbelief and disappointment just
spilling out as she sobs her way through this downtown
eatery closely followed by her boyfriend's wife.

Why is he sorry to you?

George, just wait, Iris, just a minute.

You are such a lying sack of shit!

Why are you apologizing to the hostess, John?

Why would you do this to me?

Iris—

Why would anyone do this to anyone?

John!?!

I didn't do anything to deserve this.

Just, everyone stop, George, please, Iris, I need you
to stop.

I love you!

What do you mean you love him?

Just stop please—

You can't love him, he's my husband!

George, please.

I love my husband!

But I do too.

Oh my god.

We both do. We both love him.

John?

I should have told you sooner.

Iris, shut up!

Told me what? What are you telling me?

John Fisher lies to us both.

What is she saying, John?

Iris, stop, don't do this.

Do what?

I should have told you but I didn't because I didn't want to hurt you and I thought we could be okay later when it was over if you didn't know.

I am not for you to hurt or not hurt!

But now we all know and no one can be okay.

Do you think saying this will bring us together?

Don't you get it? I'm not trying to bring us together!

John, have you been fucking the hostess?

Can't you see? I'm trying to break us apart!

How old is she, John?

I don't want this.

What doesn't she want, John?

I never wanted this!

Wanted what?

This is your secret now, Georgina. I don't want it anymore.

And George is running after Iris and they are all moving fast like a unit toward the dining room. John yelling for Damian and Ben to leave. Everyone out, he is yelling. Get out. Get out now. But there is a blizzard and there are no cabs. Where will they go?

I don't care, just get out of my fucking restaurant now.

Your fucking restaurant? *My* fucking restaurant, John.

Sweetheart, Georgina, I can explain.

George has chased Iris into the linen closet where Iris tries to pull the glass French door in front of herself because she is scared of these two people. Always has been, really.

Where did you fuck?

What?

Where have you been fucking my husband?

I don't know.

Did you fuck him in my bed?

What? No.

Well, where did you fuck him? Where? Answer me!

In my bed. It was in my bed.

My bed! A borrowed bed.

It was my bed.

All your beds are my beds! I pay you.

That doesn't make any sense.

Fucking in someone else's bed doesn't make any sense.

I'm sorry, I said I was sorry.

Fuck your *sorrys*.

It wasn't my idea.

Whose idea was it?

I don't even know how it happened.

Well, you picked a fucking genius this time, John!

Georgina—

This time?

She doesn't even know how you fucked her?

What other time was there?

What? Are you for real?

John?

You think you're special?

This time?

I suppose she's some kind of artist too.

Jesus fucking Christ, Georgina, I told you—

Who was the other? What other? What artist? What? What?

Didn't you learn your lesson with Sarah? I mean, my fucking god.

Sarah?

You think you are special or something?

John?

Sarah was just like you. Or you are just like Sarah. You have the same stupid hair!

You were with Sarah?

She really hired her replacement, hey?

Georgina.

Don't Georgina me, you fucking asshole. You promised me. You got on your hands and knees and begged me.

I can explain.

You said you would never lie to me again—

It was not like that—

Who have you told?

What?

Who have you fucking told about this, Iris?

I don't know what's going on anymore.

Did you tell your little friends?

What?

Be honest.

Me be honest?

You cannot let her tell anyone, John!

Is that what you're worried about?

They won't give us the baby.

You shouldn't get the baby!

Shut the fuck up, Iris!

How could you do this to me?

I cannot breathe. I can't catch my breath.

You're both coming at me —

Stop crying. Calm down.

Don't tell me to calm, you calm down!

Stop yelling!

Fuck you, John!

No, fuck you, Iris! You knew I was married.

I didn't, not right away!

Don't dare use that shit on me. You knew.

John, she cannot tell people, I will die.

I thought I would die this whole fucking time!

No one cares about you, you're the bad one!

I am not the bad one!

You were fucking my husband!

And you knew! You knew and didn't care as long as you could pretend!

I did not know.

Did you think your marriage problems just fucking vanished?

You don't know about my marriage problems!

Of course I do, I'm your fucking girlfriend too, aren't I?

Shut your face, Iris.

I've been augmenting your fucking life this whole time. And you knew and didn't fucking care because it meant you could have everything while I had nothing. You both got everything you wanted and I got nothing. You used me as much as he did, Georgina. You both just used me like I was nothing. And if I say nothing, you will use the next one. You will pretend it all away to preserve your fantasy while some other woman has her life blown up. Like we are collateral damage is how you act! Like we are here to serve your fiction. No. No! I'm not having it! I will make it impossible for you to keep doing this. You're not allowed to do this to people. I am a person. And I'm telling. I'm gonna tell on you.

John?

Iris, you listen to me, you are never to utter my fucking name—

But I don't have to utter your name. Children and dogs know about you.

Iris—

Everyone can see the kind of man you are. Everyone already knows. They just fucking pretend they don't because they are trained that way.

John, I will never be able to show my face again.

Iris, I've had enough of your hysterics—

Fuck you.

You are never to talk about Georgina or I—

Fuck you both.

I didn't know!

You did!

And of course she did. George couldn't help subconsciously filing away the names of all the young waitresses in her head. There were cabinets set aside in the back of her mind tavern for just this very thing. The files inside were colour-coded according to rank of availability and appeal. She had a dog-eared list going of John's new female friends that he was just looking out for because he was such a good guy.

She sifted and sorted through them regularly while in transit. Waiting for the subway. Sitting at the gate. Her brain just unlocked and quietly slid free the chain links wrapped around the small guarded drawer and George pulled it free slowly so as not disturb the other concerns milling around nearby.

Her beauty. Her career. Her fertility. Her father.

In the drift between peace and wakefulness, she slithered in there to check and recheck her filing strategy. There was always a real concern that she had missed a detail and misfiled. It was not so much that George was worried that this would negatively impact those folded into her cardboard holders. No. She could not care for them.

It was more that the very wrong people would discover what she had been hiding back here. That would undo everything. The sweet story of renewal would be recklessly unfastened if someone were to discover that George had known the real deal all along. So she was watchful of the place where she stored her truth.

She examined the possible complainants to determine who was a feasible foe. John's voice reverberating on the interior of her, shaking through the hallways, snaking up the stairs toward her tavern. And she would look over her shoulder with the files held in her hand, worried that she was betraying him in this act of distrust. Knowing that this very kind of thinking was the sort of thinking that he had been warning her against.

You know me, Georgina, he would whisper pleadingly while wearing his best pity face, practised and adjusted to meet the changing needs of feminism.

She came up with numerous reasons why there could indeed be nothing more to it. She justified why he texted them in the evening or, worse still, why they texted him. She held them up against herself in profile and decided which of them were not his type because she was his type and they were so unlike her. She contrasted their hips and waists and chests against her own, which he had readily declared his favourite kind. One was far too tall, another very large, this one here with a scar across her cheek was rather flat and immature, another too leathery and much much too old.

Though there were a couple with tight bangs high above hip frames that she couldn't bear to look at, and she considered removing herself from the whole internet to prevent further searching in their faces.

George could not google and scrutinize random women if she had no data plan on her phone. This proved unrealistic and a hindrance to her job so she occasionally found herself on the web determining why it was impossible for her oh so handsome husband to be cheating on her with all these women. Because that would make John some kind of pathological liar. It would mean the fellow she took inside her was also inside all of these other people. That could just not be so. No one would do that. Be that duplicitous. And so instead George convinced herself that she was jealous, just as John had said.

She was trying to possess him, and love was not about possession.

John, being the wolf that he is, feasted on these little bunnies, all the while telling his deluded wife that they had crushes. All these women had become of their own accord infatuated with him because he was simply so irresistible. And he was trying to let them all down easy is what he told George when she questioned the time spent alone with them.

They were deeply wounded by some other fellow, he suggested, and this suited George's purpose finely as it kept her pretty picture hanging on the wall a little longer. Her husband was the most sought-after man in town and he had chosen her above all the others, which meant she was the most talented and desirable woman.

The best woman.

And she fucking well needed that to be true after what Andrew had done. So she feigned ignorance. Even when she caught him touching Sarah's cheek in the doorway. Even when Sarah moved to the other side of the world without warning. Even then, George pretended that it had nothing to do with John.

Acknowledging for a second that John could have played a role in a woman running for her life was more than George could get a handle on. It was better to sacrifice the next round of young servers. And so George left him to it so that she could pursue George stuff. She deserved that.

Though sometimes when she ran off to conferences in Dubai, she thought, I am close to Sarah, Sarah is not far, I could ask her. But she did not dare send the woman a message because sending her a message would be like inviting the truth in. Any contact with Sarah would result in George knowing things that she did not want to know.

Namely: John is a lying cheating son of a bitch who has never been faithful to an idea let alone a woman.

And now here's Iris, screeching into the tablecloths.

John, get our coats.

CALV HAS WRESTLED Roger to the ground just beyond the delivery door.

The wind is gusting something hateful still and this had worked momentarily to Calv's advantage. He had tried hard to reason with Roger.

Calv finds it fucking infuriating when people don't listen.

His collar has always shot up hot when he says something that garners no response. People should fucking listen to him. Roger had somehow made his way to the parked truck with Calv blindly bawling down Water Street until making his way up one of them nothing side streets meant to connect you to more important streets. He tries to convince Roger that the truck will be fine tucked in there. But Roger can't be persuaded. He says he'll have a little lie-down in the truck and then drive. But that's crazy too. They can't very well both go to sleep in the parked truck idling in a blizzard on Valentine's Day.

What if they suffocates accidentally? What will everyone back home think?

So, he smacks at the keys when Roger pulls them out to unlock the doors. Beep beep goes the truck and then ba-bam! Right down across the portside of him. And it is likely that Calv's level of inebriation such as it is has made him throw in a little too aggressively and he has by all accounts given Roger the best kind of wallop. He recognizes he overdid it when Roger cowers from him with one shoulder up and arched in expectation of a beating. Calv recognizes this posture from their childhood. Roger's older brothers right regular gave him a trimming for being younger and smaller than them, like it was an offensive choice he himself had made.

What'd you hit me for, Calv b'y?

Roger says this in a timid voice and Calv almost regrets the course of action as he roots around for the keys in the slob hole where he saw them land. He's turning to explain when Roger gives his backside a little kick and he falls palms-first into the wet snow. It is freezing and full of grit from the ground. Roger is demanding his keys back. He is standing up in the fucking moonlight with his hands hung but Calv can see him curling and uncurling his wrists hung alongside that blown-open ski-doo jacket.

I hates your fucking coat!

Calv don't know he is saying it until it is well gone out of his mouth, and the effect it has on Roger is one of shock. That was not what he was expecting, and the combination of information and countering narcotics delays his reaction long enough for Calv to gain his purchase and start off across the road. Roger is travelling behind him bawling slurry gibberish about just taking a nap in the cab of the truck. But Calv don't believe it. Cause Roger is a jesus liar. He always has been. Since they was boys and playing guns out behind the shop.

Gets them in over the tops of their rubbers every time.

They were liable to die in the fucking truck, Calv is yelling back after him. That's how people commits suicide. Don't you fucking know anything? Jeremy's older brother in the gear shed in he's Camaro that time in high school. That's what he done. And Roger stops momentarily to take this in cause he never knew that before.

Really?

Yes, Jesus!

Why'd he do that?

Cause he was low minded.

I would never do that.

I knows you wouldn't.

No one would believe it.

Sure they would.

No b'y.

Found dead together from carbon monoxide on Valentine's—

Go on.

—they'll say we're queers.

No, they wouldn't.

Yeah, they would. You knows they would.

The delivery door opening surprises Roger and Calv into silence. And the blowing blistering gale provides a temporary shake tent of sound that they hide inside until they hear the door close shut again. The emerged person tries to light a cigarette, hands up, flick, flick, but no flame proceeds from the raw scratches. He stands there swearing and shaking the lighter to release that last bit of life-giving fluid.

Damian had been inside listening to the triangle walls come apart in the kitchen.

He had been quietly eavesdropping, a forefinger to his lip, facing Omi, who was trapped in the adjacent dish pit afraid to run the water. Through the crack in the swing door, he could see Ben across the hall with his back pressed against the wall and his arms crossed over his chest.

The linen cupboard had grown quiet so Damian had thought the worst had passed. He motioned to Ben that he was going to have a cigarette at which the bartender waved him off, bewildered that anyone could think of smoking at a time like this.

That's what he knows, Damian thinks to himself. When shit goes down, Damian is filled with an almost destructive urge to shove a whole pack in his gob and light the works on fire. What do he need them lungs for? He's not running any marathons, is he? The people that do only seems marginally better off anyhow. Listen to George out there in the dining room quietly crying as a member of her staff sobs into the table linens. She don't exactly have her licked out there just cause she can run twenty odd jesus miles.

I knows you.

And Damian let the lighter drift in the direction of the voice and now he has no lighter. The words through the snow startled him. These words full of conviction and rage. Deep and foreboding, just loud enough to reach him through the weather. Followed almost immediately by another voice.

You don't know him, come now we goes.

Damian had suspected that Calv had recognized him. All afternoon and evening. He had been certain of it because Calv had been sober when he walked in and out of the hotel that night.

He was working there.

Yeah, course. We just ate there.

No, not there. There.

Roger b'y, you're loaded b'y.

You was working at that hotel, wouldn't you?

And Damian says nothing.

Wouldn't you? Before Christmas.

406

Because what can he say?

We had a party there one night.

Come on, Roger b'y, let's go, I'm froze.

We had one of them little tarry hookers.

And rage is weird. Sometimes it feels like getting sick. Or like you're physically exploding. Like your guts and bile and blood are trying to fast escape your body. Every hair on end, rising, like striking an electrical field where everything becomes heightened. And you are hyper-aware of yourself and the moves that you make or don't make and time is moving but immovable and it is like you are once again a small child with the will to rip the head off your sister's Barbie because you wanted a Barbie but they won't let you have one.

The night you raped the shit out of her, he says.

And rape is a powerful word well-despised by rapists the world over, because they rightfully don't like being called out for what they are or what they do as it will for sure impact their ability to continue doing so. Not full on prevent them from continuing to rape, but it is a kind of inconvenience in life moving forward.

Roger has Damian's staff shirt hauled over his head before he has time to elaborate. Had Damian played hockey past Peewee, he would have seen that obvious move coming. But he didn't because, like Roger is informing him now, he's just some fag. And Roger is giving him the boots straight over his ribs with the full motion of one side of his whole body weight, back and forth, contact, breakage.

I never raped no whore you fag.

Never raped no whore you fag.

Raped no whore you fag.

No whore you fag.

Whore you fag.

You fag.

And the details are lost in the night as Damian feels the blood come into his mouth and thinks with a quiet confidence that he deserves this. He deserves all of this. Every bad thing that happens to him is because he deserves it.

Thwack.

It is a strange hard noise a cold metal fan hood makes clipping a drunk man across the jaw. It reverberates and echoes in the wind. The crunchy noise of the sharp corner connecting with bone followed by the bellow of pain and confusion as they all look up to see Omi holding junk metal, heaving his chest, full of adrenalin upon discovering two men murdering his co-worker in the alley.

This is what Omi is thinking as Calv drags Roger away from the smoking nook.

Omi is thinking that he has saved Damian's life. He is watching the trail of blood left behind, half expecting more to emerge from behind the snow. He is standing there holding the fan hood up, his trunk rising and falling, ready to strike again if need be. Damian never stacks his plates properly and pretends to not see the full garbage bag but he is a friend.

And Omi doesn't let a friend get beaten to death in the snow.

JOHN HANDS GEORGE her coat.

She pulls it on over her shoulders and places her hands in her pockets. But it is not right.

There is something wrong-feeling. She wraps her right hand around a familiar piece of plastic and her left around a small peanut-shaped biscuit. These are correct feelings, but across the shoulders is all wrong. She pulls both hands out and holds them out in front of her. The blue plastic bag is perforated every six inches and attached to another blue plastic bag for tearing. It is covered in little bones, an unnecessary decoration that George has thought amusing and altogether tacky. She has always, until now, smiled pulling these bags from her pockets. Dog bags everywhere. Everywhere. But she is not smiling now.

This is not my coat.

What?

This is not my coat.

Of course it is.

No, it's not.

It looks like your coat.

It's not my coat.

It's my coat.

And of course it's Iris's coat. And of course he doesn't know them apart.

All coats look the same to him.

And George remembers herself less than twenty-four hours ago feeling triumphant for having gotten home. She had gone to airports hours early in Toronto and then Halifax. She had placed her name on lists and paid change fees, bartered politely with the airline staff. George had done everything to get home to John for Valentine's Day.

She had flown through bad weather for him not once but twice.

The first flight turning back to Halifax just as they reached Bell Island. Then circling, the quick plucks upward, George gripping the armrests, her gel nails digging into the hard plastic. All the hopeful women trying to get home staring at the tiny airplane on the little lit screen, willing it not to turn around until it does. The moans from the cabin, even a small groan from a member of the cabin crew behind them and out of sight. George remained hopeful until the pilot announced they had to turn back to Halifax. And then the crying from the disappointed knowing that it would be days now before they actually reached their destination. Well past any point of romance.

Missing their chance.

And the attendants at the customer service desk had no time or patience for silly soft-hearted women trying to get home to their partners because they weren't home either so they had no empathy to share around. Instead, they chastised the rumpled passengers about the realities of flying in February as if every Canadian didn't already know that flying in the winter was a punishment. As if there was any other way to get to Newfoundland. As if feelings were rational.

They were forced to ready themselves for the Dartmouth Holiday Inn, order terrible pizza and search Nova Scotia basic cable for HGTV. But not George.

Different kinds of planes can land in variable weather conditions, so George booked all the planes. Stayed at Stanfield the whole time, which is Eastern purgatory for haughty Newfoundlanders. Some feel a part of civilization just being in an airport, but George is seasoned and not impressed by the offerings. Fast food. A fountain. It is vaguely skeety. But she stayed there in the event that something could get off the ground, and travelled to get home to a husband who seemed startled to see her.

Surprise, she said.

Surprise, he said weakly and kissed her on the side of the mouth.

He had kissed her on the side of the mouth, avoiding her ready-puckered and persistent lips. She assumed something horrible about her sleepy breath.

But it was because he had been with Iris. George sees that now. He had been with Iris and Iris had been walking her dogs.

You walk my dogs.

And Iris just doesn't want to face this kind of hurt in another lady so hides her eyes in her hands.

You walk my dogs.

John's locus of control is legless as he searches for a quiet way to remove them from this place.

You walk my dogs!

Sometimes.

My dogs.

Sometimes I walk your dogs.

They can't run after they eat—

I know—

They're barrel-chested.

I know.

You know?

An hour. To prevent bloat.

Bloat can kill.

Yes, yeah, I know.

And when the dogs run into the restaurant wagging their tails it is to see Iris. And when she saw Iris walking them last winter it meant she had been walking them last winter. How many months was that? How long ago? George's vision blurs. And there was a night before that, a Basia Bulat concert, George had been unable to go, Board of Directors meetings for RANL, so John had gone with people from work, he said. That was before the winter. That was in the fall. October. Two Octobers ago. The BOD meeting had been cut short because the Chair's children were sick and throwing up. George had been so careful to not touch anything. She had a trip to Singapore she just could not miss. So she went to find John and the people from work. They would be easy to spot.

But when she got there she could not see them. She walked around and around. She drank a Blue Star on an empty stomach. She texted John. When finally she spotted him, he was leaning over Iris at the bar by the bathrooms, whispering something in her ear. She had her elbows on the bar behind her, her hips jutting out. When George walked over, John looked surprised but put his arm around her and kissed her on the side of her mouth. Leaned into her ear. Said, it is really loud in here.

Later, he left.

He left the bar without telling either of them. Iris said he was not feeling well. Headache. Gone home probably. George texted John. He said he needed some quiet. But she didn't go home. She stayed out with Iris. Stayed right beside her the whole night. Needed to befriend her.

Needed Iris to know her because knowing her would prevent it from happening. George only realizes this now. Only now knows why she followed Iris from bar to bar that night in October even after it started to rain. George never stayed out when it rained. The rain made her bangs go funny.

You bought me a beer that time.

I did.

You were on a date with my husband.

And then I was on a date with you.

Putting her fist through the first pane of glass brought shock. George's capacity for it was shocking. But like any good student, George learned to lean into it as she smashed each individual pane of glass in the French door over Iris. The shards of glass cutting her arm from wrist to oiled elbows. Coconut oil would not fix this. The broken panes ripped at her flesh as she tried to push the broken glass in on Iris, toward her, closer, toward her neck and face. It was not Iris specifically George wanted to slice apart but the conditions that brought them so low. All of them. George wanted to smash that knowing intangible thing up. She wanted to sweep it into the trash. Have it taken out. Take it outside. Drag it off to the dump. Incinerate it. But the ways of being cannot be scorched as easily as a French door held fast closed by your husband's girlfriend can be smashed in her face. Larger pieces of glass landing at her feet. She's no socks on in her ballet flats. No fucking socks.

John has broken her heart for a woman without the sense to wear socks in winter.

And John is there with her real coat. He is pulling the

wrong one off. He is wrapping his shattered wife in her real coat. Bundling her hands in tea towels that she hates. They're neon green and synthetic shammy material.

I hate these tea towels.

I know.

Why do you do things I hate?

And John has no answer to that.

John, where are you going?

I have to take my wife to the hospital.

But John —

She's hurt.

But I'm hurt too!

You can take care of yourself.

But John —

Stop saying my fucking name. Never say my fucking name again. We're done here. I'm done. I have no animosity toward you but I am done it is over.

You have no animosity toward me?

No. I have no ill will toward you —

John, there's blood —

It's not your fucking ill will to have toward me, you fucking maniac!

John, I'm bleeding on the floor.

Iris —

John! Stop talking to that woman!

Yes, I'm sorry, Georgina, I'm sorry. Let's go.

I'm your wife. Your wife is bleeding.

I know, I know, let's go.

Do you love her? Is that it? Do you love her, John?

No, no, of course not. She means nothing to me.

There it is. Finally.

She means nothing. Meant nothing. Means nothing. Is nothing to me. It was nothing. Iris means nothing to me!

And if Iris means nothing, then he hurt George for nothing. And if she means something, then he is hurting himself, too.

Hard to say who is the most or worst hurt when you treat people like nothing.

The fallout is catastrophic.

IRIS WAITS UNTIL she hears the front door close.

Then she waits a little longer. Then she stands.

Tiny pieces of glass fall from her. She thinks all the linens will have to be laundered. And then she thinks, that's not my job anymore. And her life is different. Everything has changed again. She walks over to the corner picture windows and looks out toward the harbour.

There is some new feeling swimming inside Iris.

Not a feeling she can grasp with any certainty. It is still too squishy slick, slipping free like a codfish onto the haul of a boat after being jigged up by its same own tail. The tail-jigging part being another betrayal as this groundfish had not even sincerely chosen to take the bait. Properly and definitively caught up, it was.

This fishy feeling of Iris's has been captured and thrown down at her feet.

Iris is relieved and horrified to be alone now with it as it slowly suffocates, the laboured gills pulling up and down for possible contact with the measly store of damp salt she dribbles along its once-shiny backside. She needs to keep it alive long enough to identify it.

She sits aboard herself and plays witness to the struggle. Pays it respect deserving of its heroic determination. The will to survive in this dry dock surrounded by the bodies of feelings long silenced: there was hope, optimism, pride, even love.

But they are gone wretched now. Dead and rank. Too strong-smelling to have any help in their removal. Iris is left to wash this mess down on her own. And she wants to, really, she will scrub the last of the guts clear, scrape off every small scale stuck to the side with her very own chipped fingernails, as soon as she can get this final wily fish feeling up.

Iris puts her heel down over the skull of it. She knows this means waste, but she is too tormented. Killing this feeling is the only way, and Iris feels murderous.

And what is worse is she understands her mother now.

This: another gutting that awaits her ashore if she is ever capable of steering this dory inland. She grabs hold the rudder and decides her decision.

Iris walks to the bar phone, takes a whisky bottle from off the shelving and places her cellphone face up. She has clung to it for nearly two years. She had grown wholly convinced that her survival depended on this small shiny slip of a thing. It would be her defence against whatever else came, but she sees now it had been a shackle. She was handcuffed to bad decisions, the worst ones, the accidents, her hateful, desperate pleas, it was all housed inside this singular device so that she might have evidence later when accused of some great sin. But what of it now?

Those who could pretend it all away could pretend away anything.

It did not matter in the least whether or not Iris could prove she had been misled. They cared not a speck for her. They wanted the Johns and they would believe anything to have them. And so let them have him, Iris thinks as she brings the back end of the whisky bottle down over the phone face. She does so repeatedly until it is mere shards before walking to the hostess phone and dialling a landline number she can remember because it used to be her landline, too. When she lived there with them. She leaves her message after the beep. She imagines her voice echoing through the dark kitchen.

I'm drunk and have no money. So am walking over. Please let me in, okay?

And then . . . click.

Jo hears it. And gets up. Pulls on her snow pants over her Scottie pyjama pants. Chris tells her she's crazy. He begs her not to go because she is three months pregnant. But Jo goes anyway. She will get Iris and bring her home.

Iris puts the phone down on the bar. She doesn't need to worry that it is not on the cradle as John likes. Because he is done with her now, he said so. He is finished with her now. No hard feelings, he said.

Actually, John, all the hard feelings.

And who is John to think he can dictate what feelings Iris has, believing he's a self-appointed party DJ spinning her feelings for entertainment, turning them up and down and off however he pleases like some tune on the radio. And the playlist hits the tail end of the album. Leave your home. Change your name.

Some day all the songs that play will be songs they have never heard together.

And Iris already can't fucking wait for that day.

She will walk to Jo's. She will make Jo forgive her. She will take Harry to the park. She will not lose him. She will call her mother. She will tell her she loves her. She will find Olive. She will apologize for never being there. She will move out of that shit apartment. She will paint. She will only date nice men. She will never lie again. She will not let this ruin her life. She will never ever let this happen again. She will move on. Move forward. She will forgive herself for doing this. For letting this happen. For not being genuine. For putting him first. She will get over this. She will be new. She will not die. Because she does not want to die not even a little bit not even at all.

Iris wants to live.

She steps off the sidewalk into the street because it is easier to walk there and her feet are already wet and freezing in the ballet flats. She is so caught up in the promises she is promising herself that she doesn't see the figure walking toward her also on the street. Waving. Olive sees Iris a ways off. She sees her moving through the intersection. She can see her coming across the steep slap of hill. And she sees the truck lights come up through the blowing snow. Olive sees the lights fall on Iris. And she hurries toward her screaming her name. Iris has her head down. Iris cannot see the truck. Calv does not see her until he has already struck her. Roger is bleeding all over the seat. Calv was looking at Roger bleeding all over the seat.

Iris's shoes come free as she is dragged through the intersection by her coat before coming clear of the truck.

She looks up as she falls, sees the brake lights move away, then nothing.

Then Olive.

Olive did not recognize the truck. But she recognized the driver.

Olive takes off the snow boots and places them gently on Iris's feet before sitting down next to her in the road. She takes Iris's hand in her smaller hand and blows warm air into Iris like her grandmother did when she was a girl. Olive thinks this is love and Iris needs love now. Olive blows more love into Iris. Each breath is like hope. Iris is holding what little hope Olive has left in her cupped right hand. Olive gives her more. Olive gives all she has, rocking back and forth, chanting, it's okay, Iris, you're okay. Olive wants to believe that's true. Just like she has always wanted to believe in happy endings. Ever since she was a girl. Ever since forever.

Olive, like Iris, is a kind of forever girl just like all of girls who had their girlhood trampled.

Olive looks toward the truck. It is still braked in the road. The red lights are lit just long enough for Olive to think perhaps he will help them. But the truck drives off.

The snow is heavy with moisture.

It clings to them as Olive pushes Iris's hair from her wet face and wipes the snowflakes from around her shiny mouth. Her own hands are growing cold but she doesn't feel her own hands. Or feet. Knelt down in the slush. It is all texture void of temperature. Olive doesn't feel the snow drifting in around them. She cannot hear the swooping wind. The world has been robbed of external sight and sound.

There is just still-beating hearts once thought broken.

Not broken though.

Still beating.

And Olive wills for something good to happen because Iris deserves to be shown some kindness having had nothing but hurt for herself. She deserves better than the cold road. And Olive wants to howl out but soft-cries over Iris's buckled body, knowing her ancient anger in this moment would cause fright when she means to comfort. So she leans in close, as close as she can be to battered Iris, and through the white noise, wafting and wavering, she assures and reassures in cobbled-together confidence that someone will come, someone will help.

Iris says, I hurt myself. Like a deer in the road. But we don't have those.

Olive offers, I saw a pink caribou once.

And Iris nods and says, I want to be like that. After. I want to be a whole new animal.

And then she says, I'm sorry, Olive.

And she is sorry because Olive's germs are her germs. Iris and Olive have half the same germs. Iris had been only young and always scared and mostly angry when Olive told her. It had been hard to look into a little face and find her father's face staring back.

The knowledge that they would always share his fixed features stung Iris through and her jealousy left her too sore to overcome. So Olive did not get a big sister. And Iris did not get a little sister. They were hairline fractured this way and lonely for it their whole young lives.

Olive knows Iris is sorry. Has always known it. Olive is sorry too. But that's not the apology they have been yearning for. Perhaps now, they will stop waiting for some man to make it right.

Iris imagines her and Olive together travelling concrete along the backs of optimistic towns built to house former baymen, taking the second right-handed turn before swinging round the bend, a tight ushering westward, cutting through the thin rocky ridge, an otherworldly scape.

Fully forging inland and over interior, this stolen ghost land, fog, mesmerizing silver birches, an ancient scenic green bay, lakes, rivers, bodies of water to cross, quick and continuous, finally rearing from the stress of living, a great wave of relief crashing north beyond the mountains atop a road called for visitors rather than kin, norse, men.

Everyone kept moving through the thickness of the centre by a need to be further out of reach, that welcome release upon the first sighting, an awakening, freedom felt when finally reaching the shoreline's windy break to emerge from the trees and breathe again, make up for all that shallow gasping, salt in your lungs and along the lines of your face, fullness.

There stretching out, shimmering lean and fierce, their razored coastline, windswept and weather-beaten, a Strait of Belle Isle, bountiful and hardened, this the place that made them, all the good bits plaited broadside the bad, unknowingly mixed, indivisible, a savage braid surviving the ragged shore, stronger still, a threat, a comfort, a forgiveness, always.

I want to go home.

And Olive shakes her head in agreement. She too wants more than riches to be off this city's winter road and out of harm's way for once. It is written all about her person. They share the sense of it passing between them, a true longing to be some elsewhere.

Please don't leave me here, Ollie.

The nickname, a hug sealing the pair, is a precious incantation, making them, suddenly in a word, belong to each other. Sisters. Olive holds Iris's pale hand between her same but darker hands and she doesn't let go and she doesn't leave. Olive stays.

ACKNOWLEDGEMENTS

I WOULD LIKE TO EXTEND my sincere gratitude to Sarah MacLachlan for believing in an idea not yet fully formed. Perhaps that idea was me. I would also like to thank my editor, Jane Warren, as well as managing editor Maria Golikova and all of the team at House of Anansi for their patience and generosity. Wela'lin to Stacey Howse and miigwech to Michelle Porter for your sensitive, necessary and thoughtful comments.

Much appreciation to everyone at Riddle Fence Publishing and Eastern Edge Gallery for their understanding and support. Thank you to my UBC classmates for their feedback and to my thesis advisor, Maureen Medved, for her ready ear and unflinching encouragement. My tireless agent, Samantha Haywood, regularly entertains my raging about art and capitalism long distance, and for this I am always appreciative.

A special thank you to my big Newfoundland family: aunts, uncles and cousins. Always to Melissa, Chelsie and Alicia; sister is my favourite word because of you! To my mom and dad, Della and Nelson Coles, wild horses the pair of them.

Also, to my pop, Stephen Dredge, for his gentle and constant care. And to my nan, Susan, who tries desperately to protect us from the world's worst bits in her devoted and strong-willed way. I am so lucky to be your dollie. When I am driving home, I am driving home to you, constantly stopped steady by your affection whenever I speak of Nan, which is every day and all the time, such is your overwhelming impact and influence on my life.

All my love and loyalty to my friends for their kindness with shout-outs to Emma, Robert and Elisabeth. As is the way in adulthood, some people were accidentally lost during the writing of this hurt monster. Some new humans appeared then purposefully to fill me in and help me up in the misplaced's stead. Regardless of our current relationship status, though, I am grateful to all for the time and attention you paid my soft and savage heart. It did not go unnoticed, even if sometimes it went unsaid. And that's on me.

Thank you especially to my Katie Lauras for always answering the phone. And to Maria, who hangs on to me for our dear lives through every heartbreak and retelling and draft and hunger-strike. I would not know how to be in the world without you.

To all the people who have kept me alive these thirty-seven years: thank you and I love you.

ArtsNL and the City of St. John's financially supported the writing of this novel through project grants to professional artists. Sadly, Canada Council did not. I was very poor.

Oh, and #metoo. Obviously.